A BEAUTIFUL BREED
OF EVIL

ANDY MASLEN

TYTON PRESS

ALSO BY ANDY MASLEN

Detective Ford:

Shallow Ground

Land Rites

Plain Dead (coming soon)

DI Stella Cole:

Hit and Run

Hit Back Harder

Hit and Done

Let the Bones Be Charred

Weep, Willow, Weep

Gabriel Wolfe :

Trigger Point

Reversal of Fortune

Blind Impact

Condor

First Casualty

Fury

Rattlesnake

Minefield

No Further

Torpedo

Three Kingdoms

Ivory Nation

Crooked Shadow (coming soon)

Other Fiction:

Blood Loss – A Vampire Story

For my parents

When we are born we cry that we are come to this great stage of fools.

   William Shakespeare, *King Lear*

1

LONDON

Stella stared at the bloody lump of flesh and wondered what it meant. If you wanted a man to keep a secret, removing his tongue would do it. But why do it after he was dead?

Again, the answer presented itself. Because you wanted somebody else, maybe the whole world, or your part of it, to know he squealed when he shouldn't have.

But what on earth could Tomas Brömly, an elderly Swedish ex-diplomat, say that would be worth killing for? Any political or business secrets he may once have possessed would surely be out of date now? And if he'd been an intelligence operative, the Swedes would have arrested and prosecuted him for breaching whatever their version of the Official Secrets Act was.

The former ambassador was seventy-nine. Stella didn't write off the possibility of a jealous lover. Though the odds were against it.

Would a woman scorned really procure and use a firearm? And what about the business with the tongue? If it *had* been a woman, Stella would have expected any post mortem mutilation to have taken place south of there.

The other possibility was a religious maniac. Stella puffed out her cheeks and tugged on her ponytail, running the thick hank of brown hair through her clenched fist until it hurt. Motive would have to wait. Facts were more important.

This felt like a targeted hit, rather than a random or chaotic killing. Brömly had been shot dead. Probably by a handgun. The killer would have needed planning, considerable forethought and the smarts to get hold of an illegal weapon.

She stared at the tongue. The tattered root, far from being neatly severed, had clearly been wrenched out. Blood had stained the open pages on which it rested.

Stella turned to the nearest CSI.

'Any chance you could move the tongue?' she asked. 'I'd really like to take a look at the Bible.'

The CSI shook his head. 'Sorry, Ma'am. The pathologist said to leave it. He had to go back to the mortuary. Said he'd be back by three.'

Stella checked her watch. Five to. She began a walk-through of the apartment.

She'd called her estate agent brother-in-law earlier to ask him what flats in Upper Brook Street went for. Jason told her two-bed apartments went for three or four million. The most expensive sale in the previous twelve months had been for eighteen.

The room she'd just entered was huge, at least thirty feet by forty. Standing in a corner on a deep-red Turkish carpet was a full-sized grand piano. A wall of large plate-glass windows gave onto Hyde Park: she saw trees waving in the wind outside.

She walked over to the piano. A Bechstein. A double-spread of sheet music lay open on the stand above the keyboard. Stella read the title: *Piano Trio No. 4 in C Major* by Franz Berwald. A Swedish-sounding name. Natural for an expat to feel nostalgic for his homeland, however happily settled he might be in his adopted country.

She surveyed the paintings and drawings on the walls. Art had never been her thing, but she could recognise quality when she saw it and these works were very definitely quality. Strike that. These were Quality.

At the window, she looked out across the park. A pair of

mounted police officers trotted along one of the paths through the park, their chestnut horses steadfastly ignoring the waving tourists trying to distract them for selfies. She tried to bring this elderly Swede into sharper focus.

A cultured man. A wealthy man. A man who, though retired from the diplomatic service, had stayed in England. Had he enemies? Did senior diplomats live the sorts of lives where they pissed people off badly enough to want them dead?

Why not? Anyone could. Until you added in the wild card of the tongue.

Tongues had two main jobs, as far as Stella could see. Eating and talking. Maybe three, if you included their erotic potential. You could eat without a tongue, she supposed, if only soup and liquids. You could kiss, do all the things people got up to behind closed doors. But talking? No. That came to a stop.

She entered the master bedroom, another impressive space. The lower halves of the walls were clad in pale-wood panelling. Above that hung more exquisite works of art, including a fleshy female nude by Lucian Freud. A sleigh bed in a rich russet colour that suggested cherry wood to Stella took up half the floorspace.

She opened a door that led to a walk-in wardrobe the size of the spare bedroom in her own, far more modest flat. She saw a dozen or more expensive-looking suits in soft sober-coloured fabrics.

She checked the label in one of the jackets and recognised the name of a famous contemporary tailor based in Savile Row, where well-heeled English gentlemen, and their imitators, had bought their suits for centuries.

Dress shirts hung in a coordinated row from white through pale pink to pale and then darker blue. High-end shoes sat on the carpet in pairs. She stooped to check the makes. Crockett & Jones, Grenson, Tricker's. All high-end English brands.

She had Brömly pegged. A member of that tribe of foreign settlers who fell in love with London and became more English than the English.

She turned to the nightstand and opened the drawers one by one. The top drawer held a slim leather-bound book that, when she

3

flicked through it, contained contact details for hundreds of men and women, with a great many possessing British-sounding names.

A CSI poked their head round the bedroom door.

'Ma'am? The pathologist's here.'

Stella walked back to the room where Brömly's cleaner had found his body. Fitted out with dark-wooden furniture and an old-fashioned writing desk, with framed vintage Grand Prix posters on the walls, the study was a very masculine space and larger than the living room in her own flat in Lisson Grove.

The man bending over the tongue with a magnifying glass was her favourite of the Home Office pathologists working out of Westminster Mortuary: Dr Roy Craven. He turned as she approached, pulled his face mask down and smiled.

She returned his smile and pointed at the tongue. 'What can you tell me? Apart from the obvious.'

'What would you consider obvious?' he replied, eyes twinkling behind his glasses.

Realising she'd strayed into a trap, Stella refused to blunder forwards into its waiting jaws.

She pointed at the body. 'I see a human male corpse missing its tongue.' And at the grisly specimen on the desk. 'I see a tongue, which appears to have been torn free of its moorings, on top of an open Swedish Bible.'

'And?'

Craven cocked his head on one side like a heron eyeing a fish in a pond: eager to catch a mere police officer out in an assumption unsupported by evidence. He wanted her to put the two facts together and come up with a third. That the tongue belonged to the dead man. She wouldn't give him the pleasure.

'From which *some* people might conclude that the tongue belonged to the dead man,' she said, locking eyes with him. 'But can we really be sure? Perhaps the killer took the tongue away and left an animal tongue behind to confuse us.'

Craven nodded. 'Perhaps.'

They'd played out this ritual before and both enjoyed it. It was their way of getting an initial feel for a case.

'Though intact, the tongue *appears* to have been torn out, rather than cut free,' Stella said.

Another nod.

'Therefore, an *inexperienced* detective might decide the killer lacked knowledge of anatomy or surgical techniques.'

'But you?'

'But I consider that our killer could just as easily have been a consultant maxillo-facial surgeon disguising their knowledge.'

Craven offered an ironic clap of his gloved hands. 'Bravo.'

'Was it removed before or after death?' she asked.

Craven shook his head again.

'Surely you don't expect me to offer an opinion *before* my investigation?'

'Just thought it was worth a try. When's the post mortem?'

'Tomorrow. First on my list. You'll be there?'

She nodded. 'I'd really like to get that Bible.'

'And so you shall. I'm done with it for now.'

And with that, the grand panjandrum of Westminster Public Mortuary's Iain West Forensic Suite left her to it, trailing behind him a faint, fruity aroma of pipe tobacco.

Stella beckoned the closest CSI.

'Could you secure that, please. Then get it to Westminster Mortuary.'

The CSI fetched a plastic box. When he lifted the obscene lump of tissue away from the Bible, the page beneath lifted.

'It's stuck. Hold on, I'll have to remove the page as well.'

'No! I want that. Try to free it without damaging the paper.'

The CSI nodded before disappearing to another room briefly and reappearing with a small scalpel in his hand.

Stella stretched out a hand and closed her gloved fingers on the tongue. The surface gave a little, making her wince. She raised it a couple of centimetres so the CSI could get the scalpel in.

With a series of gentle strokes, like a watercolourist applying paint, he managed to separate the tongue from the thin sheet of bloody paper without damaging either. It came free with a whisper and the page settled back.

The CSI placed the tongue in an evidence bag, sealed and labelled it, and placed the whole thing in the plastic box.

Shaking her head, Stella peered at the blood-soaked page. Through the staining she could make out the type but that was all. No, not all. She looked closer. One of the verses had been underlined. Important, then. But to whom? Brömly? Or his killer?

She pulled her phone out and took a picture.

Stella looked at the multicoloured strips poking out from between the pages. They were either yellow or green and bore greasy marks and furred, tattered corners. Except one. Pink. Fresh-looking, with crisp edges and sharp corners. She touched it. It had to be another important verse.

Stella turned the pages until the marked page fell open. A single verse had been underlined. She took another photograph.

She'd have to get them typed up and translated by a Home Office-approved interpreter or any evidential value would crumble. But for now she was happy to use an online translation tool for a quick reference. She made a mental note to do it as soon as she got back to Paddington Green.

Stella left the flat using the common approach path of yellow plastic tread plates and crossed Upper Brook Street to the designated motorcycle parking bays. Her metallic-blue Triumph Bonneville waited for her at the end of a row of mopeds. It looked comically oversized next to the spindly two-wheelers with budding taxi-drivers' clipboards fixed to their handlebars.

Over the years, she'd had to endure a certain amount of good-natured piss-taking from her colleagues. They'd suggested, variously, that she should join Traffic, or possibly go undercover with the Hells Angels.

Truth was, Stella loved bikes. She'd always ridden them, even owning a Harley for a while. She'd ended up ditching the Fat Boy for something British and more suited to London's narrow streets.

Throwing her right leg over the wide, comfortable saddle she settled herself then twisted the key in the ignition and thumbed the starter button. The big engine caught with a cough and a roar.

She toed the gear lever down for first and pulled away, heading back to Paddington Green police station. That meant turning left onto Park Lane and going all the way down to Hyde Park Corner, before swinging north again and heading up beside Hyde Park itself to Marble Arch.

As she rode the big Triumph back to the station, Stella was thinking about the lack of damage to the flat's door. That could mean one of two things.

Either Brömly knew his attacker. True in ninety-five percent of murders. Or the attacker was a stranger with a plausible story that got him admitted.

Of the two hypotheses, she leaned towards the latter. People one knew well enough to admit to one's home tended not to be psychopaths with a penchant for DIY oral surgery.

She thought back to the time she'd forced a High Court judge to remove one of his own teeth with a pair of pliers. Leonard Ramage was the one who'd killed Richard and Lola. The trigger man. Even though his weapon of choice was a Bentley. He'd deserved it. They all had. Especially her old boss, Adam Collier. Rounding Hyde Park Corner, she scowled at the memory.

Four thousand and twenty eight miles due west of her position, Collier was about to get a new lease of life. Or, at any rate, death.

2

PRESTON, MINNESOTA

The unnamed lake outside the town limits was Jimmy Lindqvist's favourite spot for trying out new big-air tricks. No likelihood of fans, rivals or the media catching him or his three-thousand-dollar BMX bike on video.

Upside down and grinning with exhilaration, Jimmy looked at the blue-green water, glittering in the sunlight. His mood changed in an instant. And he screamed.

He plunged beneath the surface, mouth still stretched wide, looking straight down at a human skeleton. It lay fifteen feet away from a black SUV. It was lying on the lakebed as if parked.

Although he had only been underwater for five seconds, he broke the surface gasping as if he had been close to drowning.

'Oh shit oh shit oh shit!' he gasped between breaths. 'Oh holy shit!'

Arms and legs flailing in an ungainly crawl, he struck out for the shore. He heaved himself out of the water onto the wooden jetty, from which the practice ramp curled upwards like a great curving tongue, and ran for his truck. The dark-brown footprints he left on the wooden planks began fading immediately. He snatched his phone off the Dodge's dashboard and dialled 911.

* * *

Chief Andersen, who'd known Jimmy since he was a baby, climbed out of the car and hitched up his belt. He strode over to greet Jimmy.

'You OK?'

'Yeah, Chief. Just shocked, I guess.' He turned and pointed at a spot maybe twenty feet from the shore. 'It's down there. My bike, too. Will they be able to get it out?'

Andersen laid a meaty paw on the kid's shoulder.

'We'll get it, Jimmy, don't worry. I'm going to need you to come in to the station and give your official statement. We'll give you a ride and have your bike back at your house before you are. That OK?'

'I guess. Am I in trouble?'

The chief laughed, grateful that on this bright summer morning there was at least one piece of good news he could dish out. 'No, Son. You're the hero of the hour.'

Thirty-five minutes later, the lakeshore was Jimmy's private domain no longer. Diesel engines chuntered. Walkie-talkies crackled. Cops were chatting. Behind black-and-yellow crime-scene tapes, a few dozen bystanders stood, phones aloft, capturing the scene for posterity, or Facebook at least. The chief had sent Jimmy to wait in his truck.

A silver-and-yellow Manitowoc mobile crane towered above the white CSI van, two black-and-white prowl cars and the chief's Cherokee. The thrum of its huge Diesel engine set up a sympathetic vibration in the chief's chest.

He sent a couple of divers down to attach a lifting rig to the SUV and recover the bones. They popped up now, like seals, gave the circled finger-and-thumb for OK, and flippered back to the shore. Between them bobbed a black body bag.

The divers hauled themselves and their burden out onto the warm planking. The lead diver unzipped the bag, letting the lake water stream out. The chief peered in and the sightless eye sockets of a human skull stared back at them.

The chief signalled to the crane driver, pointing at the water and giving him the thumbs-up.

For good measure, he yelled, 'Go get it!'

The tone of the engine deepened under the load. Slowly, roof first, then windows, sides and finally wheels, the black SUV emerged. Water sluiced over the hood and spattered the lake surface.

With the SUV secure on the shore, a gum-booted CSI strode forwards, lifted the driver's door handle and stepped back smartly. The pressure of the water inside the vehicle swung the door out, narrowly missing her right hip. And in a great flood, several hundred gallons of lake water rushed out onto the deck.

But it wasn't the water that caused gasps and salty expressions. Nor the four-foot-long mottled-brown flathead catfish that came out with it, slithering across the planks before splashing back into the lake.

What drew the sounds from the lips of the assembled law enforcement officers were the scatter of human bones that the outrushing water deposited at their feet. The skull, perforated between the eye sockets, bobbled and rolled to a stop at the chief's booted feet.

'Looks like we got us a real puzzle, eh, Chief?' a detective asked, pointing at the skull.

'Uffda! You betcha!' was all the astonished chief could manage.

* * *

The following morning, Andersen stood looking at the two skeletons on their side-by-side stainless-steel tables in the ME's autopsy room.

Using an extending chromed pointer, Dr Cory Pleasaunce tapped the female skeleton's ribcage on the left side.

'Your divers found a .40 S&W jacketed hollow point that matches the Glock. Right where her ribcage was lying.'

'No surprise there.'

'No. But you want to know what *is* surprising?'

Andersen smiled. He and the ME went way back and he knew how much she enjoyed trying to trip him up.

'Go on then. Surprise me.'

Pleasaunce tapped the male skeleton's skull, a little to the right of the bullet hole. Andersen found it unsettling the way its top had been cleanly sawn off and now lay beside it like a gruesome ashtray. He peered in, noting the scoring and multiple fractures on the inner surface, imagining a JHP round pinging around the murderer's brain like a pinball.

'We found that round, too. It wasn't hard. It was sitting waiting for us inside the cranium.'

'So far, so *un*surprising. Come on, spill the beans,' the chief said with a smile.

She returned the expression.

'It was a Speer Gold Dot jacketed hollow point.' She paused for a beat. 'In a thirty-eight special. You're looking at two guns. The Glock and a thirty-eight. Probably a revolver. And I'll tell you what. I have never heard of a murder-suicide where the doer used two guns.'

Chief Andersen called up the dive team again. After forty minutes of fingertip searching, they surfaced with a Smith & Wesson.38 'Airweight' revolver. He sent it off to the ballistics lab in Minneapolis and the techs there emailed him back to say it was a match for the slug recovered from the male victim's skull.

A trace on the Glock 22 came back with a weapon registered to the FBI. Specifically to the armoury at the Chicago field office.

Cory had removed a gold wedding ring from the male corpse's right hand. Inside it bore the engraved text:

Adam & Lynne 24.5.97

A smaller ring recovered from the lake floor had an identical inscription.

Chief Andersen ran the SUV's plates. It came back first registered to an Adam Collier, resident in Chicago.

With a pile of evidence before him, he rang the Feds in the

Windy City. After taking a few details, the receptionist routed his call.

'This is Special Agent-in-Charge Eddie Baxter. What can I do for you today, Chief Andersen?'

'Well now, I've got a couple skeletons up here. We just recovered them from a lake. One male, one female. The male was sitting in a black Ford Explorer SUV registered in Chicago beside a Glock 22 registered to your field office there.'

SAC Baxter drew in a sharp breath.

'Everything OK?' the chief asked.

'Yes. Go on, please,' Baxter said in a tight voice.

'Well, we also recovered two wedding rings. Same engraving on both. Adam and Lynne. Twenty-four, five, ninety-seven. Which strikes me as the British way of writing our dates.'

'I'm going to need you to hold everything securely for me, Chief. I'm coming up to see you. Where's the nearest airport?'

'That would be Rochester International. I had one of my guys look up flights for you already. You can get the four-fifty-five American Eagle flight. Gets in at quarter after six. When were you thinking of coming up?'

'Today.'

The chief put the phone down and blew out his cheeks. The Feds. In Preston. Well, it would be one for the grandkids, that was for sure.

3

LONDON

Back at Paddington Green, Stella went to see her boss. Detective Chief Superintendent Calpurnia 'Callie' McDonald looked up as Stella entered the spacious office.

'What's up, Stel? You've got a glint in your eye,' she said.

'New case. Weird one. More than usually weird,' she added, to forestall Callie's telling her that 'weird' went with the territory in the Special Investigations Unit.

Callie pursed her lips, today a darker shade of red than her signature scarlet.

'Go on then. Gie me a wee case of the heebie-jeebies,' she said, roughening her genteel Edinburgh accent to something sharper.

Stella outlined the basics.

'Odd, but not weird. What aren't you telling me?'

'Like our Lord, I've saved the best till last.'

'Och, so now you're blaspheming, too? Spit it out, woman!'

Reflecting that Callie's turn of phrase was unpleasantly appropriate, Stella did.

Callie nodded. 'That is weird,' she said finally.

* * *

Stella convened a briefing with her team. Joining her in the meeting room were her bagman, DS Garry Haynes, plus DI Roisin Griffin, DS Barendra 'Baz' Khan, DS Stephanie Fish and DC Camille Wilde. Other members of the team had either transferred out, retired if their thirty was up or were simply busy on other investigative teams within SIU.

She'd set up a laptop connected to a projector and beamed a photo of the dead man's blood-besmirched face onto the screen. Over the next twenty minutes she gave them all the information she'd acquired so far, which included that from the West End Central Murder Team who'd caught the case initially.

'Robbery gone wrong?' Cam asked.

'His phone and laptop were still there, plus a very nice watch, a wallet with credit cards and two hundred in cash, and a bunch of extremely expensive paintings. Plus assorted gold and silver cufflinks and his gold wedding ring.'

'Sex crime?' This from Baz.

'Apart from the tongue, I saw no other injuries or mutilations. Nothing sexual, either. No perv stuff in the bedroom.'

'You think it's a serial, boss?' Garry asked.

'I bloody hope not. But if it is, we'll have to move fast. I don't want to see headlines blaring out at me from every newsagent's window about a "senior slayer" terrorising the old and rich.'

Stella looked down at her notes. So what did they have? Not a robbery. Nor a thrill-kill. Up to the point the tongue had been removed, and despite the use of a firearm, the whole thing smelled like another murder in Normaltown. But the mutilation moved it into a new postcode: W1 3RD.

'The tongue, guv,' Cam said. 'Was it taken out before or after he was shot?'

'Good question. Doc Craven wouldn't commit, but if it was *ante-mortem*, as he'd probably say, then we're looking for a sadistic psychopath. If it was post-mortem, it means something else, though what I have no bloody idea at this point.'

'How about forensics?' Roisin asked.

'West End Central are turning everything over to us once their team are finished. Lucian, can you prioritise it as soon as it arrives, please?'

Lucian nodded. The senior CSI at Paddington Green, Lucian Young was one of the people at work Stella counted as a friend, as well as a colleague. He was also a computer genius who'd sold a company he'd started with friends while at university before even leaving for the world of practical science.

'Which version of the Bible, guv?' Cam asked.

'Swedish. Someone, probably the killer, underlined one verse and put Brömly's tongue right on top of it. The other one was bookmarked in a different colour from all the others picked out.'

She projected the two verses onto the screen along with their English translations.

*Ordspråken/*Proverbs 11:12

Den som förminskar sin granne saknar förnuft, men en förståelsesman förblir tyst.

He who diminishes his neighbour lacks reason, but a man of understanding remains silent.

*Ordspråken/*Proverbs 28:13

Den som döljer sin synd blir aldrig lycklig, men den som bekänner den och ångrar sig möts med barmhärtighet.

He who conceals his sin is never happy, but he who confesses and repents is met with mercy.

'So they're significant to the killer?' Cam asked.

'Or the victim. Or both. Can you get onto the National Crime Agency and ask for two accredited Swedish interpreters to give us evidence-grade translations, please?'

'Some nutter's gone biblical,' Rosh said.

'It's a line of enquiry, certainly.'

'"And if thy right eye offend thee, pluck it out",' Rosh said. 'It's obvious!'

Stella shook her head, already anticipating another blow-up from the DI. 'I don't think it is. Something about this points in a completely different direction.'

The two women had clashed many times in the past, and after Stella had caught Roisin leaking details of an investigation to a journalist had delivered a bollocking that had almost reduced Rosh to tears.

'What direction, boss?' Def asked.

DS Stephanie Fish had won her nickname after her initial moniker of 'Definitely Fit' had been shortened to something more manageable.

Stella inwardly thanked the blonde DS with the supermodel looks. Def was a shit-hot interviewer. She was also the team peacemaker, and often poured oil onto the turbulence Rosh and Stella stirred up whenever they were in the same room.

'I think he was killed to silence him. I think the killer left the tongue there as a message. "Talk and this is what happens."'

She wrote up the others' suggestions, from a straight contract hit to a bizarrely staged domestic and assigned tasks accordingly. Cam to get the Bible verses to accredited interpreters. Baz to start working the address book, contacting friends and any family. Rosh to make contact with the Swedish expat community. Garry to secure the dead man's medical records. And Def to run a search on the National Homicide Database for murders where tongue removal was a feature.

'My first guv'nor told me something once,' Stella said after finishing the distribution of jobs. 'If you can find out how the victim lived, you can find out how they died. I want to know everything about Tomas Brömly from the moment he was born to the moment he carked it.'

She finished work just after six-thirty. Some of the other female detectives were heading to a nearby Italian place called *Buccia di Limone*. The occasion was a monthly meet-up called Good Girls

Drink Plonk. Once a dismissive nickname for female officers, Plonk had been proudly reclaimed.

Stella had been a regular attender but since meeting Jamie, she'd started missing the odd session. This was one of those times. It was her turn to stay at his place tonight. She smiled at the thought of her boyfriend's cooking, and his taut, slim body pressed against hers in bed.

She swung her leg over the Bonnie's saddle and pushed the starter button. The engine started with a glorious bark that reverberated around the underground parking garage and brought a smile to her lips. She blipped the throttle, just for fun, and pulled away, the rear tyre screeching on the grey-painted floor.

* * *

Roisin knew she wasn't a brilliant detective. Even though she hated Stella, she recognised in her that rare and indefinable skill that marked out the truly great thief-takers from the also-rans.

But Roisin also knew that technical competence wasn't always the best or fastest route to promotion. Being good enough could keep you in post. Being *connected* could get you higher up the greasy pole than any number of solved cases.

She'd made it her business since arriving at Paddington Green to cultivate those connections she thought would best help her in her ambitions. And she used one now.

As she sat at the long candlelit table in *Buccia di Limone's* private dining room, Roisin raised her glass of Chianti. She turned to her neighbour, Assistant Commissioner Rachel Fairhill. One of the rules of 'Good Girls', as its members called it, was that rank was forgotten.

'Cheers, Rachel,' she said.

'Cheers. How was your day?'

Roisin nodded and sipped her wine.

'Good. Can I ask you something?'

Rachel smiled. 'Ask away.'

'I love my job at SIU, but the opportunities for promotion are pretty limited on account of we're so small. I just wondered, if anything comes up where you need some help, would you keep me in mind?'

'Of course. After sitting in for me on that *dreadful* community relations committee, I owe you. Nothing at the moment. But I'll make a mental note. Ah,' she said, smiling up at a waiter, 'here's my *pollo cacciatore!*'

Roisin wished her *buon appetito* and poured more wine. As she drank, she offered a silent toast to her own career.

4

CROWTHORNE, BERKSHIRE

Stella pulled off the road and gentled the Bonneville across the pavement and onto Jamie's drive. The house itself was a red-brick Victorian rectory: two main storeys plus a loft conversion in the steeply pitched tiled roof. A wrought-iron balcony extended out from the master bedroom. She loved to drink an early morning cup of tea or an evening gin and tonic out there.

She found Jamie at the black granite kitchen counter, perched on a bar stool. He was reading a report of some kind, a slender-stemmed glass of red wine at his elbow. He was wearing chinos and a soft, faded Levi's denim shirt with mother-of-pearl press studs. His feet were bare.

She planted a kiss on the back of his neck. He turned and returned the kiss, full on the lips, lingering over the embrace.

'Well,' she said when he let her go, 'somebody's had a good day.'

He grinned. '*The Journal of Criminal Psychiatry* accepted my article on childhood attachment disorders in serial murderers.'

'That's brilliant! When's it coming out?'

He shrugged. 'It has to be peer-reviewed first. Then they'll take a proper look at it and possibly send it back for revisions, but hopefully this side of Christmas.'

'Is that good?'

'For the JCP? It's fast-track, believe me. Wine?'

He poured her a glass and clinked rims with her.

'Apart from the good news, how was your day?' Stella asked him.

'I have a new patient referred from the High Court. Found not guilty of murdering his elderly parents with an axe by reason of insanity,' he paused. 'He believed they were sent by the devil to poison his Weetabix.'

Stella snorted, narrowly missing spraying wine over Jamie's shirt. 'Oh god, sorry, darling. I know it's not funny.'

'It kind of is,' he said, smiling. 'For Broadmoor, that counts as light relief. As I think you know.'

Stella did know. When your boyfriend worked at one of the UK's special hospitals for the criminally insane, seemingly innocent enquiries like hers yielded tales that would have most people looking for the exit.

'How about your day?' he asked.

'New case. Really weird.'

He frowned. 'Isn't that rather why Callie set up the SIU?'

'That's what she said. What do you make of this?'

When she finished speaking, Jamie blew his cheeks out. Then he tapped his index finger against his pursed lips. It was a signature gesture of his. It reminded Stella of her initial feeling that this was about silence.

'Did someone on your team latch onto the religious nutter angle?' he asked eventually.

'I did to start with. Then I dismissed it. Rosh was sold on it, though.'

He took another mouthful of the wine. 'Why did you dismiss it?'

'Look at the MO. Brömly was shot. Most likely with a handgun. That's a pro's weapon. And extremely difficult to get hold of. Your average religious maniac wouldn't be able to lay their hands on one. Let alone an undiagnosed schizophrenic or some poor sod off their meds. I'm also thinking it's a man.'

Jamie nodded. 'In my experience as a forensic psychiatrist—'

'Soon to be published in a very prestigious academic journal…'

He grinned. 'Religiously inspired killers tend to go for more, what shall we say, baroque methods of killing. Think of Robey.'

'I'd rather not,' Stella said, massaging a place on her left bicep where the serial killer Jamie had just mentioned had cut deep into her flesh with a machete.

'My point is, they tend to select weapons with religious resonance. Knives, usually. Ropes, occasionally. Even home-made gadgets they've constructed from drawings in old books,' he said. 'They often see themselves as conducting some sort of sacred ritual of cleansing or consumption. Now, if your killer had eaten the tongue, or part of it, that would be different. But a pistol? No. Too modern.'

Jamie had confirmed her own initial feelings about the case. Killers who used pistols tended to score way down on the religious nutcase scale.

'So, what else?' Stella asked, sipping her wine.

'Well, tell me about tongues. What do they signify?'

This was why Stella enjoyed talking shop with Jamie. He wasn't Job, but close enough to be able to discuss any detail of a case, however gruesome, without getting a fit of the vapours. Plus he came at things from a different angle to cops. And that made it interesting. Invaluable, sometimes.

'Tongues signify more than just speech,' Stella said. 'If you stick your tongue out, that's offensive. Lick your lips and it's erotic. Maybe Brömly had sexually abused his killer in the past.'

Jamie nodded. 'If you want a motive beyond a jilted lover, that's where I'd look.'

'I'll add that as a line of enquiry. But I still see the silencing angle as the best right now.'

'I agree. It's the most straightforward. And don't be put off by thoughts of having seen it in the movies,' he said, making air quotes. 'Most murderers lack imagination as well as self-control.'

'Thanks.'

Jamie smiled. 'You're welcome. Now, how about some food? I'm hungry.'

They stayed up late, discussing work and a holiday they'd been talking about. Jamie wanted to visit the Lake District to do some walking. Stella wanted somewhere they didn't speak English and where she wouldn't need to pack anything warmer than a sarong.

They tumbled into his king-sized bed at just after midnight.

Stella yawned luxuriously.

'Sleepy?' he asked.

'Not yet,' she said, reaching down for him under the sheet.

* * *

Stella woke to the buzzing of her phone. Jamie rolled over.

'What time is it?' he mumbled.

'Six-thirty.'

'What? We normally get up at seven.'

'I know,' she said, backing into him. 'But today we need a little longer.'

'Again, Ms Cole?'

She responded by pushing her bottom against his groin. She sighed with pleasure as he slid his hand between her arm and ribcage to cup her breast.

The memory of the sex took her, still smiling, into London and on to the post-mortem. Standing beside her in Examination Room 3 of the mortuary, Garry nodded to her.

'All right, boss?' he asked.

'Yeah, you?'

'Me? Fine. Yeah, tip-top.'

'What's going on?'

'Get some this morning, did you?'

'What?'

He grinned. 'You heard! You had that smile on your face when you came in.'

'I have no idea what you mean.'

'Yes you do. It was an "I had a pre-work shag" smile.'

Shaking her head, she pointed at the sheeted body before them. 'Inappropriate.'

24

'I'll take that as a yes, then.'

Joining them at the dissection table, Dr Craven cleared his throat. 'If our colleagues from SIU have finished their *banter*, perhaps we could make a start?'

'Sorry, Doc,' Stella and Garry choroused.

Beside Dr Craven stood his assistant Verity Carr, her willowy figure disguised by her baggy scrubs. She glanced at Stella and shot her a wink from behind her Perspex visor.

One of the rituals Craven performed at his post-mortems was to say a short prayer.

'Lord, help us bring clarity where there is doubt, light where there is darkness and order where there is chaos. And, above all, let us uncover the truth behind Tomas Brömly's death and bring the perpetrator to justice. Amen.'

'Amen,' Garry murmured.

Craven clapped his double-gloved hands together. 'Right! Let's crack on, shall we? Verity, my trusty PM40 scalpel, if you please.'

As he drew the large blade in from each shoulder to a point at the sternum, then continued down to make the classic Y-incision, Craven kept up a running commentary into a mic dangling centrally above the table on a curly wire. Stella had attended dozens of post- mortems as a detective. Although she wasn't shocked by what she saw anymore, she still felt a thrill each time the pathologist revealed the workings of the human body.

Craven opened the chest cavity. He cut through the rib cartilage each side of the sternum with what looked like a high-tech version of garden secateurs. Each rib parted with a crack like a snapping stick.

He freed the heart from its attachments and pointed to a huge wound.

Stella looked closer. The right side of the heart had been virtually destroyed. Cause of death would have been massive internal bleeding. Craven handed the ruined pump to Verity, who weighed it and placed it in a plastic container.

The lungs came next and Craven showed them to the assembled observers. Apart from Stella and Garry, they included Lucian, a photographer, the crime scene manager and the coroner's officer. The bullet had ripped through the left lung, turning its upper half into a mass of shredded pink, foamy tissue.

The chest cavity was full of blood. Unasked, Verity brought a suction pipe into play. With the pipe gurgling as she moved it deliberately around the chest walls, Stella peered at the internal surface of the entry wound.

It resembled a grotesque flower. Petals of burnt flesh folded back on themselves above a hole that led through the ribs and the broad triangular muscle beyond to the breach in the skin.

'Where's the bullet, Doc?' Garry asked.

'That is precisely what I am trying to ascertain,' Craven said. 'Verity, would you be so good as to have a poke around in the heart for me?'

Stella observed the way Verity inserted a long gloved finger into each of the remaining chambers of the heart. She looked up as she probed, relying on feel alone.

'Not in the heart, Doctor,' she said after a minute or so.

'Very well. Where else might we look?' Craven asked. 'Anyone?'

'The lungs?' Garry asked.

'The wound track suggests only a single pass through the lungs. I believe it entered through the *latissimus dorsi* muscle, smashed its way between the third and fourth true ribs just to the left of the T3 and T4 vertebrae,' Craven said with all the authority of a twenty-year veteran of the autopsy room. 'From there, it travelled upwards at a slight angle, penetrating the left lung, before entering the right ventricle where it caused the fatal injury.'

'Chest wall?' Stella offered.

'That seems probable.' Craven took a smaller scalpel and probed the great flap of flesh lying on the corpse's left side.

'The interior surface of the left *pectoralis major* bears every sign of a penetrating wound. And if we just...' As Verity had done, he glanced upwards, using feel rather than sight. 'Forceps, please.'

Using the narrow-nosed forceps Verity placed in his palm, Craven poked and prodded for a few more seconds. Nodding, he pulled them clear. They made a tiny sucking noise.

Gripped between their serrated tips was a deformed bullet, its splayed tip resembling a ragged-edged mushroom. Craven dropped it with a clink into the stainless-steel kidney bowl Verity held ready.

'*Voilà!*'

Verity held the bowl out so Stella could see the bullet. It looked to her like a jacketed hollow-point round from a nine-mil. She'd keep her counsel until the techs had done their stuff.

Craven pointed to the face and nodded at Verity. She hooked her right index finger into the corpse's lower jaw, pulling down to open the mouth then taking half a step backwards to give Craven space.

Craven leaned closer and brought his face almost within kissing distance of the corpse. Stella shuddered.

'The killer did not use a knife, scalpel or any other type of blade to remove the tongue,' Craven said, probing the lower surface of the open mouth.

'What *can* you tell us?' Stella asked. 'How much strength would it take to pull out a man's tongue?'

'Yeah, Doc. Could a woman do it, for example?' Garry added.

'To tear the tongue away from its four anchor-points and separate it from the soft tissue would require a great deal of force. But it would certainly be possible for a woman if she were determined enough. However, the principal obstacle to the successful evulsion of the tongue would be saliva.'

'It's too slippery, right, Doc?' Garry asked.

'Precisely. One would need gloves and pincers of some kind. In fact, let's take a look at the abused organ and see what we can deduce about the killer's method.'

Verity walked to a large stainless-steel fridge, one of three ranged along the back wall. She returned holding a plastic container.

Garry nudged Stella. 'Crap! I brought my lunch in one just like that.'

Stella rolled her eyes.

Craven lifted out the tongue and placed it on a second, smaller examination table. Everyone moved over to gather round.

Craven tapped a Perspex rod against the upper surface of the tongue. Stella looked closely. Craven was indicating a sharp-edged rectangle of depressed flesh, inside which, running left to right, were a series of deep parallel cuts.

What would have created marks like those? Grips, she thought. Or pliers. She had some basic tools in the flat for the Bonnie. She thought one of them could have made similar cuts.

Stella and Garry stood aside as the photographer stepped closer and took a series of close-ups of the marks.

'Could you email those to me as soon as you can, please?' Stella asked the photographer, who nodded in reply.

Craven returned to his examination of the body. He pointed at a purplish-red area of bruising on the corpse's forehead. It looked like a honeycomb: interlocking hexagons studded with irregular blotches. A shoe print of some kind. Probably a running shoe. Something athletic, anyway.

As Craven worked and kept up his commentary, Stella began to see how Brömly's murder had unfolded.

The killer had buzzed the intercom for admittance, then knocked or rang the doorbell. Brömly had let him in, probably with a smile, as he knew him. They'd talked.

The killer had bided his time and, when Brömly's back was turned, shot him in the back with the nine. Brömly had fallen. The killer had rolled him onto his back, put his foot on Brömly's face, grabbed the tongue with a pair of grips and then yanked. Hard.

Craven picked up the right hand. She looked at the pale digit gripped in Craven's gloved fingers. The nail was trimmed, the edge smooth, not ragged. Not a biter. She looked at the knuckle. On its left side, roughly where it would touch the index finger, she saw a raised bump.

'What's that, Doc?' Garry asked. 'Arthritis?'

Stella saw it. A writer's callus. She recalled the cluttered writing desk in the study. Most people these days used keyboards or touchscreens. Brömly preferred a pen.

After establishing with Craven that the rest of the post-mortem would be largely routine, Stella excused herself and Garry.

'You'll have my report by day's end,' Craven called after them.

Which would be fantastic. But she was already working angles, formulating theories and drawing up a new list of lines of enquiry she wanted to pursue. One of them meant a return to Brömly's flat.

She sent Garry back to Paddington Green and made her way to Upper Brook Street. Once through the cordon, Stella entered Brömly's office and sat at the desk. She began surveying the space where Brömly had done whatever retired ambassadors did at their desks.

A large, old-fashioned blotter pad occupied most of the space in front of her. The gold tooling on the burgundy leather surround was worn on the right-hand side nearest the front edge. Brömly must have been right-handed. The pale-blue paper in the centre bore a few doodles: mainly spirals and crosses, no words.

The rest of the desk and the dinky wooden cubbyholes against the wall were cluttered with all sorts of pens, old-fashioned wooden rulers, pencil pots and bottles of ink.

She pushed the chair back and squatted in front of the desk. Reaching up, she switched on the Anglepoise desk lamp and angled its conical shade until the light spilled across the blotter at a shallow angle.

She dipped lower, grateful that her running regimen kept her quads in good shape, and looked along the surface of the blotter. There! Faint impressions denting the soft, fibrous paper. She ran her fingers over them, just brushing the surface.

5

LONDON

Stella called the Swedish embassy and, after explaining why she was calling, was put straight through to the ambassador. Ten minutes later, she was passing through several layers of embassy security.

The junior diplomat who escorted Stella to the ambassador's office wore a beige skirt suit and nude high heels. In her bike jacket and black jeans, Stella felt distinctly underdressed. The diplomat knocked softly on the door and waited.

The door opened inwards to reveal a man in his late forties with thick, dark hair swept back from his forehead. He smiled.

'DCI Cole? I'm Anders Johansson, please come in. Thank you, Nilla.'

He led Stella to a pair of armchairs flanking a glass-topped table. The plate-glass window beside it gave onto Montagu Square, a neat little park with trees, flowerbeds and well-maintained benches.

On the table sat a chrome coffee pot, two white china mugs and a jug of steaming milk. Beside them, a plate of dinky chestnut-brown spiral buns.

He sat and gestured for Stella to do the same.

'Please, help yourself to a *kanelbullar*. Coffee?'

'Thank you.'

Stella took one of the little buns and bit into its warm, doughy centre. The way the cinnamon and sugar combined with the sliced roasted almonds on the top made her groan involuntarily.

'That is delicious! Where do you get them from?'

'Our chef makes them fresh every morning. I recruited him personally from the best bakery in Stockholm.'

'I hope you're paying him well.'

Johansson laughed. 'Believe me, I will make sure he stays here as long as I do.'

Stella placed a folder on the table between them. Johansson's gaze flicked down before returning to her.

'The man who was murdered. His name was Tomas Brömly,' she said.

Johansson's eyebrows shot up. 'My god! You mean *Ambassador* Brömly?'

'I'm sorry. We need to track down his next of kin. Is that something you could help with?'

'He was widowed. Anna died ten years ago. They never had children, but I'll have someone look into it for you.'

'Thank you. Did you know him well?'

Johansson wiped a hand across his mouth. His face had paled.

'Fairly well, yes. He was my predecessor-but-one. The Swedish community in London isn't large, and the diplomatic community is smaller still. We used to see each other socially maybe once a month.'

'Can you think of anyone who would have had a reason to hurt Mr Brömly? To the point of killing him?'

Johansson frowned. He didn't answer at once, instead standing and walking over to the floor-to-ceiling window and staring down at the square.

'I'm sorry,' he said. 'I need to compose myself. This is a great shock.'

He drew a handkerchief from his breast pocket and pressed it to his eyes. He blew his nose. He turned back to Stella, though he remained standing.

'Tomas was what you might call a diplomat in the classic mode. He was unfailingly courteous to everyone he met, from heads of state to the office cleaners. I don't think in all the time I knew him I ever heard him raise his voice.'

'None of that excludes the possibility of an enemy,' Stella said as gently as she could.

'I know. But I am struggling. After he retired, he settled in London. He told me once he had fallen in love with Britain and wanted to live out his days here. I suppose at least he got his wish.'

Johansson returned to the table and sat down again. He finished his coffee and poured some more.

'If he did make enemies, I don't see that he could possibly have made them in London.'

'Did you know him socially?' Stella asked.

'A little. We saw each other at church and at the Swedish Social Club on Balfour Place. He was a very good bridge player.'

Stella had been making notes as he spoke. She'd underlined 'church' and 'social club'.

'His flat was in a very expensive part of London,' she said. 'And he had some expensive art on his walls. I didn't know diplomacy paid so well.'

Johansson shook his head. 'I'm afraid you're barking up the wrong tree. Tomas was not poorly paid as a diplomat, and the Swedish government is generous with pensions,' he said. 'But it was Anna who had the real money. Her family built a sizeable industrial company supplying aerospace industries around the world. He inherited her fortune when she died.'

Mentally crossing off money as a line of inquiry, Stella returned to more mundane matters.

'Do you have his CV on file?'

'Yes. No harm in sharing it with you, now's he's dead. I'll have it emailed to you.'

Stella passed him one of her Met business cards.

'I'd also like to speak to the minster at the church he attended. And someone at the social club,' she said.

Johansson nodded. 'I'll add that information to my email.'

In the face of his evident distress, Stella tried to offer some comfort. 'If it's any consolation, I am sure Ambassador Brömly didn't suffer. Death would have been instantaneous.'

As she uttered these reassuring words, Stella hoped they were true. Only once she'd read Craven's report would she know for sure exactly how much Brömly had really suffered.

By the time she got back to her desk in SIU, the email from Johansson was waiting in her inbox. He explained that finding the next of kin might take a little longer, but he could give her Brömly's CV, and the two names she needed, right away:

Karin Malmaeus, priest, Svenska Kyrkan (Swedish Church)

Lars Bjorling, secretary, Svenska Vänskapssamhället (Swedish Friendship Society)

She noted down the names and contact details. She sent Bjorling's details to Roisin, then turned to the CV.

After twenty minutes of reading, and re-reading, she had built a truncated timeline for Brömly's professional life.

1942 Born (17 Jan)
 1960 Left school
 1963 Graduated from Stockholm University with degree in Demographics and joined civil service
 1971 Took sabbatical to do voluntary work in Tanzania
 1976 Joined diplomatic service
 1997 Appointed ambassador to UK
 2002 Returned to Sweden
 2007 Retired
 2008 Moved to London
 2021 Murdered

. . .

His early career looked like a civil service recruiter's wet dream. But then she took another look at what she'd written. And she realised she'd missed something. It was so obvious in the shortened form of his career, but it had been lost amidst all the detail of his actual CV. The sabbatical.

How long did people do voluntary service overseas for? Six months? A year? But five years? Really? Mid-career? That was a lot of time away from the greasy pole.

She left her office and stood in the middle of the open-plan area of SIU.

'Sorry, everyone. Your attention, please, for a moment!' She waited while those not on the phone swivelled in her direction. 'Anyone ever do any VSO?'

'I did, boss,' a DS from a neighbouring team called out.

Stella crossed to his desk. 'Where did you go?'

'Cambodia. Straight after uni. It was awesome.'

'How long were you out there for?'

'It was three months, give or take a week.'

She returned to her office and circled the item on her timeline. She added a note: Too long?/multiple placements?

If there were a Swedish equivalent to the British Voluntary Service Overseas charity, would it still have records from the mid-seventies? Stella thought she knew the answer.

Instead of digging further into the CV, she called the priest at the Swedish Church.

'Hello, this is Karin?' A lilting voice, with an undercurrent of seriousness.

'Ms Malmaeus, this is DCI Cole. I'm with the police. I was given your name by the ambassador, Anders Jonasson?'

'Oh, yes. Jonas is a good friend. And it's Mrs by the way.'

Once more, Stella explained what she was doing. Malmaeus agreed to see her at once.

* * *

The Swedish Church occupied a central position on Harcourt Street, just a few minutes' ride from Paddington Green. The white stone frontage soared upwards, dwarfing the three-storey office buildings to each side. A copper spire, weathered to a vivid green, stretched higher still, surmounted by a golden weather vane. A Swedish flag fluttered from a pole set into the white stone to the right of the ornate portico over the front door.

The woman in clerical black and dog-collar who met Stella at the church had a bony forehead, a long, narrow nose and a heavy jaw. Stella felt she could almost see the bones of her skull beneath her pale, smooth, un-madeup skin. Her dazzling pale-blue eyes seemed out of place in such a rough-hewn face, like the pretty flowers one might find growing among the rocks of a sea-cliff.

'DCI Cole, I am sorry not to be welcoming you to our church under happier circumstances. Please, follow me. We should talk in my private office, yes?'

Having been offered, and refused, coffee and cakes, Stella sketched in the details of the murder. This time she did mention the mutilation.

'I must ask you to keep that detail a secret. I don't know if there's a Lutheran equivalent of the confessional, but this is highly confidential.'

Malmaeus nodded. 'We believe very strongly in confession and absolution. It is called the Office of the Keys. But in any case, yes. I give you my word as a priest.'

'Two verses in Mr Brömly's Bible were highlighted. If I show them to you, could you tell me if they might have any particular significance? Perhaps especially to a Swede?'

'Do you have them with you?'

Stella passed a sheet of paper bearing the two verses across the desk. She waited while Malmaeus placed a pair of black-framed glasses on her nose and read the brief passages of Swedish.

'There's nothing that makes me think of a particular relevance to Swedes,' she said, handing the sheet back to Stella. 'Sin and absolution are universal experiences.'

Stella stared at the Swedish verses, the English translations reverberating in her head in Malmaeus's quiet, strong voice. Was her hunch on the money? Was this about Brömly wanting to speak out and his killer wanting to silence him?

'Did Mr Brömly give you any cause to think that something was troubling him? That he had something on his conscience?'

Malmaeus smiled sadly, and the expression transformed the misshapen face.

'I am sorry. I cannot reveal anything to you about Tomas's confessions.'

'Of course. I understand,' Stella said. She frowned. How could she get the information she wanted without forcing Malmaeus to choose between trouble with the cops or trouble with her faith?

'How about outside of the confessional? Had he changed in any way recently?'

Malmaeus nodded. Her smile was more open, free from the concern that had lent her previous expression a sad edge.

'He had started to appear distant. And he smiled less. Not to the point of rudeness. Tomas was never impolite. But I would just say he had something on his mind.'

Stella thanked the priest for her time and Malmaeus showed her out. They had to squeeze to one side as five children barrelled along the passageway, laughing and trailing balloons behind them on coloured ribbons.

Malmaeus smiled at Stella. 'A family christening. Sometimes the little ones get bored.'

Stella smiled back. She watched the little girl at the rear of the group and felt a distant ache.

* * *

Later that afternoon, she assembled her team in a conference room. With variations, depending on which aspects of his life they had been investigating, everyone gave the same information.

Brömly was some kind of modern-day saint. A generous giver to Swedish charities. A regular churchgoer. A pretty sharp bridge player, but, as he and his friends only played for matches, gambling as a motive was off the table. One of the card players told Baz that Brömly had been off his food recently.

'Not much, I know, but he also said Brömly used to be a great one for those cinnamon buns.'

'*Kanelbullar*,' Stella said.

'Didn't know you spoke Swedish, boss,' Garry said.

'The ambassador's giving me lessons,' she said, winking at Cam.

'Oh yeah? Good-looking, is he?' Garry asked. 'Blonde hair, blue eyes, proper Nordic type?'

'Actually he was the complete opposite. More Italian-looking. Mind you, I wouldn't kick him out of bed for eating crispbreads, know what I mean, ladies?'

'Anyway,' Garry said, raising his voice over the female laughter, 'I got his medical records. And I think I know why he'd lost his appetite. He had terminal prostate cancer. I've got contact details for his oncologist. She's at St Thomas'.'

'That would certainly account for him being self-absorbed, which is what the priest said.'

Finally, Stella turned to Def. 'What news from the world of perverted, fucked-up murderers?'

Def smiled, brushing a stray lock of long blonde hair away from her face. 'Since 1950 there have been seven murders where part or all of the victim's tongue was removed. Four were bites that just removed the tip. Two involved a knife to remove part of it. And in one, the whole tongue was cut out and left on the victim's chest.'

'Any of the doers possibles for Brömly?'

Def shook her head. 'Four of them died of natural causes. One was killed in a gang hit in 2014. One's ninety and has dementia, is living in a care home. One's in Holloway serving time for modern slavery.'

'On paper, Brömly's clean,' Stella said. 'But nobody's that good. We know that, right? And speaking of paper, there's this one thing on his CV I want to look into a bit more. From 1971 to 1976 it says he was doing voluntary work in Tanzania.'

Rosh frowned. 'Sounds like more of the same to me.'

'Yeah, but that's a hell of a career break, don't you think? The guy looks to be making solid progression in the Swedish civil service for eight years, then he ups sticks and buggers off to Africa for half that time again.'

'Maybe that's it,' Baz said. 'Almost a decade pushing paper in some government office block and he got a bit of wanderlust.'

'Maybe,' Stella said, though she wasn't convinced. 'Right. He had cancer. I'll take his oncologist. Garry and Baz, can you try and dig up anything you can about those four years in Africa? Rosh and Cam, keep talking to the local Swedish community. Nobody's *that* good. Maybe drop down a couple of levels.'

'I've got a CI who moves in expat circles,' Rosh said. 'Mainly Eastern Europeans, but I'll ask him if he knows anyone from Sweden.'

'Good. OK, thanks, everyone. I know you're all working flat-out, and I appreciate it, but remember to take care of yourselves. Get home at a reasonable time and get some sleep.'

The briefing broke up with a chorus of general assent, although everyone knew they'd be ignoring Stella's instruction. Including Stella.

Just as she was leaving for her meeting with Brömly's oncologist, Craven's PM report dropped into her inbox. She printed it out and tucked it into her bag. She'd read it later. The covering note put her mind at rest on one important topic. Brömly was already dead when his tongue was removed.

6

STOCKHOLM

Annika re-read the online article about Brömly's murder.

Tomas Brömly, 79, a former Swedish ambassador to London, was found dead in his £12.5m Mayfair flat on June 10th. Police are treating Mr Brömly's death as suspicious. A source close to the investigation confirms that Mr Brömly's body was mutilated, and a body part was left on an open Bible.

Closing her eyes, Annika let herself travel back in time to that dreadful day in '75. Her sixteenth birthday. She could remember it as if it had happened yesterday. No, like it was happening to her all over again, right here, right now…

* * *

…her stomach is fizzing with excitement at the thought of the school bell at the end of the afternoon. She's arranged to meet Juliana for a coffee at that new place in town. After coffee, they're going to get their ears pierced together, then go to the record shop on *Nygatan* and listen to the latest releases. Juliana loves ABBA, but Annika's into David Bowie. *'Rebel Rebel'* is literally her favourite single ever.

The last lesson is English. Normally, Annika enjoys the sound of the unfamiliar words as they escape her lips. But her eyes have been tiring throughout the day. Plus, the classroom is so hot half the class are falling asleep. It's the heatwave.

The chalked words on the blackboard are so fuzzy she can't make them out. Is that 'chair' or 'chance'? She can't tell. She needs glasses. But that dope Andriesson at the children's home says she'll grow out of it. What an idiot!

Miss Petersson, with her crow's voice and sleek black hair, has this witchy ability to find the one girl who's fearful and pick on her to read from the board. Annika tries to pull her head down between her shoulders, like a tortoise.

Pick Pia! Pick Sophie! Pick Linnea! Pick anyone you like, but please don't pick me!

'Annika Ivarsson. Stop hiding, girl, and read the next line.'

Annika's belly flips, but it's not excitement this time. It's terror. She knows she'll be in trouble again. She squints at the board, forcing her aching eyes to focus just enough on the line of poetry that she can hazard a guess.

Around her, her classmates are watching her over their shoulders, or whispering to each other just out of her sightline. She hears a suppressed giggle. It sounds like that bitch Maja Jacobsson. Then her voice cuts through the chatter and Annika is sure it's her main tormentor.

'Don't they have books at the children's home?'

'Come on,' Miss Petersson caws, 'we haven't got all day.'

It's no good. Try as she might, the chalked words in Miss Petersson's spiky scrawl stay blurred.

'I can't, Miss,' Annika says, finally, dreading what must inevitably follow.

'What do you mean, "can't"?'

Miss Petersson loves this, Annika can tell from the triumphant smirk on the woman's face.

'My eyes, Miss. They're tired.'

Miss Petersson raises one finely plucked eyebrow into a perfect arch. She puts the tip of her finger to her thin lips.

'Tired? My dear girl, you should have said so earlier,' she says, pulling the corners of her mouth down. 'If you're tired, of *course* you mustn't participate any further in the lesson. After all, it isn't as if William Shakespeare has anything to teach *you*, now is it?'

Her sarcasm has infected the rest of the class. They're giggling openly, not even hiding their whispers from Miss Petersson behind their hands. No need, when she has made it totally clear whose side she's on.

'I didn't mean that, Miss,' Annika begins. 'I—'

'I don't care,' Petersson snaps. 'You are excused.'

Pale cheeks ablaze, Annika gathers her things, stuffs them into her camo-patterned backpack and scuttles out of the classroom. She fights back the tears that threaten to burst their banks before she has reached the sanctuary of the corridor. She won't give Maya the satisfaction.

The following day, at 7.45 a.m., she heads for the front door, ready to begin the three-mile walk to school. But the warden's office door opens and Mr Andriesson steps out to bar her way. He is wearing his usual outfit: skanky tweed jacket with leather elbow patches, sludge-brown corduroys and those weird shoes that look like they're made of brown pastry. God, he's so uncool.

'Ah, Annika,' he says. 'My office, please.'

Frowning, she turns away from the front door and follows him into the office. Where a young, good-looking man in a dark pinstriped suit is waiting. He's taller than Mr Andriesson. Ha! That's not hard. He has thoughtful eyes and the way he looks at her makes her think he is clever. Like he can see things about her nobody else can. She decides in an instant she likes him.

Mr Andriesson points to a thinly upholstered armchair. 'Sit,' he says.

What is she, a dog? Arsehole!

Annika takes the chair and looks at the stranger.

'Who is he?' she asks Andriesson.

'My name is Tomas,' the man says. He holds out his hand. 'I'm pleased to meet you, Annika.'

Puzzled by the warmth in his voice, she stretches out her right hand and shakes mechanically. Nobody's ever done that before. She enjoys the sensation of his warm, dry hand enfolding hers.

'Mr Brömly is the regional administrator for all the children's homes in Umeå,' Andriesson says.

'And?' she replies, jutting her chin a little like Juliana taught her.

'Miss Petersson says you've been having trouble reading.'

'No. Not reading. I read loads of books. Just from the blackboard.' She looks at Tomas. 'My eyes get tired. I think I need glasses.'

Andriesson smiles icily as if she's just asked for a thousand kronor to spend on sweets.

'You're to go with Mr Brömly. He helps girls like you.'

Now she understands. Or thinks she does. There must be some sort of government programme to give out free glasses to, what's the official phrase? Ah yes, 'children from non-standard backgrounds'. Yes, well, that just about covers it. Dumped into the care system aged five and left to fight it out with all the other losers.

Tomas smiles at her and stands.

'Come on, then. I have a car outside.'

She follows him. No bus for Annika today. Instead, a ride in this smooth-looking guy's bright-yellow Saab 900. It's one of those cool ones with a black fabric roof.

She settles herself in the passenger seat. It's black leather and smells new. It's hot on the backs of her bare thighs. There's a funny cardboard strawberry hanging from the mirror. It adds a sweet perfume to the smell of hot leather.

She looks down. Her school skirt has ridden up and she unsticks her skin from the seat so she can pull it down a little. She glances across, but Tomas has his eyes fixed firmly on the road.

They all know what goes on with children's home kids. It's no secret. Some even claim they get paid for it. But Annika doesn't want it. Not one bit. She's a virgin and she intends to stay that way. At least until she gets married. But if she *was* going to do it, she thinks Tomas would be the kind of man who'd be all right. Kind. Gentle.

'Buckle up!' he says, in a fake American accent that sounds like he learned it off the TV. She smiles to show she thinks it's cool.

Then he puts the car in gear and drives away from the home.

* * *

...The rest is a blur. Try as she might, and over the years she has, many, many times, she simply can't remember.

Various therapists have tried to help her. But one after another they have all given up. The usual explanation is that the trauma prevented her from making any long-term memories.

She opened her eyes and wiped away the tears that had wetted her cheeks. She ground her teeth together. With Brömly dead, she'd have to work fast. If the others had any sense, they'd be talking precautions now.

She pulled up the second profile she was working on and looked at the woman's kindly face. She looked like a grandma. One who baked *kanellbullar* for her grandchildren and pinched their cheeks, rosy with cold after a morning sledging at *Mormor's* house.

She read the first line:

Inger Hedlund, 73. Former govt. lawyer.

'Brömly is gone. Now you, *Advokat* Hedlund, will know something of the pain you caused,' she said aloud in her empty flat.

7

LONDON

The next morning, Stella looked over Jamie's shoulder as he read the paper on his iPad. When she reached the sentence about the mutilation, she swore loudly.

'Bloody Roisin Griffin! I'll kill her, Jamie, I swear to god!'

He turned away from the screen and held her by the hips, pulling her towards him.

'You don't know it was her,' he said.

'Yes. I do. She was the mole when we were hunting Robey and I bollocked her then. Now she's up to her old tricks again.'

'It could have been anyone. Didn't you say the cleaner found his body?'

'Yes, but— '

'Couldn't she have been approached by the media?'

'She was interviewed and advised not to reveal that detail to anyone.'

'She's probably not making much money, even if her Mayfair clients do pay above the minimum wage,' he said. 'If *the Guardian* waved some cash under her nose and promised anonymity, she might well have decided it wouldn't hurt to sell the story.'

'Don't be so bloody reasonable!'

'I work in a caring profession, what can I say? I see every side of a person's character. Anyway, the article doesn't say which body part, so you can screen out the attention-seekers who ring in to confess.'

Stella conceded the point with a kiss. But inside she was still fuming.

'Got to go. Have a good day. See you at mine tonight?'

'Is it Friday?'

'It is.'

'And are we spending the weekend together in London?'

She poked him in the chest, grinning. 'We are.'

'Well then. I'll see you at yours. I'll buy a nice bottle of wine.'

'What makes you think I haven't got a nice bottle of wine already?'

'I think you'll have *a* bottle of wine. But I feel like celebrating. I'll go to that independent wine merchant on Marylebone High Street.'

'All right. I'll be home as soon as I can manage.'

On the ride in to work, Stella turned over Jamie's words in her head. On one level, the purely rational level, she knew he was right. Well, she knew he was right that it could have been anyone.

But *anyone* also included Detective Inspector Roisin-bloody-Griffin. Plus there was the small matter of the non-rational part of Stella's brain. The intuitive, emotional part that could see beyond the surface to what lay beneath.

If Brömly had been trying to atone for some sin of the past, she doubted it could be worse than hers. Thirteen people dead by her hand, in a variety of MOs ranging from straightforward shootings to methods altogether more medieval.

She pushed the thought aside, because it was always followed by the same horrible idea. That one day, she would have to confess to Jamie what she'd done.

Her feelings for him were the real thing. And although she hadn't used the L-word, either to him or to herself, she knew that was the truth of it. She loved him. And she couldn't bear the thought of losing him. But the idea of confessing – that word again – to being a multiple murderer?

How could he stay with her after that? Even if her actions had been sanctioned at the highest level, he couldn't look at her the same way again after that. Could he?

Overtaking a string of London-bound commuters with a flick of her wrist, she focused on the immediate future instead. Specifically the meeting she had planned with Roisin.

The meeting took place at 8.43 a.m., as soon as Roisin appeared in SIU. Stella beckoned her over to her office.

'Close the door,' she said.

Roisin sat facing Stella, arms folded. Ignoring the dangerous look on her DI's face, Stella flopped a copy of that day's *Guardian* in front of her, folded to the page with the report of Brömly's murder. Roisin glanced at it then back at Stella.

'Am I supposed to know what's going on?'

'A body part resting on a Bible. The one detail I wanted keeping back. And there it is in black and white.'

Roisin's eyes flashed. 'What, and you think I leaked it. Is that it?'

Stella's pulse was bumping uncomfortably in her throat. 'Well did you?'

'No! I didn't. And it doesn't say tongue, does it?'

'No. And that's about the only mercy, to coin a phrase, in the whole thing. I told you before what would happen if you crossed me.'

'Yes, you did,' Roisin said, raising her voice to match Stella's. 'And I haven't. It could have been anyone. You know what crime scenes are like. How many CSIs were in that flat? Uniforms milling about? The photographer? Dozens of people saw that disgusting thing. So why are you picking on me again?'

Stella couldn't believe what she was hearing. She let her temper have its head. 'Why? Why do you think? You were taking bundles of cash in brown envelopes from that shitbag at the *Sun*, that's why!'

Rosh jerked her chair back and stood up.

'I don't have to listen to this. You're totally out of line. I'm going to complain to my Fed rep.'

'Good! Do that! And while you're about it, tell them you've been kicked off this case. Now get out.'

Roisin slammed the door so hard the noise made Stella's ears ring. She watched Rosh storm over to her desk, grab her things and then march out of SIU.

Her pulse was racing and she felt sick. Ordinarily she'd make for the ladies to splash water on her face, but she had a shrewd idea Rosh would have beaten her to it. Instead, ignoring the worried glances directed at her, she headed straight for Callie's office.

Callie looked up with a smile. It vanished as Stella pulled out the visitor chair from under the desk and fell into it.

'What's up, wee girl? You look like you lost a tenner and found a severed tongue in your handbag.'

Stella laughed despite her roiling emotions. She wasn't at all sure Callie's bizarre image wasn't preferable to what had just happened. She explained how she'd just blown up at Roisin and booted her off the case. As she relayed the details, the certainty she'd felt on the ride in to work disappeared. In its place, a sick feeling that she may have completely over-reacted.

She watched Callie's face for a sign. But her boss was as inscrutable as ever. Her deep-red lips a straight line. Her eyes giving nothing away. Her complexion pale, as it always was.

Stella cracked first.

'Well?'

'Well, what?'

'What do you think?'

Callie leaned forward and steepled her fingers under her nose.

'You're a DCI. You're an SIO. I can't think of any more bits of alphabet soup but I'm sure you've got some. I know you and Roisin never saw eye to eye. She'll create a bit of a fuss, but I'll try to contain it.'

'I can't work with her anymore. I want her gone.'

'Leave it with me. I need to figure out how best to contain the fallout.'

'Speaking of fallout, she said she was going to talk to her Fed rep.'

Now Callie did smile. Briefly.

'Aye, well they all say that, don't they? Look, Stel. You get results, which is what I care about,' she said. 'Leave Roisin to me. I'll have a word with her. Maybe I can iron things out.'

As it turned out, Callie's ironing took care of itself. An hour after Stella left her office, her desk phone rang.

'Ma'am, I've got Assistant Commissioner Fairhill for you.'

Callie stood. Always better to have room to breathe when the brass called you. Funny. She knew as far as SIU was concerned, *she* was the brass. But nobody in the Job could look up and see clean air. A snatch of a poem her mum used to take pleasure in reciting came back to her now. *Big fleas have little fleas upon their backs to bite 'em, and little fleas have lesser fleas, and so ad infinitum.*

Callie stopped trying to puzzle out where in the flea biting-order she belonged.

'What can I do for you, Ma'am?'

'It's bit of an odd one, actually. Could you come down to Scotland Yard? I'd rather explain in person.'

Half an hour later, Callie found herself sitting opposite Rachel Fairhill in her luxurious fifth-floor office. A desk the size of a tennis court dominated the light, airy room. In front of it, not one but three black leather chairs waited for a visitor to choose between them.

In a mark of the Met's architectural as well as organisational hierarchy, AC Fairhill also had space for a circular conference table that would seat six. A leather sofa and two matching armchairs grouped informally around a steel-and-glass coffee table completed the furnishings.

Rachel gestured for Callie to take one of the chairs at the conference table, and joined her there after a brief handshake. Rachel pushed a petrol-blue folder forward.

Callie opened the folder. The first sheet of paper inside bore a logo that immediately piqued her curiosity. A blue-and-gold seal enclosing a red-and-white-striped shield surmounted by the scales of justice. The design was strong, eye-catching, and familiar to anyone with half an interest in American law enforcement, let alone a senior Met detective. The legend spelled it out for the rest.

DEPARTMENT OF JUSTICE
FEDERAL BUREAU OF INVESTIGATION

Callie's brain went into overdrive. Why was Rachel showing her an FBI file? A nasty memory, which she tried to keep buried, scrabbled its way upwards into her consciousness.

Adam Collier, correction, *the late and unlamented* Detective Chief Superintendent Adam Collier, had transferred to the FBI Field Office in Chicago seven years earlier. Stella had gone after him. And whilst she'd never explicitly told Callie what had happened, her meaning was unambiguous. Collier would never be returning to the UK to cause trouble.

To the right of the FBI seal, the letterhead proclaimed the memo, or whatever it was, had come from the desk of Edward H. Baxter, Special Agent-in-Charge, FBI Chicago Field Office.

She turned it over.

The next document, a full-colour photo, occupied her for much longer. A human skeleton on a stainless steel autopsy table, labelled John Doe. She moved it to one side. The next sheet bore a similar photo, this time labelled Jane Doe.

She turned over once more. A black SUV, clearly one that had not been looked after, sat in what appeared to be an inspection bay of some kind. Its windscreen was shattered.

The final set of images showed two handguns. Turning back to the autopsy photos, Callie looked up at her boss, eyebrows raised in question, not trusting herself to speak.

'I had a call yesterday evening from SAC Baxter,' Fairhill said. 'He insisted I call him Eddie. You're looking at the skeletons of Adam and Lynne Collier.'

Callie's gasp was entirely natural. If Stella had been clear about Adam, she had been entirely opaque about Lynne's fate. Callie felt a pang of shame. Nobody had given any thought to Collier's wife.

That included her. The focus, and the urgency, of the op had all been on erasing Pro Patria Mori from the face of the earth.

'Are they asking for our help, then?' Callie asked.

Rachel nodded. 'They've requested someone senior to fly out there. I want you to send Roisin Griffin.'

Callie managed to maintain an expression of professionalism and calm. But inside she was panicking. Sending the one DI who regarded Stella as her enemy – Oh, yes, she'd heard plenty of canteen gossip to know the truth of it – could bring the whole edifice of secrecy crashing down about their heads. Not to mention putting Stella in a situation from which there were no good exits.

The fact that Stella had just thrown her off the Brömly case added petrol to an already merrily burning fire.

'Callie?' Fairhill was looking at her with raised eyebrows.

'Sorry. It's just we're understaffed as it is and Roisin's a great detective. I'm not sure we can manage without her.'

It was a lie, but a necessary one. Out of the two evils, having Roisin inside the team causing trouble was infinitely preferable to have her doing the same thing but from the outside.

'I know you took a hit in the last budget round, but needs must. Send DI Griffin to see me this morning.'

Outside in the fresh air again, Callie drew in a breath and exhaled noisily. She permitted herself a brief expletive, drawing the curious gazes of a couple of police staff re-entering the building. A black Jaguar XF saloon drew up beside her with a whisper of rubber on hot tarmac. She climbed into the back seat, grateful for the aircon.

'Back to Paddington Green, Ma'am?' the driver asked.

'Yes, please, Bash. Take the scenic route, though, eh?'

Kamal "Bash" Bashir had been with her for five years now, and had a good driver's ability to sense when his boss needed to talk and when she wanted quiet. He used it now.

'Everything all right?' he asked as he nodded to the gate guard and joined the southbound traffic on the Victoria Embankment.

'You know when people say they're between a rock and a hard

place? From where I've just been put, a rock-and-hard-place sandwich looks like a bloody nice place to be.'

'That bad, eh?'

Under stress, Callie's refined Edinburgh tones slid towards the rougher tones of the docks down in Leith. They did so now.

'Och, Bash, ye've no bloody idea!'

'You want me to recite the Serenity Prayer?'

'Ye want me to kick you up the bloody arse?'

Bash laughed. He pulled away from the traffic lights holding them back from Hyde Park and drove west along Birdcage Walk. As they cruised down the tree-lined avenue, Callie compiled a mental pro/con chart for Rachel's news.

Pro

1. It gets Roisin out of Stella's hair for a bit.
2. Roisin feels she's got a high-profile case all to herself.
3. She gets to salve her wounded pride.
4. Callie gets a tick from the Assistant Commissioner.
5. Roisin is a solid but unexceptional DI: maybe she'll come up empty-handed.

Con

1. Where do we bloody start?
2. The FB-bloody-I have just found Adam-bloody-Collier's bones.
3. And his wife's.
4. AC Rachel Fairhill has sent Stella's sworn enemy to investigate.
5. The FBI are giving her her very own Junior Special Agent Kit.

6. Roisin might be unexceptional but she is dogged, and extremely highly motivated.
7. The whole shit-show is coming back to the UK.
8. Where I, Gordon Wade and god knows who else will be royally screwed.

When Bash dropped her at Paddington Green, Callie did not return immediately to her office. Instead, she walked up Edgware Road for a few hundred yards until she found a quiet little side street. She turned into it and continued until she found a tiny park, enclosed on all four sides by black iron railings.

In the centre of the park stood a graffitied bandstand, a relic of an earlier age, when folk might congregate on a Sunday afternoon to sing along to patriotic songs. Its sole purpose nowadays was as a meeting place for kids bunking off school and, at night, winos and druggies. At this time of day, though, it was deserted.

Callie pulled out her phone and called her old boss, Gordon Wade.

'We've got trouble,' she said, as soon as he answered.

'Explain.'

She explained.

'Can you keep it contained?'

'I'm not sure. I think it's going to end up back here.'

Wade paused for a few seconds, and she could hear his breathing down the crystal-clear line.

'Then we have no choice. Cole gets burned.'

'We can't just throw her to the wolves! The media'll take her to pieces. It could kill her. You know what happened before.'

'Aye, I do. And I also know the committee agreed to suppress it. For ever, hopefully,' he said. 'But if anything popped up from the mire—' He hesitated for a second. 'I'm sorry, Callie. It's the only way.'

She knew he was right about disavowing Stella. In her head, if not her heart. Writing her off as a maverick cop with a vigilante complex was the safest course of action. But she also felt the bitterest sense of being a betrayer of the woman she regarded as a friend.

Callie agreed to go through with the contingency plan, and ended the call.

On the short walk back to Paddington Green, she reflected ruefully on the discussions that had occupied her time a few years back. She'd argued vehemently that they should protect Stella. But, in the end, the bigger fleas had simply bitten back harder.

* * *

Several hundred miles to the north, Wade called a contact on a freshly purchased burner phone.

'We may have trouble.'

'PPM?'

'What else?'

'God, will it ever end?'

'Cole could be exposed. They've found the Colliers.'

'Would she talk if they arrest her?'

'I don't know.'

'Better not take any chances, then.'

'Disavowal?'

'I think we both know that's not watertight. She needs to go. Permanently.'

'We can't!'

'We have no choice, Gordon. I'll sort somebody out for the job.'

Wade finished the call. Pulled a bottle of single malt from a desk drawer and, with shaking hands, poured a very large glass.

8

LONDON

Stella tugged on the end of her ponytail. Something about the murder said that she wasn't looking for a psychopath. This was a murder committed for a specific reason. Against a specific individual.

The motive wasn't in the present – their initial research had failed to find a shred of evidence anyone had a grievance against Brömly. So it had to be in the past. He'd been murdered because of who he was, or what he'd done, not because he fitted some psychopath's idea of the perfect victim type.

Her PC pinged. An email from Lucian. Relieved to have something new to read, she opened it and scanned its contents.

Thorough as always, and blessed with imagination and creativity as well as analytical skills, Lucian had come up with something.

He'd used electrostatic detection apparatus on the blotter from Brömly's desk. The ESDA had revealed traces of writing impressed into the soft paper. They'd been in Swedish, but Lucian had run them through Google Translate and then, in square brackets, added his own best guesses for the remainder.

. . .

[I'm going] to make a full confession of my involvement in the Project.

[This will] reveal your complicity as well as my [own]

[It's nothing] compared to the evil in which we all [took part]

[I'm going to give a full] and frank account of our actions

[Then I'll be] able to face my death, and my maker, with [acceptance/courage/grace?]

[listen to/consult] your own conscience

Lucian had also found three names on the blotter: Ove, Kerstin and Inger.

He also confirmed Stella's initial opinion about the tool used to remove Brömly's tongue. According to the Met's toolmarks database, which Lucian had confirmed by buying a pair and using them on a pig's tongue, the killer had used a set of Teng Tools 12" flat-jaw grips.

Stella looked Teng up on the web. Interesting. The company had been founded by a Swede and was the bestselling tool brand in Norway and Sweden. Of course the tools were available everywhere, but Stella didn't believe in coincidences.

The CSIs had recovered a dark hair from the crime scene, picked up on adhesive tape from the carpet. Brömly was grey, which ruled him out. The hair had a root, which would be useful for obtaining DNA should they get a suspect in custody. For now, though, Lucian had filed it with the other exhibits.

They'd also pulled crumbs from the carpet that contained butter, flour, sugar, cinnamon and a single caraway seed. Now what did that suggest? *Kannelbullar*. The sweet buns every Swede seemed to have tasted along with their mother's milk.

Of course, one could buy them all over London. Add the fact that they were found in the flat of a Swedish national and their evidential value looked even shakier. She herself had eaten one in the ambassador's office. Although maybe the caraway seed would lead somewhere. She didn't remember tasting any in the bun the ambassador had provided. She made a note to check into it.

The same went for Teng tools. She was sure the guys who maintained the Bonneville for her used them. She'd seen the distinctive scarlet tool trolley with the glaring yellow eyes logo in their workshop.

Despite all that, something was telling her the killer was Swedish. The five-year absence from his career was niggling at her. Too long for a standard period of volunteering. Yet Brömly had returned to Sweden and picked up where he'd left off. Given his spotless record and matching soul, as described by everyone they'd so far interviewed, whatever the project was, she thought it must have happened in that half decade.

She pulled the team together for a briefing and wrote up new lines of enquiry on the whiteboard. She pointed to the three Christian names Lucian had revealed with the ESDA machine.

'I think I know who they are.'

She flicked a switch to display Lucian's recreation of Brömly's letter onto a large white screen pulled down over one section of wall.

'Brömly refers to a project. He calls it evil,' Stella said. 'He tells the others he's going to make some sort of confession, so he can die without it on his conscience. I think it happened between seventy-one and seventy-five.'

'Do you think they were all involved in something dodgy?' Def asked. 'In Africa?'

'Yes to the first question, no to the second. I'm not even sure he was in Africa. I think it was just a conveniently vague line on his CV.'

'A smokescreen?' Cam asked.

Stella nodded.

'It's going to be hard to find out anything more from here,' Garry said.

Stella nodded. She'd already decided to visit Stockholm in the next couple of days, as soon as she could square it with Callie.

'Lucian turned up twenty-nine murders where the murder weapon was a nine,' she said. 'Garry, I want you to pull the files and see what you can find out about the weapons in each case. We know some dealers do a roaring trade renting pistols out. Can you work with Lucian, please?'

He nodded. 'Sure.'

'Then there's the pastry fragments the CSIs lifted from the carpet in Brömly's flat,' she said. 'Baz, I want you to look into that. See if there's any variation in recipe among local suppliers.'

Baz nodded.

'Don't start sampling them all for research purposes,' Cam said with a smile.

'Yeah, or the missus'll have you on a diet till the end of the year,' Garry added.

Over good-natured laughter, Stella ended the briefing. She had a couple of hours until her meeting with Brömly's oncologist and she needed to update the murder book with the new lines of enquiry.

She turned her attention once more to the two questions she was sure held the key to solving his murder. What was the precise nature of the 'evil' project Brömly had taken part in? And what were the identities of the other three Swedes? She sat back and rolled her shoulders, frowning as the joints in her neck clicked.

Closing her eyes, she strove to imagine how things might have played out, and smiled as a picture started to emerge.

Brömly had written to three people announcing his imminent confession. It felt to Stella like he'd kept the secret all the way from the seventies until now.

So, including Brömly, those four people were the only ones who knew of The Project. He'd written to them spelling out his plans. If it was as evil as he seemed to think, his confession, and presumably the bad publicity that would follow, would drag them down into the shit with him. Easy to imagine at least one of them preferring to stay out of it.

The conclusion was obvious. One of the other three had murdered Brömly: Ove, Inger or Kerstin. Unless Jamie was right, and they should be looking for someone Brömly had abused in the past.

9

STOCKHOLM

Tracking down Kerstin Dahl had been easy. And now Annika sat a few tables away from the elderly woman in her local cafe. Dahl had ordered her usual, a strong black coffee and a slice of chocolate and almond cake. Annika was nibbling on a lemon and poppy seed muffin while sipping from a latte.

Both women were nose-deep in their laptops. But whereas Dahl was engrossed in whatever she was reading, Annika was merely hiding behind her screen. Dahl's face betrayed her feelings. Her forehead was creased and her left hand covered her mouth.

Annika rose from her table and asked her neighbour to watch her laptop for her. The young girl agreed with a friendly nod then went back to her own screen. Annika wove between the tables in the direction of the restrooms.

The route she chose took her directly behind Dahl's table. She paused to check her phone, using the opportunity to look over the older woman's shoulder to see what she was looking at.

She was on the website of *Svenska Dagbladet*, the newspaper so many Swedes turned to for their daily update on matters domestic and international. The headline told Annika all she needed to know.

. . .

Former ambassador found murdered in Mayfair flat

Beneath the headline a large colour photo of Brömly took up the rest of the laptop's screen. A kindly, smiling, elderly man, obviously once handsome. Annika felt revulsion knotting her insides.

In the toilet, she leaned on the counter housing the sinks and splashed cold water on her face. She shook her head, sending droplets flying left and right, then went to dry her cheeks with a paper towel.

On the way back to her table, she paused again behind Dahl. She imagined holding a loaded gun to her head. What she had planned for Dahl would be infinitely sweeter. For Annika, at least.

10

LONDON

The meeting with Brömly's oncologist was brief. She told Stella that, thanks to inoperable prostate cancer, Brömly had only a few months to live.

'And when you spoke to him last, how did he strike you?' Stella asked.

The woman looked up for a few seconds before returning her gaze to Stella.

'Philosophical. Some people go to pieces when they get a terminal diagnosis. Understandably. But Tomas seemed resigned to his fate. Almost as if he'd been expecting it.'

'Did he say anything at all that struck you as odd?'

The doctor pursed her lips. 'Only once. About a month ago. I mentioned, as I had to, that there were risks to fertility with surgical interventions.'

'He was a bit old to be worrying about that,' Stella said.

The oncologist nodded. 'We still have to explain to a patient all the potential side-effects and complications following treatment. Anyway, when I mentioned fertility he grew, well, I would call it agitated. He said, "How ironic," or something like that. He didn't elaborate and I didn't ask him to.'

From the meeting with the oncologist, Stella rode back to Jamie's place. After dinner that night, they curled up on the sofa together. While he watched a football match on TV, she pondered the implications of what the oncologist had told her.

A dying man, correction, a *devout* dying man, wanting to set his mind at ease before going to meet his Maker. She could understand that quite easily.

But what was it specifically about the mention of fertility that had unsettled him?

Jonasson had mentioned that Brömly and his wife were childless. Was that it? Even after all these years, could his infertility have been causing him pain? She resolved to check his medical records. And those of his wife.

Maybe they weren't child-free by choice. But if they were, something else had agitated the old man.

* * *

Midway through the following morning, Stella managed to get hold of Brömly's British GP. As far as he knew, Brömly had never enquired about his own fertility. He'd inherited, if that was the right word, Brömly's Swedish medical records, and they told the same story. As for Mrs Brömly, Stella would have to contact the Swedish authorities.

She'd just made herself a coffee and taken it to her desk when Callie called her in to her office for a chat.

Stella knocked and entered. Callie looked up when she came to sit down opposite her, but she didn't smile. In fact, she looked as if she might be about to throw up. Her skin, always pale, had acquired a sickly cast. Every muscle in her face appeared to be straining to stay still.

Callie swallowed. 'They found Adam.'

Stella gripped the arms of her chair. Her stomach churned and now it was she who felt she might need to excuse herself and rush to the ladies.

She'd been expecting blowback from her kicking Roisin out of the team. Or pressure from the brass to solve the case. But not this. Never this.

'How?' she croaked out.

'A kid practising BMX stunts over water, if ye can bloody believe it. He called the local cops and they called the FBI. Jesus, Stel, I'm sorry.'

Stella opened her mouth to speak, then closed it again. *Sorry? Sorry for what?* OK, so the FBI had discovered Adam, and presumably Lynne, in that lake in the snowy wilds of the Minnesota countryside. But that was a long way from its coming back to bite her in the arse. Wasn't it?

'Why are you sorry?' she asked in a quiet voice, suddenly fearful.

'The FBI asked for a liaison officer from the Met. AC Fairhill's sending Roisin. There was nothing I could do,' she said. 'She went over my head, or behind my bloody back. Either way, the damned woman's outflanked me. Us.'

'Fuck!'

'Stel, I have to ask. Did you kill Lynne Collier? Because they found her bones in the water alongside Adam's.'

Stella closed her eyes. Felt the chill of the icy wind blowing off the lake outside Preston. The snow, thick underfoot, compressing with a soft *crump* with every step. A faint tang of wood smoke in the air.

She'd lured Adam Collier out there by kidnapping his wife. Now she stood facing him across a few dozen feet, with Lynne in front of her as a shield.

She'd pushed her towards Adam, expecting her to run, giving Stella enough time to run for cover before shooting him. But things had taken a shocking turn. Collier had shot his own wife dead to give himself a clear field of fire.

Eyes open, she looked Callie straight in the eye. 'No. I didn't. That was him.'

'Why? Why would he do that?'

'I think he was desperate. He would have killed me if he could, then fled. Probably gone over the border into Canada.' Stella sighed. 'He was backed into a corner, Callie. By me. I didn't pull the trigger, but Lynne's death is on me, just the same.'

Callie inhaled deeply and let the breath out in a rush. 'Oh, Jesus, Stel, what a fucking great slaister!'

The stress, and the glitch in her understanding caused by Callie's sudden drop into low Edinburgh slang, unhooked something in Stella's mind. For the first time since she'd arrived back in England after killing Collier, she experienced a feeling of

unreality

she knew she was sitting in the visitor chair

                           opposite Callie, in Callie's office and

beyond that, the open-plan

space occupied by SIU

the floors of administrative staff and detectives in other units and

forensics
    the armoury exhibits room
    custody
    suite

                              and all the other

functions a

busy central london police

station
needed

but right now she felt herself

becoming detached from all of that hard-edged reality and floating

NO! not now not ever

she would never allow that to happen again

collier was dead lynne's death was tragic but she was not going to allow
either of them to reach out from beyond the

grave

and drag her down with them all the way to—

Stella ground her jaws together until a high-pitched whine in her ears pulled her back to reality. No. Not going to happen. She was a survivor.

She sat straighter. Below the level of Callie's sight, blocked by the desk, she was pinching the skin between her left thumb and forefinger with the nails of her right hand. The pain was intense, but it was keeping her focused on the here and now.

She had no desire to witness herself from a vantage point up on the ceiling. Her days of out-of-body experiences while Other Stella committed murder were behind her.

'Can you help at all? Or have you been warned off?' she asked, as reality asserted itself in sharp edges and rubbish odds.

Callie looked sad. 'I'll try. But I'm in the wrong place to run interference. Too senior to be monkeying around at the detailed level, too junior to steer the investigation in the wrong direction.'

'It's fine,' Stella said at last. 'I'll handle it.'

Callie frowned. It wasn't hard to read her thoughts.

'Don't worry,' Stella added. 'I won't go after Rosh with a meat cleaver, if that's what's worrying you.'

She went for a smile but it felt as though someone had injected Botox into her cheek muscles. She wasn't sure they'd responded the way she meant them to. Callie's expression suggested they hadn't.

'It had crossed my mind.'

'I'll be a good girl. Look, if it all goes to shit, you'll back me though, won't you? I mean, I appreciate you can't interfere in the investigation,' she said. 'But if she comes looking for me, you can put a word in higher up the food chain. After all, it was you and Gordon Wade plus some very important people who let me get on with everything.'

Callie was avoiding Stella's gaze, fidgeting with a stapler. A spring popped out and a slide of staples shot across her desk, pinging off the base of a lamp. Callie looked up guiltily.

And in that moment, Stella saw with great clarity the nature of the world she'd moved into after expunging PPM from the face of the earth.

'You're going to throw me under the bus, aren't you?' she said, hardly believing she was hearing the words her lips were forming.

Callie appeared to be in physical pain. Her face twisted and her lips, coloured their usual deep red, narrowed to a thin line of discomfort.

'I tried to protect you, wee girl—'

'Don't you dare "wee girl" me! Gordon Wade sent you after me and you told me I was in the clear to carry on,' Stella said, struggling not to shout. 'I *murdered* for you, Callie,' she hissed. 'I cleaned up the whole shitty lot of them. Ramage, Fieldsend, Howarth, Ragib and Collier. And you let me. You bloody well *let* me!'

'I know. I know. I'm sorry. I told Gordon at the time that what we were doing was wrong. I shouldn't even be having this conversation with you. But if Roisin does come for you, there's nothing I can do.'

Callie hadn't even riposted that Stella had been murdering the members of PPM for herself, not Callie and Gordon Wade and their shadowy paymasters much higher up the tree. That worried Stella even more.

'I could go quietly. Plead not guilty and have my day in open court,' Stella said. 'How would Gordon like that? Because, believe me, the headline wouldn't be, "Rogue cop turns vigilante". I'm thinking more along the lines of, "Senior politicians sanction one-woman death squad".'

Callie's eyes were glistening. The sight of the tears frightened Stella.

'I don't think they'd let you,' she said.

Stella felt a cold hand clutch her heart and squeeze. She found she was struggling to breathe. Dark wings closed over her vision then flapped wide again.

'What? You don't mean what I think you mean, do you?'

Callie dashed the tears away with a clenched fist. 'If Rosh comes for you, please just go along with it.'

Stella cursed herself. What had she expected? Really?

That, having discovered a death squad in their midst, top government lawyers, cops and politicians would send in an assassin to wipe them out and protect her if she were ever to be caught?

When she'd trained as a cop, she'd envisioned justice as a solid, hard, square-edged object with non-slip grips you could carry securely with you throughout your career. Now it turned out it was more like an eel, slimed with ambiguity and always wriggling free of your grasp.

Stella stood up. Let Roisin come for her if she might. Stella had friends. Vicky, the journalist. Lawyers who'd known Richard and specialised in human rights law.

Sure, she'd killed. But so, by association, had a great many other people. That made them liable to charges of conspiracy to murder. They might send someone to silence her. But, she reflected with grim amusement, that hadn't worked out so well for PPM, now had it?

She stood, ignoring the way her legs were shaking. 'I have a murderer to catch.'

Callie surprised Stella by coming round her desk and enveloping her in a hug. In all the years they'd known each other, Callie had never once engaged in physical contact beyond a handshake. For a slim woman, her grip was fierce and Stella felt the breath being squeezed out of her.

Callie pushed her away but gripped her by the shoulders. She stared at Stella, her eyes blazing.

'You are the best fucking detective I have ever met. If it was a choice between you and fifty Roisin Griffins, I'd choose you every time,' she murmured. 'I'll do what I can for you. I promise.'

Stella left, closing the door with exaggerated care behind her.

11

LONDON

Stella got back to her flat in Lisson Grove at 7.15 p.m. All the way on the brief journey, she'd been worrying about Roisin's upcoming trip to Chicago.

She didn't think she'd left a trace of her trip to murder Adam Collier, but of course the odds were that she had. Damn! It wasn't fair. How could they have let her track down and kill the PPM leadership and then wash their hands of her? And Callie, too!

She put her helmet in the cupboard in the hall, shucked off her jacket and hung it on a hook in the hallway and more or less ran into the kitchen.

Jamie was uncorking a bottle of white wine. She strode across the floor to him and hugged him tightly, before leaning back just enough to plant a kiss full on his mouth. He returned it with passion, then, eventually, stepped back. He was beaming.

'Well, that was a nice way to start the evening,' he said with a wide smile.

She looked into his eyes. He really was a very nice-looking man. Not model-handsome, all chiselled cheekbones and designer stubble. But he had a rough-edged charm. Best of all, something in his eyes radiated understanding. She wished she was sure enough of herself to test that empathy now.

'Wine, please,' she said, fetching a glass and holding it out.

Jamie poured a couple of inches into the glass. 'Now, I want you to savour this. It's a very superior—'

She took a huge gulp, swallowed noisily, then finished the remainder.

'Fill 'er up, Joe,' she said, holding her glass out.

'—Marsanne from 2016. Good with white fish and asparagus, apparently, which I bought for our supper. But also for slugging back unaccompanied.'

She waggled the glass in front of his nose until he gently pushed her wrist down and refilled it.

'Sip it,' he said. 'That's an order.'

She raised the glass to her lips and sipped dutifully, rolling the wine around her mouth and making appreciative noises.

The alcohol was working one of its kinds of magic inside her. Not the I-feel-great-let's-party kind. Nor the this-is-nice-let's-watch-an old-movie-together kind. This was more the I-feel-a-muffled-version-of-the-me-that-wants-to-scream kind.

Jamie frowned. He put his own glass down. Gently placing his hands on her arms he pushed her back onto one of the high stools beside the counter.

'Something's bothering you. Tell me.'

Was something bothering her? Stella supposed that was a fair description of her state of mind. She looked at Jamie. Well, where should she start? She'd told him Richard and Lola were killed by a hit and run driver. And that it had driven her temporarily insane. What she hadn't told him was the rest.

And now her sworn enemy in SIU had been seconded to the FBI to investigate.

Stella opened her mouth to speak.

'It's the case. It's a bugger.'

He frowned. 'And that's all?'

She managed a smile. Took another sip of the chilled wine,

which, she had to admit, was delicious. She tasted peaches and vanilla.

'Yep. So, you're cooking, are you? Get your apron on, then. Nothing sexier than a man in a pinny.'

Stella managed not to gulp her second glass of wine. She watched Jamie take out from the fridge two thick fillets of cod, the flesh beneath the sage-green and silver skin firm and translucent. He chucked a thick slab of butter into a skillet and as it sizzled, added a slug of olive oil.

'Open the window, would you? The fish is going to smell a bit.'

She slid off her perch and pushed the casement window wide. The kitchen overlooked the road at the rear of the block. The sounds of children playing floated up through the trees. An exchange of children's laughter and squeals for the smell of frying fish: it seemed like a good deal to Stella.

With the cod sizzling in the pan, skin-side down, Jamie laid a handful of fat asparagus spears onto a smoking griddle pan. He added a drizzle of olive oil, some ground black pepper and a sprinkle of sea salt flakes.

He prodded the two fillets in the frying pan, lifting them in turn to inspect the skin beneath the now-white flesh.

Stella laid the table while Jamie finished cooking. He plated up their food and laid hers before her with a flourish. She bent her nose to the fish and inhaled the gorgeous aroma. The skin had turned a golden-brown and was crisp to the touch.

She took a forkful and placed it gently onto her tongue, closed her mouth and chewed.

'Oh my god, that is good,' she said after swallowing the succulent fish.

'Thank you,' Jamie said with a smile. 'So, I have some news.'

Stella put her cutlery down and looked across the table at him. He was struggling to contain a smile, she could see that. So it was something big.

'Go on, then,' she said, 'what is it? The article?'

He shook his head. 'I've been headhunted.'

'What? By whom?'

'The Institute of Forensic Psychiatry and Neuropharmacology. It's a new private research and treatment facility. It's based at the Maudsley Hospital.'

'What's the job?'

'Clinical Director and Deputy CEO.'

'Jamie, that's fantastic!' Stella leaned forward and grabbed him so she could kiss him a second time.

'I have to give Broadmoor three months' notice, but after that I'll be working in London. Oh, and they've almost doubled my salary.'

'Wow! You're not sorry about leaving Broadmoor? I know how much your work there means to you.'

He sighed. 'Honestly? I've been starting to feel like I might be burning out there. You know what it's like. The kind of people I have to treat,' he said, serious, suddenly. 'They *are* ill, and it's my sworn duty to try and heal them. But then what? If I *do* achieve a measure of success, all that happens is some fucked-up child-murderer or serial killer leaves us and goes straight through the revolving door and into the penal system. Which is probably where they belong, to be honest.'

'And the new job will be different.'

He nodded vigorously, biting the tip off an asparagus spear. 'Completely. At IFPN, which is what we're calling it, by the way, I might be able to prevent the evil from ever happening,' he said. 'It's a research post as well as a clinical one. I hope to combine both strands of practice so we get a deeper understanding of the causes of the personality disorders that create the Fred Wests and Dennis Nilsens of this world.'

They finished their meal with some rich chocolate ice cream Jamie had bought at an Italian deli on the Edgware Road.

'I bought some champagne to celebrate,' Jamie said.

He brought out a bottle of Bollinger from the fridge, collected two flutes from the dresser and turned to Stella.

'Balcony?'

She nodded, smiling. 'Balcony.'

Outside, the sound of traffic replaced the delighted screams of the children playing out the back. Jamie fired the cork with a pop into the foliage of the plane tree directly opposite the balcony.

He grinned as he filled their glasses.

'I know the posh way is to twist the bottle, but I'm not posh. And I like the noise.'

'Fine by me,' Stella said. 'I'm not posh, either. As you may have noticed.' She raised her glass. 'Jamie Hooke, here's to you and your wonderful new job. Congratulations, darling, I'm really pleased for you.'

They clinked glasses and drank. Compared to the rich, oily white burgundy they'd drunk with the fish, the champagne was crisper, drier though still fruity – stewed apples rather than peaches.

Stella set her glass down carefully on the table. What had Jamie called his patients? Fucked-up? He'd said they belonged in prison. That sounded like a hard-headed realist talking. No flaky 'they're not bad, just vulnerable' nonsense. Would he understand the bind she was in and what had led her to kill Adam?

'I was thinking,' Jamie said. He stopped and took a gulp of his champagne. He smiled nervously. 'I don't really need my house in Crowthorne anymore. I was wondering, what would you say to selling this place and us buying somewhere together?'

Jamie's questions set emotions bursting free inside her like the cork escaping the champagne bottle.

How amazing that Jamie wanted them to move in together. But she'd have to lie to him about her past for the rest of her life. She loved him, she was sure of it. Could he love her once he knew she was a killer? Should she tell him?

Fear mixed with a devil-may-care attitude in which she heard the faint echo of another version of herself.

Go for it, babe. What's the worst that can happen?

Stella finished her champagne. Jamie picked up the bottle but she shook her head. She weighed up the odds. Didn't like what she saw. But at the same time, wanted desperately to win and win big.

Confessing to Jamie could finally free her from her violent past. They could move on, together, buy somewhere together. Maybe in a leafier part of London. Get married. Maybe they could even—

Then the downside risks barged into the party.

He could call the police.

He could thrust her away from him, horrified – revolted – by what she'd done.

She'd lose him for ever. Turn into a broken-down, alcoholic cop and die alone. If she lived that long, given what Callie had intimated was waiting for her.

She felt she was standing at the head of a craps table in some sleazy West End casino. Drunken gamblers clustering round her as she clenched the two translucent blood-red dice in her fist. All or nothing on the biggest gamble of the year. Cheering her on, not caring if she won or lost. Their money wasn't at stake. Only hers.

Jamie frowned. 'Stella, what's wrong? I knew something was bothering you the moment you walked in. It's not just the case, is it?'

'Bloody headshrinkers,' she said with a cock-eyed and, she realised, drunken grin. 'Our heads are all made of glass to you, aren't they? You can just look straight inside and see what we're thinking.'

She crushed the sharp-cornered dice in her fist. The muscles in her arm were bunching, ready for the throw.

'No. But I can tell something's on your mind. Why don't you tell me?'

Stella felt a tear welling in her eye. 'Oh, Jamie, because I'm terrified that if I tell you, I'll lose you and I don't want that. I do want to move in with you. I can't think of anything I'd like better right now.'

He got up from his chair and came round the small table to crouch at her feet. He looked up into her eyes.

'Then tell me. It can't be any worse than what my patients tell me day in, day out at work, can it?'

The tear dropped from her chin onto his shirt and she stretched out a fingertip to touch the wet place on the soft denim. Her tear had turned the pale blue to a darker shade.

The realisation dawning in his eyes was as visible as the dark lashes that fringed them. As his curved eyebrows. As his curly hair, brown but streaked with grey, above them. She had time to take in each feature while she tried to find the right combination of words that would explain and exonerate in one sentence.

'My god,' he said in a quiet voice. 'It *is* worse, isn't it? Stella, darling, what have you done?'

She sniffed. Rubbed a finger under her nose. Then she hurled the dice down the table, watching them bounce and skitter over the payout zones then rebounding towards her off the end wall, drops of blood flying off and spattering the baize.

'I've killed— ' she was about to say *people*, but at the last moment she panicked. The dice she thought had settled on lucky seven had come up snake eyes: two beady black dots eyeing her soul hungrily — 'someone.'

He nodded, a sympathetic half-smile on his face.

'Darling, I know. Remember, you told me before? But Robey was attacking you. It was self-defence. That sort of thing scars a person, but I don't blame you. No need for the tears.'

Stella shook her head, realising she was crying. She dashed the tears away with her fist.

'I meant somebody else. Before.'

His brow furrowed. 'Who? When?'

Treading carefully, she decided to test her resolve with a single confession. 'The man who killed Richard and Lola. He murdered them. The whole hit and run was a set-up.'

Jamie sat back in his chair. He passed a hand over his face.

'I can't believe this. What do you mean you killed him? Was he attacking you, too?'

'No. He was the head of a conspiracy. Richard was about to expose them. I, I shot him.' She watched him processing this revelation. Didn't like what she saw. 'I *had* to,' she blurted. 'He would have got away with it. And the balance of my mind was disturbed. You know. Post-grief psychosis. I saw a psychiatrist. It's an actual diagnosis.'

'I know,' he snapped. 'But, you killed a man in cold blood, Stella. You murdered him. Taking the law into your own hands. I thought I knew you, but this…'

He trailed off. Stella watched the muscles in his face moving beneath the skin. They fired in sequences that set his lips twitching, then compressing. His eyebrows would move up, then draw together before relaxing. A couple of times, he opened his mouth but then closed it again.

Reeling from his reaction, she resolved in that moment never to tell him about the others, the *many* others.

'Let's go inside,' he said, finally.

He stood, without letting go of her hand and led her to the sitting room. There, she sat on the sofa, hoping he'd join her. He took an armchair and her ashy hopes, which needed just a little breath of tenderness to ignite, guttered fitfully.

He leaned towards her, hands clasped between his knees.

'How did you get away with it?' he asked, finally. 'Wasn't there an investigation?'

She explained how Callie and Gordon Wade had covered it up.

'I shouldn't even be telling you. I signed the Official Secrets Act. They could throw me in jail just for this.' She tried for a smile, but it was stillborn on her lips. 'You do understand, don't you?'

Stella tried to cling to the hope she'd been feeling. Blowing gently on that pitiful flame in an attempt to bring it to life. What Jamie said next extinguished it altogether.

He spread his hands wide. 'It's too much to process. I need some time.'

'Of course, darling! I know it's been a shock. A huge shock. You should take as much time as you need. But I was doing their dirty work, and they let me. You can see that, can't you?'

Even as she spoke, Stella heard how desperate she sounded. She'd interviewed enough murderers and rapists to be familiar with their self-pitying litanies of excuses. It was an accident. We were just playing. It was consensual. She was asking for it. They wouldn't stop crying. Aliens in my TV told me to do it.

Jamie shook his head sadly. 'That's not what I meant.'

'Then what did you mean?'

But Stella already knew. A pit had opened up before her and she felt powerless to avoid tumbling headlong into its gaping maw. What did that philosopher say, 'Be careful when you stare into the abyss, because the abyss stares back out at you'?

Jamie stood. 'I can't be with you right now. I'm going to find a hotel for tonight. Then I'm going back to Crowthorne first thing.'

'But you're coming back tomorrow night, like always, aren't you? It's the weekend.'

'I can't. I'm sorry. I have to go.'

Stella watched, helpless, as Jamie went into the bedroom to gather his things together. He emerged a few minutes later with a small bag and headed towards the door. He turned just before he left.

'I'm sorry.'

And then he was gone. Just like that.

The door clicked shut. And Stella was left alone in her flat. The ruins of a delicious celebratory supper on the kitchen counter. A half-drunk bottle of champagne on the balcony table, and a rip in her soul.

She went outside and poured another glass of champagne and sat there drinking until the bottle was empty and her heartache was numbed and the moon illuminated the city with a white glow.

12

LONDON

The following morning, after forcing herself to eat a breakfast of toast, peanut butter, coffee and painkillers, Stella walked to work. She could feel the alcohol still poisoning her system and dimly remembered hitting the vodka after the champagne was all gone.

Sleep had come upon her like a train. But then she'd woken at 2.55 a.m. and not slept since. She had no worries that Jamie would report her. After all, she'd explained that her actions had been officially sanctioned. But the pain of losing him – that was too much to bear.

As she arrived in SIU, massaging her right temple, Cam buttonholed her.

'Morning, guv, you look rough as old boots and the big boss wants to see you.'

Stella grimaced. She'd seen her face in the mirror already and hadn't enjoyed the sight. Cam's judgement, truthfully delivered in her raspy South London accent, only fed the flames of her self-loathing.

As Stella walked up to the door of Callie's office, she heard an unfamiliar voice, and accent, coming from inside. She knocked and entered.

Sitting with Callie was a man who gave off maximum-strength cop vibes. She thought it was probably the slouchy body language. Or the worn black leather jacket, black Levi's and scuffed black boots. He stood.

He was on the short side, wiry build, lank, dirty-blonde hair swept back from a high, domed forehead. Haunted blue eyes under heavy brows. And a straggly blonde beard and moustache. All in all, she thought he was the ugliest man she had ever seen.

The male cop shook her hand. 'Oskar Norgrim, pleased to meet you.'

His English was flawless, without a hint of an accent. The gentle, warm voice contrasted oddly with the imperfections of his face.

'Hi. I'm Stella Cole. Callie, what's this all about?' Stella asked as Callie motioned for them to sit.

'Detective Inspector Norgrim is with the National Operations Department of the Swedish Police Authority. Ambassador Jonasson summoned him to help with our investigation.'

Norgrim swung round in his seat to smile at Stella. 'I'm here to offer any assistance you might find helpful, DCI Cole. You don't need to hide your toes away. I won't be stepping on them in my size twelves.' He frowned. 'Is that how you say it?'

'Close enough. But we're fine for resources, boss, honestly. I really don't think we need to complicate the investigation with an outside force.'

'Nobody's saying you do,' Callie said, flashing Stella a brief warning with her eyes. 'But this has come down from on high via the Foreign Office.'

'Ambassador Brömly was a Swedish national, murdered on British soil,' Norgrim said. 'I can coordinate things from the Swedish end to ensure you don't miss anything in your investigation.'

Stella felt a flash of heat rise from the collar of her shirt. She knew she shouldn't but she could feel a strong sense of territoriality washing through her.

'I can assure you, we wouldn't miss anything, whether or not we had outside assistance.'

'No offence intended, DCI Cole. I am only here to help. Perhaps you could tell me where you have got to in your investigation,' Norgrim said.

'Fine,' she said, hearing the petulant tone and unable to do anything about it. 'Come and meet the team. I'll brief you over there.'

They rose and as Stella turned to say goodbye she raised her eyebrows enquiringly at Callie. *Why?*

Callie's level gaze spoke volumes. *Don't ask.* And, *You look like shit. Also, Are you all right?*

Leading Norgrim away from Callie's office, Stella waved him to a chair at the cluster of tables SIU used as a conference space. She called the others to join them.

Once the introductions were out of the way, Stella asked each member of the team for a brief update.

'I called the Swedish embassy and spoke to the chef. The one from Stockholm,' Baz said. 'He said there's only one baker in London who uses caraway seeds in their *kanelbullar*. It's called Kafé Valhalla. I called first thing this morning. The manager said they only make them with caraway on Thursdays. It's some kind of regional speciality, apparently. Their CCTV is cloud-based. Our IT guys are hooking up a link so we can review it here.'

'Excellent work, Baz,' Stella said. 'How's the firearms angle coming, Garry?'

'There are just two guys in London known for supplying nine-mil, hollow-point ammo,' he said. 'One's doing a ten-stretch in the Scrubs, the other one's been keeping a low profile of late. I've put the word out I want to talk to him.'

'Sorry to interrupt,' Norgrim said. 'What is the "Scrubs"? A prison?'

'Yeah. Officially, Wormwood Scrubs. Over Hammersmith way.'

Norgrim turned to Stella. 'What is your working hypothesis?'

'I think he was murdered to shut him up. He was dying of cancer and had apparently decided to confess to some sort of misdeed in his past. It looks as though three others were involved. He wrote to them shortly before he died.'

'Do you have their names?'

'Only their first names. Ove, Kerstin and Inger.'

Norgrim shrugged. 'Very common Swedish given names. Do you have his phone or computer?'

'We do. They're both password-protected. I've put in a request with Apple to get the phone unlocked but that could take weeks. Our digital forensic team are looking at the laptop but he didn't use a *password* or 1234 so it might take a while.'

'How can I help?' Norgrim asked.

'Can you ask around the local Swedish community? We've made a start but maybe they'll open up to you.'

'Can you sort me out with a desk? A computer, maybe?'

Stella nodded. 'We've had some cutbacks recently.' She pointed at a handful of swept-clean desks. 'Take your pick.'

She left Norgrim talking to the others and retreated to her office.

Inside the space she so rarely used, she closed the door and crossed the brief expanse of grey carpet to reach her desk. She slumped into the chair and rested her forehead on her fists. She knew she was being unfair on the Swedish cop, but she couldn't help it.

How had it gone so wrong, so fast? One minute Jamie was suggesting they move in together – basically halfway to a proposal – then she'd royally screwed everything up.

What had she been thinking? That confessing would lead to Jamie's opening his arms wide, growling, 'Come here, tiger,' and a night of drunken sex before deciding on soft furnishings for their new place? Stupid, stupid woman!

She pulled out her phone, intending to message him, then realised she had zero idea of what to say and pocketed it again. Though it was costing her plenty, she decided to let him make the next move. Her last had been devastating enough.

She distracted herself by calling the Swedish embassy to find out if they'd located Brömly's next of kin. It turned out he had a younger brother, Anders, living in Uppsala. Stella thanked the researcher, took a note of the brother's phone number and prepared herself to make the call.

He answered on the fifth ring and, after asking him in rapidly memorised Swedish if he spoke English, Stella got to the meat of the call.

'I'm afraid I have some bad news for you.'

She explained about Brömly's death, and that until the case was brought to court the coroner wouldn't be able to release the body. Her questions about enemies proved fruitless. Anders and Tomas had not been close, he explained, and apart from seeing each other at Christmas and Midsommar, only kept in touch by email.

'I'm sorry for your loss,' she said. 'If you think of anything, you can call me on this number.'

Sighing, she ended the call and went to see how Baz was getting on with the CCTV from Kafé Valhalla.

'How's it going?' she asked, settling into a chair beside him.

'I've done the Thursday before last. Now I'm on last Thursday.'

'The day of the murder.'

'Yeah, and so far I'm seeing a lot of people smiling and chatting with the staff but nobody who stands out. The manager said he mostly sells the specials to regulars,' he said. 'Apparently it's a bit of a thing and they all know to arrive as soon as the *kanellbullar* come out of the oven.'

'Nice pronunciation,' Stella deadpanned. 'Who taught you? Norgrim?'

Baz frowned. 'You don't like him, do you, Guv?'

Ignoring him, Stella jabbed her finger at the screen. 'Go back.'

Baz moused over the on-screen controls and paused the playback. He hit Fast Rewind, stopped it and pressed play again. Stella leaned closer. Their heads almost touching, they watched the bakery's customers coming and going for a couple of minutes. Sun streamed in through the big display window, casting strong dark shadows. Stella pointed at a figure.

'There.'

The figure wearing a baseball cap froze in the act of reaching across the counter to accept a bag of pastries. From this angle, Stella couldn't tell their sex. But what she picked up was a person wearing a coat on a hot summer's day, with a cap pulled down to hide their face from the camera.

'Man or woman?' Baz asked, echoing her thoughts.

'Can't tell. Play it on and let's take a look at the gait.'

The customer took the pastries, turned and left. On the short journey from counter to door, Stella couldn't see anything that strongly suggested a male or female walk. The customer's clothes didn't help. A long dark trench coat worn unbelted flowed out from the shoulders, effectively disguising what might have been female curves.

Baz pointed at the chest area. 'Is that a boob?'

Stella wrinkled her nose. 'Or a crease in the fabric? I can't tell. Bugger!'

'I'll go and talk to the manager,' Baz said. 'Maybe if they usually sell the specials to regulars, that guy stood out. They might have someone who served him and remembered the outfit or maybe how he spoke.'

Stella shook her head, then winced at the burst of pain it set off behind her eyes. 'No. I'll go. I need to get out for a bit.'

13

LONDON

Sitting with Kafé Valhalla's manager at a window table, Stella showed him the screen grabs she'd printed out of the mystery customer.

'Do you remember this person?' she asked.

The manager scratched his thin beard as he studied the photograph. Stella watched the way he touched the paper, as if trying to divine Cap'n Coat's identity by direct contact with the image.

He looked up at Stella. 'Sorry. He looks vaguely familiar, but if you've seen the CCTV footage you know how busy we get on Thursdays.' He looked over at the serving counter. 'Natasha was on last Thursday. I'll go and get her.'

He sent over a young, skinny black girl wearing round turquoise glasses.

'Hi,' she said. 'Joff said you wanted to see me?'

Stella motioned for her to sit down. 'Yes. We're trying to trace this person,' she said, tapping the printout. 'They came in last Thursday to buy your special *kanelbullar*. Do you remember seeing them?'

'Why are you saying *them*? Are they, like, trans?'

'No,' she said with a smile. 'I mean, not necessarily. But we don't know if they're male or female.'

She studied the photo.

'I think I do. I mean we were really busy, you know? But I remember her coat and the cap because it was a really hot day. I thought she must have been boiling. And she said she loved the *kanelbullar* with caraway because they reminded her of home.'

Stella experienced a mental jolt as the young woman's words sank in. She?

'You're certain it was a woman.'

'I think so.'

'You *think* so?'

'Well, she said her husband liked them, too. I mean that doesn't mean anything, right, but I just thought…'

'How about her face? Can you remember what she looked like?'

She frowned. 'I'm sorry. I have this condition. Prosopagnosia? I can't recognise faces. But it means I pay more attention to clothing and stuff to help me fix people.'

Stella smiled. 'Is there anything else you remember. Or anything else she said?'

Natasha wrinkled her nose. 'She had a really strong Swedish accent. I could tell because I listen to a podcast called My Swedish Life. I'd like to live there one day.'

Stella smiled again. Aiming for maximum reassurance. If Natasha was right, she may have been one of the people who spoke to the murderer on the day of the killing. Maybe the only person, apart from Brömly.

'Think about her voice some more. How did it sound to you?'

Natasha closed her eyes and Stella could see the movements behind the lids as she swivelled them up, left, right and back again. Without opening them, she spoke.

'Kind of light. Not high, but, you know, smooth. Not gruff or gritty like a guy's voice. Gentle.'

'And with a strong Swedish accent?'

'Yeah,' she said, eyes open again. Then they widened, an effect magnified by the lenses of her glasses. 'Oh. She did say something strange. She asked me where the nearest tube station was. Only she called it the metro.'

Stella thanked them both and headed back to Paddington Green, picking up half a dozen *kanellbullar* on her way out.

Stella found Baz in conversation with Garry and the Swedish detective. She offered the buns round. All three men took one. She told them about her conversation with Natasha and outlined her conclusions.

The woman was a Swedish national. Her strong accent and reference to the 'metro' suggested she was a recent arrival. Either Inger or Kerstin had received Brömly's letter, then flown to London to dissuade him from going public. He'd refused and she'd shot him. The tongue was a message to the other two.

Baz had been busy on his phone. 'Guess how many Swedish nationals fly to London every month.'

'Surprise me.'

'Fifty thousand.'

Stella straightened her shoulders. 'Right. As SIO, I'm calling this one,' she said. 'Everyone keep chasing down these lines of enquiry. I'm going to Sweden. That's where we'll find Brömly's killer.'

Norgrim nodded. 'I'll call the embassy now. Do you need any help with credentials for the Swedish Police Authority?'

'No thanks. I'll get onto CPS. They'll issue me a letter of introduction. Can you get hold of Anna Brömly's medical records?'

'What am I looking for?'

'I want to know if she ever received treatment for infertility.'

On the way to Callie's office, Cam stopped her. She'd taken on Rosh's responsibilities and told Stella her confidential informant had come up with nothing. Stella didn't care. She was convinced the answers lay far from the grimy fringes of the London underworld.

Callie authorised the trip immediately, concurring with Stella's view that the killer – or the clue to their motive, and identity – would be in Sweden. The meeting had been tense, with neither woman wanting to acknowledge the threat hanging over Stella. Instead they'd concentrated on the case. Only as Stella was leaving did Callie crack.

'Watch yourself out there, Stel.'

Stella nodded and closed the door behind her.

* * *

Stella woke at 4.15 a.m. the next day. She'd booked a seat on a BA flight leaving for Stockholm from Heathrow at 1.35 p.m. She knew sleep would elude her if she closed her eyes again. She pulled on some pyjama bottoms and a black T-shirt.

She made a cup of coffee and some toast with peanut butter. She took her breakfast out onto the balcony and watched the sky lighten over west London.

Despite the promise of another hot day, the air still carried the chill of night. She wrapped her hands around her mug, enjoying the contrast between the heat of the coffee and the cold enveloping her.

Just as fast as it had arrived, the feeling of pleasure left her. She'd well and truly ruined her relationship with Jamie. He'd said he needed time. But that was what people always said. What they really meant was they needed to run a million miles in the opposite direction.

She sighed. Because as if trashing her love life wasn't bad enough, she now had a vengeful and highly motivated Roisin Griffin on her case, literally.

What would she do if Roisin confronted her after her trip to the US? Bluff? Deny everything? Or arrange to meet her somewhere quiet and kill her in cold blood? Find a chainsaw and a pig farm?

Callie had intimated what would happen if Stella didn't go along to get along. They'd send someone for her. Make it look like an accident, or a random nutter with a hard-on for cops. She'd like to see them try. Hadn't worked out too well for Moxey, now had it?

No! She couldn't, wouldn't go there. Not yet.

Maybe Rosh wouldn't solve Adam and Lynne's murders. Maybe her plane would crash on the way home. Stella laughed harshly. Maybe, maybe, maybe. *Make your own luck, Stel.*

She went and changed into her running gear and was racing through Regent's Park fifteen minutes later, alternating sprints with slow jogs, then dropping to the ground to do sets of ten press-ups before sprinting off again. She thought for a worrying moment that a white transit van was following her, but after checking over her shoulder to see it going down a side street, she relaxed. *Getting jumpy, Stel.*

At 8.30 a.m., she called her best friend and arranged to drop by an hour later. Vicky Riley was a journalist.

The first time they'd met, Stella had thought she'd been having an affair with Richard. It transpired that, before Richard's death, she'd been working with him on a piece that would have exposed the rats' nest of PPM conspirators.

They'd silenced Richard and made an attempt to frighten Vicky off, too. She'd helped Stella go after the conspiracy's leaders. Over the months and years that followed, they'd grown close.

Vicky opened the front door and smiled. Then she frowned.

'Is everything OK?'

'Not really.'

Frowning with concern, Vicky hugged her then pulled her inside and closed the door. Stella followed her into the kitchen. Vicky had married her fiancé the previous year. Her new life suited her. Still slender, with a bum Stella was openly envious of, she was more relaxed and had lost some of the anxiety creases around her eyes. She'd had her long blonde hair cut into a choppy short style that emphasised her cheekbones and china-blue eyes.

Damien was sitting at the table, mug of tea at his elbow, staring at his laptop. He rose from his chair when Stella appeared. Coming round the table he hugged her.

'How's our favourite murder detective?' he asked, his Yorkshire accent unaltered by his time living in London.

She forced a smile. 'Off to Sweden this afternoon.'

Damien smiled. 'So you're an *international* murder detective now. Maybe I should get our features department to do a profile for the Saturday paper.'

Stella glanced at Vicky, and was glad to see she picked up the message.

'Leave Stel alone, darling. In fact, shouldn't you be off to work? *The Guardian* won't write itself, you know.'

He grunted as he slapped his laptop shut. 'Huh. The way AI's going, it probably *will* before too long.'

She grinned at him. 'Yeah, but an AI can't get drunk with politicians until three in the morning, can it?'

Once Damien had gone, slamming the front door behind him, Vicky poured Stella some tea from the big brown pot on the table. She looked at Stella, arching her eyebrows.

'PPM isn't dead,' Stella said, simply.

Vicky's eyes popped wide open.

'What? I thought—'

'That's the problem. I *did* kill them all.'

'Then what? I don't understand?'

Stella explained what had happened.

'What are you going to do?'

Stella shrugged. Even though her plight was just as bad as before, telling Vicky had punched a hole in the lowering grey clouds that had gathered over her head. A few rays of sunshine speared through, showing her a possible route.

'Keep on working the case. Hope Rosh comes up with nothing that links me to their deaths. Hope for the best, prepare for the worst.'

'What can I do?'

Stella looked up at the ceiling then back at Vicky. 'Honestly? I don't know. If she comes up with any evidence linking me to the murders, she'll want it splashed all over the media. It'll make her career. But the people pulling her strings want the exact opposite.'

Vicky nodded. 'They'd hardly want you in the witness box on murder charges. Too risky.' Then her expression changed. Her mouth dropped open. 'You think they're going to try to kill you, don't you?'

There! Vicky had externalised what, until now, had been one of the blackest thoughts to have entered Stella's mind for years.

She nodded. 'I do. Callie pretty much admitted it.'

'But they can't! After all you did for them. They should have given you a bloody medal or a pension for life.'

'I don't think that's the way their minds work.'

'Bastards!' Vicky spat out. Then she smiled. A sly expression like the one she employed when ordering another round of cocktails when they both had work the next day.

'What?' Stella asked.

'I know what to do. How to protect you.'

'How? And don't say expose them. It won't work and I'll be as much in the spotlight as them.'

Vicky shook her head, then ran her hand through her hair again.

'That's not what I mean, although it does involve my journalistic skills, which, as I think you know, are incredible!'

Stella laughed. 'OK, Mrs Pulitzer Prize, what *do* you mean, then?'

Over the next twenty minutes Vicky outlined a plan to keep Stella safe for the rest of her life. And, as she outlined each stage, Stella felt more holes being punched through the leaden clouds over her head until the sun burnt off the remaining tatters and flooded the kitchen with light.

14

CHICAGO

Roisin scanned the reception area. So this was the FBI. She felt a low-level buzz of adrenaline as she waited for SAC Baxter to come and collect her.

Sharply-dressed agents marched through the gleaming white space. If the dress code for the Feds had eased up, as the briefing she'd read on the plane suggested, it must have been in incredibly subtle ways.

The men all wore conservatively cut two-piece suits in a rainbow of shades from navy through charcoal to black. White shirts predominated and the ties were, if it was possible, even less flamboyant than the suits. Black, navy and grey were favourites, though she did see one guy sporting a burgundy number.

For the women, the memo must have been headed: You can't go wrong in a trouser suit. She supposed trousers were more practical. But these girls really needed to lighten up. Presumably trying to outdo the men, they stuck to a sober palette taking in black, gun metal and dark tobacco with an occasional beige number to lighten the mix.

For the ones wearing skirts, American Tan tights were the order of the day, slipped into sensible low-heeled court shoes.

She glanced at a couple of bulging jackets and oddly-kinked jacket flaps. Then it hit her. Every bloody person in the building was carrying a gun. No need for urgent calls to SCO19 here. You needed tactical support? You *were* tactical support. Would she be issued with a gun? Or, what did they call them, a sidearm? She thought about it briefly and realised she was hoping the answer was yes.

A cheerful male voice snapped her out of her nine-millimetre calibre daydream.

'Detective Griffin?'

She looked towards the source of the greeting and stood. Striding across the polished floor towards her was a man in his late forties. His ginger hair was a few shades lighter than her own, and immaculately cut, parted with laser-like precision on the left. His moustache gave him the look of a country and western singer. He was smiling. One of those dazzling American smiles: all teeth, underpinned by a genuine good humour towards visitors.

He shook her hand.

'I'm Special Agent-in-Charge Baxter. But please, call me Eddie.'

She smiled. He was an easy man to smile at.

'Thanks, Eddie. Roisin.'

'Hey, Roisin,' he said, not stumbling at all over the Christian name so many of her British colleagues seemed to find incomprehensible, despite only being two syllables long. 'Welcome to Chicago, and welcome to the Federal Bureau of Investigations.'

He led her over to a set of lifts – *Elevators*, she mentally corrected herself – and a few minutes later they were sitting in a light, airy office on the top floor of the building.

He arranged coffee and biscuits – *Cookies, Rosh!* – and motioned for her to take a seat at a table by a plate-glass window that gave onto an expanse of manicured parkland that stretched to W. Roosevelt Road.

After a couple of minutes of small talk, he pushed the conversation into a higher gear.

'You've read the file, so you know where we're at. What else can I tell you?'

Roisin had spent most of the eight-and-a-half-hour flight thinking about how best to work the investigation.

'Can you take me to the crime scene?'

He nodded. 'Not personally. Too much admin, I'm afraid. But after we're done here, I'll introduce you to the agent I've assigned to you for the duration of your stay.'

'Where's the SUV you recovered?'

'We have a fully equipped auto analysis facility on site.'

'Has it been examined?'

'Only superficially. Once we realised the bodies were Adam and Lynne, I put everything on hold.'

At his use of their Christian names, Roisin remembered something Rachel Fairhill had said to her. Adam had been seconded to the FBI at Eddie's invitation.

'I'm sorry, by the way,' she said. 'I know you and Adam knew each other.'

He grimaced. 'Thank you. We weren't close friends. But, honestly? It's been quite a few years since he came out here. Things move on, you know?'

She nodded. 'Are the guns here, too?'

'In our ballistics lab.'

'Can I see them, too?'

'Sure you can. I've arranged for you to have full access to the evidence locker, the armoury, the works.'

'Thank you. One last thing. Will I be issued with a firearm while I'm out here?'

His ginger eyebrows flickered upwards. With surprise, she assumed, But he hid it well.

'I thought you Brit cops were all anti-gun?'

She grinned and thickened up her accent. 'Well, for a start, I'm Irish. A proper Colleen. And also, some of us believe in protecting ourselves.'

The reality had nothing to do with self-defence. Roisin doubted she'd be allowed to get anywhere near trouble while under the care of the FBI. She just wanted to know what it felt like to walk around with a pistol on her hip.

Eddie grinned back.

'Do you have any experience with firearms?'

'I have my Met firearms proficiency certification. I keep it up to date. I brought it with me, if you want to see it.'

He smiled. 'There are some formalities to go through, but we can issue a temporary permit and a sidearm for you while you're here. You won't be able to carry it unless an FBI agent is accompanying you.'

'That's fine. Thanks, Eddie.'

'All right then. Any more questions at this stage?'

Roisin shook her head, making sure she kept her eyes on Eddie and powering up the gaze her sisters called the Green Lantern.

'None for now.'

He reached for his desk phone. 'Let me call Simone and she can give you the tour.'

He spoke briefly then replaced the handset. 'She'll just be a couple of minutes. One other thing. How are you fixed for tonight?'

She shrugged. 'Eating in my hotel, I guess. Early night. I hadn't really thought.'

'Let me take you to dinner.'

She glanced at his left hand. Saw a gold band. 'That would be lovely.'

'Sure. We can discuss the case. I'll make sure you get some of the best food Chinatown has to offer before you depart for the land of a thousand cheeses.'

'Thanks. I look forward to it.'

'I'll pick you up at your hotel at six-thirty.'

Roisin remembered that Americans reputedly ate early. Eddie's suggestion confirmed it.

At a knock on the door, Eddie rose from his chair. 'That'll be Simone.'

He opened the door to admit a striking black woman. She stood at least six feet in her heels, which meant she towered over Eddie.

Smiling broadly, she came to shake Roisin's hand.

'Hi. Special Agent Simone King.'

'Detective Inspector Roisin Griffin. Nice to meet you.'

'Oh, you have such a great accent,' Simone said.

Roisin smiled. She felt like a visiting member of the Royal Family instead of a DI for the Met's unlovely outpost in Paddington.

Agreeing to meet Eddie in the lobby of her hotel, Roisin let Simone lead her away and back towards the elevators.

Visiting the evidence store meant a trip out of the main building along a covered walkway to a separate facility, where Simone escorted Roisin through three levels of security.

After introducing her to the supervisor, Simone requested the two handguns from the Collier case. She led Roisin along a corridor to a locked room she accessed with her swipe card. There, she laid the guns on a table topped with white laminate.

Seeing the guns, Roisin's heart rate accelerated. She was looking at the weapons used to kill Adam and Lynne Collier.

Simone pulled out a chair and sat down, gesturing for Roisin to join her. She put on a pair of nitrile gloves, got Roisin to do the same, then picked up the larger of the two guns and handed it to Roisin.

'Know what that is?'

Roisin turned the gun this way and that. It weighed more than she'd expected. She found the mass of it reassuring. She inspected the barrel and found the maker's engraved logo.

'Glock 22?'

'Chambered for .40 calibre Smith & Wesson rounds. This is the gun used to kill Lynne Collier.'

Roisin picked up the smaller gun. Its steel parts were dull with age but it was clean and undamaged. Compared to the bulky, squared-off Glock, it felt like a child's toy. About half the weight of the pistol, it sat snugly in her hand. She wondered what sort of bullets it took.

As if reading her mind, Simone pointed at the cylinder.

'You've got five .38 Special rounds in there.'

'How close would you have to be to be sure of killing someone with a gun like this?'

Simone shrugged. 'It depends what kind of a shot you are. This thing'll group at five inches out to fifty yards if you're good enough.

But if I wanted to be sure? And I was under stress? In a fast-moving situation? The closer the better. Certainly no more than ten yards. Probably less.'

'Do you have a theory as to how it happened? I've studied the schematics and the whole thing just looks weird.'

Simone nodded and smiled at Roisin.

'I know, right? Two weapons, two bodies. Everyone at Preston PD assumed it was a murder suicide, or a suicide pact. But when I started looking at it, the whole thing fell apart pretty rapidly.'

Roisin nodded excitedly. Simone had voiced her own thoughts. If Adam had shot Lynne first with the Glock, that would account for the .40 S&W round recovered from her skeleton.

But then he would have had to switch to the Airweight to account for the .38 Special inside his skull. So why was the Airweight recovered *outside* the SUV?

Then again, if Lynne had shot herself with the Glock, she couldn't have gone on to shoot Adam with the Airweight. And if it was a suicide pact, why not sit together in the SUV? And why drive out onto the ice?

'So the only explanation that makes sense is—' Roisin said.

'A third shooter,' they said together.

Grinning, Simone got to her feet. 'Come with me.'

Bemused, Roisin followed Simone along the corridor, where she dropped off the Glock and the Airweight at the counter.

Simone stopped off at her desk and picked up a cardboard carton from underneath. From the way she lifted it, Roisin didn't think it could be too heavy. It certainly wasn't full of more hardware, even if that had been allowed, much less stacked with documentation.

15

STOCKHOLM

Whether it was the hotel bed, or the distance she'd put between her and the troubles she'd left behind in London, Stella slept better than she had for days.

She checked her phone on waking. No messages from Jamie. Again. Sighed. Holding to her vow of silence was proving hard. She sent a quick text.

How are you?

Uncertain of the Swedish police dress code for detectives, but feeling a degree of decorum from a visiting Met DCI was appropriate, she dressed in a smart navy jacket and khakis over burgundy loafers.

Her white shirt was crisp from the iron in the hotel room. She even stood for a minute by the lift, buffing the tops of her shoes under the shoe polishing machine.

After a hurried breakfast of toast and peanut butter plus an apple from a glass bowl overflowing with fruit, she headed out for the headquarters of the Swedish Police Authority on *Kungsholmsgatan.*

Halfway to the station, she began to wonder whether she'd have been better off getting a cab. The heat was intense and it was only eighty-thirty in the morning. Her shirt was sticking to her back and inside her trousers her legs were prickling with sweat.

Hoping for some shade, she crossed into a park called *Kronobergsparken*. Landscaped with rolling hills and plenty of broad-branched trees, it offered a respite from the sun and a shortcut to the SPA building. Ten minutes later, having crossed the park via a series of winding tarmac paths, she arrived at the main entrance. The HQ consisted of a whole block of buildings, faced in red granite panels.

Oskar came down to reception to meet her and ten minutes later she was sitting at his left hand in a large conference room filled with Swedish cops. Stella glanced around, noting that the uniformed cops wore sidearms on their hips. Presumably the detectives wore weapons too, in shoulder holsters. Or on their belts. Oskar stood.

'Good morning everyone,' he said, speaking English. 'Before we start, I'd like to welcome Detective Chief Inspector Stella Cole. She's from the Met in London and she's leading their investigation into the murder of Ambassador Brömly.'

The assembled cops offered a variety of greetings, all in English, accompanied by smiles and nods.

Stella felt embarrassed by the Swedes' language skills. She couldn't have introduced Oskar to SIU in Swedish and, even if she had, how many of her team could have welcomed him in his mother tongue? She knew the answer. None. She resolved to learn as much Swedish as she could during her stay. No time like the present, she thought.

'*Tack*, Oskar,' she said to him, then turned to address the room more generally. '*God morgon*. I hope I can repay your hospitality with some helpful insights while I'm a guest in your country. And work with you all to catch Ambassador Brömly's murderer.'

Her semi-prepared speech went down well, earning her a few more nods and grunts of appreciation. She was experienced enough to know that a senior officer flying in from not just another force but another country, was as welcome as a boil on the bum.

After all, she'd hardly behaved herself when Oskar had turned up in London. She had no intention of provoking rivalry or worse before she'd even reached her first coffee.

Oskar spent twenty minutes outlining the evidence they'd gathered in London, and, more importantly, the gaps he wanted filling. Once the meeting dispersed, he turned to Stella.

'Time to introduce you to my boss.'

He led her through the bustling CID room to a wall of glassed-in offices. On the way he informed her that there was nothing in Anna Brömly's medical history about infertility treatment. She nodded her thanks. Maybe the couple had remained child-free by choice. In which case, why was he so bothered about the issue?

Oskar knocked at the door of the leftmost of the glassed-in offices and entered. She followed him in.

Sitting behind the desk was a woman in her late forties or early fifties. She smiled and rounded the immaculate desk to shake Stella warmly by the hand.

'You must be DCI Cole. Welcome to Sweden and Stockholm Region Murder Squad,' she said. 'I'm Detective Chief Inspector, Malin Holm. Call me Malin, please.'

'And you must call me Stella.'

'Please, sit,' Malin said.

Stella took in Oskar's boss in a quick, appraising glance. Her auburn hair was cut short in a pixie crop, not a million miles from the look Stella had adopted on her trip to kill Collier. She wore no or little makeup and the overall effect, from intelligent gaze to strong jawline, was of a determined woman who put professionalism ahead of everything else.

'Why don't you fill in Malin on where we got to in England,' Norgrim said.

Stella nodded, deciding in the moment to use Brömly's former title as Oskar had at the team briefing. When she finished, Malin acknowledged the concise summary with a quick nod.

'You said "she" just then. This wasn't in Oskar's report. Has there been a new development?'

Stella explained how her interview with the cafe server had

yielded the new piece of intelligence. Malin narrowed her eyes, throwing them into shadow. 'Does the MO sound like a woman to you, Stella?' she asked.

'I think, in the right circumstances, a woman could commit any type of injury on another person,' Stella said carefully.

Malin nodded. 'But statistically, isn't it more likely to be a man?'

'Yes. But that doesn't mean this one was.'

'Tell me again why you feel this individual is your prime suspect.'

Feeling more like a rookie than she had for any number of years, Stella pushed on with her explanation.

'That is a bit thin,' Malin said, when Stella finished.

Feeling defensive, Stella pushed back. 'It's the best lead we have. Everything points to the killer living in Sweden. It's why I'm here.'

Malin nodded, pursing her lips. She blew out, flapping them like a horse, an incongruous sound in the small office.

'Please don't be offended. I'm just testing the evidence underlying your assumptions.'

Stella smiled. 'I get it. And I agree, it doesn't fit what I would think of as the normal profile of a female killer.'

'So. What is the plan?'

Oskar touched Stella lightly on the arm. 'May I?' he asked her.

'Sure, go ahead. It's your show now.'

'Man or woman,' he glanced at Stella, 'the killer is here. On that Stella and I agree. We think if we find the motive, we'll find the killer. That means digging into Brömly's past.'

Malin steepled her fingers together in front of her face.

'We should discuss operational protocols.'

'Of course.'

'You are here on a letter of introduction. You are strictly limited to interviewing witnesses. If there are any arrests to be made, Swedish law requires they be made by an officer of the SPA.'

Stella smiled. 'I understand.'

Malin nodded. 'Good. Brömly grew up in Umeå, didn't he?'

'Yes. That's where we need to begin.'

'You'll like Umeå. It is sometimes called the capital of the north.

You know, they call it *Björkarnas Stad*. It means City of Birches. Oskar can explain why on your trip.'

After the meeting with Malin, Oskar led Stella to a spare desk.

'You can work here. I hope it's OK. The PC isn't new but it's not too slow, I checked,' he said with a lopsided grin.

Then he left her to it, explaining he had a court appearance to prepare for. Stella settled into the chair, which was far more comfortable than the ratty old things they had to put up with in SIU.

She fished around in the desk drawers and came up with an A4 pad and a pen. Ignoring the PC for the moment, she began making notes of the lines of enquiry she wanted to pursue in Sweden.

She got out Brömly's CV, opened a browser and started searching for phone numbers.

Stella worked the phone solidly for two hours. During a break, a text arrived from Cam. The translations were back from the interpreters. Neither added anything to the versions they'd put together from Google, and Malmaeus the priest. But at least she now had evidential-quality renderings into English.

A quiet cough made her turn round. A young female detective stood by her desk. Her long blonde hair was held back in a black scrunchie. She had a perfect heart-shaped face and lightly tanned skin, tinged over the cheekbones with pink.

Her eye colour was hard to describe until Stella remembered a semi-precious stone she'd once coveted called moss agate. Like the wet green stuff fringing river banks, it was somewhere between green, blue and grey. Her lips were full and curved upwards in a smile.

'Hi, I'm Johanna Carlsson. I just transferred in from Financial Crime. I saw you in the briefing this morning.'

Stella stood and smiled as they shook hands. 'Wow! That's a strong grip for someone who chases white-collar criminals.'

Johanna grinned. 'I work out. I can bench press thirty-five kilos.'

Stella nodded her appreciation. 'Not bad.'

Johanna cast an appraising glance over Stella's body. 'How about you? You work out, too?'

Stella laughed and shook her head. 'No. But I like running.'

'Oh, yes? What distance?'

'My personal best for a 10K is fifty-six thirty.'

Now it was Johanna's turn to nod. 'Cool. So, you want to go for a run with me? Maybe tonight after work?'

'Sure, I'd like that.'

Johanna's smile broadened. She looked genuinely pleased.

'Where are you staying?'

'*Hotel Kungsträdgården* on *Vastra Trädgårdgatan*. Sorry about my pronunciation.'

'That's a great hotel. And your pronunciation is fine. It's cute in your English accent. So, my apartment's not too far from there. I'll drive over to meet you outside. Say seven?'

Most of the day passed the way it had started, with Stella calling Brömly's old schools, researching his early years in Umeå and arranging to meet people who knew him there when he was younger. Without exception, everyone she spoke to could say nothing but good things about Brömly. She was beginning to wonder whether it had been a random killing after all.

Needing to get out and do some old-fashioned coppering, she researched the national agency responsible for coordinating volunteering in Sweden. It was called *Volontärbyrån*, the National Volunteering Agency.

She called and made an appointment to see the Executive Director that afternoon.

Anna Strömgren, fortyish, stout and with half-moon glasses on a thin gold chain, welcomed Stella warmly and led her to her ground-floor office. With its profusion of indoor plants, it resembled a hothouse rather than a place of business. Stella realised she'd left home without arranging for anyone to water her house plants.

'How can I help you, DCI Cole?' she asked.

'I'm investigating a murder. A former Swedish ambassador was killed in his London flat.'

Strömgren's expression changed. Her smile disappeared, replaced by a look of sadness.

'I read about it. You know, Tomas was a good friend to *Volontärbyrån.*'

'How do you mean?'

'He sent money every year. Quite a large amount.'

'Can I ask how much?'

'One hundred thousand kronor.'

Stella frowned. Almost nine thousand pounds. That was a lot of money for a yearly donation to a charity.

'Did he ever say why?'

Strömgren nodded. 'He told me once. He said he believed Sweden needed to be more compassionate. That it could save the country's soul.'

Stella made a note. Because it jarred with her own impression of the country. Back in the UK, people were always holding up Sweden as an example of an enlightened democracy, caring for its immigrants and with a welfare system second to none. What was wrong with its soul?

'Tomas was a volunteer himself, in the seventies,' Stella said.

'Yes, he told me. In Africa.'

'Do you have records stretching back that far?'

She shook her head. 'I'm sorry. We were only established in 2002. Before that, volunteering in Sweden was coordinated through hundreds of smaller organisations. Charities. Churches. Social clubs. I doubt, even if the one Tomas worked through still exists, that they would have records from that far back.'

Stella nodded. She hadn't really been expecting anything else. But at least she'd learned that Brömly gave a sizeable annual donation. Of course people, especially wealthy people, often gave large sums to charity. But Brömly's reasons sounded very much like those of a man trying to escape some moral failing of his own.

Towards the end of the day, during which she'd largely managed to avoid checking her phone, Lucian emailed her with a new piece of evidence.

. . .

We got a match off the shoe sole pattern database for the print on Brömly's face. It's a Swedish brand, which you may find interesting: Icebug. I narrowed it down to two models then spoke to a *very* nice product manager in their marketing department, and he told me it's their Spirit8.

I measured the spacing between the studs (which I learned are carbide-tipped btw – they're designed for running on icy trails, who knew!).

From my measurements, he thought they were probably a 42 or a 43. The 42 is the largest women's size they do, then you have to buy from the men's range.

Stella made a note, smiling at Lucian's evident delight in acquiring a Swedish contact for whom, she had no doubt, he'd fallen. She wondered whether he'd tell his partner, Gareth, a primary school teacher with a wicked sense of humour and a beautiful tenor voice.

She thought it was careless of the killer to wear such distinctively patterned shoes to a hit. But then maybe she hadn't reckoned on the need to pinion Brömly to the floor before wrenching out his tongue.

She? Or he? Was Malin right? Were the statistics against it?

Bugger the statistics! If you believed numbers over evidence and, yes, your copper's instincts, you'd do what most cops did and solve the majority of murders using the commonest assumptions and the most probable lines of enquiry.

Which was fine in the Murder Squad, where on a good day you'd have a suspect in custody before the body was cold.

But in SIU, where they dealt only with the weird ones, the off-menu ones, the ones that, statistically, shouldn't have happened at all, stats were about as much use as a Taser with a flat battery.

She'd ask Johanna what she thought. Coming from an outside discipline she'd hopefully have fewer preconceptions about what women were, or weren't capable of doing. When pushed too far.

16

CHICAGO

Simone led Roisin to an unused conference room. On the way, she explained she'd transferred in from Oakland in California a month earlier. She'd read the files but little more than that.

Inside she gestured for her to close the door as she set the box down on the rectangular wooden table.

In one corner stood a whiteboard on a tripod. Unlike those Roisin was used to, this was pristine. Its glossy surface appeared never to have been used. Or if it had, someone had used an industrial solvent to remove the blue, green and red smears that marred every single whiteboard back in Paddington Green.

God, that seemed like another world away. Did the FBI have to deal with cuts? It didn't look like it to her. Everywhere she saw new-looking office equipment, gleaming, undented vehicles, and people going about their business with the quiet confidence that came from being part of a well-resourced machine.

'Give me a hand with this, would you?' Simone asked, standing to one side of the whiteboard.

Roisin joined her and together they lifted it up and laid it flat on the table. Simone went to a side table positioned under a window and brought a white box to the table. It was full of drywipe markers, felt erasers, Post-It pads, a couple of notepads and some FBI-branded ball points.

Simone took out a blue marker and sketched in a sweeping curve down the centre of the board.

'That's the lakeshore,' she said.

With a few swirls of a green marker, she added some rough circles to the left of the shore. 'Trees.'

At last, she opened the flaps of the cardboard carton. Roisin peered inside and laughed. The box contained toys. She looked more closely. Not just toys, action figures in a variety of uniforms and civilian outfits, plus motorbikes, cars, trucks, furniture, road cones, traffic barriers – in short, everything you might need to recreate a crime scene.

'We've played this out a couple dozen different ways, but you knew the Colliers. Maybe you'll come up with something we missed,' Simone said.

Roisin bit back the answer that she hadn't known the dead couple at all. Instead, she pulled out a black SUV. Twelve inches from bumper to bumper, it had opening doors and bonnet – hood, she corrected herself. She placed it in the centre of the area designated lake by Simone's curving shoreline. Next she pulled out a male character in a grey suit. She manoeuvred him into the SUV's driver's seat.

Simone pulled out a female character wearing a blue skirt and, incongruously, a shocking-pink halter top.

'Minnesota in winter's a bit cold for this, really, but, hey, she's gonna die in a minute, anyway,' Simone said, shocking Roisin with the crudeness of her humour. Just for a second.

She lay the figure on its side about a foot from the front of the SUV. Roisin looked into the box and pulled out a male figure. She pursed her lips. Something made her want to put the male figure back in the box. She rooted around among the hard plastic figures until she found a second female. This one wore a navy bomber jacket with a bright-yellow FBI on the back. She placed it equidistant from the two others, to form a triangle.

Simone looked at Roisin.

'You don't think it was one of us, do you?'

Roisin smiled and shook her head. 'I don't know why I did that. I suppose it's too easy to assume the other shooter was a guy.'

'Good thinking. Maybe this'll help us stay unbiased. OK, so what happened? Go.'

Roisin looked down at the diorama in front of her. Adam Collier's handsome face swam into view. She closed her eyes for a second and pictured the file photos she'd studied since Rachel Fairhill had assigned her to the case.

Collier had what she thought of as movie-star good looks. Dark, heavy eyebrows above penetrating brown eyes. A regular face, clean-shaven. The hint of a sardonic smile. Lynne, by contrast, was unremarkable. Nondescript, she thought. Mousey. The kind of person witnesses would always describe as average-looking.

She opened her eyes again.

Lynne had been shot with Adam's service weapon. The odds were that he'd been the one to shoot her. It was possible the mystery person had got his gun off him and used it to murder his wife. But then, why not use it on Adam as well? Why switch to the little revolver?

Roisin scratched around under the bulkier items in the box and came up with a fistful of tiny pieces of plastic. Among the oddly detailed food items and household doodads, she saw a couple of black pistols. She picked one out with thumb and forefinger and placed it inside the SUV on the passenger seat.

She had another go but came up with chicken drumsticks, sandwiches and an orange coffee mug.

'Here, let me,' Simone said.

She picked up the box by its sides and emptied it out with a rush and rattle of hard plastics onto the table beside the whiteboard. Fifty or sixty bits of multicoloured plastic skittered across the polished surface.

Roisin spotted what she wanted. A cowboy figure complete with lariat in one hand and silver revolver in the other. She prised the revolver from his hand – his cold, dead hand, a voice intoned between her ears – and laid it beside the female figure on the ice standing, well, lying, in for Lynne Collier.

She took the FBI figure away and stood it up on the land side of the shoreline.

'This is how the Colliers were found, yes?' she asked Simone as she pointed to the two victim figures.

'Under the water, but yes. Preston PD pulled them out of the lake in roughly those positions relative to the bank and each other.'

If the Glock was Adam's then the mystery shooter must have brought the Airweight. Roisin clipped the little revolver into the FBI character's right hand. She moved the figures around on the schematic landscape, looking for a setup that fitted the evidence.

Roisin stared at the female figure, lying on its side on the ice. She realised that was how she'd begun to think of the whiteboard – as an expanse of thinning ice on a lake deep in the Minnesota countryside where two expat Brits had been murdered.

She picked up the 'Lynne' figure and brought it to shore. She laid it down between two of the trees Simone had crudely sketched in.

'Try this on for size,' she said. 'Adam, for some reason, maybe the shooter forces him to, shoots Lynne on dry land. Then he drives out onto the ice, again, maybe he's at gunpoint. The shooter kills him then runs back, drags Lynne out to the hole and dumps her in.'

Simone shook her head. 'If Adam's got a Glock, why doesn't he just shoot our mystery guy? Why go along with an order to kill his wife?'

Roisin frowned. Simone was right. She pulled out a nugget of advice from her training. If you can't figure it out, think the unthinkable.

'What if Adam *wanted* to kill Lynne? What if he killed her just before the other shooter arrived?'

Simone nodded slowly.

'He's panicking,' she said. 'He drives onto the ice to escape the shooter. But he's not used to Minnesota weather. He thinks the ice will hold him. He'll drive across or along the ice and escape further down the shoreline.'

'But the ice cracked and he went through,' Roisin said. 'The shooter followed Adam onto the ice and shot him where he sat, then the SUV sank.'

'The shooter dragged Lynne's body over and dropped it in the hole, along with the Airweight.'

Roisin nodded. It worked except that now she was faced with another mystery. If Adam had killed Lynne before the shooter arrived, it was murder. What was his motive for killing his wife? With the prospect of the investigation into the Colliers' deaths splitting into two before her eyes, Roisin turned to the little figures on the ice.

A sentence from the ME's report on Adam Collier came back to her. 'Edges of bullet hole and fractures to frontal bone indicate a downward trajectory from a shot fired straight-on.'

She picked up the FBI figure, bent its knees and placed it on the hood, arm outstretched and angled down into the cabin.

Roisin looked at the figures and the toy SUV. For some reason, Adam Collier killed his wife in the middle of nowhere. A mystery shooter arrived, having somehow worked out where to find him. The shooter's intended victim must have been Adam. If it was Lynne, there was no need to kill Adam at all. They could have vanished, leaving Adam as the prime suspect in any subsequent murder investigation. So, who had a motive to kill Adam Collier?

It would have to wait. She wanted to see the SUV.

17

STOCKHOLM

Stella emerged onto *Vasträ Trädgårdsgatan* in her running gear at 6.58 p.m. and looked up and down the narrow street for Johanna. This far north, and approaching the summer solstice, which she'd read the Swedes celebrated as *Midsommar*, the sun was still high in the sky. It felt more like early afternoon than early evening.

While she waited, a few pedestrians nodded to her and smiled. She inhaled deeply, catching a whiff of someone's toffee-flavoured vape. Despite the shit-show with Jamie, despite Roisin digging around in stuff Stella had thought literally dead and buried, despite everything, this felt good.

She found she couldn't wait to get started. Her legs were twitching with pent-up tension. She now realised how badly she needed to feel herself flowing along in that blissful state when everything became clearer, simpler and easier to understand.

A tap on her shoulder made her turn. Johanna stood beside her, close enough to smell her perfume, a light, floral scent. In her leggings and running top, cropped to show off a flat, muscular stomach, there was no escaping her incredible physique.

'*Hej*!' she said, leaning closer to kiss Stella on each cheek. 'You look great! Ready to go?'

'More than ready.'

'I thought we'd head into *Kungsträdgården* and do a couple of laps to warm up, then there's a really nice waterside circuit we can do. About 5K. That all right with you?'

Stella smiled. 'Sounds great.'

The two women set off, side by side, splitting around other pedestrians and nodding to fellow joggers heading in the opposite direction. Johanna looked as though she could run at twice the pace she'd set, though Stella was finding it easy to match her.

The park was surfaced with Astroturf. Stella wondered why the city council hadn't gone for grass. Plastic turf in somewhere as environmentally aware as Sweden struck her as odd.

She and Johanna ran round the periphery twice, picking up the pace a little on each turn.

Johanna turned her head as they completed the second circuit. 'Ready to hit the waterside?' she asked.

'Let's go.'

Johanna led her out of the park and onto *Strömgatan*. Concrete bollards linked with heavy black iron chains stood between the pedestrians and the waters of *Lilla Värtan* maybe a couple of metres below.

Stella found her rhythm easily and, as they ran almost hip to hip, she asked Johanna the question she'd been mulling over all day.

'Do you think a woman could have done it? The business with the tongue?'

'For sure! You know, in the town where I grew up, the butcher's shop was called *Petersson och Döttrar*. You know what that means?'

'Petersson and Daughters?'

'Yes, exactly! And *daughters*. I was best friends with Hanna, the older one. She and Stina, they would do all the work that their dad did. Cut up the carcases, take out the guts, do whatever was needed. And guess what they like to eat the most in their house?'

'Surprise me.'

'*Långsamt kokt oxtunga.*'

Stella laughed, dodging an elderly man using a Zimmer frame. 'I didn't get all of that, but I'm guessing *oxtunga* is ox tongue.'

'You're right. The rest means slow-cooked. We ate it with French fries and pickled vegetables. Even now, when I go back home, that's what I ask my mum to cook for me.' Johanna slowed down a little so she could turn her face to look at Stella. 'Speaking of food, do you want to get some dinner after this?'

'Love to. I haven't had anything since breakfast. I need to change, though.'

'Me too. Why don't we circle back to your hotel? You can shower and change, then I'll drive you over to mine and I'll change there, then cook for you.'

Stella hesitated, just for a second. Was Johanna coming on to her? It had never happened before. Gareth always joked that Stella sent out mega-strong 'straight-girl vibes' as he called them in his lilting Welsh accent. But the way Johanna had checked her out earlier, and called her pronunciation 'cute'? Hey, what did it matter? It was no different to a man inviting her, and she'd probably say yes to him. Just not take it any further.

'Stella?'

'Sorry, yes, thanks. I'd love to. Just as long as it's not *Långsamt kokt oxtunga!*'

Johanna laughed, revealing crooked front teeth. At last! A flaw in that irritatingly perfect face. They turned left and ran back through another park and a few more wide, clean, birch-lined streets.

'Come up,' Stella said, as she collected her key from reception. 'I won't take long, then we can go.'

Stella closed the bathroom door behind her, having left Johanna sitting in a squishy armchair reading a magazine. She glanced down at the lock beneath the handle.

Hesitating for a second, she stretched out her right hand, then, as quietly as she could manage, twisted the chrome knob to the stop. She felt silly for doing it, but shrugged her shoulders. If Johanna said anything she could always put it down to English squeamishness about nudity.

As she massaged shampoo into her hair, she looked over to the door and saw the handle inching downwards. It stopped, paused, then returned to its horizontal position. She smiled to herself.

Ten minutes later, feeling tingly from the heat of the shower and full of energy after the run, she was sitting beside Johanna in her pistachio-green Fiat 500. Johanna put the little car's transmission into first and pulled away, zipping into a gap between two looming black Audis.

'You smell nice,' Johanna said. 'What is that?'

'Miller Harris Feuilles de Tabac. It's my boyfriend's.'

Stella hadn't meant to add the second sentence. But she registered Johanna's tiny pause.

'Unisex, then?'

'I guess so.'

'How long have you two been together?'

Stella sighed. 'Er, not very long, actually. About a year.'

'You sound sad. What is it?'

'It's a long story. A glass of wine story.'

Johanna smiled. Nodded. 'We can do that.'

The evening traffic was slow and it took another fifteen minutes to reach Johanna's apartment building.

Inside, Stella marvelled at the sleek flat with its white and beige palette and the frill-free contemporary furniture. Pale woods with contrasting grains like winding black rivers dominated. A painting of a birch forest occupied most of one wall.

'Make yourself at home. I'm going to take a quick shower,' Johanna said.

A picture window gave onto an expanse of water dotted with small sailing craft and larger pleasure vessels including multi-decked, glass-enclosed tourist boats. Stella stood there people-watching while Johanna changed.

'Red or white?' Johanna called from the kitchen five minutes later.

'White, please.'

Johanna entered the living room bearing two long-stemmed wine glasses, a bottle in a wooden cooler and a white porcelain bowl of green olives on a black lacquer tray. She'd done her hair up in a loose pleat at the back of her head. A couple of tresses curled artfully down to her collar bones. She'd paired a simple turquoise shirt with pale, tight jeans. She was barefoot.

She poured them both some wine and raised her own glass. 'Welcome to Sweden, to Stockholm and to my humble abode. *Skål!*'

'*Skål!*' Stella clinked rims and took a sip. The aroma of new-mown grass and gooseberries filled her nose as she drank the lightly chilled wine.

Johanna motioned for her to sit. Stella chose an armchair – unbleached cotton stretched over a bentwood frame. Johanna took the end of the matching sofa nearest to her guest.

'What's the cost of living like in Stockholm?' Stella asked. 'All I know is alcohol is supposed to be very expensive.'

Johanna laughed. 'It's not just *supposed* to be expensive. It really is. Are you perhaps wondering how I could afford my apartment? Waterfront location, amazing views, three bedrooms, state-of-the-art kitchen?'

Stella shook her head. 'No! Not at all.' But she had to admit, Johanna was on the nose. She had been thinking just that. A detective sergeant in her early thirties living in a swanky city centre flat like this.

She didn't know what the SPA paid its sergeants, but there was no way a DS in the Met could afford a place like this.

'Most people come to the same conclusion. They think I must be on the make – is that right?'

Stella shrugged again. 'I think "take" is more usual, but they both mean basically the same thing.'

'Thanks. Well I'm not. I said I was in Financial Crime, right?'

'Yes.'

'I studied Finance at university. The crime side of the industry interested me but I also learnt enough to get into investing as a sideline. You're looking at the fruits of my own hard work.'

Stella nodded and took a sip of wine to hide her embarrassment. 'Good for you. I wish I knew how to do that.'

'It's mainly down to research. Then you just need a strategy.'

'You make it sound so simple.'

Johanna drew one leg up and folded it beneath her. 'OK, maybe a master's in International Finance and Investment helps,' she said with a smile.

Stella laughed. It felt good to be far from home, drinking a clearly expensive bottle of wine with an intelligent woman who was unafraid of going for whatever she wanted. *Whatever* being the operative word.

'Story time,' Johanna said decisively. She leaned forwards, plucked an olive from the bowl and popped it into her mouth. 'Tell me about you and your boyfriend.'

Stella gave her an edited account of her and Jamie's relationship. Meeting through work — the old story — discovering they had lots in common, from a dark sense of humour to liking Renaissance art. Keeping clothes at each other's places.

'Then what happened?' Johanna asked, as Stella petered out at the days immediately before her trip to Sweden.

She poured another glass of wine for Stella and topped up her own.

'He suggested we move in together and I felt I needed to be honest with him about something. He didn't take it so well and he left. Went to stay in a hotel. I haven't heard from him since.'

'What thing?'

Stella looked at Johanna, searching behind those grey-blue eyes for some prurient desire to know another's secrets. But she saw only unfettered curiosity. An enviable quality in a detective, but a pain in the arse from a new friend.

'Something I did that I'm not massively proud of.'

Johanna nodded, adopting a knowing expression. 'Been there, sister. Sometimes you have to draw a line, yes?'

'That's what I'm hoping.'

'Have you called him? Texted?'

'I'm letting him make the first move,' Stella said, discounting her texts as not worth the name 'move'.

'I went through something similar with my ex-girlfriend. She asked me to marry her. As we were being totally honest about our past relationships, I told her I hadn't always been a lesbian. She went crazy! My god, Stella, if you've never seen a dyke lose her shit, it's not something you'd pay to get a ringside seat for, I can tell you. Awful.'

Stella laughed loudly. Somehow, Johanna's confirmation that she was gay took all the tension out of the air. She felt herself relax, and, as soon as she did, the wine hit her and she felt a delicious warmth spreading out from the pit of her stomach.

'Were you hitting on me earlier?' she asked.

Johanna smiled. 'You're an attractive woman. You know that, right? And don't give me any of that terrible British modesty, because you are. So, maybe, yes, a little bit. But I won't anymore. We can still be friends, yes?'

'Of course. I'm just not, you know—'

'It's fine. Honestly. Probably, I broke about a million SPA rules. So, let's talk about the case.'

With the elephant in the room gently led out by its keeper, there seemed to be more air to breathe. And in the space created, something scratched at Stella's brain. Something to do with Cap'n Coat. And Johanna. It wouldn't come. Plenty of time. Let it find its own way to the surface.

'I spent all day looking into Brömly's background,' Stella said. 'I spoke to eight people, no, nine. I even tracked down a couple of his school friends. They're all old now, but some have amazingly clear memories.'

'And?'

'Nobody had a bad word to say about him. I'm surprised he wasn't nominated for the Nobel Peace Prize.'

'No sexual indiscretions?'

'None.'

'Money worries?'

'Nuh-uh. Nothing.'

'Any snags in his military record?'

'Nope. He did his national service – *värnplikt?*' Johanna nodded. 'In the tenth *Psyops-förbandet*. A lot of that's classified, but, from what I could see, his service was blameless and undistinguished.'

'Sounds like he made a career out of not giving people a reason to kill him.'

'Yes, it does, except for one thing. There's a big gap between 1971 and 1976 when all it says is voluntary service in Africa. It's like a black hole. No information escapes that period in his life.'

Johanna took a sip from her glass.

'In finance, you look for trading patterns or sudden spikes in profits or losses that can't be explained by analysis of a company's fundamental financial data. Anomalies, yes? So that's your anomaly.'

'That's where I'm at, too. We need to know what Brömly was up to in the early seventies.'

Johanna nodded. 'Come into the kitchen and we'll talk while I cook.'

'Anything I can do to help?' Stella asked in the spotless wood-and-stainless-steel appointed kitchen.

'You could make us a salad. There's loads of stuff in the fridge.'

As Stella chopped and sliced tomatoes, avocado, spring onions and fresh herbs, Johanna set to work on two rainbow trout, slitting their bellies open and cleaning them with swift, decisive movements.

After thirty minutes they were sitting facing each other across a table of spalted maple wood. The colours in its variegated top ranged from the palest sand to a dark, ashy grey. Black lines, swirls and pockmarks gave it the look of a desert criss-crossed by roads and dried-up riverbeds.

The trout was excellent. Johanna had served it simply, a dollop of horseradish cream on the side, lemon wedges and a few grinds of black pepper.

Johanna took a sip of her wine. 'Did you lose your husband?'

Stella's stomach flipped. 'Pardon?'

'Sorry. My ex always said I had no filter. It's just you're wearing a wedding ring, but on your right hand. I just thought...' She tailed off, a blush creeping over her cheeks.

Finally, after a mouthful of wine, Stella nodded. 'He was killed by a hit and run driver. Ten years ago. My baby daughter, too.'

Johanna's face fell. 'I'm so sorry. How dumb of me to ask. Did they catch the driver?'

Stella gave herself time to think by cutting another chunk of the trout and popping it into her mouth. It was a good question. But how to answer?

'He tried to evade justice. But we caught up with him in the end.'

'What's the maximum penalty for that in the UK?'

This was an easier question. She answered at once.

'Life.' Meaning death.

'Did he get that?'

She contented herself with a nod.

'I'm glad. For you. I hope it gave you some closure.'

Stella wrinkled her nose. 'Not really. He can't hurt anyone else, so that's something, but I still miss them both. A lot.'

She left Johanna's flat at eleven. The two women embraced and Stella found some comfort in the hug. She wondered if she'd ever hug Jamie again.

18

CHICAGO

Inside the FBI's vehicle investigation facility, Roisin was struck again by how much money federal-level law enforcement had at its disposal.

The garage was the size of an aircraft hangar. Marked bays accommodated eighteen-wheelers, family-sized cars, bikes and pickups. Even a couple of speedboats on steel stands. She counted nineteen vehicles sitting dead-centre in spots demarcated by yellow-and-black tape.

Most stood unattended, but a crew of mechanics in FBI-branded overalls were working on a panel van, its bodywork screeching as power tools bit and sliced through the thin metal sheets.

Simone led her to a corner where the black Ford Explorer she'd only seen in photos stood waiting. The experience of having handled its toy-sized plastic stand-in a few minutes earlier made it seem even larger than it really was.

Up close, the first thing she noticed was the smell. A dank, muddy, vegetal stink hung around it. She walked up to the driver's door and peered in through the open window. Adam Collier died in the seat she was looking at.

She tried to imagine what he must have thought in his final moments. He'd been trapped in a car sinking into freezing cold water, in the middle of nowhere. He was going to drown. He escaped that horrific fate only because someone put a bullet between his eyes.

He'd sunk with the car and then been eaten by the small things that lived in the lake. Fish, eels, crayfish? He'd rotted away in the seat in front of her until only his bones were left.

Simone tapped her on the shoulder, making her jump.

'I have to attend to a couple of things. Will you be OK here? Mike – he's the facility manager – has my number. Just get him to call me when you're done.'

Five minutes later, dressed in FBI navy-blue overalls and equipped with a torch, Roisin opened the driver's door and climbed up into the seat. She spent some time looking in the footwells, pulling back carpets, opening the glovebox and what felt like dozens of little lidded cubbyholes. At the end of the examination of these obvious places, she had nothing.

She climbed out again and went round to the SUV's front end. Placing her right foot on the bumper or, what did they call them over here, fender?, she hoisted herself up and clambered onto the bonnet. *Hood!* She aimed the torch down at the windscreen. The shooter had kneeled up here. Right where she was now. Maybe in this exact position.

She looked down and saw a series of scratches in the paintwork. They were deep enough to have scored through the surface of the paint but not hard enough to reach bare metal. She switched on the torch again and shone it down between her knees, sliding sideways across the expanse of metal to take a closer look.

The scratches were grouped into irregular sets. Each set contained parallel marks that curved, spiralled and overlapped across the black paint. Three, four, five, sometimes more. What had caused them?

The gun, gripped in the shooter's right hand and scraped across the paint as the shooter got into position? Maybe. But there were so many.

A belt buckle, if the shooter was on his or her belly? Possible. But wait. It was winter. So they surely had to have been wearing a thick coat of some kind. It might have had a zip but that would only have one point of contact at most – the tab. She couldn't see how a metal zip could cause this kind of patterning.

Boots, then. Perhaps the shooter was wearing those ice grips you could buy that fixed to your shoes with straps. It seemed the most likely explanation, even though in that case Roisin thought the scratches would have been deeper.

Returning to the cabin, she yanked on the hood-release lever. The latch sprang half open with a clonk. She went back to the front and lifted the hood and latched it onto the stay.

A black plastic cover concealed much of the engine. Visible were suspension components and the usual assortment of wires, pipes and random bits of mechanical engineering.

She ignored the engine itself and began at the windscreen. A black plastic gutter ran the width of the glass, where water would run down and away through mesh-covered drain tubes. Starting at the driver's side, and hoisting herself up to lie on her belly, she scrutinised the intricately moulded plastic, looking for something, anything, that might have been left inadvertently by the shooter.

Even though she was a detective, not a CSI, she knew of Locard's Exchange Principle, the famous forensic dictum coined by the French father of forensic science: 'Every contact leaves a trace'.

Somewhere on, or in, this SUV, was a trace of the killer. She just needed to find it.

The gutter was full of dried-out lake scum. A compacted, grey-brown mixture of silt and fragments of vegetation, presumably disturbed when the two-ton vehicle had settled into the mud.

She picked at it with her fingernail, rubbing it to a fine powder between her fingertips. Nothing. More damn nothing! She managed to make it halfway across then slithered down and went round to the passenger side.

Here she repeated the process. Inch by inch, she scraped and prodded the dried gunk from the gutter. And inch by inch she realised there was nothing there. Finally she had a two-inch section left, right in the centre.

Sighing, she prodded the muck with a fingertip. And, instantly, she felt something hard. For a second she thought of leaving it in situ while she went to find an evidence bag. Then she realised something.

This wasn't an FBI case anymore. They might call it 'extending assistance' but she knew they wanted shot of it. She didn't have to follow FBI evidence-gathering protocols. Or, come to that, Met ones either. Plenty of time to tidy up the chain of evidence later.

She pushed her thumbnail into the dirt and got it underneath the object. Gently, she levered it up and out of its cocoon of dried mud. What was it? She frowned as she rubbed it clean.

Lying in her palm was a pointed metal cone about the size of the eraser on the top of a pencil. It had once been shiny, but now its surface was dull and pitted by the water. At its base, three tabs stood proud.

She knew what it was. A decorative stud. The shooter was wearing a studded jacket. Or a belt. But then, how had this come loose? Much more likely to be a boot stud that got pulled out of the leather when the shooter was clambering onto the bonnet.

An image came to her. A biker with long, greasy black hair held back by a stars-and-stripes bandanna, grimy from working on a Harley Davidson. The biker had climbed up onto the bonnet, shot Adam Collier between the eyes and, in the process, lost a stud.

She let herself slide down to the ground and rolled the piece of metal around in her palm. Something about it felt familiar, but she couldn't place it. She wrapped it in a paper tissue and stuffed it into a pocket, then went to find Mike.

After lunch with Simone in the first-floor cafeteria, Roisin moved on to the next phase of her evidence review. CCTV. Another corridor, another swipe-card-protected office and she found herself in a familiar setup. A plain wooden table bearing a PC already loaded with a program for video review.

'How come you have this footage?' Roisin asked.

'We investigated their disappearance at the time and collected the CCTV then. But we hit a brick wall and had to park it. We kept the footage on file. Standard procedure.'

'Why didn't you request a liaison officer back then?'

'We talked to our counterparts in London, but with no bodies and no leads they said there was nothing they could add to our investigation.'

Roisin nodded. It made a kind of sense.

'You'll see we picked up an unidentified driver outside the Colliers' house,' Simone said. 'Couple of the neighbours had security cameras at the front of their properties. Thank god for Neighbourhood Watch!'

At the mention of the driver, Roisin's pulse kicked up a notch. Could this be the killer? She dismissed the thought. If it were, the FBI would surely have done something about it.

'Male or female?'

'It could be either. Have a look yourself and maybe we can put our heads together.'

Giving Roisin instructions how to find her cubicle from the video review room, Simone left with a cheery, 'See ya!'

Roisin jiggled the mouse to wake up the screen and then began the tedious process of watching CCTV footage. Which turned out not to be tedious at all. Someone had cut together the relevant sequences. Roisin found herself watching a condensed series of shots that would lead, ultimately, to the deaths of Adam and Lynne Collier.

Adam appeared in shot first, behind the wheel of the black Ford Explorer. She stared at the dark eyes and clean jawline, the mouth set in a line. Who wouldn't look tense if they were on their way to murder their spouse?

Seeing him like this, Roisin finally got a handle on the question that had been eating away at her since she first read the dossier the FBI had emailed to her in London.

How, exactly, had Lynne got to the lake in Minnesota?

If she went of her own volition, then Adam, or somebody else – the killer, maybe – must have given her a really, *really* good reason. What could he possibly have said? Oh, hi, darling, it's me. Listen I thought I'd take the day off and drive all the way up to the frozen middle of nowhere. Join me for a picnic? She shook her head. It didn't make sense.

So Lynne went under duress. Either Adam took her, or the mystery shooter did. If Adam took her, how did the mystery shooter know where to find them? Convinced Lynne was already a prisoner when Adam left the FBI building, she pressed play again.

Five more minutes passed during which Adam tracked northwest from Chicago towards Minnesota. And it became obvious that Roisin's supposition was correct. In every shot, he was alone in the Explorer.

The footage ran out at a town called Sparta in Wisconsin. A superimposed line of text at the bottom of the screen read:

Last sighting of A Collier: 5.47 a.m.

The video jumped from Adam in the black Explorer to a suburban residential street, devoid of cars except for a stationary black Ford Taurus.

A figure slouched behind the wheel, a dark baseball cap over their eyes. Visible beneath the sides of the cap was short blonde hair. The video resolution wasn't great and Roisin couldn't make out the features: a generic nose-mouth-chin combo that could belong to a person of either sex. But at least she had a nickname for the driver: Blondie.

Another jump-cut, and Blondie, minus the cap, walked up to a front door. It opened and there stood Lynne Collier. Even from across the street it was unmistakably her. She beckoned Blondie inside and closed the door.

Roisin felt a surge of adrenaline race outwards from the pit of her stomach to flood her system. Hand shaking, she rewound the video and pressed play again, slowing the playback to half-speed.

Blondie slow-walked up to the Colliers' front door. Her face – because, yes, it was a woman, wasn't it! – was in three-quarter view. Even with the blonde crop, Roisin thought she knew who she was looking at. But the walk was the giveaway. She knew someone who walked exactly like that. A slight roll to the hips. A way of thrusting them ahead of the rest of her. Aggressive.

She hit pause.

She stared and stared, and *stared* at the woman stepping onto the porch of the Colliers' house.

A lawyer might doubt Blondie's identity. CCTV evidence was always open to interpretation. Especially when hairstyles had been changed.

But Roisin wasn't a lawyer. She was a detective.

And she knew who she was looking at.

What the hell was Stella Cole doing knocking on Adam and Lynne Collier's front door?

19

STOCKHOLM

The following day, Stella arrived at SPA headquarters at 8.00 a.m. Oskar greeted her when she arrived in the Murder Squad's area of the cavernous second floor.

'I'm glad you're here early,' he said. 'Press conference in twenty minutes.'

'Really? You want me there?'

He grinned. 'No need to pull a face. Swedish journalists are very polite. You'll be fine.'

The media centre occupied a corner of the ground floor of the building. Together with Oskar and Malin, Stella sat at the usual top table, its blue baize surface bristling with microphones, their multicoloured cables snaking off the front edge. Behind them, a blue-and- yellow Swedish Police Authority banner hung from a pop-up arrangement of slender aluminium poles.

She estimated the number of journalists at fifty. The TV crews stood at the back, their professional cameras supported on robust-looking black tripods. Sound recordists held their boom mics over the heads of their seated colleagues.

Malin patted the air for silence. At once the noise level fell from a loud hubbub to complete silence. *Impressive*, Stella thought.

'*God morgon*,' Malin said, then switched to English. 'Sitting to my left is Detective Chief Inspector Cole of Scotland Yard. She will now update you on the investigation into the murder of former Ambassador Brömly.'

A volley of flashes went off, momentarily blinding Stella and leaving orange afterimages dancing across her eyes.

She cleared her throat. Inwardly she was cursing Malin for dropping her in it like this, and Oskar for not warning her they'd want her to speak.

She leaned forward a few degrees. But not because she needed extra amplification from the mics. She'd found early on in her career that the movement suggested to journalists a copper serious in her mission to solve the crime. Body language was half the battle in winning them over.

She summarised the working hypothesis in a few brief sentences. Then found a video camera and looked directly into its black eye. Imagined she was speaking to a single witness.

'We are looking at a period of Mr Brömly's life from 1971 to 1976. If you knew him at or around this time, perhaps through work, or a personal connection, I would ask you to get in touch with Stockholm Police.'

She turned to Oskar.

'There'll be a number displayed on screen and at the bottom of all articles for you to call,' he added, mirroring Stella's posture by leaning closer to the bank of microphones.

'I would like to reassure the public that we are doing everything in our power to identify and apprehend the murderer,' Malin said. 'Now, questions.'

Malin fielded the questions skillfully, selecting the journalists one at a time while cueing up the next, so people gradually stopped shouting to be heard and contented themselves with putting their hands up. Those writing for online outlets tended to keep their hands up anyway, as they all brandished smartphones.

'Rolf Tomsson, *Aftonbladet*. Why do you think the killer is Swedish?'

'We have forensics evidence plus witness statements from London that point in that direction.'

'Lydia Stenson, *Expressen*. Was Mr Brömly being investigated by the police?'

'No.'

'Susanna Bengtson, *Kanal 5*. What about suspects?'

'I'm afraid I cannot comment on operational matters.'

A woman in the front row, who had been silent so far, shot up her hand. Stella looked at her. Early-sixties. Grey hair cut short. Pale-blue eyes set close together, giving her the intense gaze of a bird of prey.

'Yes,' Malin said, pointing at her.

'Do you think Brömly's murder was related to his politics?'

Malin frowned. 'I don't know why it would be. He was not an extremist. I believe he was a lifelong member of the Social Democratic Party.'

The woman made a note in her pad and Stella caught a hint of a smile on her downturned face. She'd called the victim 'Brömly', too. That was interesting. Everyone else referred to the dead ambassador as 'Mr Brömly'. She looked up and stared back at Stella, holding her in that hawk-like gaze.

After a few more questions, Malin rang down the curtain on the conference, promising further updates as and when…blah blah… something new to report…working night and day…the usual senior officer's brush-off to the press pack.

After the press conference, Oskar took Stella to one side.

'Now we're getting to the active part of the investigation I need you to fill out one of these,' he said, producing a folded form from his jacket pocket.

'What is it?'

'Officially, a *Tillfällig Skjutvapenlicens och Ackreditering*, although we just call it a TSA,' he said. 'It means Temporary Firearms Licence and Accreditation.'

Stella shook her head. 'No thank you. If there's any shooting to be done, I'll leave that to you.'

Oskar smiled. 'Oh well. I guess that's fine. As you're unfamiliar with firearms, you probably wouldn't be any good with a gun anyway.'

He went to refold the form and replace it in his pocket.

Stella couldn't help herself. She shot her hand out. How dare he make assumptions? Oskar Norgrim was about to get a lesson in what female British cops were capable of with a pistol in their hand.

'Wait! Tell me what's involved.'

'I assume your Met firearms accreditation is still up to date? I checked with Chief Superintendent McDonald while I was in London. She told me it was.'

She looked at him. He had a nerve. Going behind her back to check up on her basic competence.

'Yes, it's current.'

'Good. So, you sign the form, we go down to the range, issue a pistol and you run through a magazine to show you're competent to handle a firearm.'

She scribbled her name and followed Oskar to the lifts.

Like a lot of police stations, Stockholm Central housed its armoury and firing range in the basement. Pretty sensible really, not letting the general public overhear gunfire while they came to report their lost dog or burgled apartment. And nowhere for stray bullets to fly except into walls backed with millions of tons of earth.

'Have you had any recent experience with firearms?' Oskar asked as they made their way down a brightly lit corridor to the range.

Stella pursed her lips. Recent? Not really. The last time she offed someone with a firearm was more than six years ago. But in her time she'd gotten pretty good at despatching those who'd wronged her. She'd become proficient with a hunting rifle, a Glock, other pistols, a sawn-off shotgun and a dinky little .38 revolver: more weapons, she suspected, than Oskar had ever used. Especially in anger. And, oh, such anger.

Swallowing, she shook her head. 'Not recent. We try to avoid them as far as we can.'

'But why, when you have armed criminals? Bank robbers? Terrorists?'

Stella smiled. 'We have a dedicated firearms command. Properly trained. They're usually enough.'

Oskar patted the pistol on his hip. 'I think I prefer to have my own weapon on me at all times. That way you can't be caught out by a bad guy.'

Stella nodded as if to show her agreement. Oskar wasn't to know just how hard it was for a bad guy – or girl – to catch Stella Cole out. Those that had tried had ended up dead, whether or not she'd been carrying a firearm.

Through the door to the range, Oskar led her to the armourer's office. Already she could smell the acrid tang of gun smoke.

The noise on the range was deafening, and Oskar handed her a set of ear defenders from a rack. She settled them gratefully over her head. Though muffled, the reports of the pistols were still loud through the layers of plastic and acoustic foam, but reduced to a manageable level.

She'd always thought it odd that Health & Safety regs meant you couldn't practice without ear protection, but nobody worried once you were out on the street and discharging your weapon.

Stella handed over her completed and signed TSA form to the armorer. An overweight man in his late forties, he stamped it then dropped it into an overflowing in-tray.

Turning his back on them, he wandered over to a steel cabinet from which the paint had been knocked or rubbed off on the corners, and returned with a dull, black semi-automatic pistol in a leather holster. He placed it on the steel counter between them and added three magazines.

He pointed at them.

'Ten rounds. Forty-calibre Smith and Wesson.'

'*Tack*,' Stella said, earning herself a brief smile.

Oskar led her to an empty booth and laid the pistol and magazines on the wooden surface of the shooting bench. Taking the pistol out of its holster, she inspected it from all angles.

The manufacturer's name and model were engraved on the barrel. Sig Sauer P229. She racked the slide twice to check the gun was empty. Then she slotted a magazine home, making sure it was latched securely. She racked the slide a third time, chambering a round.

All this time, Oskar had been watching her. She was conscious of his proximity, and wished he'd step back and give her some room to breathe. He put his hand on the top of the barrel, pushing it down onto the bench.

'Now, before you shoot, Stella, just be aware this is a powerful handgun. If you're out of practice it can be a surprise when it kicks. Just take your time and—'

Stella brought the pistol up in a two-handed grip and emptied the magazine in a few seconds.

Two shots.

Three.

Three.

Two.

The smoke from the muzzle drifted back towards her: some fluke of the AC, she imagined. The spent-firework odour from the burnt propellant entered her nose and wormed its way into her brain. A couple of cops nearby had stopped firing to watch the stranger.

The recoil was forceful. But the mass of the gun meant it was manageable. Certainly compared to the Model 38 Airweight she'd used to kill Collier. Practising for a couple of hours with the little revolver had left her hand feeling like someone had stamped on it with heavy boots.

She reached out and flicked the switch to bring the shredded paper target whizzing up the range towards them on a taut wire. The 'terrorist' had lost most of his head. And she'd blown a football-sized hole through the torso, over the heart. Turning to her right, she encountered Oskar's frank, admiring gaze.

'Half the guys on the squad here couldn't shoot like that. Where did you learn to group so well?'

She saw herself in the middle of some woods on an Ojibway

First Nations reservation in southern Ontario. Plugging away at soda cans with the Airweight. Ken White Crow standing beside her.

Then climbing onto the SUV's bonnet in the depths of a Minnesota winter. Adam Collier's face, a mixture of terror and despair as he sank into the freezing waters, the doors pinioned by still-heavy slabs of lake ice. Her pointing the Airweight's snub nose at him.

The kick as the .38 round left the barrel. The hole it punched, dead-centre between his eyes, blood pulsing out like a geyser. Dragging Lynne's body out onto the ice and pushing her down through the hole where the SUV had sunk.

And then, out of nowhere, revulsion for the object gripped in her right hand swept over her. She looked down at the smoking gun and replaced it on the bench. She didn't want it anymore. She noticed the way her fingers had cramped around the ergonomic grip. It took a physical effort to uncurl them.

'Thank you. But I'll leave it here. If there's any shooting to be done, you can do it.'

He frowned. 'You're sure? You're probably the best shot in the whole station.'

She nodded, feeling sick. 'Sure.'

As they took the lift back to the Murder Squad, Stella stared at her blurry reflection in the stainless-steel wall.

Why couldn't Collier have stayed dead? The lake floor should have held him in its embrace for ever. Now his bones were lying on some pathologist's table in the US and Roisin was coming after her.

A dark, poisonous thought occurred to her. An echo of a voice she thought she'd never again hear.

You'll just have to deal with her, then, won't you? Babe.

Her stomach turned over. She'd killed enough people. Then a flash of her last kill lit up her brain: Robey sinking into a pit of used engine oil, impaled on a metal fence post.

That was ruled lawful killing and had been one hundred percent in the line of duty. It didn't bother Stella. She knew it was a confused position. But it was the best she could manage.

Back at the desk Oskar had sorted for her, Stella pushed all thoughts of her murderous past aside and went on with the series of calls she'd drawn up for herself. First on her list was the Ministry of Foreign Affairs. It was the last government department listed on Brömly's CV.

She listened to a lot of hold music over the next thirty minutes as she bounced between different teams, records units, departmental secretaries and compliance directors. Finally she reached someone who seemed willing, or able, to help her. He introduced himself as Fredrik and told her he worked at Central Records.

Once again, she explained who she was, what she was doing in Sweden, and that she was in possession of a letter of introduction from the British prosecuting authorities. She told him that she was working closely with the Swedish Police Authority to solve the murder of a Swedish citizen.

He put her on hold. A few minutes elapsed during which she nodded to Johanna who placed a coffee in front of her, mouthing '*Tack*'. Johanna beamed her a toothy grin in return.

'Hello, DCI Cole?'

The young man was back.

'Yes, I'm here.'

'So, Mr Brömly's career in the civil service was quite illustrious. He served in a number of ministries: Foreign Affairs, Education and Research, the Prime Minister's Office, and Employment.'

'Is there any record of his being employed in any of those ministries between 1971 and 1976?'

'Hold on, let me check.' A pause. Stella heard a keyboard clicking. The young man hummed as he typed. 'That's odd. In late '70 he was working in the Ministry of Employment. In '76 he turns up again at Education. But in between there's a gap.'

Stella's heart sank. 'Yes, we believe he may have been working overseas. Volunteering in Tanzania.'

'I don't think he can have been.'

Her pulse picked up. 'Why not?'

'His employment record is uninterrupted for that period. He would have had to resign for anything more than a short sabbatical. A month might have been acceptable, but not five years.'

There. Stella felt it in the pit of her stomach. The first flickering of a fresh investigative trail. She was getting close. She could feel it.

'Can you double-check?'

'Yes. I am already looking at his... yes...I cross-checked to his Personnel records. He was receiving his monthly salary as normal right through that period.'

Stella thanked the helpful young man and went to find Oskar. She found him talking to Johanna.

'*Hej,*' Johanna said as Stella arrived. '*Du ser ut som en ren som åt alla lingonbär!*'

'*Hej*. What does that mean?'

'You look like a reindeer who ate all the lingonberries,' Johanna said with a grin.

Stella smiled. 'I think I did. Or at least a nice little bowl of them.'

'What did you find out?' Oskar said.

'Brömly never left government employment. His pay cheques kept going into his account and there's no record of him ever resigning or being re-employed.'

'So he was never in Tanzania?'

'Doesn't look like it. I can't imagine your government would have been content to pay a relatively junior civil servant for five years if he wasn't doing any work.'

Oskar furrowed his bony brow. He scratched at his stubble.

'We should go and talk to the two ministries where Brömly worked before and after the gap.' He turned to Johanna. 'Jo, can you and Stella check in with...' He looked at Stella. 'Where was he in '70?'

'Employment.'

Oskar nodded. 'I'll go and see——'

'Education,' Stella supplied.

'Let's meet up here afterwards to compare notes.'

'Our flight's at three-fifteen, remember,' Stella said.

'It's fine. Police can skip the queue. We'll leave for the airport at two-thirty. Plenty of time.'

Stella frowned. It didn't sound like lots of time to her. But

Stockholm Airport was a lot smaller than Heathrow. Presumably it was quicker to get through, as well.

Five minutes later, she was sitting beside Johanna in a silver Volvo estate pool car. Johanna drove skillfully, and fast, and they arrived at the Ministry of Employment on *Herkulesgatan* ten minutes later.

The civil servant into whose spare but elegant office they were ushered rose to greet them. She wore a long grey wool tunic over dark trousers. The stylish look continued with narrow copper-framed glasses that magnified already-large grey eyes, and a string of oversized amber beads across her chest.

She rounded her desk to shake hands, first with Stella and then Johanna.

'Hello. I'm Maria Östergren, Deputy Director of Human Resources. Would you like coffee?' she asked. Stella and Johanna both declined. 'Then how can I help?'

'We're trying to trace the career path of a former civil servant.'

'Tomas Brömly.'

'Yes, that's right.'

The woman smiled. 'No need to look surprised. I watched the press conference online. How precisely can I assist your investigation?'

Johanna consulted her notebook. 'We know Mr Brömly was working at this ministry in 1970. Could you find out for us where he went after that?'

The woman leaned back in her chair, puffing out her cheeks.

'I don't imagine there's anyone around now who would have known him. I'm afraid to say, many of his colleagues and probably more of his superiors are dead, but perhaps I can find out something about his responsibilities.'

'That would be really helpful. Thank you.'

Stella exchanged a glance with Johanna as the woman pulled her keyboard towards her and began typing. Johanna raised her eyebrows. Her meaning was clear to Stella. *Do you think we'll get anywhere?* Stella shrugged.

'Here we are,' the woman said. 'In 1970, Mr Brömly was responsible for children's homes in Umeå. Is that useful?'

Stella and Johanna exchanged another glance. *Oh it's useful all right.*

20

CHICAGO

Roisin restarted the playback and watched, hunched forward over the screen, as the seconds, then minutes ticked by. She yawned. Then pinched the skin on the inside of her wrist to wake herself up. *Jesus, Mary and Sweet Joseph, Roisin, if there was ever a moment to be wide a-fucking-wake it's now!*

Then it happened. The moment when Roisin caught the biggest break of her career. Stella Cole, her arm around a curiously unresisting Lynne Collier, emerged from the front door, walked her across the street and then out of shot. But she knew where Lynne was headed. The inside of Stella's car.

Roisin's insides squirmed with an unsettling mixture of foreboding, puzzlement and pure, unalloyed joy. Stella was toast. And not just the nicely browned all over variety. She was burnt, blackened and smoking. Her career – ha! – was over. And so was her freedom.

Roisin rewound the footage and played it again. She looked closely at Stella's coat. It was a long, formal garment, in scarlet, with a belt and buttons. Not a stud in sight.

She was about to move on when she remembered with a flash of clarity exactly why the tissue-wrapped stud in her pocket felt so familiar. She replayed the footage a second time and froze Stella in mid-pace across the road.

Her right foot, extended at the end of a stride, was shod in a black boot on which she could make out the glitter of chromed studs. Those bloody Prada biker boots she was so proud of. Well, they were going to hang her now. She zoomed in, but the boots disappeared into a haze of pixels.

She pressed play again. The montage spooled on, with several more clips of Stella heading northwest towards what Roisin now knew was a fatal rendezvous with Adam Collier. And in every shot, she was alone in the front of the car.

Stella must have stashed Lynne in the boot. That wobbly walk of Lynne's as they came out of the house. Had Stella drugged her? It would explain her passivity. All Stella would have needed was some way of keeping her from freezing to death as she transported her to Minnesota and it was game over.

The playback switched abruptly to black. White text informed her the video was property of the FBI.

Roisin sat back and ran her fingers through her hair. Breathing deeply she thought her way through the events she'd just watched. Something about the timings of the short sequences troubled her.

She rewound and watched again, this time at quadruple speed. Adam – Adam – Adam – Adam – Stella – Stella – Stella and Lynne – Stella – Stella – Stella – Stella—

The timings! She'd watched Adam first and inferred he'd started driving before Stella. But that didn't make any sense. She snorted. Yeah, right. Because everything else made *perfect* bloody sense.

No, Stella must have phoned him and told him she had Lynne.

She slowed the playback and started noting time-stamps. And then she had it. Stella had drugged and kidnapped Lynne first. Got clear of Chicago, then phoned Adam.

Questions piled in on themselves like a rugby scrum. Or, she supposed, since she was in the Land of the Free, an American Football tackle.

What possible motive could Stella have for killing Adam Collier?

Did she identify herself to him or disguise her voice somehow?

How could she have got a firearm?

How did she get to the US?

Did she leave a trail?

Where did she go after killing him?

Why did Adam kill his own wife?

And then other, hideous, questions interposed themselves. When Callie announced that Stella wasn't dead after all, had she known all along what she was doing, and where? Why did she promote Stella to DCI and not Roisin? Was it payback? A reward? Oh god, was Stella *sent* to America to kill Adam?

Suddenly feeling nauseous, Roisin got up and left the room in a hurry, looking for the Ladies. She splashed cold water on her face and dabbed it dry with paper towels. Then she shut herself in a cubicle and sat there for thirty minutes.

Desperate to get back to the UK, Roisin made it through the rest of the day by reading every single document assembled by the FBI during its inconclusive investigation into the murders of Adam and Lynne Collier.

Like her, they'd identified the figure she knew to be Stella Cole and even given her the same nickname: Blondie. Their supposition was that Blondie had kidnapped Lynne, driven her to Preston, then lured Adam out to the frozen lake.

Like her, they'd war-gamed a number of scenarios before concluding that Blondie was responsible for at least one of the Colliers' deaths.

Like her, they had noted down a raft of questions, from motive and means to, most tellingly of all, Blondie's true identity. They tried running facial recognition algorithms. They looked for fingerprints on the SUV and the firearms, despite their immersion in lake water. They ran ballistics on the Airweight.

The face was a blank. The only fingerprints on the SUV were Adam's plus a valeter and a mechanic at the FBI field office. The Airweight was clean. From the serial number, they surmised it was a Vietnam-era weapon, manufactured in the tens of thousands and distributed widely over Southeast Asia.

Unlike her, they then closed the file.

Unlike her, they wanted rid of a case that was an embarrassment.

Unlike her, they hadn't solved the case within a single working day.

Over dinner – thick, juicy steaks and spicy home fries – Eddie Baxter asked her how she wanted to handle her forthcoming trip to Minnesota. She begged off. How could she hope to discern anything new when the entire resources of the FBI's Chicago Field Office had been devoted to the case? The flattery worked on Eddie who shrugged and admitted he couldn't, personally, see the point, but, hey, he wanted to offer every courtesy, yada yada yada.

She told him she had gotten – pleased with herself for using a small piece of American grammar – everything she thought she could from the evidence here. She requested that the whole lot, excepting the SUV, which was too big, be shipped lock, stock and barrel to London.

She asked him to thank Simone. Requested that the SUV be retained should a British forensics team want to re-examine it if she managed to ever get any further forward with the case. Rolled her eyes. Huh! Fat chance! Felt the reassuring little lump of tissue-wrapped, chromed steel in her pocket all through dinner and on the cab ride back to her hotel.

In her room, she booked a flight back to London for the next day. She opened two miniatures of vodka from the minibar, added ice and sipped her drink reflectively as she watched an old movie starring Charles Bronson as a family man turned vigilante. *Death Wish*.

21
UMEÅ

Stella and Oskar arrived in Umeå at 4.20 p.m. that afternoon. Oskar rented a car and they drove straight to the police HQ on *Ridvägen* to introduce themselves to the locals. The building itself, an untidy design of brick, aluminium sidings and plate glass, was reached via a sprawling carpark.

The local cop assigned to help them was a *Detectivinspektor* William Ekland. Stella thought that if a Viking donned a blue suit and cut his plaits off, he'd look like Ekland. He was well over six foot, broad-shouldered and the possessor of red hair and a magnificent copper-coloured moustache.

The meeting was short. They agreed to keep Ekland informed of their actions in Umeå. He promised cooperation, though he didn't miss the chance to complain about 'those penny-pinchers in Stockholm' starving his department of resources.

Stella and Oskar checked in at the Scandic Plaza on Storgatan. They agreed to meet in the bar for a drink then venture out to find somewhere to eat.

Stella unpacked, and put her clothes away. She ran a bath and while she waited for it to fill, she checked her messages. A text from

Callie asking how she was getting on. Various emails from SIU team members. A Snapchat message from her niece Polly, now twelve and at secondary school. But nothing from Jamie.

A sense of melancholy washed over her. They'd been happy together. They did everyday things together. Loaded the dishwasher, and bickered about who did it 'properly'. Went food shopping. Took walks in the countryside if they were at Jamie's. A normal, everyday life. And now he was blanking her.

Anger surged through her. Not at Jamie, although she was beginning to feel as though he could at least have the decency to fob her off with an 'I'm still processing it' message. But at Ramage and the rest of his evil gang.

They'd started Stella down a very dark street, a street that had almost become one way with her own suicide at the end of it. Without them, there'd have been nothing to confess to Jamie.

And what about Gordon Wade, Callie and their political paymasters? Because Stella had no illusions on that score. Given what had very nearly blown up in their faces, Stella had pulled all their nuts out of the fire. And the first, and only, time she'd asked for help they'd basically walked away, tossing a casual, 'Sorry, babe, you're on your own on this one,' over their collective shoulders.

She called Jamie. It went straight to voicemail. She cleared her throat.

'It's me. I understand if you can't bear to talk to me, or answer my texts or emails. But can you at least let me know you're all right and haven't been attacked by one of your patients? Please.' She hesitated, swallowed. 'I love you.'

Sighing, she put the phone on the desk and undressed for her bath.

She stepped into the water, hissing a little as her toes entered the water. Little by little, she eased herself in. The heat made her inadvertently suck in her stomach muscles, still flat from running despite having hit the big four-oh two years earlier.

She'd left the bathroom door wide open and could see the blue sky outside the window. It struck her as funny that she should be inching her way into a painfully hot bath in midsummer.

And then she was in. She lay back and let the water close over her belly. She exhaled in a long, grateful sigh. She felt her breathing slowing, an enjoyable sensation. She relaxed deeply. Maybe for the first time since the case began. As sweat broke out on her forehead she let her eyes close.

She and Johanna were naked, and swimming underwater. Sunlight lanced down through the greenish lake water, painting flickering curves across Johanna's pale skin as she kicked towards the bottom. 'We're going to kill Brömly and tear his tongue out,' she said in a stream of silvery bubbles that wobbled their way to the surface.

Then she grinned and darted downwards. Stella followed her, then panicked as something reached up out of the dark and grabbed her right wrist. She was staring into Tomas Brömly's ruined face. He was grinning at her from inside the cabin of a black SUV. Johanna was struggling to release her from Brömly's grip.

He opened his mouth wide and a fat, muscular eel shot out towards Stella. In his free hand he held a long, curving knife. He swept it sideways, slicing Johanna's head from her shoulders and releasing bright-red blood that curled away into the water like smoke.

She woke with a start, coughing up water, her hair soaking wet and cool bathwater streaming from her face. Gripping the twin chrome handles, she levered herself up to a seated position and got out.

Dry and dressed in jeans and a T-shirt, she stepped out onto the narrow balcony and stared out across the city.

The dream was troubling her. She'd never solved a case in a dream, but she strongly believed they were a route to connections her subconscious might already have made. Ones that, if she could access them, might provide a new way of seeing things. What was this one trying to tell her? Was her working hypothesis off the mark? Should they be looking for someone Brömly had hurt, rather than one of his co-conspirators? Someone who'd waited until now to exact their bloody revenge?

She checked her phone again. Her pulse jumped. Jamie had replied to her text. She opened the messaging app.

No attacks so far today.

Five minutes later, he'd sent a second message.

Sorry for blanking you. Give me time. Still struggling.

She smiled. That wasn't a final brush-off. That was a holding message. Feeling happier than she had done since Jamie had left her alone in the flat, she headed out of the door.

Oskar was sitting up at the bar, a bottle of beer by his right elbow. He was chatting to the bartender, a mixed-race guy with ginger dreadlocks tied into a complicated knot on top of his head and wound round with strings of multicoloured plastic beads.

Stella slid on the neighbouring stool and ordered a glass of Sauvignon blanc for herself.

Oskar took another swig from his beer, emptying it. He gestured to her glass. 'You want another for after that one?'

'I'm fine, thanks.'

He ordered another beer. Then turned to Stella. 'I've been thinking about the five-year gap he erased.'

'Me too. He was in charge of children's homes. In the UK there've been a spate of allegations of historic sexual abuse. A lot of it took place in children's homes,' she said. 'Kids who were already vulnerable put under pressure by people who had power over them, almost of life and death.'

Oskar was nodding as she spoke. 'We have the same problem here although the authorities were slow to admit it. Do you think he abused a child in the seventies and for some reason they decided to kill him after all that time?'

'Could be. Say you were ten in seventy-five. You'd be fifty-six now. No reason why you couldn't be capable of the physical side of it,' Stella said.

'We should look into this.'

'I agree. First thing tomorrow.'

He nodded and smiled, and Stella realised he was halfway to getting drunk. She was catching up fast as the wine hit her empty stomach.

'This wine's going to my head,' she said. 'Let's find somewhere to eat. Why don't you take me to somewhere typically Swedish?'

Oskar smiled. 'I was hoping you would say that. I already booked us a table at *Sjöbris*. It's pretty cool, actually.' He pointed out of the window. 'You see that row of birch trees down by the water's edge?'

'Yes.'

'It's just on the other side.'

'What would you have done if I'd said I fancied Thai?' she asked.

He grinned lopsidedly. 'I don't know. Tried to win you over with descriptions of their succulent pickled herrings?'

She laughed. It was the unlikeliest line of persuasion she could imagine.

A three-minute stroll took them to a gangplank that led up to a white-painted boat acting as the reception area. A smiling waitress in a black polo shirt bearing the restaurant's white and orange logo showed them to their table, right by a huge window that gave onto the Ume River.

Stella asked Oskar to order for both of them, a task he accepted with an enthusiastic nod. After scanning the menu for a few minutes he signalled to the waitress and spoke to her rapidly in Swedish. She smiled widely, revealing pretty turquoise braces, and left.

'I ordered their chef's seafood platter,' Oskar said. 'We get a little of everything. Lots of herring, plus salmon, trout, crab, shrimps. It is very traditional.'

The food, when it came, did not disappoint. Stella tried some herring cured in lime juice with lingonberries. The combination of sweet, tart and the sea-fresh taste of the herring made her exclaim with pleasure. 'God, that's good!'

'I'm glad you like it,' Oskar mumbled through a mouthful of shrimps.

Later, after Oskar had settled the bill by explaining he'd claim it on his expenses, they walked the short distance back to the hotel.

Stella declined his invitation to a nightcap in the hotel bar and headed up to her room. She undressed for bed and lay back against the cool cotton pillows. She checked her phone. No more messages. Not ready for sleep, but equally not ready to try calling Jamie again, she called Vicky instead.

'Hola!' Vicky said. 'How are you?'

'A bit drunk. I'm in Sweden. A lovely little place called Umeå,' she said. 'Also known as,' she inhaled, 'Bee-yer-car-nas-stad.'

Stella gave the pronunciation her best attempt, though from Vicky's laughter it appeared she'd come off more like the Swedish chef from *The Muppets*.

'And that means?' Vicky asked.

'The City of Birches. It's very pretty.'

'Are you still on the Brömly case?' Vicky asked. 'That's what took you to Sweden?'

'Yeah. We think the killer's here somewhere.'

'We?'

'Me and Oskar.'

'Oskar, eh? Who's he? Some tasty Swedish detective?'

'He's my colleague,' Stella said, 'and he's not, actually, very good-looking.'

'Jamie's got nothing to worry about then?'

Stella felt sudden hot tears running down her cheeks.

'Oh shit!'

'What is it?'

Stella sniffed. 'I didn't want to say anything before. But I told him, Vicky. I told Jamie I killed Ramage. And I was going to tell him about the rest, but stopped myself because he was so freaked out.'

'Oh my god! What did he say?'

'Not a lot. He basically walked out of my flat and that was that. He texted me, but it was just a holding message. I think I've really blown it and I don't know what to do.'

She heard Vicky sigh at the other end of the line.

'I don't think there's anything you *can* do. Not right now. But you said it was a holding message. So he hasn't broken up with you?'

'No. But—'

'Give him time. It's not the sort of thing you hear every day, is it? That the woman you love shot a High Court judge dead. Like you said, good job you didn't tell him about the other eleven.'

'Twelve.'

'Eh, eleven, twelve. Once you pass ten it's just a number.'

'Vicky!'

'Sorry. Bad joke. I've had wine, too.'

'Hey, did you just say he loved me?'

'You did know, right?'

'I hoped he did. We've not said it yet. To each other, I mean. It's only been a year. But he said we should move in together. He's got this new job in London.'

'There you go, then.'

'That doesn't mean much these days.'

'Maybe not. But he told me.'

'When?'

'Last month when we had that drunken dinner. You, me, Jamie and Damien.'

'What did he say? The exact words.'

'He said, "Vicky, I really love Stel, but I don't want to frighten her off. Do you think it's too early to tell her." Word for word.'

Stella swallowed down the lump in her throat that felt as big as an avocado stone.

'I don't know if that makes me feel better or worse.'

'Look. Give him time. I'd have thought, with his job, it wasn't the facts that he was struggling with so much as that it was you. You told him why you had to kill them, right?'

'I did! Probably in too much detail, but yes. I explained everything.'

'There you are, then. He just needs to wrap his head around it, like I did.'

'I hope you're right. I really do.'

'I am. Now, it's late. You've got a murderer to catch and I've got a deadline to meet.'

'Thanks, mate.'

'Laters.'

Stella fell into a dreamless sleep. She awoke with a hangover, took two painkillers with a pint of water and went for breakfast.

At the police station, she started calling children's homes in Umeå.

22

UMEÅ

Initially, the people Stella spoke to were quick to point out that releasing records would be an infringement of the children's human rights. Once she explained why she was calling, and that the records she and Oskar needed related to the seventies and not the present day, they became less defensive.

With one exception, they promised to start digging out the records, although, as they all pointed out, records back then were all paper. It might take a few days to find the relevant files.

Stella leaned back in her chair. If Brömly had been an abuser, it would certainly provide a strong motive for someone to kill him. Maybe they'd read the business with the tongue all wrong.

It didn't take a forensic psychiatrist to explain it. Anyone who'd ever had a French kiss, whether or not they enjoyed it, could relate to the idea of the tongue as a sexual organ. Maybe that had been Brömly's 'thing' and his killer had torn out his tongue as a final, horrific statement of his guilt.

She went to find Oskar. He was holed up in a corner of the CID main office, head in hands, staring at a computer screen.

'I need to look up records of any prosecutions for child sexual abuse in children's homes in Umeå,' she said.

'What year?'

'Same as our missing gap for Brömly: 1971 to 1976.'

Oskar nodded. He opened a new window on the PC screen. A few moments later, he leaned forwards as an SPA-branded database screen brightened in front of him.

'This is the Swedish Police Authority database on historical sexual abuse of children,' he said.

He typed in a couple of search terms and hit return. The hourglass symbol spun for perhaps ten seconds, then stopped.

NO MATCHES

'It doesn't mean no abuse occurred,' he said.

Stella nodded her agreement. But in the absence of prosecutions, they couldn't identify whether Brömly was a perpetrator.

'I've asked for lists of children who were resident at the homes for that period,' she said. 'They're all paper. It's going to take a few days for them to arrive and god knows how long to go through them all.'

Oskar sighed. 'By the way, William says we have a press conference in thirty minutes. Can you be there?'

Stella nodded. 'Of course. Maybe we could put out an appeal for people who were in care for that five-year period to contact us.'

Unlike the Stockholm media centre, the room allocated for the press conference in Umeå was plainer, shabbier, and a lot smaller. Still, it currently held around twenty journalists, all hoping for an angle on the case they could make their own.

It smelled strongly of pine. Stella wondered whether the cleaners used it to mask the stink generated by crowded media briefings in badly ventilated conference rooms.

As William introduced the speakers, Stella swept her gaze over the journalists. A familiar face peered round a tall, bearded male journalist in the centre of the room. Pale-blue eyes and the intense stare of a bird of prey. The woman who'd asked about Brömly's politics at the Stockholm press conference. *Must be following me and Oskar*, she thought.

When Oskar turned and introduced Stella, she issued her appeal, which she'd agreed with William and his boss.

'*Tack, Inspektör Eklund*,' she said, earning a few smiles from the journalists, before appealing for people to come forward if they'd been in the system in the first half of the seventies.

The sixtyish woman didn't ask any questions this time. Stella decided to speak to her.

Stella excused herself once William wrapped up and hurried outside. She found the female journalist standing off to one side of the main entrance to the station tapping on her phone's keyboard.

She looked up, startled, when Stella approached her.

'You were at the press conference in Stockholm,' Stella said. 'Are you following the case?'

'Yes.'

'You called the victim Brömly. Everybody else I've spoken to called him either "Mr" or "Ambassador". Why is that?'

'Because he did not deserve that level of respect from me. Or anybody else,' she added with a bitter twist to her mouth.

'Why is that?' Stella asked, feeling a familiar sensation: that she was on the brink of a breakthrough.

'My name is Annika Ivarsson,' the journalist said. Her eyes, in which the irises seemed to fade into the whites without a demarcating edge, burnt in her thin face. 'I grew up in a children's home here in Umeå. Brömly arranged for something terrible to be done to me on my sixteenth birthday.'

Stella felt a cold chill sweep through her. Was this it? Had Brömly sold a young girl's virginity to the highest bidder? That, and worse, had happened plenty of times in the UK.

'Do you know who killed him?' she asked.

Ivarsson's voice took on a raw edge. 'No. But if you need a motive, I suggest you Google "Swedish eugenics".'

With that, she turned and left Stella staring at her back.

Stella returned to her desk, and launched a browser. She typed in the exact phrase Ivarsson suggested. As the results popped up, she sat back in shock. Page after page of hits. But not about sexual abuse in children's homes. Forced sterilisation in Sweden from the 1930s until 2012.

This was it. This was the evil project Brömly had written of to his three friends. Including his murderer.

She started with the first article. As she read, her mouth dropped open with shock. She couldn't believe what she was reading. Drawing on ideas of racial purity originally developed in America, and seized upon with genocidal fervour by the Nazis, the Swedish government had ruthlessly sterilised over 60,000 of its own citizens.

How could this be? Sweden was human rights central. Everyone knew that. Yet from 1934 onwards, the Social Democrats had selected kids in children's homes, those with behavioural problems, petty criminals, people with learning disabilities, prostitutes, unwed mothers, even children who simply needed a little extra help at school, like a pair of reading glasses. And prevented them from ever having children.

The date that leaped off the screen as Stella read another shame-filled article by a Swedish journalist was the date the programme was finally shut down: 1975. The year Brömly's unexplained absence from public life in Sweden ended.

Stella sat back in her chair. It all made sense. This wasn't about child sexual abuse at all. Her cop brain kicked up a gear. They'd speculated that the killer's motive might be revenge for something that had happened between 1971 and 1976.

Stella saw more of the picture, as if changing the batteries on a flickering torch in a night-time search. Brömly had been involved in the eugenics programme. After the news broke in the mid-nineties, he must have found a way to doctor his past to erase the connection.

Then a quite different thought occurred to Stella. Ivarsson had more or less told her that Brömly himself had taken her to be sterilised. Maybe Ivarsson wasn't a journalist at all. She hadn't shown her press card. And it seemed anyone could get into a press conference out here. The Swedes didn't ask for ID. Probably part of their famed culture of openness. She snorted. Except when it came to forcibly sterilising children, that was.

She felt a surge of disgust. If he hadn't been dying of cancer, would Brömly have been happy to live out his years in his swanky Mayfair apartment? Free to enjoy his art and play his grand piano? Go to the Swedish church and enjoy beating his friends at bridge at the social club? Never acknowledging, still less atoning, for his involvement in such a barbaric scheme?

First he'd laundered his past, then he'd been trying to launder his soul. Fresh and clean in time to meet his maker.

So she had the motive. And, as she thought back to her encounter with Annika, she wondered if she'd just met the perpetrator. It was a classic tactic of an over-confident murderer. Involving themselves in the police investigation. Even offering help.

Ivarsson looked to be about the same height as the woman in the Kafé Valhalla CCTV footage. But so much of her face had been obscured by the cap and the raincoat, that was all Stella felt confident about.

Parking the thought for now, Stella returned to the central question. Who were the three other Swedes Brömly had written to?

To run a national eugenics programme would have called for a vast administrative apparatus, just like the Nazis erected. They'd have needed record-keepers as well as policymakers, doctors and, for all she knew, police and social workers.

If he was going to expose his former colleagues, that would be plenty of motive for murder. Presumably they'd all forged equally blameless careers since the seventies, and availed themselves of the same reputational deep-clean as Brömly had. They'd all be retired by now, old and comfortable, living out their lives free of suspicion like Nazis in South America.

Well, guess what? Now they weren't. Stella wasn't a Nazi-hunter. But she could sniff out evil and she had the scent now. She also had her suspect pool. Ove, Kerstin, Inger. And Annika. Whether it was fear of exposure or revenge for what happened, the roots of Brömly's murder were now exposed to the light.

Part of her thought it might not be a bad thing if Brömly's three associates, old as they surely were, died prematurely, as he had. But the police part wanted to bring the killer to justice and close the case.

Back at the station, she briefed Oskar and William on her conversation with Annika, and what she'd discovered about Sweden's shameful past. It turned out they, like most Swedes, knew all about the scandal but in an effort to face the future had tended to sweep it under the carpet as something that had happened 'back then'.

William was all for bringing Annika in and, as he put it, 'getting the information out of her, one way or another'.

Oskar argued against it. He put forward the same argument as Stella had formulated. Annika might stand on her right to silence, and, as a journalist, could probably stir up a 'whole shitload of trouble for us'.

They agreed, William grudgingly, to leave her alone. 'For now.'

23

LONDON

Of all the types of evidence Lucian had to deal with, passive data from mobile phones was his least favourite.

Blood and body fluids, hairs, soil samples, footprints, fingerprints, insects, ballistics: all were susceptible to scientific analysis. If the presiding CSI or analyst conducted their analysis with sufficient rigour, the evidence would yield its secrets. But phones were another story. Especially when the owner was deceased.

He'd given up trying to crack the password and had gone for Plan B, contacting the manufacturer to ask them for an access code. Apple was known for being helpful to law enforcement agencies, foreign as well as domestic. Just not for being fast.

Lucian had submitted the relevant forms and accompanying paperwork. He'd proved he was who he said he was, and that he worked for who he said he did. And he'd been waiting for almost a week.

Now, though, he was smiling. That morning, he'd received an email from someone named Yan, who was based in the company's Legal Department (International). And Yan, bless him, or her, had supplied a sixteen-character access code for Brömly's phone.

The Legal Department's IT manager had done something clever to the box in which the code was displayed, which meant the code couldn't be copied and pasted from the email. Instead, in a move that struck Lucian as ludicrously old fashioned, not to mention open to the worst excesses of Fat Finger Syndrome, he had to retype it.

He checked each four-character group as he entered it, then rechecked the whole thing. Holding his breath, he hit the blue ENTER button on the phone's screen.

The entire display turned black.

His stomach clenched.

He stared at the screen, willing it to come back to life. He'd reached seven in an internal countdown to some serious swearing, when the display flickered, flashed royal-blue, then popped into life.

He exhaled noisily and went to work.

He opened the messaging app and began scrolling back through Brömly's texts and instant messages for the past few months. Plenty of conversations, but grouped into very few threads. One with the priest, Malmaeus; one, a group text to what appeared to be members of his bridge club; and one with the secretary of the Swedish social club he belonged to.

Deciding to hand over detailed reading to the detectives, he moved on to the emails. And immediately struck gold. The last email Brömly had sent was to a group. Here were the people who his ESDA analysis had only identified by their Christian names. Ove Mattsson. Kerstin Dahl. Inger Hedlund. He noted down the names.

The text of the email, once he'd got it translated, revealed little they hadn't already worked out.

Dear Ove, Kerstin and Inger,

I am sorry I have fallen out of touch with you all. Please look out for my letter, which will arrive in the next few days.

Cordially,

Tomas

.   .   .

Lucian returned to the Mail app and systematically checked each folder. The drafts folder under Gmail had a '1' beside it. He tapped the arrow, feeling a flicker of excitement. He was not disappointed.

The folder contained a single email. He ran it through Google Translate and also sent it to one of the interpreters Cam had found.

Lucian began reading. The ESDA had revealed the essence of it, but here was the full story. A devoutly religious man nearing the end of his life had decided to wipe the slate clean. He intended to confess some long-buried act he'd come to consider evil. Clearly, Mattsson, Dahl and Hedlund were involved.

The exact nature of their shared evil, he left to Stella to discover. Not so much above his pay grade as not relevant to it. Dozens of officers working multiple cases needed his support, and that of the small team he managed. If he stopped to ponder the whys and wherefores, rather than the whats and whens, of each piece of evidence he analysed, he'd be crushed by the weight of those unanswered requests.

The translation came back from the official interpreter at 6.00 p.m. He emailed Stella the names and attached Brömly's draft email. He took a wander round the department, checking in with each member of his team. He reached the desk of his latest hire. Anna had joined from the Police Service of Northern Ireland the year before.

She looked up from her computer screen.

'I was about to come and find you,' she said. 'I just got the results back from the hair we recovered from Brömly's flat.'

She opened an email from NDNAD. The DNA profile came with a note explaining that the donor was

a) male

b) of Nordic extraction

c) NOT Tomas Brömly

Sadly for the investigation, he didn't show up on the database itself, so had no criminal record in the UK.

No use for now, then, but if Stella – he corrected himself – *when* Stella had someone in custody, they'd have a reference smile to compare against their DNA. Putting them at the primary crime scene would be a start down the long road to a murder conviction.

24

UMEÅ

Towards the end of the afternoon, Stella's phone pinged with an incoming email. She read Lucian's email, transferred the attachment from her phone to the PC's hard drive, and opened it on screen.

Dear Ove, Kerstin and Inger,

I am dying. My oncologist informs me I have between three and six months left. Prostate cancer. (I suspect she may have been being optimistic to spare my feelings.)

We talked about getting my affairs in order. I suspect she thought that meant a will and so forth. In truth, my 'affairs' have long been tied up: without an heir, everything goes to the Church of Sweden.

But these are merely the material aspects of my life. For some years now, it is the spiritual side of things that has needed not so much tidying up as releasing.

I have reflected on my – our – past and prayed for guidance. (There is a small but very lovely Church of Sweden congregation here in London, shepherded by an excellent minister.)

Will God accept me into his ever-loving embrace with an unclean conscience? I fear not. So, as a good Lutheran, I have decided to make a full confession of my involvement in the Project.

I know you may feel this is a selfish act on my part, as in doing so I may lead people to look for others who were involved. But faced with eternity, I find it is the lesser, by far, of two evils. (And as nothing compared to the evil in which we all participated so eagerly.)

I have some contacts in the media here, most notably the BBC. I intend first to write a full and frank account of my actions between '71 and '75 and then explore the possibility of an interview.

With this burden finally lifted from my heart, I know I will be able to face my death, and my maker, with fortitude and, I hope, with grace.

I am sorry that this may not be welcome news. So I leave you with an exhortation. Consult your own conscience!

I am dying, and doing it this year. But we are all old. Even those of us without terminal cancer have the greater part of our lives behind us. Is it not better at least to try to atone for our sins?

'For on that day shall atonement be brought unto you, to cleanse you; ye shall be cleansed from all your sins before the LORD.' Leviticus 16:30

Cordially,

Tomas

She sat back. What utter crap. Fear of hell dressed up as piety. She forced herself to reread it, slower this time. She was looking for anything that might point her towards the murderer's identity. She went to find Oskar.

'Ove, Kerstin and Inger are Mattsson, Dahl and Hedlund,' she said. 'And I've got the text of the letter he sent them. I'll print it out. It might help us fill in some gaps.'

Stella dragged over a chair and sat beside Oskar as he started accessing government databases, entering his police ID then the three names.

Oskar's initial trawl brought up encouraging numbers. Four men named Ove Mattsson, six women called Inger Hedlund and three women named Kerstin Dahl.

'Try narrowing it down by age,' Stella said. 'They're all likely to be in their seventies at least.'

Oskar nodded. His fingers tapped out a brief sequence of commands and he hit Return for the second time.

'Better,' he said.

They were looking at two, three and two, for Mattsson, Hedlund and Dahl. It would be barely an afternoon's work to contact all seven, but Stella fancied another throw of the dice.

'Try putting in Umeå as their city of birth.'

Oskar nodded and typed. He looked at the screen then turned to smile at Stella. The screen showed one each for Mattsson, Hedlund and Dahl.

'Could you put a profile together for each of them?' Stella asked.

* * *

Later that afternoon, Oskar came over to her desk with some stapled sheets of paper.

'Background on Mattsson, Hedlund and Dahl. A doctor, lawyer and county governor,' he said. 'I also put Johanna onto backgrounding the others on the list. None had the right kind of jobs to be involved in the eugenics business. These are the three you need to talk to.'

She skimmed Mattsson's file. He'd taken a different path to Brömly: clinical medicine then academia. He was now Professor of Genetics at Umeå University. It fitted with the idea of genetic engineering and eugenics.

She realised her heart was racing. Yes, she was excited by the discovery. But it was also the coffee. How the Swedes drank so much of their high-octane brew without passing out was beyond her. Compared to the liquid speed they drank by the bucketful, the stuff most Met officers swilled down was Valium.

She made a note of his address. On her way out, Oskar looked up from his laptop.

'Who are you going to see first?'

'Mattsson. Do you want to come?'

He shook his head. 'Do you mind if I don't? I've got some stuff to do on other cases. Malin's pushing me to close a couple. I can access my files remotely from here.'

'It's fine. I'm happy to go on my own.'

'Just bear in mind, your letter of introduction means you can take witness statements, but you can't arrest anyone,' he said.

'I'll try to remember that.'

He grinned, and the expression changed his mis-assorted features into something more pleasing.

* * *

Mattsson lived in a large timber-framed house on the outskirts of the city, amid hundreds of the birch trees that had given Umeå its nickname. To one side of the house stood a separate garage with wide double up-and-over doors. Like a lot of the wooden buildings in Sweden she'd seen, it was painted in the striking shade of plum-red called Falun.

She parked her rented Volvo on the gravel drive to one side of the front door. A stiff breeze had blown up, which kept the temperature cool, despite the sun beating down on the top of Stella's head from a crystalline-blue sky.

She rang the doorbell. After a minute or so, it swung inwards to reveal an old man. Mattsson looked in good shape for his age, though. He was about five ten. His bearing was erect and though he had a paunch distending the front of his white linen shirt, he had decent muscle mass.

He looked at her with raised eyebrows, as white and bushy as his hair. '*Ja?*'

She fought down an urge to grab him by the shirt front and scream, 'Why?' into his open, enquiring face.

Instead, she showed him her Met ID card. '*Pratar du engleska?*' she asked, pleased with how fast she was picking up Swedish phrases.

He smiled. 'Yes, I speak English. But thank you for asking.'

'I'm Detective Chief Inspector Stella Cole. I'm with the

Metropolitan Police. I am working with an Inspector Norgrim of Stockholm Murder Squad.'

'How can I help you?'

'I'd like to ask you a few questions in relation to a case I'm working on.'

'A case? What sort of case?'

'I'm investigating the murder of a man I believe you knew. Tomas Brömly?'

His face fell. 'Poor Tomas. I read about it, of course. Come in.'

That was interesting. He hadn't admitted to receiving the letter.

She followed him down a wide hallway hung with framed photographs to a large kitchen. Mattsson led her into a garden that stretched down to a river. More birch trees swayed in the breeze, framing a long lawn interrupted by clumps of tall plants tipped with flame-orange blossoms.

Halfway down the garden, a pale wooden easel stood. Beside it lay a paint-splodged wooden palette threaded through with a handful of brushes.

Mattsson gestured towards the river.

'We have a couple of comfortable chairs down there.'

The carved wooden armchairs, padded with striped cushions, were not only comfortable but afforded a superb view across a sweeping curve of the river towards the far bank, fringed by yet more birches.

'Please make yourself comfortable,' Mattsson said. 'I'll go and fetch us coffee.' He strode towards the house, calling over his shoulder, 'We have herons!'

Stella shaded her eyes against the sun, which was still high in the sky, and watched for herons. After a couple of minutes during which her eyes gradually adjusted to the confusion of swaying branches, reeds and lush undergrowth on the far bank, she caught a fleeting movement.

Stalking majestically out into the reeds, a grey heron appeared, its dagger of a beak pointing towards the water as it moved its serpentine neck this way and that.

With a darting movement, it stabbed down into the water. When it drew its head up again, she could see a glittering flash of silver in its beak. It tossed its head back and snapped its beak around the struggling fish before swallowing it and returning to the hunt.

You and me both, she thought.

'Here we are!' Mattsson said.

She looked up, forcing a smile. On a black tray painted with pale-pink peony flowers stood a coffee pot, two white mugs and a couple of small plates. The other was taken up with a plate of pale, sugar-encrusted biscuits.

Mattsson poured them both a mug of coffee. He sat down and leaned forwards, watching her. She realised he was expecting her to take one of the biscuits. She took one and nibbled off a corner. She tasted almonds, and lemon.

Stella drank some of the coffee, which, mercifully, wasn't as strong as the normal brew she'd been offered since arriving in Sweden. But her pulse was elevated all the same. She looked at the old man opposite her. Was he Brömly's murderer? She was there to find out.

'How well did you know Tomas?' she asked him, pulling out her notebook.

Mattsson blew out his cheeks. 'We were close, once. We grew up together, you know, here in Umeå. We kept in touch during our national service and university careers, then I went into medicine and Tomas entered the civil service. After that, we drifted apart, as school friends often do.'

'Did you have any contact after that?'

'We exchanged Christmas cards, birthday messages, that sort of thing. But recently, not really at all. Not since he moved to London.'

'So his letter must have come as a shock, then?'

Mattsson's eyes widened, just for a moment, but enough for Stella to catch the expression of surprise.

'What letter is that?' he asked.

'We found evidence that suggests he hand-wrote a letter to you and two others, Inger Hedlund and Kerstin Dahl.'

Mattsson pushed out his lips in an exaggerated pout and shook his head.

'I'm sorry. I received no such letter from Tomas. All we get these days are those infernal circulars and begging letters from charities. It's all email now, isn't it? Do you suppose he might have drafted this letter but never sent it?'

Stella made a note. He was right about email, which also had the virtue of being traceable. Even for a letter sent by registered post, there was no practical way for anyone other than the sender to check it had ever been delivered.

'It's possible.' It was indeed, and she cursed herself for leaping to the conclusion that a letter written was a letter posted, delivered and read. 'Do you know either of the two women I mentioned?'

'Sorry, their names again, please? My memory isn't so good these days. Age,' he added with a rueful smile.

'Inger Hedlund and Kerstin Dahl.'

He furrowed his brow. Looked up into the cloudless sky. Back at Stella.

'I'm sorry, neither of those names means anything to me.'

'Do you have any idea why Tomas would have grouped you three together in an email distribution list?'

He shrugged. 'I'm afraid I have absolutely no idea. As I said, we fell out of touch when he moved to London. They could be colleagues from his days in the diplomatic service, I suppose.'

Stella nodded. 'In the letter, he mentioned something called the project. He described it as being evil. Does that phrase mean anything to you?'

Another shake of the head. He leaned forward to retrieve his coffee and took a long drink. 'You would have to go a long way to find a man purer in thought, word and deed than Tomas,' he said. 'Once, at school, he found a ten-kronor note in the playground. One of the old ones with Gustav the First on it. Guess what? He handed it in to the teacher. Poor *Frökken* Pärsson didn't know whether to pat him on the head or send him to see a psychiatrist!'

Stella smiled. 'I appreciate that you hadn't been in touch for a few years, but please try and help me out, here, *Herr* Mattsson. You see, in the letter—'

'Which, as I said, I didn't receive,' he interrupted her, with a genial smile.

'Exactly. But in it, he wrote that you, *Fru* Hedlund and *Fru* Dahl were equally guilty. He used the word "complicit". I wonder, do you have any idea at all what he was referring to?'

'None at all. I hate to ask this, but, as a medical man, I must. Do you know if poor Tomas was suffering from dementia? It can play hideous tricks on the mind.'

Stella realised they hadn't considered the possibility at all. An oversight for which she delivered a swift imaginary kick up her own rear end.

'We're reviewing his medical records, but, at this point, there's no evidence that he was in any way lacking in mental capacity.'

What a pompous phrase, she thought, as the words left her lips. Was it because she was aware of being the foreigner being addressed in her mother tongue? This falling back on stock police phrasing that wouldn't sound out of place in the High Court?

'People don't always get a diagnosis,' Mattsson said. 'Especially in the early days.'

'No,' she conceded, 'they don't.'

Mattsson smiled and pushed down on the arms of his chair. 'If you have any more questions, I will try my best to answer but I would really love to get back to my painting. The light is perfect at this time in the afternoon. It lends itself particularly well to painting outside. What the French call *en plein air.*'

Stella rose too. 'Nothing else.'

She offered her hand. He grasped it and pulled himself to his feet. 'Thank you. I'll show you out.'

On the way through the hall, Stella glanced at the photos. One caught her eye. A group of four people, in their thirties, it looked like. Two men and two women. One of the men could have been a younger version of Brömly, the other Mattsson.

'Who are they?' she asked, pointing at the photo.

He peered and then smiled. 'That's me,' he said, tapping the man on the right of the group. 'The others were friends from medical school.'

'Is that Tomas?' she asked, tapping the glass over the face of the other man.

He shook his head. 'Tomas wasn't at school with me. He went into the civil service.'

She shrugged. 'You all look happy.'

He smiled. 'They were good days. By the way,' he added, 'did you see any herons?'

'Yes, one,' she replied.

'Beautiful, aren't they?'

She nodded her agreement as he squeezed past her to open the front door.

On the drive back into the city centre she made a list of new lines of enquiry opened up by her conversation with Mattsson. She needed to check Brömly's medical records and speak to his GP if possible.

If he was developing symptoms of dementia then a horrible possibility would raise its head: their whole case might have been based on nothing more than the ravings of an elderly man's disordered mind. Perhaps he'd doctored his CV for some other, entirely innocent, reason. Then she'd be back to square one. And to London.

She realised with a jolt that she didn't want to return home. The thought of being alone again frightened her, yet surely that was now more than likely given Jamie's reaction to her confession.

She hit the steering wheel in her frustration, clipping the horn boss and earning a reproachful hand gesture from the car in front. Because Jamie had reacted as any normal person would, hadn't he? He had every right to leave like he did. Who wouldn't, after their girlfriend had just told them she was a stone-cold killer?

It just wasn't fair. Soldiers could be married and they killed. AFOs did it and nobody flounced off in a huff to stay in a hotel. She felt a twinge of guilt at the way she'd characterised Jamie's retreat from her flat. But it was true, wasn't it?

Shaking her head, she forced herself to return to the questions thrown up by the interview with Mattsson. What about his alibi for the day of Brömly's murder? She hadn't wanted to go there on a first, casual meeting. But she'd come back to it when they spoke again. Because she strongly suspected that they would be. And his career. If she examined his record, would she discover a hole from 1971 to 1976? Were the quartet in the photo the four Swedes whose lives and death she was now investigating?

And Mattsson was a doctor. Now a lecturer in Genetics at the local university. They'd have needed doctors to conduct the sterilisations, wouldn't they?

The civil servant she'd spoken to had said Brömly was on the payroll for that whole time, so was unlikely to have been simultaneously in Africa, doing good works. But what if he'd been on long-term sick leave? Had he had some sort of breakdown? Was that why he'd altered his CV?

The more she thought about it, the more she could see a completely new narrative emerging.

A highly ambitious, driven and, by all accounts, competent civil servant pushes himself too hard, has a breakdown and is put on sick leave for four years. Was that possible?

She realised she didn't know enough about Sweden's employment laws. But they were renowned for their high-tax, high-benefits system. She resolved to ask Oskar after seeing Hedlund.

25

UMEÅ

Stella pulled off the forest road onto a single-track road, little more than a grass track, really, and trundled the Volvo through still more birches, their delicate leaves shimmering pale-green then gold in the sunlight.

She had the aircon switched to full, yet guiltily opened all four windows. She inhaled a sweet, sappy smell of summer growth and smiled. Despite the pressure to find Brömly's killer, there was something about the Swedish countryside that gladdened her heart.

Hoping she wouldn't meet anyone coming the other way, she noticed a slender arc of flattened vegetation to one side of the road. From the tyre tracks, she saw others before her had used it to squeeze past each other.

The track widened out into a V before merging with an area of grass in front of one of the prettiest houses Stella had ever seen.

It was painted the same shade of red as Mattsson's. The doors, windows and a balustraded veranda were picked out in a contrasting white. An old fashioned 'sit-up-and-beg' bicycle that looked as if it weighed as much as the Volvo leaned nonchalantly against one corner of the house. She parked beside a dusty Audi A4 saloon, its metallic-grey paintwork speckled acid yellow by pollen from a nearby tree.

Here was another summer cottage facing the pristine waterfront of Lake *Nydalasjön*. She thought ruefully of her own urban flat, traffic thrumming beneath her window for twenty hours out of every twenty-four, and felt a pang of envy.

A wooden slatted table and two chairs sat beneath a tree that cast dappled shade over the two people sitting there, each with a mug before them. Inger Hedlund and her husband, Erik. She recognised them from their driving licence photos, which the Swedish Government thoughtfully made available to police officers with the necessary clearance.

She called out to the old couple, not wishing to startle them.

'*Hej!*'

They turned, both smiling, and rose from their chairs. They manoeuvred themselves into an upright position with that care for aging bones and stiffened sinews old people took.

'*Hej!*' they called back in unison.

Inger Hedlund's round face was smooth and plump. None of the dry, weathered look that smokers developed or careless sunbathers. Here was a woman who had looked after her skin. Her blue eyes twinkled and she projected a grandmotherly air.

Erik Hedlund matched her in eye colour, although his skin bore the marks of a life spent outdoors. Dark patches that might once have been melanomas spattered his bald head. His face bore the effects of the sun: deep lines and a leathery, teak-coloured complexion.

With the introductions out of the way, and her police ID produced, examined and returned, Erik offered coffee and 'a little something to go with it'.

Feeling as though she might burst if she consumed any more food that day, yet desperate not to offend the hospitable couple, Stella smiled.

'I've come straight from talking to another witness. They were just as hospitable as every other Swedish person I've met. Would you mind if I said no?'

Erik Hedlund laughed, a warm, whisper-edged sound that spoke of a man enjoying life and slow to take offence.

'Of course not! We Swedes like to feed our guests, but if you're full, then of course you must say no.'

Stella smiled, glad her small piece of genuine flattery seemed to have gone down the right way.

Inger turned to Stella and placed her plump hand on her arm, just for a second. The twinkle had left her expression and the skin around her eyes had tightened.

'This is about Tomas, isn't it? I read all about it online. *Svenska Dagbladet* covered it. *Dagens Nyheter*, too. And of course *Västerbottens-Kuriren*. It's our big local newspaper. Did you know Tomas was from here?'

Stella nodded. 'Do you know of anyone, anyone at all, who might have wanted to hurt Tomas?' she asked.

Inger's eyes slid sideways to her husband.

'Tomas was a good man,' she said firmly. 'I only met him a couple of times before he moved to London. But he had what we call in this part of Sweden *en själ lika ren som sjövatten*. A soul as pure as lake water.'

Stella nodded. 'Everybody I've spoken to says more or less the same thing. Although none quite so poetically.'

Erik smiled. 'I myself was once rather a good poet. In fact I had two collections published by Norén & Beck.'

Inger laughed and shushed her husband with a finger to her lips.

'Erik! Honestly. The *Detektivinspektor* didn't come here to listen to you boasting of your literary career.'

He spread his hands wide and looked at Stella, a smile cracking his weather-beaten face.

'You'd think after being married for fifty-one years, she'd let me have a brief moment to relive past glories. But no! I am to be silenced in the name of modesty.'

Stella smiled. 'Do you have copies of your books here?'

His eyes widened. 'Of course I do! The publishers were kind enough to send me fifty of each. I think I have a couple left.'

Inger snorted. 'A couple! Huh. He has lots. He gives them away and orders more when he runs out.'

'I'd love to see one,' Stella said.

Erik nodded and got to his feet with less care than before, she noticed, and walked back towards the house. She watched him go. Now she had Inger on her own, it would change the dynamic between them.

'We didn't release this detail to the media, and I'm sorry to tell you something that might distress you, but the murderer, after shooting Tomas, pulled his tongue out.'

Inger's hand flew to her mouth. Stella continued, monitoring the old woman's reaction carefully. Eager for any tell-tale sign of foreknowledge.

'Did you receive an email or letter from Tomas in the days before he died?'

There. That was the killer question. Mattsson had denied it. Would Inger?

She took her hand away from her mouth. Her eyes, so merry when Stella had first arrived, were now filmy with moisture. She nodded.

'Do you still have the letter?'

She shook her head. 'I burnt it.'

'Why?'

'It was horrible. Poor Tomas, I think he must have been acting out some sort of fantasy. It was full of all these mysterious accusations about this evil,' she made air quotes around the word, 'we'd all done. I couldn't make head or tail of it, to be honest.'

Stella recalled Mattsson's question. *Do you know if poor Tomas was suffering from dementia?*

She was beginning to think he might have been. Except for one thing. That reference to 'Poor Tomas'. Inger and Mattsson both used it. That might mean nothing. It was a common enough phrase. But she'd formed the impression the trio had lost touch. It seemed a strange expression of sympathy for a man neither was particularly close to.

'What job did you do before you retired?' she asked, knowing the answer already from Oskar's profile.

'I was a lawyer for *Västerbotten* County Council.'

'What did that involve?'

Inger looked up. 'Oh, well, it was all sorts of things. In a regional government it could be drafting procurement contracts, disputes with suppliers, employment law, anything.'

Stella decided to push deeper.

'When did you retire?'

Inger frowned, perhaps surprised at the sudden change of direction, which was Stella's intention.

'It was 2015. They threw me such a lovely party,' she said with a smile. 'I'd been there forty years, you see. We had cake, dancing. I probably drank too much champagne.'

'Were you ever involved in settling compensation claims from the victims of the forced sterilisation programme?'

Inger rocked back in her chair as if Stella had punched her. The colour left her face and she swallowed convulsively three times, then clamped her hand across her mouth. Stella half-rose, hoping she hadn't just caused a helpful witness to have a heart attack.

She heard footsteps and half-turned.

'What's the matter?'

It was Erik, returning to the table with a couple of slim paperbacks in his right hand. He knelt in front of his wife. 'Darling, are you all right?' He turned to Stella, his eyes ablaze. 'What happened? What did you say?'

'Get her away, Erik!' Inger hissed from between her fingers.

'I think you should leave. Right now,' he said. His voice was shaking as he took a step towards Stella.

Stella nodded, retreating without wanting to turn away from him. He was old but looked more than capable of landing a punch. Malin Holm wouldn't take it well if her visitor became involved in a fight with an elderly Swedish citizen after almost poleaxing his wife with an ill-judged, if pertinent, question.

'Thank you,' she said. 'I'm sorry for upsetting your wife.'

'If you have anything else to ask, come back with a warrant,' he snapped as he knelt beside Inger and commenced patting her hand.

Back in her rental, Stella executed a hasty three-point turn during which she almost got the Volvo's rear tangled in a hammock slung between two birches. She drove away, simultaneously ashamed and elated. She was onto the truth now. She could feel it.

Back in Umeå, she parked behind the police station. She'd drunk so much of the strong Swedish coffee the Swedes loved that her heartbeat felt fluttery and too fast, as if she were about to hold a press conference or give a speech. Instead of heading inside, she walked to the nearby park and pulled out her phone to call Garry.

'Boss! I thought you'd gone dark on us. How's it going?'

'It's going well, though I'm starting to miss the station coffee.'

'Bloody hell! That bad, eh?'

'Not so much bad as strong. Jesus, Gary, if I drink any more of it, I won't need a plane to fly me home. I'll just flap my arms.'

He laughed. 'Did you need something, or is this just a social call? Not that I mind, of course.'

'I did need something. Can you look into Brömly's medical records for me? I need to know if he had dementia. Oh, and any history of mental illness. Something serious enough to have caused delusions.'

'Blimey! You think he was losing it when he wrote the letter?'

'In one. One of the people he wrote to suggested it today. I'm sceptical but we need to dot the i's all the same.'

'Leave it with me.'

'Thanks, Garry. How are things there?'

She could hear the shrug in his voice as he answered. 'No new cases this week, which is good. Callie's on the warpath about cutting back on external consultants and forensics labs.'

'Any news of Roisin?' she asked, keeping her voice light.

'It was the talk of the station,' a beat, 'for about five minutes. Then those muppets in Traffic won the station sweepstakes on the new Home Secretary and bumped her off the front page.'

'Where is she now?'

'Haven't seen her. Rumour is, she's gone to the US on some jolly for the brass. As far as I know, she's still out there.'

'No emails on what she's up to?'

'Radio silence. Why?'

'Just curious.' Stella stared at a pigeon, hopping closer and closer to her left boot. She kicked out at it. She focused on the here and now. 'Email me when you know about Brömly.'

The conversation with Garry had done her good. She felt calmer. The sun was hot on her skin and she turned to meet it head on, closing her eyes and allowing her upturned face to act as a solar panel.

'You look happy.'

She opened her eyes, blinking away the blue afterimages that danced in her vision. Oskar was standing in front of her, carrying a takeaway cup and a brown paper bag.

She pointed. 'Lunch?'

He looked down at his provisions. 'Very late. Or maybe it's dinner. I don't know. How did you get on with Mattsson and Hedlund today?'

'Do you mind walking while we talk? I really need the exercise.'

'No. If you don't mind me eating while you talk.'

He pulled out a filled roll from the bag and took an enormous bite. Stella could see a flap of smoked salmon poking out of the bread, which was dotted with poppy seeds.

'Mattsson denied ever getting Brömly's letter. Hedlund got it but said it sounded like he was, I don't know, mired in some fantasy.'

Oskar frowned. 'Sorry, what was that word? Mired?'

'Oh. Sorry. It means sunk in. You know, like up to your knees in soft mud.'

'*Tack*. Go on.'

Stella took him through both interviews, mentioning that she was checking Brömly's medical records. Oskar nodded and swallowed another mouthful of his roll, washing it down with a swig of coffee.

'So when you asked her about the sterilisation programme she, what, fainted?'

'Almost. I thought she was going to have a heart attack. Then her husband asked me to leave.'

'We should take a look at their employment history. See if they have gaps for the same years Brömly did.'

'Kerstin Dahl, too.'

'Yes, of course. I'll call Johanna and ask to her to get onto it. When are you seeing Dahl?'

'The day after tomorrow.'

'I may have to go back to Stockholm for a day or two. Will you be all right working solo up here?'

'Sure. I've got plenty to do and I can always hit the gym.'

Oskar grinned. 'Finding *fika* a bit much?'

'It's a national obsession! I mean, I know us Brits love our cups of tea, but the amount of cake I've had to eat! And that coffee! Do you get *any* sleep?'

He laughed. 'You get used to it. I sleep pretty well. Apart from when the new baby wakes me.'

'How old?'

'Nine months.'

'Boy or girl?'

'Boy. We called him Gustav.'

'He was the king, right?'

'One of them. Six in total.'

Something caught at Stella's memory. Something Mattsson had said about King Gustav the First. What was it? The banknote. That was it.

'When I interviewed Mattsson, I asked him about Brömly and he said his memory wasn't good. But then he told me this story about Brömly finding a ten-kronor note in the school playground and handing it in. It had a portrait of Gustav the First on it.'

'You think he was lying?'

'Old people can have deficient memories in one area and good elsewhere. But I would have thought long-term memory for a bank note would work the same as long-term memory for the schoolfriend who found it, wouldn't you?'

Oskar nodded. 'You going to talk to him again?'

'I was going to anyway. I didn't ask him for an alibi. Inger either, come to that. I'm sure one of them knows more than they're saying. And they both called him "Poor Tomas". It sounded off to me, staged. Like they'd agreed to refer to him that way.'

'If there's anything you need while I'm away, just call me. Or Johanna. She likes you.'

Stella scrutinised his face for a sign he knew what had passed between her and Johanna, but saw nothing.

They made their way to the station, where Oskar collected his stuff and headed back out, promising to return two days later.

Later that day, Garry emailed. The news was good. Brömly had enjoyed perfect mental health. No anxiety or depression, no psychotic illness and, at the time of his last consultation with his GP, no dementia.

The letter could still have been a fantasy of confession, forgiveness and redemption, but it was the product of an ordered mind. As such, Stella was inclined to dismiss the idea. He and his former friends had been involved in something he came to regard as evil. Putting two and two together, she kept coming up with the same answer.

26

LONDON

Roisin left Paddington Green, darted through a gap in the traffic on the Edgware Road, walked north for a couple hundred yards, then turned right into Church Street. Despite what she was about to do, she felt no nerves.

Instead, her heart rate had accelerated from pure adrenaline. She was closing in on the biggest case of her career. Hell, anyone's career in living memory.

The serial killers always got the headlines. But a killer cop? That made headlines *and* careers. Principally, Roisin's.

As she walked past dry cleaners, delis and shops selling everything from plastic laundry baskets to cans of fly spray, she turned to the question that had been plaguing her since she'd recognised Stella on the CCTV in Chicago.

Why?

What could Adam Collier possibly have done to Stella that would have warranted his murder? The risks she'd taken were off the scale. And yet she'd gone ahead and done it anyway.

Walking through a street market, the backs of the stalls clad in green-and-white striped sheeting, she thought harder about the woman she was sure had murdered the Colliers. What did she know about her? Really?

Stella was tough, Roisin gave her that. If Adam had tried anything that smacked even faintly of sexual misconduct, she'd have slapped him down, probably literally. Any professional slights she'd have sucked up and worked her way past. So not professional, then. That meant it was personal.

Nobody knew much about Stella's private life. She wasn't standoffish. But she didn't regale the canteen with tales of emotional disaster – or triumph – either. It wasn't her style. Not since that dreadful business with her family.

They knew she had a new squeeze, but that was about it. By all accounts, Jamie Hooke was her first relationship since that little toe-rag Edwin Deacon had killed Richard and Lola in a hit and run.

She stopped at a crossroads. A lunchtime drinker stumbled out of a pub on the northeast corner and swerved to avoid crashing into her.

'Sorry, love,' he said.

She waved him away with a smile. That was interesting. She knew a version of herself that would have had to fight down an urge to hit him, or swear at him for his clumsiness at the very least.

She turned right into Lisson Grove, enjoying the play of sunlight on her skin through the shade cast by the plane trees. The drunk had interrupted her thoughts. She regathered them into a coherent sequence.

Stella had killed Adam for a personal reason.

Hooke was her first relationship since Richard died.

Edwin Deacon had killed Richard and Lola in a hit and run.

That had to be it, didn't it? The single worst moment in Stella's life. She was a fast-track, graduate-entry girl. Promoted and promoted and promoted, over Roisin's head in the end. Yes, she'd made mistakes, and had setbacks. But only the kind that stiffened a copper's sinews and made them stronger for the next time.

Had Adam been mixed up in Richard's and Lola's deaths somehow? If he had, and Stella found out, wouldn't that give her plenty of motive for murder?

Roisin knew it would if *she'd* been the grieving wife and mother. Da's words would have bounced off her steely resolve like plastic arrows. 'Slow and steady?' Fuck that! She'd have wanted blood.

But what could Adam have done that Deacon hadn't done already? The guy had confessed and gone down for it. The sentence was a joke, but he'd been arrested, charged and convicted in record time.

Unless Adam had set Deacon up. But now the story started taking on unimaginable dimensions. Why would Adam have commissioned Deacon to murder Richard and Lola? It didn't make sense.

She turned off the pavement and approached the front door to the block of flats where Stella lived. Without a second thought, she pressed three buttons on the intercom panel in rapid succession. After a few seconds, a woman answered.

'Police. Open the door, please,' Roisin said in a stern, authoritative voice.

The latch clicked and she pulled the handle towards her. Inside, the building was a few degrees lower than the humid air outside. Roisin rested her forehead against a painted wall, letting its smooth surface cool her skin.

She called the lift and stepped in as soon as the doors opened. She caught a wisp of another woman's perfume. Better than the smell of piss that usually greeted her whenever she had to venture into a lift in a block of flats. But then, she thought, as she ascended to Stella's floor, they weren't usually swanky blocks in an expensive tree-lined street in central London.

The doors opened. A man made to step in, then noticed Roisin, smiled and stood back.

'Thank you,' she said with a smile.

She turned and waited until the lift doors had closed and the machinery in the shaft emitted a refined hum. Then she walked along the corridor to Stella's flat.

* * *

The conference on genetics and mental health was fascinating, but after an hour-long speech by a Hungarian psychologist on genetic factors affecting psychopathy, Jamie felt the need to get out into the real world for a bit.

Lunch was scheduled for an hour and a half: he decided to check on Stella's flat. He knew she was in Sweden, and as he was in town it seemed the least he could do. Her plants would need watering and although he felt sure she would have asked a neighbour to pop in, he felt a tug to be in her space.

Her revelation to him over dinner had unnerved him so thoroughly that he'd bolted rather than try to explore it with her there and then. Was it because his relationship with Stella was personal – *no, say it, Jamie, romantic* – rather than professional that he'd reacted so emotionally?

After all, he spent his days talking to men who had done things just as bad, and, sometimes, considerably more deviant than murder people in revenge for the death of their family. In fact, compared to their warped psychology, Stella's actions had been those of an entirely rational being.

And, as she'd said, she'd been suffering from grief-induced psychosis. The literature was full of such cases. Hell, he'd written a paper on it himself: *Brief Psychotic Disorder With Obvious Stressor: Grief, Loss of Control and Homicide in Women under Thirty.*

A niche subject, to be sure, but one of the first he'd had published and a rung on the ladder that stretched ever-upwards in front of every ambitious clinician.

Yes, those afflicted were more likely to be women already suffering from a serious mental illness. And Stella was older than thirty when Richard and Lola were killed. Nevertheless, she was still in the central hump of the bell curve for that type of breakdown.

He hailed a cab outside the university hosting the conference. With a hum from its electric motor, the cab pulled away.

The silence inside the spotless interior seemed tailor-made for thinking. Jamie returned to the problem of Stella's behaviour.

A high-level conspiracy had snuffed out the lives of her husband and baby daughter because Richard was getting too close. Stella had secretly re-investigated and discovered the truth. And then, the part he struggled with emotionally, though not intellectually, she had killed its leader in cold blood. Jamie shook his head.

The trouble wasn't that he couldn't understand why she'd done it. The trouble was that he could.

He looked at the back of the taxi driver's head. Saw ripples of flesh between his shaved scalp and the white collar of his polo shirt. Imagined if the driver had been responsible for murdering Stella. Saw his right hand gripping a pistol, pressing its muzzle to that sun-reddened flesh and pulling the trigger.

Not only could he understand what Stella had done. On some primal level, he approved.

27

UMEÅ

In the end, Erik's fussing drove Inger to her sewing room. He meant well. But because he didn't know what had upset her so badly that she'd almost passed out, he ended up getting on her nerves. Which were hardly capable of functioning as it was.

She shut the door behind her, sat at her sewing table and massaged her temples with the pads of her fingers.

How much longer could she go on ignoring what they'd done? For the rest of her life? She wasn't old. Not really. These days, seventy-three was counted as late middle age. Her mother had died aged ninety-nine. Inger might have another two decades with a monstrous secret eating away at her. Two decades to add to the four and a half so far.

They said stress could cause cancer. She believed it. But even if she didn't get cancer, living with the secret was turning her soul into a pitiful, blackened, diseased *thing*. She could feel it, squatting inside her like a troll under a bridge waiting to devour the unwary traveller.

When Tomas's letter had arrived, it was as if a perfect Swedish Sunday afternoon in midsummer had been ravaged by a storm. She hadn't told Erik, explaining away her depressed mood as news of a schoolfriend's death.

'Will you go to the funeral?' he'd asked.

'No. She lived in England. We lost touch a long time ago.'

Then, a miracle. She'd read online that Tomas had been murdered. The killer had done something dreadful to his body. They weren't specific. Just a nasty phrase including the word 'mutilated'. Somehow imagining what might have been done to him was worse than knowing for sure.

But maybe Tomas was right after all. Maybe confession wasn't just good for the soul, but essential for its very existence.

Oh god, why had they done it? They'd all been intelligent, democratically-minded citizens of a country widely regarded in international circles as enlightened to the point of soft-heartedness.

She couldn't remember. They'd just got on with it, swept along on the tide of memos from central government and, she admitted, their own fervour.

She felt sick as she remembered the detailed records they'd kept, the reports she herself had written for the national leadership of the party and the government. Sicker still as she remembered the hospital visit she'd made to see for herself what was being done at their behest.

The British detective seemed remarkably well-informed. When she'd asked about the Project, Inger hadn't needed to feign her discomfort. It had been real enough, and she'd felt sure she was about to faint.

Thank god Erik had returned when he did, clutching his poetry books. She swore if they got through this, she'd never joke about them again.

She batted the sides of her head with her palms, trying to still her mind long enough to figure out what to do.

When the pain jolted her mind into some semblance of calm, she placed her smarting palms together in front of her and rested her forehead on the first joints of her thumbs.

She searched inside herself for that quiet place she could reach in church or at the end of a long, peaceful day.

Father, this is your daughter, Inger Agnes Hedlund.

I pray that you will guide me.

You know that Tomas is dead. I am frightened, Lord. I am frightened that whoever murdered Tomas will come for me, too. And for Ove and Kerstin.

Tomas was going to confess. He urged us to as well. Was he right? Should I accept my sin and hope for redemption?

I want to be free of this fear, Lord. But I also don't want to die before my time. I want to live.

Guide me, please.

Amen.

Her breathing felt easier than it had done since she learned of Tomas's murder. Through the open window she could hear birds singing in the birch trees.

God would answer her. He always did. But what would he say?

When the answer came to her, she was shocked. She wanted to resist. To cry out against the unfairness. But then she accepted it. Because it made sense.

No, more than that. Making sense was for choosing the right replacement dishwasher or car insurance policy. This was about doing the right thing. Finally. And to hell with the consequences.

She would have to tell Erik, of course. He would be shocked. Horrified, even. But they'd been married for forty-three years. She felt sure the marriage would survive.

What about Ove and Kerstin? They deserved to know. She might even be saving their lives. By voluntarily confessing, as Tomas had wanted her to, she would draw the sting from the murderer's rage.

Forgiveness was a very human need. More, perhaps, than revenge. She prayed it was. And she could ask for police protection too, once it was out in the open.

Tears pricked at her eyes and then burst free, wetting her cheeks and dropping from her chin onto the sewing table. The lightning bolt she'd released when she unsealed Tomas's aerogramme had sundered the wall of denial she'd built around her past. Now she saw, *truly* saw, the Project for what it was.

They'd thought they were creating a beautiful breed of people. But what they'd done was evil.

Silently, she wept for all the harm she'd done. She wept for all her – she realised with a kind of painful joy that she could finally use the word – *victims*.

Finally the tears dried. Perhaps she'd run out. It certainly felt that way. Practical problems presented themselves.

How did one confess? Not like in church, where everything was secret. But in public. Should she approach the press? Do it on social media like the youngsters did everything these days?

She decided against that course of action. She wanted a clean soul, not a torrent of hate mail and death threats. Although she supposed she might get those anyway. But better death threats than actual death.

Maybe Erik would know. She'd ask him. She'd plead for his forgiveness first, though. For having deceived him all these years. And if he couldn't cope? If he left her? No. He wouldn't. Couldn't. They were too old for that sort of thing. They'd find a way through it.

Before any of that, there was one person to whom she felt she owed an explanation.

Ove would try to persuade her out of it. Maybe he could cope with the idea of a murderer hunting them all down, but Inger couldn't. She decided to visit him in person. That way he'd have to hear her out.

She went downstairs and told Erik she was going for a drive to clear her head.

Fifteen minutes later, she rolled up to Ove's house and cut the engine. Even though it was after nine in the evening, the sun was as bright as day. *Midsommar* wasn't far off. She flapped a fan in front of her face as she approached the front door and rang the bell.

Ove answered, dressed in some sort of white silky pyjamas, like a martial arts outfit. Baggy trousers cut off at mid-calf and a belted jacket. She frowned. So did Ove.

'Inger? It's been years. What are you doing here?'

'Can I come in, please?' she said. 'And what on earth are you wearing?'

He made no move to stand aside or beckon her in. Instead, he looked down. 'They're Japanese. Very cool in this heat. Sigge brought them back for me on his last trip.'

She frowned again. Sigge? A grown-up son? An assistant of some kind? She realised how little she knew of Ove's life. A man with whom she once collaborated on the Project, working side by side for almost six years.

'Sigge?' she prompted.

'My husband.'

'Oh.'

He smiled. 'You disapprove?'

She shook her head, aware he was already seizing control of the conversation and distracting her from her purpose.

'Not at all. I have gay friends. Can I come in, please?'

'Why? I told you when we all went our separate ways, contact between us was a very bad idea.'

'Please, Ove?'

He stood aside, rather ungraciously, she thought, and let her precede him down the hallway and into the kitchen. His lack of manners didn't end there. Even though it was a hot evening, and he must be able to see she was sweating, he didn't offer her a drink. Though coffee would have been unwelcome, she needed a cold drink.

Swallowing her pride, she asked him. 'May I have some water, please?'

He turned from her and filled a glass from the cold tap, handing it to her and indicating she should sit at the table, where he joined her.

Once she'd taken a long draft of the water, she set the glass down.

'Tomas was murdered for what he did,' she said.

'Yes,' he said. 'I don't mind telling you, it really shook me. Especially after his letter.'

'Whoever killed Tomas is going to come for us. I can't bear it.'

He shook his head. 'You don't know that. Maybe they only knew about Tomas. We were careful. You know that. I helped you.'

'Yes, and you helped Tomas, too. It didn't stop someone finding him and shooting him and then,' she gulped down some more water, suddenly feeling sick, 'doing something afterwards.'

'He must have got careless. Maybe he let it slip before he wrote to us with his absurd notion of confessing.'

'Why absurd?'

'He was getting soft in the head. If there *is* a god, which, as a scientist, I don't for one moment believe, then do you *really* think he would grant absolution to someone like Tomas Brömly?' he scoffed. 'Poor old Tommy could have crawled on his hands and knees from Umeå to Santiago de Compostela and he'd still have ended up in Hell.'

Inger couldn't help herself. Her mouth dropped open.

'How could you say such a thing? He genuinely wanted to repent. Do you know your Bible? "There will be more rejoicing in Heaven over one sinner who repents than over ninety-nine righteous persons who do not need to repent."'

Mattsson smiled. 'I think I'd prefer to enjoy my life here on earth than worry about what they think of me in Heaven. Besides, it didn't do Tomas much good, did it? He died before he had a chance to wipe the slate clean. I dare say he's somewhere hotter than we are right now.'

'You shouldn't say that.'

'No? I'm in my house. I think I can say whatever I damn well please. Now for the final time, why are you here?'

She inhaled deeply and spoke on the out breath. 'Tomas was right. You are wrong. We took part in a great evil. I'm going to tell Erik tomorrow night,' she said. 'After dinner. Then I'll ask him to help me work out how to confess publicly. I hope if I do that then Tomas's murderer will see I am genuinely sorry and leave me alone.'

Ove sat back on the hard kitchen chair. He didn't say anything. Inger had imagined he'd bluster or try to bully her into agreeing to maintain her – their – silence. She watched his eyes flicking left and right as if inventorying the contents of the kitchen. Finally he spoke.

'I think you're wrong. But it's your life. Throw what's left of it away for the promise of peace in the afterlife if you want. But I make one request of you.'

'What's that?'

'Leave me out of it. I've more living left to do. I'm content to take my chances. Both here and in the next world.'

So, surprised that he'd not made any attempt to talk her out of her own confession, Inger readily agreed.

'I promise. And I'll leave you alone after this. You won't see me anymore. I wish I could have met Sigge, though.'

'He's picking up supplies at ICA for *Midsommar*. There's a party in the village.'

'Oh well. Thank you for being so understanding.'

He got up and she followed him back to the front door. She turned on the threshold.

'Do you still think what we did was right, Ove?'

He looked her in the eye. 'Goodbye, Inger.' Then he closed the door.

28

LONDON

As a young girl, Roisin had helped Ma with her dressmaking. She loved it when Ma would ask her to thread needles, sew on seed pearls or do the delicate bits of embroidery for First Communion dresses.

Now those same nimble fingers worked a pair of lock picks as she crouched outside Stella's front door. Twenty seconds and she was in, closing the door behind with a soft snick from the mechanism. She sighed out a breath. That was the hard part over.

Inside, she could relax and start looking for the boots. She walked down the hallway, opening each door in turn. A room kitted out as a home office. A sizeable sitting room with a dining table in one half. A bathroom. A separate toilet. And a bedroom. She went in, skirting a tall ficus plant in a glazed pot.

The bed had been made: a plumped-up duvet and matching pillowcases in an off-white, pocketed cotton that looked as though someone, surely not Stella, had ironed each pleated square.

The wardrobe occupied one whole wall beside the bed. She rounded the bed and slid the mirrored central door to the left. It revealed a row of garments on hangers: shirts, tops, trousers, skirts, a couple of long dresses. She moved the dresses to one side, but saw no shoes.

She slid the heavy door back the other way and followed it with a solid door, patterned with a limed-oak design. Shelves stretched from waist height up to the top of the wardrobe. They housed plastic boxes full of T-shirts and knitwear, underwear and tights. On a white wire rack below the lowest shelf were the shoes.

Roisin squatted and checked the pairs of trainers, ankle boots, flats and heels. She worked her way methodically along four rows but already her heart was sinking. Her eyes had run ahead of her fingers and she could see there were no studded biker boots.

She sat back, leaning on the bed. No! They had to be here. Then a horrible thought struck her.

What if Stella had taken them with her to Sweden? She was forever going on about how comfortable they were, like a second skin. It would make sense. You were travelling, you'd want to be wearing comfortable shoes.

She still had the final third of the wardrobe to check. She reached forward and slid the two doors back the way they had come. Stella and Jamie had obviously been playing house together. The space was mostly taken up with men's clothes. A couple of suits, some jeans and dark trousers, and a handful of dress shirts.

More for form's sake than anything, she rummaged around in the bottom of the space. She found size ten running shoes and a pair of brown lace-up boots that were clearly Jamie's. But no damned biker boots.

She got to her feet, knees popping as she straightened. She realised she was grinding her teeth and forced herself to unclench her jaw. This wasn't over. All she'd done was try one wardrobe in one room. She needed to be more methodical. Stella could have put the boots anywhere.

Wait a minute. Stella had that stupid motorbike. But Roisin hadn't seen a crash helmet. So where was it? And the leather jacket with the orange stripe?

She darted out into the hall. She'd walked straight past the coat rack. She riffled through the jackets and longer-style coats and –

Oh, Sweet Jesus! – she found it. The thick leather that met her questing fingers promised her success.

Just to be sure, she dragged the jacket out from between a navy pea coat and a tan trench. If the jacket was here, surely the helmet and boots couldn't be too far away. She turned around and saw a door set flush into the painted wall opposite the coat rack. A utility cupboard of some kind.

She pulled the door open and came face to face with a matte-black bike helmet. She saw her face reflected in its curved Perspex visor, distorted so that her mouth stretched disgustingly from one side of her face to the other.

She looked down. At her feet, toes-inwards as if too shy to meet her gaze, were the boots.

She bent to grab them and froze. Footsteps were approaching the other side of the front door. She closed the cupboard and fled down the hall, still holding the boots. *There!* The unmistakeable sound of a key hitting the surround to a lock then slotting home.

It must be a cleaner. How could she have been so careless? So sure she was about to find the silver bullet that would take Stella down she'd forgotten to check if anyone was due to come to the flat.

She raced back into the master bedroom and closed the door behind her. Then, panicking, realised it had been open when she'd arrived. She pulled it open a little then turned, desperate to find a hiding place. The wardrobe? No room. She knew that, didn't she? She'd only just searched it. Stupid woman!

Her heart was racing. *Come on, Roisin, think!*

She went down on her knees and looked under the bed. Perfect. Just a couple of shoe boxes and a baseball bat. Naughty!

Figuring that if Stella's cleaner was anything like her own, she'd hardly be the type to bother vacuuming under a double bed, Roisin went flat on her belly and shuffled in on her elbows, keeping the boots in front of her.

Heart thumping, she forced herself to breathe slowly, straining to listen to the sounds beyond the bedroom door. The carpet was furry with dust and hair: soft little balls of tumbleweed on a desert of oatmeal-coloured twisted wool. Her nose started tickling. She wrinkled it and pushed her knuckle hard against her top lip, terrified she'd sneeze.

Her heart sank as she realised the reality of her situation. The cleaner would be there for what, one hour? Two? Three? She couldn't stay under here for that long. But what other option did she have? She could hardly emerge with a cheery, 'Afternoon, all', flash the warrant card and let herself out, now could she?

Then everything changed.

'Hello? Anybody there?'

She'd only met Jamie once, but she recognised his voice. Her stomach flipped over and all thought of sneezing vanished.

If he found her here there'd be no chance of blustering her way out as she might past a confused and possibly fearful cleaner. He'd start asking questions. Hell, he might even make a citizen's arrest. She wouldn't put it past him.

She flattened herself into the pile of the carpet, wishing she could disappear between its fibres.

She heard Jamie humming, then a kitchen cupboard opening. The noise of plastic containers knocking and clattering onto the worktop. His swearing. Brief and humorous. Stuff being restacked. The tap running. Something filling.

What the hell? Was he about to burst in and chuck a jug full of cold water under the bed to flush out a burglar?

She got ready to fight. It was the only option. If she hit him hard and fast enough, she could knock him out or at least temporarily blind him before he recognised her. He'd call 999, but, by the time the uniforms arrived, she'd be long gone and sorting out an alibi.

Then, nothing. What the hell was he doing? The humming had morphed into singing. He had a terrible singing voice. Flat, almost completely out of tune. She'd have laughed if her situation wasn't so dire.

She could hear him going into the different rooms. Everything would go silent for a minute or two, then he'd emerge. She prayed that whatever he was doing he wouldn't need to do it in the bedroom.

Keeping her head down, she focused on the boots under her nose. This close she could smell them: leather and a solvent-y top note that might have been some kind of waterproofing product they sold in shoe shops.

She turned the right boot over in her hands. The simple pattern of studs was uninterrupted. Then it must be the left. It *had* to be.

She examined the upper. The tiny metal cones extended left and right in unbroken lines. The heel revealed more of the same. The she turned it to examine the outer edge.

She missed it the first time she looked. Jamie had just walked past the bedroom door, sending her heart into a fluttery rhythm she felt in her throat. She looked again, tracing the pattern with her finger. And there, a third of the way along, her fingertip dipped into a gap between two studs.

She closed her eyes and rested her forehead on the carpet and released a pent-up breath.

Jesus, Mary and sweet Joseph, it was there!

The evidence she needed. Right in front of her. All she had to do was avoid being discovered hiding under the bed like a teen in an eighties horror movie.

The bedroom door opened. She heard its lower edge brush over the carpet. She saw Jamie's feet, encased in tan brogues below the rolled cuffs of indigo jeans. Her heart stuttered in her chest.

'Now, then,' he said.

This was it. He'd bend down and peer beneath the bed and she'd hit him straight in the eyes with clawed fingers. It was a brutal move and she could permanently damage his sight, but it was better than the alternative.

She'd back out from under the bed and come round to kick him in the belly to drive his wind out. Then she could escape. And if she didn't gasp or grunt he'd probably think he'd been attacked by a man.

'Has anyone been giving you a drink or did Stella forget?'

What the hell! Who was the man talking to? For a dreadful second she thought she'd left a foot sticking out from beneath the bed. She drew both feet in as much as she could. And waited.

Holding her breath, she watched his feet move in front of her and towards the window. Then she heard the sound of water pouring. What the hell was it? A trickle for a few seconds. Then a pause. Then another splashing.

Was he pissing? No. He was watering her houseplants!

She wanted to laugh. She tightened her stomach muscles until they hurt, but the effort squashed the hysteria building in her gut.

A minute more and he was gone. She waited until she heard the front door close behind him. Waited a minute more in case he'd forgotten something. Sure he was gone, she struggled out from her hiding place and sat on the floor, her back to the bed.

In the light, she could examine the boot more closely. Where the missing stud should have been were three little slits, each no more than two millimetres long. She fished around in her pocket until she could bring out the stud in its protective tissue wrapping.

The tabs at the base of the tiny metal cone were bent. She straightened them with her fingernails, cursing as one broke near the quick. She bit it clean off and spat it out. Swearing at her carelessness, she stretched out to retrieve the ragged sliver and pushed it down into her pocket.

She lined up the stud with the slits in the leather and pushed it home. Nodding with satisfaction, she took a series of photos of the boot, both with the stud and without.

She considered taking it with her but realised it was premature. If Stella had kept it this long she obviously hadn't realised she'd lost a stud, or, if she had, thought it had come off while riding. Either way, she hadn't dumped it yet, so it was safe to assume she wouldn't now.

The stud, she rewrapped and pocketed. *That* was staying with her, along with the FBI's analysis of the lake mud in which it had been embedded.

Back at Paddington Green she called Rachel Fairhill and asked for a letter of introduction for the Swedish police.

29

UMEÅ

Annika stared at her laptop. Inger Hedlund's Facebook profile occupied most of the screen. Her smiling, grandmotherly face twinkled with good humour.

The photos were of her and Erik enjoying retirement. Canoeing on Lake *Nydalasjön*. Holding glistening rainbow trout aloft, hers bigger than Erik's. A humorous caption, 'Now who's the expert?' Drinking beer from tall frosted glasses with a group of other happy, elderly, complacent, look-away-and-it-didn't-happen Swedes.

Annika herself didn't have a Facebook account. Or Twitter. Or Instagram. She'd had them all, once. But when her plan started to take shape, she realised it would be better to become less easy to find.

She didn't know, but she suspected the quartet of evil-doers still had connections. Powerful connections. The kind of connections who wouldn't think twice about silencing a woman for reaching down elbow-deep into the muck to drag out long-buried secrets.

When she'd been married to Ulf, everything had been fine. He'd accepted her inability to have children with good grace and even suggested they adopt. But the state agencies turned them away with vague phrases about Annika's 'suitability'.

She knew what it meant, even if Ulf didn't. Those bastards hadn't just torn part of her womanhood away from her. They'd poisoned her file so nobody would ever trust her with a child, whether her own or someone else's.

Oh, she'd spent years, decades, trying to access her records. But even with Sweden's so-called Freedom of Information law, it turned out there were some kinds of information that just didn't qualify for the freedom.

Then Ulf had been taken away from her, too. No drawn-out illness. No car crash or sporting accident.

He'd been shopping in *Östermalm* Market Hall in Stockholm and a man, an immigrant from one of those war-torn countries somewhere in the Middle East, had starting hacking at people with a machete.

The police shot him dead but not before he'd seriously injured five people and mortally wounded two. One, Mika Aronsson, a student nurse, died at the scene.

Ulf lasted for an hour after the ambulance rushed him to Karolinska University Hospital. He died on the operating table from blood loss.

That's when the idea came to Annika. There was so much random evil in the world, one couldn't hope to do anything about it. But the evil that they had perpetrated against her, and the tens of thousands of others, had been anything but random.

They'd thought about it. Studied it. Planned it. And then they'd damn well gone ahead and implemented it.

With Ulf gone, and nobody else to care for – Lord knew, she hardly cared about herself – she decided then and there to take revenge.

She finished the profile on Inger Hedlund later that evening. She sat at her desk sipping a freshly made cup of coffee.

The sleek weapon she would employ to destroy Hedlund sat before her, gleaming in the light from her Ikea desk lamp. Designed in America but manufactured in China, every single part was there for a purpose. No waste, no decoration, no frills. But in the right hands – hers – devastating.

She leaned back in her office chair and kissed the air at her cat, Ziggy. He twitched his whiskers and jumped up onto her lap. Scratching him absentmindedly behind the ears, she stared at the face of the woman on screen. Inger was smiling. She wouldn't be smiling for long.

Purring so fiercely that Annika felt the vibrations on the tops of her thighs, Ziggy chose this moment to extend his claws. Annika winced as the needle-points penetrated her corduroy jeans and pricked her skin.

Gently, she lifted his paws, one at a time, cooing to him until he retracted his claws. 'Naughty cat!'

30

UMEÅ

Inger awoke to sunshine streaming through the curtains. She rolled to her left and stretched out her arm for Erik, but found only rumpled cotton, cool to the touch.

She levered herself into an upright position and slipped her feet into her soft Moroccan leather slippers. Erik had bought them for her in the souk on their holiday before last. He'd bargained for them hard, but good-naturedly, with the stall-holder. The elderly man with brown skin like a wizened apple had nodded enthusiastically as they dickered, revealing missing teeth in his friendly grin.

She crossed to the window and drew the curtains. Erik was down on the dock, his old split-cane rod in hand.

He'd concealed his abundant white hair beneath a floppy, sun-bleached hat in which were hooked a dozen or more rainbow-coloured flies.

He always claimed mornings were the best time for trout, when they rose to take insects from the surface before the heat drove them into deeper waters.

She wrapped a thin cotton dressing gown around her and went downstairs to make a pot of coffee. Once it was brewed, she assembled crispbreads and honey on the tray and carried it all into the garden. There, she sat down to watch Erik.

After a few minutes, she saw a silvery splash in the lake a dozen or so metres from the dock. Erik jerked the rod back. He'd caught a fish. Maybe she'd change her dinner plans and cook it, if it was big enough.

Catching a lake trout always put Erik in a good mood. With the addition of a nice bottle of white wine, she could frame her confession in a way he'd at least hear out.

He played the fish with his customary skill and grace, never trying to force it into the shore, but allowing it to run, then reeling it back whenever it tired. The reel fizzed each time the fish took off.

Holding the rod in his left hand, Erik reached down for his landing net. In a single, flowing movement borne of long practice he scooped the net under the inbound fish and brought it, writhing and flipping, clear of the water, dripping water like diamonds onto the worn boards of the dock.

She rose from her chair and walked down the garden to join him. If it was a nice fat lake trout, she'd stuff it with lemon, garlic, parsley from the garden and breadcrumbs, slice some almonds on the top and roast it.

'*Hej!*' she called. 'What did you catch?'

Erik turned, his weathered face creased from smiling, and held the glittering fish aloft, strong fingers hooked through its gills. She smiled back, seeing the boy she'd first fallen in love with back in the sixties. He'd had such long hair then. Dark, too. Not like now, white and—

Erik's head exploded in a pink mist.

His body fell backwards, splashing into the lake. The trout dropped to the dock, flopped a good forty centimetres clear of the wet boards and twisted off the edge to join Erik.

Inger was too shocked to scream. Her mouth opened wide but nothing came from her stretched lips.

A sharp sound impinged on her consciousness. A crack like a branch snapping in winter. A shot! *Someone shot my Er*—

The second bullet entered her own skull at the inner corner of her left eye. It killed her instantly, sparing her the sight of her own blood filling the air around her head in a scarlet cloud.

Nor did she hear the second gunshot, which echoed off the side of the cottage Erik had inherited from his *mamma* and *pappa*.

31

UMEÅ

Stella sensed something big had happened the moment she entered the CID general office at just after 9.00 a.m. People were grouped round William Ekland, taking notes.

She saw plenty of uniforms with their black pistols strapped to their hips, as well as the full complement of detectives. Oskar was already there, seated towards the back of the group. He beckoned Stella over.

'What happened?' she whispered.

'Inger and Erik Hedlund were murdered this morning. Shot,' he added.

William looked over in their direction, frowning. 'Good morning, Stella,' he said, switching to English. 'Did Oskar just explain what happened?'

'Yes. Who found them?'

'A neighbour. She'd gone round to talk about planning for the village *Midsommar* party.'

'Oskar said they were shot. Any mutilations?'

He shook his head, visibly pale. She guessed murders of elderly couples weren't a common occurrence in Umeå.

'No. The bodies were intact. Well, apart from most of their heads being missing.'

'Something high-powered then?'

'Yes. We haven't found the bullets, but I would say a hunting rifle is most likely the murder weapon. The pathologist agrees.'

'Do many people own those round here?'

'Thousands. Mostly for elk,' he added. 'There are over thirty-one thousand licensed firearms in Umeå. Many more if you widen out to *Vasterbötten* County.'

'What do you think, Stella? Do you think they're linked to Brömly?' Oskar asked.

She nodded. 'Hundred percent.'

William continued with the briefing, switching back to Swedish with an apologetic smile for Stella. It didn't matter. She knew what sort of orders he'd be giving. House to house. Search teams. Background checks on the victims. Enemies. Debts. Identify next of kin. But her mind was forming other connections.

Whoever killed Tomas Brömly had also killed the Hedlunds. That made it urgent she speak to Kerstin Dahl. If they thought she was the killer, they needed to bring her in to custody before she could kill Mattsson.

On the other hand, if she wasn't the killer, her life was in real danger. Oskar might want to take her into protective custody. Or at least arrange a safe house.

After the briefing broke up and the teams of detectives and uniforms scattered to their allowed tasks, Stella and Oskar went to see William, who had retreated to his office.

'Brömly's murder is a British case,' William began, still standing. 'But the Hedlunds were murdered on Swedish soil. That means we have jurisdiction. I'm afraid from now on you will need to be accompanied by a Swedish officer at all times. We must keep the prosecutors happy.'

Stella nodded. 'Of course. We need to find out whether Kerstin Dahl or Ove Mattsson have rifle permits,' Stella said as they sat down.

'I already did. Kerstin doesn't but her husband, Josef, does. Ove does, too. So either of them could have done it. Do you still believe your killer could be a woman?'

Stella nodded. 'There's no reason why not. A rifle's an easy weapon for a woman to use. No need for brute strength. No need for close-quarters combat. Not that either of the Hedlunds could have put up much of a fight.'

William shook his head. 'I don't know. I'm struggling with this, I have to admit it. A woman? Really?'

Stella had already come to the same conclusion. Yes, she still thought it could be a woman. But the odds were against it. She thought back to the hard evidence they'd already got. The running shoe print across Brömly's face. The tool mark of the Teng grips. The witness evidence from the girl at the coffee shop. The hair found in Brömly's flat.

The hair was male. The girl said she thought the stranger was a woman. But as her medical condition meant she couldn't recognise faces, that was shaky. The running shoe was of a size that could be a man's or a woman's. The tools said nothing. Nothing pointed conclusively to the sex of the killer.

'If our killer is seeking revenge for being sterilised, then the probability is we're looking for a woman,' she said. 'I've been researching the forced sterilisation scandal,' William winced, 'and female victims vastly outnumbered men.'

'Can you really see a woman doing all this?' William asked.

'I can. And I have,' was all she said.

'What about your other theory? That this is one of the four trying to silence the other three?'

'Then it's either Mattsson or Dahl.'

'Unless there's another member of the group,' Oskar said. 'One we don't know about.'

'But then, why didn't Brömly write to them as well?' William asked.

'I don't know,' Stella said, trying to marshal her thoughts. 'Maybe I'm reaching. Let's stay focused on the original four for now. I need to interview Kerstin.'

* * *

Annika stared at her computer screen. She re-read the news alert that had just popped up. She felt mixed emotions. Pleasure in the death of another of her torturers. And a mounting sense of urgency. Mattsson and Dahl would be taking precautions by now. She had to get her skates on. She snapped the laptop shut with a scowl and went to make some coffee.

32

LONDON

Roisin knocked on the door and entered Rachel Fairhill's palatial office at Scotland Yard. For the second time, she took in the expanse of carpet, the new-looking furniture, the plaques and commendations, and the photographs with government ministers. She imagined how those images might look with her own face smiling out of them. And the captions…

Commissioner Griffin cuts the ribbon on the Met's new headquarters.

From a childhood in rural Ireland, Roisin Griffin now holds one of the most powerful jobs in British policing.

Dame Roisin Griffin at the palace after accepting her award.

Ever since she'd been a girl, she'd been able to daydream while remaining conscious of what people were saying to her. So when Fairhill offered her a seat, she smiled, nodded, and said, 'thank you'. Reluctantly, she let the fantasies fade. For now.

'How was your trip?' Fairhill asked.

'Good, Ma'am. Really good.'

Fairhill smiled. 'That sounds encouraging. What did you find out?'

Ah. Well, now. That was the big question, wasn't it? What *had* she found out? That one of the Met's most senior working detectives was a murderer? Possibly a double-murderer? Of a fellow officer and his wife?

Before she dropped the bomb, Roisin wanted to be absolutely sure she had enough evidence to put Stella not just in the dock, but away. For a long time.

Get it right and the publicity alone would catapult her onto the radar of the most powerful people not just in the Met, but in the places where the policies affecting the Met were made.

Get it wrong… She shuddered. Put it this way, if there *were* any photographs of Roisin in the media, they wouldn't be taken outside Buckingham Palace.

'Slow and steady wins the day, Roisin.' That's what her Da used to say when his fiery-tempered, red-headed daughter was all for charging off all guns blazing.

'I uncovered some evidence that suggests the killer is a police officer,' she said, eventually.

It was true, which helped. It was also vague enough that she didn't have to point the finger at Stella. Not yet, anyway.

Fairhill's eyebrows arched. 'American?'

'British.'

'What kind of evidence?'

The woman in front of Roisin could light the blue touch paper under her career. Or, just as easily, extinguish it for ever. Desperate not to lie to her, Roisin delivered the line she'd worked on during the flight home and most of the previous evening.

'I think Detective Chief Superintendent Collier and his wife were lured to their deaths, Ma'am,' she said. 'I believe the killer had inside knowledge of British police procedures. It's how they were able to get under his guard.'

'Could Lynne have been the target, do you think? With Adam as collateral damage?'

It was a good question. Fairhill hadn't completely sunk into the swamp of admin, finance and politics that consumed so many able detectives once they made the leap into senior management.

'It's possible. But my background research really didn't suggest anything in Lynne's past, or even the last year or two, that would suggest a motive.'

'They lost their son, Theo, some years ago, when he was just a student. Did you know that?'

Roisin nodded. It was one of the first things she'd discovered when she began investigating the Colliers' murder. 'The man who killed Theo committed suicide eight years ago. His wife remarried and is living abroad. I don't see that there's a connection.'

Fairhill's forehead wrinkled and she pursed her lips. 'And do you have any idea who, precisely, this British police officer might be? Or why they might have felt it necessary to pursue Adam and Lynne Collier halfway across the world to murder them in the middle of nowhere?'

'Not at this stage of my investigation, no, Ma'am. Although the Met seems the likeliest force in terms of supplying a possible motive.'

'Oh, well, that's all right then, isn't it? That narrows it down to a mere forty-four thousand people!' Roisin flinched. Fairhill shook her head and frowned. 'I'm sorry, Roisin, that was uncalled for. It's just, this is a lot to process. You've done a fantastic job so far. What do you need from me?'

Roisin spread her hands. 'More time. Your continued support. And, Ma'am?'

Roisin readied herself for the big ask. The one that would give her the freedom she needed.

'Yes?'

'It would be really helpful if you could talk to Detective Chief Superintendent McDonald on my behalf. Tell her I'm working directly under you for the time being. Until the case is solved.'

'You sound confident.'

'I am, Ma'am.'

'Despite the size of the suspect pool.'

'Yes, Ma'am.'

Fairhill fixed Roisin with an X-ray stare. 'And you're telling me everything?'

'Everything concrete, Ma'am.'

'What about what's not concrete?'

'I think it's best not to overload you with every speculative idea, Ma'am. This is obviously a highly sensitive case. The wider ramifications for the Met are losing me sleep,' Roisin said, for once speaking the whole truth. 'I don't want to put you in the position of having to confirm something that might blow up in your face later if I'm off-beam in my suspicions.'

Fairhill leaned back in her chair. She smiled, though Roisin didn't detect much mirth in it.

'A very astute political judgment. One I'd expect to come from the lips of a much more senior officer. Leave it with me. I'll speak to Callie for you. Anything you need, anything at all, you come to me.' She reached into a desk drawer and pulled out a slim black leather wallet and extracted a business card. 'That has my personal mobile. Use it. Day or night.'

Roisin accepted the card with a nod and a small smile, the phrase 'a much more senior officer' as loud as a siren in her head.

'Thank you, Ma'am.'

Fairhill nodded. 'I think you'd better call me Rachel from now on.'

Roisin parked her car beneath Paddington Green and made her way to SIU. She felt like her grin might split her face open and tried to dial it down a little in case people started wondering if DI Griffin had truly lost it.

The general office felt smaller than when she'd left. Then she realised; the whole *operation* felt smaller.

After just a couple of days working with the FBI, her eyes had opened to a world of possibilities that stretched far, far beyond the solving of murders. Even murders of the most horrific kind that were the bread and butter of SIU.

The budget was being cut to ribbons anyway. Would there even be a SIU in a year's time?

She looked around, saw detectives pecking away on grubby

keyboards, speaking into ancient desk phones, wandering about with chipped mugs of disgusting coffee. And she thought back to the crisp atmosphere at the FBI Chicago field office. The place radiated energy. And she wanted more of it.

Yes, she'd been economical with the truth when speaking to Rachel – Rachel! – but it wasn't a lie to say Roisin was protecting her from any fallout if she'd called it wrong.

If? Ha! Stella was as guilty as hell. It was only a matter of time before Roisin could prove it. And then, slap on the cuffs, slam the cell door and call a press conference, ladies and gents, because DI Roisin Griffin has landed the catch of the century.

Callie was in her office. Roisin decided to make the first move. She crossed the room, nodding to Garry who was leaning back in his chair, phone clamped to his right ear.

Callie's door was open, but Rosh knocked anyway.

Callie looked up and beckoned her in. 'How did it go?'

Roisin gave Callie a similar story to the one she'd told Rachel. But she soft-pedalled on the idea that they were looking for a cop.

'AC Fairhill has asked me to stay on it for now. I hope that's OK. I know the recent cuts have left us short-handed.'

Callie groaned. 'Aye, well that's one word for it. It seems murder's just not fashionable these days. All the glory – and the bloody budget – goes to cyber-crime and counter-terrorism just now.'

Roisin nodded. Formed her features into a grimace of understanding and frustration. 'I know. Still, everything goes in cycles at the Met. We just need to wait until someone famous gets murdered then we'll be the flavour of the month again.'

'Sadly, I agree with you, Rosh. And that's a very astute assessment, by the way.'

Roisin smiled. Two compliments on her wider appreciation of Force politics in one morning. She took it as a good sign.

'Is Stella around?' she asked. 'I wanted to update her on where I'd got to in the States.'

Callie rolled her eyes. 'No, and that's another reason we're short-staffed. She's in Sweden.'

'The Brömly case?'

'The very same.'

'Where in Sweden?'

'Stockholm. She's working with an Inspector Norgrim over there. It looks like the murderer's a Swedish national.'

Back at her desk, Roisin launched a browser and started researching flights to Stockholm.

* * *

Rachel Fairhill called a contact in Scotland.

'We may not need plan B after all. Griffin's on Cole's trail. She thinks she's about to make the arrest of the century. I played dumb. She thinks I'm just brass, so far up in the clouds I don't know what's happening on the ground.'

'Where is Cole?'

'Sweden.'

'Cops carry guns there, don't they?'

'Yes, they do. I have a contact over there. I'll make sure he equips Griffin with everything she needs. If Cole decides not to come quietly, we might get lucky.'

'Keep me posted.'

Smiling, Fairhill replaced the handset. Oh, she'd keep him posted all right. And then, maybe, this whole bloody business would be behind them once and for all.

33

UMEÅ

Kerstin Dahl sat beside her husband, Josef, watching the lunchtime news. The lead story jerked her upright. She slopped hot coffee into her lap and cried out.

Josef growled. 'Ssh! I want to hear this.'

He didn't have to worry. Kerstin had no intention of moving from her seat. She ignored the coffee burning her through her light summer trousers. It could wait.

Saskia Persson, the regular newsreader on the midday news, was frowning as she spoke. Normally a pretty young woman, with a professional blonde bob, the serious expression turned her face darker, somehow. It suited the news she was delivering.

'Police have revealed that two residents of Umeå were murdered early this morning. Inger and Erik Hedlund, both former government lawyers, moved permanently to Umeå in their retirement. The senior investigating officer, Detective Inspector William Ekland, said that the couple, who had no known enemies, were both shot to death. We go live to our reporter, Sophie Gyllenborg, from the cottage by Lake *Stenträsket*. What can you tell us, Sophie?'

Standing in front of a white plastic tent that snapped in the breeze, the young reporter assumed a serious expression.

'Thank you, Saskia. I'm standing outside the retirement cottage on *Norra Kullavägen* owned by the Hedlunds…'

As the reporter twittered on inanely, adding nothing but neighbourhood gossip, Kerstin's thoughts were racing around in her head, tripping over their own feet, colliding, splintering into dozens of new ones. All of them bad. She rose from the sofa.

'I need to blot this before it stains,' she said, pointing at the splotch on her thigh.

Josef grunted, but didn't take his eyes away from the screen. She ran upstairs, took the trousers off and kicked them into the corner. Then she sat on their double bed and put her face in her hands.

What was happening? First Tomas, in London, then Inger. Erik, too. It could have been a coincidence. As a government minister in the nineties, she'd had no time for aides or civil servants, or her own ministerial colleagues, come to that, who suggested things sometimes happened for no reason, or out of coincidence.

Tomas, Inger, she and Ove had all taken part in the Project. *No! Be honest, Kerstin, for once in your life!* They hadn't taken part. They had *run* it in Umeå.

Others had taken part. Others who'd worked for, and reported into, the four of them. And they'd all taken care to erase their involvement once Ove had seen which way the wind was blowing.

Ove was always the smart one out of the four of them. As a young, ambitious doctor, he'd manoeuvred his way to the chairmanship of the Coordinating Committee for Racial Biology and Purity in Umeå. There, he'd pursued the Project with fanatical zeal. And they'd all fallen into line behind him.

Kerstin had always feared the day would come when their wrongdoing was exposed. Those bloody hacks at *Dagens Nyheter* had dug and dug and *dug* until they'd uncovered every sordid detail.

But, mercifully, they'd focused their fire on the national politicians. Local and regional functionaries like the four in Umeå had mostly escaped the spotlight.

They'd fled from it, sometimes literally, moving abroad. Or into the great darkness, taking their own lives in shame. Or, as she, Tomas and Inger had, under Ove's calm leadership, into corrupt anonymity, thanks to contacts, bribes and, in some cases, threats. And, for forty-six years, it had worked beautifully.

Then she'd read the news story about Tomas. They didn't keep in touch anymore. Ove had said it was better if they stayed out of each other's lives. But from time to time she used to look up the other three online, feeling her stomach flip with a mixture of guilt and nerves every time one of their names came up on a Google alert.

She needed to talk to Ove. He'd know what to do. Because she and he were the only ones left. And someone they'd – she couldn't bring herself to use the actual word, even now – *treated* had evidently decided it was time for retribution.

She thought she knew why. They must have been watching Tomas, stalking him somehow. Maybe online. They could do anything nowadays. When he'd told them of his intention to confess, the murderer had seen the letter and acted before Tomas became a public figure again. He'd be too visible to kill and get away with it.

The only other possibility was someone who'd been a junior functionary in the Project. She, Ove, Inger and Tomas had taken care to expunge that shameful episode from their pasts, so they were in the clear. But who knew who else had been less successful and now feared public exposure and disgrace?

Josef called up the stairs. 'You all right, love? You're going to miss the weather.'

'I'm fine,' she shouted back, alarming herself at the crack in her voice. 'Just putting some cream on my burn.'

She looked down at the irregular red mark on her thigh. Like a slap from an unseen chastiser. She scrubbed at the throbbing skin with her fingers as if she could wipe it off like ink. Or blood.

Later, after Josef had left for his regular Tuesday afternoon card game with his hunting buddies, Kerstin raised a trembling finger and tapped a number into her phone. She didn't keep it stored in

Contacts. Another one of Ove's smart ideas. But she'd memorised it, along with the others.

His phone went straight to voicemail. She swore, but she didn't leave a message. Something told her it was unwise to leave a record of her involvement in the Project. Even on Ove's phone.

She went downstairs again and poured herself a glass of wine.

Kerstin did not sleep well that night. Her dreams were inhabited by young men and women, hollow-eyed, naked and screaming, clutching their genitalia. One young woman, little more than a girl, really, bony ribs sticking through her skin like a concentration camp victim, came up to Kerstin.

'I want a baby,' she said, over and over again, weeping snotty tears. 'I want a baby.'

She woke at 5.47 a.m. to find her cheeks encrusted with salty residue. Wrapping her summer dressing gown around her, she went downstairs. She made coffee and took her mug into the garden. Sitting in a lawn chair, she made a decision.

Somehow, she managed to get through breakfast. She made Josef his usual oatmeal porridge, adding blueberries and raspberries, his favourite. He looked up from reading *Svenska Dagbladet*, and smiled in appreciation.

'Thanks, love,' he said, picking up his spoon.

Dear, sweet Josef. He hadn't noticed that in place of her own regular breakfast of *knäckebröd* spread thinly with English marmalade, she'd limited herself to a mug of coffee. In truth her stomach was churning so much, she doubted she'd be able even to finish it.

At ten minutes to eight, she got up from the table. She kissed Josef on the top of his head.

'I'm going into town this morning,' she said. 'Do you want me to fetch you anything?'

He shook his head. 'Nothing, thanks. Anywhere special?'

'No. I thought I might see if Gertrud's free for *fika* at ten.'

'OK, well, send her my love,' he said, then returned to perusing the sports section while spooning porridge absentmindedly into his mouth.

* * *

Annika had been planning to confront Dahl at home. Having the husband there to witness it would make things easier, she felt. Less able to blow back at her.

From her car, an ageing, pine-green Toyota Camry, she watched the house through binoculars. She wanted to be sure they were both in before she walked up that neat suburban front path and rang on the doorbell to end their lives.

Then the door opened. Annika started, before realising that she was a good fifty metres away and only the binoculars made the woman she'd pursued all these years seem closer.

Dahl was dressed for town, in pressed trousers and a smart navy blazer with gold buttons. She'd tied a yellow and blue scarf over her hair. How patriotic!

Annika swore under her breath. Now what? Dahl extended her arm towards the gold BMW on the drive. The indicators pulsed. Dahl climbed in. A moment later, she was reversing out onto the road.

Annika started her own engine and stuck the Camry's notchy transmission into first. As Dahl pulled away in the direction of town, Annika indicated and swung out onto the road behind her.

* * *

The police officer on the front desk seemed happy to listen as Kerstin began laying out her enquiry.

'So, you see, because I'm not feeling safe, I really do need to speak to a detective.'

The officer smiled up at her. 'Could you wait over there, please? I'll see if there's someone free to talk to you.'

Kerstin did as she was asked, flicking through the previous day's edition of *Svenska Dagbladet* and trying to slow her breathing, which was speeding along like a horse in a trotting race at *Solvalla* stadium.

'Mrs Dahl?'

Kerstin looked up. A young man wearing a horrid brown suit

was smiling down at her. His long-lashed eyes were magnified by his glasses, giving him an eager, enquiring look.

'My name is Mikael Olin. I'm with the Criminal Investigation Department. Would you like to come with me, please?'

Kerstin followed the detective through a set of double-doors and along a corridor smelling strongly of disinfectant. He turned and smiled at her.

'Sorry about the smell. A prisoner threw up late last night.'

He opened a door and beckoned her to precede him into a small but friendly room. It contained a coffee table and a couple of low armchairs upholstered in a charcoal-grey fabric. It looked stained to Kerstin as she sat, placing her hands flat on her thighs then wincing as the movement rubbed the thin fabric against her burnt skin.

Olin smiled again and took out a notebook. 'Let's start at the beginning. You say you're not feeling safe. Why is that?'

She nodded, smiled and cleared her throat. She tried to remember that, once upon a time, most likely before this kid in front of her was out of short trousers, she'd been a powerful woman.

'It's about the Hedlunds. You know?'

He nodded. 'What about them?'

'I knew Inger.'

He sat up straight in his chair and scribbled a note. The casual air he'd affected vanished, replaced by something altogether steelier. Maybe she'd misjudged him.

'When? How well?'

'Oh, not for a long time. But I knew her very well once. The thing is, I believe she and Erik were murdered by the same person who killed Tomas Brömly in London last month. And I think they might be coming for me, too. I want protection,' she said, trying to inject a note of authority into her voice. 'For my husband, as well,' she added.

He frowned. 'We don't really have the resources to offer protection to members of the public. What makes you think the murders are connected?'

She looked at him. So, now it came to it. Her years of peace were at an end. There would be reporters, gossip, hate-filled glares, maybe graffiti on their home. She'd have to leave social media for good. Social media? Ha! That was rich. They'd have to leave Umeå! Maybe even Sweden. Find somewhere far away to live out their remaining time together.

'Tomas Brömly and Inger Hedlund were responsible for implementing the eugenics programme here in Umeå in the seventies,' she said. 'I think someone they...'

Kerstin paused, suddenly uncertain how to complete her sentence.

His face had changed once more. His lip curled as he spoke. She saw contempt in those cow-like eyes with their long lashes. It distressed her more than she could explain to herself that he made no attempt to hide it.

'Sterilised? Is that the word you're searching for?'

'Yes,' she replied, unable to hold his gaze despite promising herself she would. 'I think someone they sterilised killed them in revenge.'

She felt tears welling up. She reached for a tissue then remembered she hadn't packed one of the little polythene-wrapped packs in her blazer pocket.

'And you know this, how?' he asked, making another note.

He knew. She could see it in his eyes. But he was going to make her say it out loud. To punish her. So be it. God alone knew, she deserved to be punished. She swallowed.

'Because I was involved as well. There were four of us in charge. Me, Tomas, Inger and a man called Ove Mattsson. He was a doctor. He works at the university now, as a Professor of Genetics.'

At the final word, Olin actually snorted. 'Appropriate,' he said. 'To be clear, then. You say that the four of you were responsible for mass sterilisations in Umeå. When, exactly?'

'From 1971 to 1976.'

He made another note. 'And now you believe that, somehow, after all this time, one of those you abused has taken it upon themselves to seek revenge by killing you all? That about the size of it?'

'Yes.' She felt as meek as she had at school when summoned for a 'serious talk' with the headmistress for one of her rare transgressions against the rules.

'I need you to give me a contact number. Preferably a mobile. I'll talk to my boss. He may want to interview you. In the meantime, I'm sorry but I can't authorise any protection. As I said, we don't have the resources.'

She felt panicky. Stars flicked around the edge of her vision.

'But what if they come for me? And Josef? He's done nothing wrong. Surely you can protect him somehow?'

Olin got to his feet and snapped his notebook shut.

'I'm afraid not. Look, if you're worried the best thing you can do is keep to your house. Stay indoors. Don't open the door to strangers. Maybe your husband could get away for a few days. Stay with friends.'

* * *

Annika checked her watch. Dahl had been inside for thirty minutes. Surely she couldn't be taking much longer. She'd be telling some detective she thought Brömly's and Hedlund's murders were connected. It was obvious. It's what Annika would do in her situation. Well, tough. Too late for the first two and too late for her as well. And Mattsson.

The reflections of the birch trees in the plate-glass doors of the police station shimmered and swerved away from each other as the doors opened. There you are! *Time we had a little chat. While we still can.*

Annika grabbed her bag, checked she had everything she needed, then climbed out, slammed the heavy door and locked it. Dahl was looking up and down the street as if unsure which way to go. Annika lengthened her stride.

She was close enough now to pick out the pattern in the headscarf, which Dahl had just re-tied. Anchors and chains and little Swedish flags.

She thought it an appropriate motif for the woman she'd vowed to destroy. The flags for the evil she and her friends had perpetrated in the name of a racially pure Sweden. The anchors for the way the past was about to drag her down.

She came to a stop a metre away from Dahl. Who turned and started as she saw Annika.

Annika reached into her messenger bag.

34

UMEÅ

Kerstin looked down at the object in the woman's right hand and her stomach flipped. The plastic ID card carried the text *Journalistförbundet* – Swedish Union of Journalists. In large capital letters, in English, it said, PRESS. She tried to read the name but the letters swam before her eyes.

'Kerstin Dahl?'

'Yes. What do you want?'

Kerstin's heart was racing. She felt as though she might faint. Her knees were wobbling. She realised she was hyperventilating and tried to slow down her breathing.

'I want to buy you a coffee,' the woman said. 'Maybe a cookie, too.'

If there was something Kerstin wanted less right now than *fika* with this slightly built woman pushing a press card in her face, she didn't know what it was.

'No, thank you. Can you get out of my way, please?'

She moved to walk around the woman but she sidestepped, blocking her way.

Kerstin briefly considered pushing her out of the way, then realised that though slim, the woman looked fit. One of those bloody women who was forever cycling or sailing or playing tennis. Trying to keep age at bay. Whereas Kerstin had long ago given up the unequal fight. And besides, how ridiculous would it look, two old women fighting in broad daylight?

The woman put her press pass back in her bag. She shook her head, never taking her eyes off Kerstin's. Kerstin wished she'd stop staring at her like that. It was unnerving. So very un-Swedish. She looked sad.

'It was my sixteenth birthday.'

'What are you talking about? Get out of my way.'

From somewhere, Kerstin found a shred of courage. She stepped towards the younger woman and pushed her. Pain shot up her right arm. She cried out. The woman had her wrist in a bony grip.

'That butcher Mattsson was so clumsy, I bled for a week,' the woman hissed.

Now Kerstin knew. She felt panicky. Black spots swam in her vision and she really did think she might pass out. She felt the woman leading her away from the police station.

The murderer had come for her at last. The police would find her body and that sneering young detective would have to explain to his superiors how he ignored the plea of an old woman for police protection.

On heavy legs she stumbled along, dimly aware that the woman had transferred her grip. Now she was squeezing Kerstin's hand so hard she could feel the thin bones grinding against each other. She'd have bruises tonight, for sure. How would she explain them to Josef? He was bound to notice.

The woman folded Kerstin's arm up in front of her, still crushing her hand, and held her elbow with her other hand. She felt powerless, propelled along like one of those doddery old dears you saw on the TV in reports on care homes.

A horrible thought struck her. Was *she* a doddery old dear? Is that how a passerby would view her? An old bird with incipient Alzheimer's being taken for a walk by a friend two decades her junior. Out for the morning and a nice spot of lunch together.

'Where are you taking me?' she croaked.

'I said. Coffee and cookies. If you don't want a cookie, have a croissant. Or nothing. I don't care.'

Somehow she managed to stay on her feet. The woman had eased off the pressure on Kerstin's right hand and the pain had subsided. But her grip was still firm and Kerstin had no doubt any attempt by her to free herself and escape would be met by renewed force.

The woman led her to a cafe she'd seen many times but never visited. It looked too studenty for her tastes. *Ask & Embla*, it was called, after the first two humans in Norse mythology.

The interior reflected the theme the owners had chosen for the name. One wall featured across its entire length a beautiful mural of *Yggdrasil*, the tree at the centre of the cosmos, surrounded by the nine worlds.

In niches set into the facing wall stood realistically modelled and painted figurines of the various Norse gods. She spotted Thor with his hammer. A red-haired female with ridiculously large breasts who might have been Odin's consort, Frigg.

'What do you want?' the woman asked, pushing Kerstin down into a chair at a vacant table.

'I'm not hungry.'

'Have a coffee at least. And don't look so worried. I haven't come to kill you.'

Kerstin didn't know that she believed her. But surely she wouldn't try anything in the cafe? Not with half a dozen witnesses. Could she signal to the barista somehow? Or ask to use the toilet then text Josef that she was in danger?

'A latte, please.'

The woman nodded. 'Good. One latte coming up. And please don't think of leaving before I get back. I know where you live and I'll just come to find you there.'

Somehow the woman's words were all the more frightening for having been delivered in such a reasonable tone. Kerstin nodded. Her legs didn't feel strong enough to get her to the door, let alone all the way back to her car.

The woman returned a few minutes later. For the first time, she smiled.

'Table service. It's one of the reasons I like this place. That and the crazy artwork.' She pointed to the mural. 'I know the artist. He's a very talented young man.'

'Who are you?' Kerstin asked at last.

The woman took a sip of her coffee and bit delicately into her *kanelbullar*.

'Delicious,' she said. 'Best in Umeå.' She brushed a crumb from the corner of her mouth. 'My name is Annika Ivarsson. Ove Mattsson sterilised me at University Hospital of Umeå on my sixteenth birthday. Tomas Brömly drove me there in his new yellow Saab. It had black leather upholstery and it smelled of strawberries.'

'What are you going to do to me?'

'I thought I'd interview you.'

'What?'

'I'm writing a lengthy article on the forgotten children of Umeå. Those of us who grew up in children's homes and were sterilised under your bloody rule during the seventies,' she said. 'Mattsson, you, Brömly and Hedlund. Of course it won't carry quite the same punch now the last two are dead, but I've come too far in my research to give up now.'

Kerstin could feel herself relaxing. She had to fight down an urge to laugh, right here among the arty types sipping their coffees and nibbling on cakes and pastries.

'You're really not going to kill me, are you?'

Ivarsson smiled. 'Is that what you thought? No, I'm not going to kill you. Though I hope I can ruin what remains of your lives – you and Mattsson – by exposing you to the glare of publicity.'

Kerstin opened her mouth. Then she clamped her lips. Hold on. Why on earth should she talk to this woman? This *journalist*?

She'd always made a point of avoiding them whenever possible when she'd been a minister, and it hadn't done her any harm in the nineties. Why start now?

She sipped her coffee. Student hangout or not, they made a

lovely latte. As her fear left her, she realised she was hungry. No, not hungry, ravenous.

'I think I'd like that cookie now, please,' she said, smiling sweetly at Ivarsson.

Tutting, Ivarsson rose from her chair and fetched back a double-chocolate cookie from the counter on a white plate with a shiny stainless-steel knife wrapped in a bright-yellow paper napkin.

Kerstin thanked her then made great play of unwrapping the knife, laying the paper napkin on her lap and cutting the delicious-smelling cookie into two equal pieces.

She halved one of the pieces again and popped a morsel of still-warm and slightly gooey chocolate into her mouth. She chewed slowly: the sweetness was punctuated by grains of sea salt and her mouth flooded with saliva.

As she swallowed, she regarded the woman sitting opposite. Perhaps Ivarsson *could* ruin her reputation. But so what? A minute or two ago she'd been convinced the woman intended to murder her.

Kerstin was eighty-one. Three years older than her mother had been when she died. Every year now was a bonus, that was the way she looked at it.

Compared to a life with Josef, free of the illnesses that had robbed her remaining friends of any pleasure in their last few years on earth, she thought she could cope with a few disapproving stares. After all, plenty of people high up in Swedish society, including some very powerful media executives, would be equally anxious to let sleeping dogs lie.

She finished her coffee and stood up, delighted by the newfound strength she could feel in her legs. And the expression on Ivarsson's face was worth all that fear and anxiety. Her eyes, wishy-washy blue in yellowing whites, popped wide. And her mouth opened, revealing grey, uneven teeth.

'Where are you going?' she asked.

'Shopping. By the way,' Kerstin said, turning in the act of leaving the table, 'where are you publishing this…article?'

Ivarsson frowned. There! Kerstin caught it. The first sign of nervousness. She struck.

'You're a freelance! I saw it on your press card. You haven't even sold the story, have you?'

'I won't need to,' Ivarsson retorted. To Kerstin, her voice lacked conviction. 'When I take it to an editor they'll pay me anything for it.'

Kerstin smirked. 'I somehow doubt that. The eugenics story is old news. *Dagens Nyheter* did it to death in ninety-seven. Nobody cares about it anymore. Sweden has moved on. It's such a shame you can't.'

Smiling, and feeling as if she could actually skip out of the cafe, she left Ivarsson at the table. 'See you later, alligator,' she called over her shoulder, not caring that two youngsters sitting by the door grinned at each other as she passed.

By the time she reached home, her earlier confidence had dissipated. What if Ivarsson did find an editor willing to run the story? Even if the nationals wouldn't touch it, she thought the editor of *Västerbottens-Kuriren* would go for it.

She could just imagine the local paper's lurid headlines. 'Eugenics butchers living among us.' 'Hiding in plain sight: the "racial purity" fiends.' 'Former minister masterminded abuse of vulnerable children.'

Even though it was she who'd made up those brief but horrifying lines, Kerstin's heart sank at the last of them. It was true, after all.

Without getting out of the car, she called a number she had memorised long ago.

'I told you never to call me.'

She felt a little of her former steel enter her spine again. She wasn't about to be shafted by a muckraking journalist. Nor was she willing to let Ove Mattsson speak to her like that.

'I don't care what you told me, *Professor* Mattsson. Because unless you're tired of being addressed by that title, I'd shut up and listen if I were you.'

Gratifyingly, Ove's tone changed at once.

'What is it?'

'A journalist just bought me coffee. She's writing an exposé of the Project here in Umeå. She's going in for the kill, Ove. Me,' a beat, 'and you.'

'Shit!'

After a ministerial career rich in invective, Kerstin swore rarely these days. But she permitted herself a brief indulgence now.

'"Shit" just about covers it. I don't know about you, but I do not intend to have what little time remains to me ruined.'

'Agreed. Listen, I'm sorry for speaking sharply a moment ago. Did she say who she was working for?'

'No and that's half the trouble. She's freelance.'

'Name?'

'Annika Ivarsson. Apparently you sterilised her yourself. On her sixteenth birthday, no less.'

Ove paused. She took it as a good sign. It meant he was thinking.

'Leave this with me. I still have some friends in the media. I'll make a few calls. Don't worry, Kerstin, by the time I've finished, nobody will want to touch her story. It'll be radioactive.'

'How? What will you tell them?'

'Never mind. Best you don't know the details. Leaves you in the clear.'

Kerstin ended the call feeling as if she'd escaped an onrushing thunderstorm. Ove had hidden their involvement for almost fifty years. She trusted him to do the same until both of them had died of natural causes. And then, who cared?

35

UMEÅ

Stella and Oskar drove out to the Dahls' lakeside house in possession of a valuable piece of intelligence. The previous day, Kerstin Dahl had entered the police station and requested protection. It gave her an advantage in the upcoming conversation.

Every few hundred metres, a gap would appear in the forest and Stella could see sun glinting off the lake. Here and there she glimpsed yachts and small sailing craft scudding across the ruffled surface of the water.

She pulled off the main road and onto the Dahls' drive. Here was yet another beautiful Swedish lakeshore house: two storeys, with a pretty balcony at the back looking over the lake. This one had been left in a natural timber, which had silvered over the years to a soft, grey sheen.

Parked outside was a big BMW estate car, its gleaming gold paintwork reflecting the trees that towered over the house. From habit, she peered in through the windows, but the cabin was spotless. The only item visible that had not been fitted by the factory was a single bottle of water slotted into a holder between the front seats.

They walked up to the front door and Oskar rang the bell. Stella recognised the opening bar of the Swedish national anthem. It opened immediately. Kerstin must have been waiting for them. Once the introductions were out of the way, Stella asked if she and Oskar could come in.

Attractive now, Kerstin Dahl must once have been beautiful. High cheekbones and a wide mouth. An aristocratic nose, neither too large, nor too small and slightly uptilted. Fine lines fanning out from the eyes that bespoke a lifetime of good humour and pleasant conversation.

Her skin was smooth and plump: no thread veins or leatheryness that would point to one or more bad habits involving alcohol or nicotine.

But today, worry clouded her features. Without any makeup, she looked washed-out. Was it guilt or fear? Stella intended to find out.

'Would you like some coffee?' Kerstin asked as she led the two cops through the house – lots of pine panelling, simple country-style furniture – and into the garden.

'That would be nice. Yes, please,' Stella said, looking at Oskar with raised eyebrows.

He nodded.

In reality, Stella thought she'd maxed out on caffeine a day or so earlier, but conversations in Sweden seemed to go better with mugs of that infernally strong brew in everybody's hands. As she had limited police powers in Sweden, she needed all the allies she could get. If the cost was another sleep-deprived night, so be it. She'd sleep when she got home.

Kerstin reappeared with coffee after a few minutes. Her eyes were red. Had she been crying? Stella resolved to go carefully. She opened her mouth to ask her first question, but Kerstin didn't give her a chance.

'I know why he killed Tomas and Inger,' she blurted. 'I think Ove and I will be next.'

'Why?' Stella asked, feeling that her suspicions were about to be confirmed.

'We ran the forced sterilisation programme in Umeå in the first half of the seventies. I was the vice-regal governor of *Västerbotten*

County at the time,' she said in a halting voice. 'Ove headed the medical team at University Hospital in Umeå. Inger maintained all the legal paperwork. Tomas managed all the logistics.'

Stella's stomach flipped over. Had the elderly woman sitting opposite her at a slatted wooden garden table just referred to the mass forced sterilisation of girls and boys as young as fourteen as 'logistics'? She bit back a caustic remark.

'Go on,' she said, instead.

'Obviously, someone that we…' she hesitated, and Stella had time to wonder what verb she would pick, '…someone whose life we ruined, has waited all this time and now they want to take revenge on us. I understand why, but I don't want to be murdered. I want to find a way to stop them. You have to find them. To arrest them. I'll do what I can to make amends, but you have to find them!'

She uttered the last few words in a rush, the pitch of her voice rising to something approaching a suppressed shriek.

'Tell me,' Stella said, pulling out her notebook, 'do you have any idea who the killer might be? You said "he" a moment ago.'

'No. It could be anybody. There were thousands of them!'

Kerstin's cheeks blanched, then suffused with a blush, as the enormity of what she'd just said hit her.

'Where were you when Mr and Mrs Hedlund were murdered?' Oskar asked.

'Here with my husband.'

'What were you doing?'

'I think in the garden. Pruning, weeding, you know.'

'Did you see anybody besides Josef? Did anybody come to the house?'

Kerstin looked skywards as if hoping for divine help answering the question.

'No. No,' she repeated, shaking her head. Then her eyes widened. 'No, but we saw our neighbours on their boat on the lake.'

'What time would this have been?'

'About eight-thirty? Maybe a little later.'

Stella made a note. 'What are their names?'

'Axel and Jenny Söderström.'

'Do you have an address for them? Or a phone number?'

'I have both. I can get them for you?'

'Let's leave that for now. Do you remember where you were on the second of this month?'

Kerstin frowned. 'Not exactly. I mean, here, obviously, in Umeå. I'd have to look it up in my diary.'

'Not in London?'

'No. Definitely not.'

Something about Kerstin's answers persuaded Stella that she was interviewing a potential victim, rather than the killer. Not just the way she looked her in the eye, but the speed and lack of evasive phrasing. And, after all, would a killer really ask for police protection? It made a little kind of sense as a diversionary tactic, but she didn't see it.

In any case, her alibis would be easy enough to check out. And Stella had already calculated the time needed to get to the Hedlunds' place from the spot where she was sitting.

Given the pathologist's confident – and tight – estimate for time of death, if Kerstin had been at home at 8.30 a.m., she simply couldn't have made the round-trip in time to commit the murder.

'We think there's a chance that the murderer was afraid Tomas was going to confess to his involvement in what he called the Project,' Stella said. 'Which we now know was the forced sterilisation programme in Umeå. I'm assuming you received his letter?'

Kerstin nodded. 'I did.'

'Was there anyone else involved at your level, apart from the four of you?'

Kerstin shook her head. She ran a hand through her tousled blonde hair, which Stella saw in the harsh sunlight was actually a very skilful dye-job. Then she looked straight at Stella.

'You think it's Ove, don't you?'

'Do you?'

Kerstin didn't answer straight away. Instead she looked off to one side, staring out at the lake. Stella followed her gaze. In the distance she saw a couple of white-sailed boats heeling over in the breeze.

'Do I think Ove might be a murderer?' she asked as she looked out towards the lake. Stella waited. 'I suppose he could be. Why not? Is it such a big step from preventing lives from ever starting to cutting them short once they've begun?'

'Do you or your husband own any rifles?' Stella asked.

'Josef owns one, yes. For hunting. Do you want to see it?'

'Yes please.'

'Come with me.'

Stella and Oskar followed Kerstin inside. Kerstin took a key from a varnished wooden board on the kitchen wall and used it to unlock a cupboard behind the door. Standing in a rack beside a pair of knee-boots were two rifles with polished wooden stocks.

'We'd like to take these to Umeå police station and have them analysed,' Oskar said.

Kerstin nodded mutely, flapping a hand in the direction of the rifles.

'Take them.'

It was another tick in the column marked Not Guilty that Stella was building in her mind.

36

STOCKHOLM

Roisin decided to walk from her hotel to the police headquarters on *Kungsholmsgatan*. She'd emailed ahead to let them know a Met detective inspector with a letter of introduction was arriving on their turf. So this was a formality.

The receptionist asked her, in flawless English, who she was there to see. When Roisin told him it was Assistant Police Commissioner Olsson, the young man's eyes widened momentarily. He smiled up at Roisin and nodded.

'I'll call his assistant for you. Please, take a seat.'

His expression said it all. Visiting British detectives were a rarity in themselves. But when one turned up with an appointment to see so senior an officer, that was big news.

Roisin was enjoying the sense of power that came from travelling with not just a letter of introduction from the CPS but also a personal letter of introduction from Rachel.

The receptionist issued her with a visitor pass on a blue lanyard and directed her to a seating group beneath a picture window giving onto the street.

She wandered away from the reception desk and chose an armchair facing the sweeping staircase to the mezzanine floor. The lifts were housed in a short corridor to its right, so, whichever way her host arrived, she'd have advance warning.

She saw a couple of uniformed cops laughing and chatting as they headed out of the main doors. One, the female, was black, the other was a male cop wearing a deep-blue turban. Somehow she'd been expecting that all the cops would be blonde and blue-eyed. Then she realised how stupid that was and reproached herself.

In fact, she saw uniformed officers in as diverse a range of skin tones as she'd become used to in the Met. Plenty of plain clothes too, though that made it hard to tell who was a detective and who a civilian employee, or even a member of the public.

The sharp, efficient click of heels on the gleaming floor tiles grabbed her attention. She swung her head round, already getting to her feet, to see a suited woman of about her own age striding towards her.

Now, here was a specimen of exactly the type she'd been imagining populated the Swedish Police Authority.

Six foot in her heels, pale-gold hair done up in a sleek, pinned style from which not so much as a single strand trailed loose. And eyes of a pure cornflower blue that put Roisin in mind of summer meadows.

On her left jacket lapel she wore an enamelled Swedish flag, its jewel-like panels of yellow and blue the only bright flash of colour in her otherwise sober outfit.

'Detective Inspector Griffin?' the woman asked.

'*God Morgon*,' Roisin said, extending a hand and smiling at her host.

She received a wide smile in return.

'Your accent is very good, but you won't need it. I'm Rebecka Wistrom, APC Olsson's Executive Assistant. Come with me, please. Nik is expecting you.'

If Rachel Fairhill's office was a tribute to how far she'd climbed the Met's greasy pole, APC Olsson's office was an altogether more practical affair. Half the size of Rachel's and crammed with basic, functional furniture, its sole window gave onto a carpark at the rear of the building.

It spoke of a puritanical mission to root out corruption so all-pervading, its occupant couldn't even bear to allow himself the luxury of a view of the park.

A single picture broke up the featureless expanse of beige-painted wall: a photograph of uniformed police officers at some sort of parade.

Rebecka introduced them then withdrew, promising to return shortly with coffee and pastries.

Olsson had the hungry look common to a lot of extremely thin men. His dark eyes seemed to bore into hers as he bade her sit. He wore a crisp white shirt with the sleeves rolled up to just past his bony elbows. On his shirt's button-down epaulettes, black shoulder boards bore the insignia of his rank: a crown surmounting two narrow gold bands enclosing a wreath of oak leaves.

He'd kept his tie on even though, she knew from reading the SPA's Wikipedia page, ties were optional in hot weather. And, Sweet Mary, Mother of God, the weather outside certainly qualified.

'Thank you for seeing me, Sir,' Roisin said, to kick things off. 'Assistant Commmissioner Fairhill asked me to send you her personal regards. She said she remembers fondly the dinner after the Europol conference.'

At this, Olsson's eyes widened and he smiled. The effect was magical. The hungry look disappeared, replaced by a twinkling expression that suggested he was thin because he burned off any spare energy having fun.

'She's lucky. I can barely remember it at all. Send my regards back to Rachel, won't you? And, by the way, before we go any further, no need for all the titles, and "Sir" business,' he said. 'Makes me feel like some stuffed shirt. I'm Nik. Short for Nikodemus. My parents thought it was a good name to live up to.'

'I guess it is. He went to Jesus to discuss his teachings. "Now there was a Pharisee, a man named Nicodemus" John 3:1.'

Nik smiled. 'You know your Bible.'

'I'm a good Catholic girl, what can I say? I had it drummed into me as a young girl.'

'Then do you know John 7:50?'

'"Our law does not judge people without first giving them a hearing to find out what they are doing, does it?"' She smiled. 'Not a bad verse for a cop who investigates other cops.'

It seemed a nice, simple way to draw the conversation around from the pleasantries to the reason she was in Sweden. And in the spartan office of the most senior internal affairs cop in the country.

Because Nik was the head of *Avdelningen för särskilda utredningar* – the Special Investigations Division. Roisin had researched his department before leaving the UK. His and Callie's had such similar names, yet the people they investigated couldn't have been more different.

Serial killers and bent cops. Roisin knew which species of wrongdoer she regarded as the greater danger to society. Despite the lurid headlines when one of the outliers made the news, the average serial killer only murdered three people before being caught.

But a bent cop undermined the whole fabric of the police. They eroded public trust and with it the whole basis of policing by consent. That way anarchy lay and Roisin would have none of it.

She'd been approached before by internal affairs cops in the Met looking for recruits, and had always rebuffed their approaches.

Not because she hated them, as so many of her colleagues did. But because she'd always thought the route to the brass was shorter and more direct through the ranks of CID.

But with the scent of blood in her nostrils and the praise from Rachel and Callie still fresh in her mind, she wondered, for the first time ever, whether she was wrong.

Nik nodded his thanks to Rebecka, who had just placed a tray with coffee and buns in between them on his plain-topped desk. He pushed a mug and plate towards Roisin, then loaded his own with a couple of cakes and bit one in half, washing it down with a swig of coffee.

'Rachel was typically discreet when she called me. Why are you here in Sweden?'

Roisin explained. 'I believe the killer was another serving officer,' she concluded.

Nik steepled his fingers underneath his beaky nose. He regarded her steadily with those close-set eyes, and all of a sudden she saw how he had risen so far in the SPA. Something predatory lay behind them. A hunter's instinct. And she'd just given him the scent.

'And this…officer,' he said, slowly, 'is in Sweden at the moment?'

She nodded. 'They are.'

Nik smiled, a tight grin that, unlike his assistant's, didn't reveal his teeth. Roisin suspected they were sharp. Pointed. The kind to fasten onto something and not let go.

'You said, "they". You don't want to reveal this officer's gender. You play your cards very close to your chest, Roisin, as a good internal affairs investigator should.'

She nodded, finding time to register that upon mentioning her chest, he'd not allowed his gaze to slide over her breasts as most male cops would, unconsciously or not. She sensed she was in the presence of a man for whom work was one hundred percent about professional duty.

She glanced at his left hand, saw a wide gold band on the fourth finger. Doubtless he was as faithful in his marriage as he was in his work. Or was he one of those hypocrites – 'whited sepulchres', Ma used to call them – who preached continence and moral purity in public, then committed all manner of foul misdeeds in their private lives? *Like those disgusting priests with their hands down choirboys' trousers, eh, Ma? You never would hear a bad word about them, now would you?*

'I'm sorry, Nik. Probably just being over-cautious,' she said.

'That's all right,' he said, sipping from his mug and regarding her over the rim. 'But if you were to reveal this officer's gender, I wonder, would it be female?'

He'd surprised her, but she hid it by taking a sip of her own coffee. It was so strong, she felt her pulse jolt as it hit her stomach. Her guts squirmed unpleasantly.

She nodded a second time.

Had he guessed? It was a fifty-fifty call after all. No, of course it wasn't. She didn't know the proportion of female to male officers in the SPA, but in the Met it was just over a quarter.

Nik leaned back in his chair. He looked pleased with himself. 'A female officer with the Metropolitan Police, in Sweden, right now?'

'Yes.'

'Not you, obviously.'

'Obviously.'

'But attached to the same unit as you.'

My god. He knew. She swallowed. Was he going to be an asset? Or had Callie done something to ambush Roisin before she'd even got properly started.

'Yes.'

'So, putting two and two together, which is about the level of my mathematical ability, I am assuming you are investigating Detective Chief Inspector Cole, who turned up here a few days ago on the trail of the murderer of our former ambassador to London.'

Roisin moistened her lips. One thing she doubted about Nik was his false modesty over his maths abilities. She had a strong suspicion he could solve quadratic equations in his head while eating his breakfast. Probably something wholesome. Plain oatmeal. Unbuttered toast. Or, just possibly, raw meat. She made a decision.

'Yes, that's her. For reasons I don't yet know, she followed, or I should say pursued, Detective Chief Superintendent Collier to the US, lured him out to a deserted spot in rural Minnesota and shot him dead, along with his wife.'

The double-murder was a stretch, but he didn't have to know that. All he needed to do was help her apprehend Stella Cole.

Nik rubbed the point of his chin. In the silence, Roisin could hear the faint whisper of his fingertips on the close-shaved skin. He looked at her.

'Obviously, this is a matter for you and your colleagues in the Met. But if there is anything, *anything*,' he repeated, eyes ablaze, 'that you need while you are here, ask.'

The last word came out like an order. He meant it.

Roisin nodded, looking him in the eye. Yes, here was one of those rare creatures, though commoner in some departments than others: the utterly driven cop.

She suspected they could take away his pension rights, dump him in a windowless office in the basement and let the beautiful Rebecka be snatched away by a functionary in Communications or

HR, and still Nik would turn up for work, wearing a tie in ninety degree heat, pursuing his vocation.

'I need a car,' she said. 'And a gun. I brought my Met firearms accreditation with me along with my letter of introduction.'

Nik nodded. He picked up his desk phone and asked Rebecka to come in and take a few notes.

37

UMEÅ

Killing Tomas and Inger was obviously necessary. They were part of the original quartet. Erik was collateral damage and couldn't be helped. His thinking had a nice, closed quality to it.

But now the plan has broken free of its original confines. It's – he doesn't use the word 'spiralling'. Because the next phrase would be, 'out of control'. But if he acts fast, he can seal off the loop again before killing Kerstin.

Tracking down Ivarsson wasn't as easy as he'd expected. She had no social media accounts and her website only listed an email address. In the end, thanks to a little help from a friend in the police, he managed to get her address. She'd been ticketed for speeding five years earlier.

He hasn't put her address into his satnav or phone. He's not stupid. But he has memorised it.

He's been sitting at a pavement cafe opposite her apartment block all afternoon. He's read literally every word in *Svenska Dagbladet*, including the obituaries.

And his patience has just paid off. She entered the building five minutes ago, clutching a couple of bulging ICA carrier bags. So she's just done her weekly supermarket shop and now she'll be inside, putting everything away.

He leaves a bill and some coins on the table under his coffee cup, signals to the waitress that he's leaving and calls a cheerful, '*Tack, tack!*' and crosses the road. As he does, he shrugs on the black raincoat and belts it around his waist. It draws a couple of looks from people crossing in the other direction, but he doesn't care.

He hangs back from the front door, waiting for another resident to appear. Coming or going, either works.

It's a ten-minute wait. He's just starting to get nervous when a young woman with a baby in a stroller approaches from the direction of the shops. She fishes out a key from her pocket and opens the door.

'Here,' he says, stepping forward with a smile, 'let me hold it for you.'

She smiles with gratitude. He's pulled the peak of his cap down low over his eyes but he further obscures his face by the simple move of leaning over to smile at the baby. The baby smiles back and curls its pudgy hand into an approximation of a wave.

She pushes the stroller into the hall, and straight into a ground-floor apartment. While she's occupied opening her own front door, he inches the toe of his right boot forward to prevent the outer door from locking. Now she's gone, he slips inside and waits for the door to click shut behind him.

Lift or stairs? No contest. He takes the lift. He's getting on, and, although fit, wants to conserve his strength for what lies ahead.

Ascending to the third floor, he readies himself. He had to think hard how best to kill Ivarsson. The rifle was out. Urban shootings would draw a full-on armed counter-terrorist squad and he really felt he could do without that.

No, this one had to be close-in, like Brömly. It was a shame he had to dump the pistol in the Thames. With a silencer he could have fabricated in his workshop, it would have been perfect.

In the end the idea came to him while he was polishing the car.

The lift pings and the doors part. He steps out onto the landing, turns left and walks down the hallway to her apartment. Rings the bell.

He strains to hear her and is relieved when he detects her footsteps approaching the door from the other side. He assumes an expression he feels appropriate for the role he's chosen to play.

She opens the door.

'Yes?' she says.

'Annika Ivarsson?'

'Yes. Who are you?'

'I have some information that you will find extremely interesting. It relates to certain events in Umeå in 1973. Can I come in, please?'

The bait works perfectly. He'd thought it would. Picking the mid-point date guaranteed she'd nibble at it. But she's cautious. Rightly so.

'What kind of events?'

'Events that would spell disaster for some extremely well-respected members of the community here. I work at police headquarters in the data department. It's how I know what you're working on.'

Her eyes flick past his left shoulder. She moistens her lips with her tongue. He waits, breathing slowly and evenly. The lie is both vague and, perhaps as a result, convincing.

'Come in,' she says, finally.

From then on, things happen more or less as he planned. He sticks the stun gun's twin terminals against the nape of her neck and presses the button. She convulses like a fish and flops to the floor, giving her skull a hefty smack against the skirting board on the way down.

He closes the door with his heel and pulls the rest of the stuff he needs out of his backpack. Swimming cap, mask, decorator's overalls and gloves first. Then the plastic bag. He stoops beside her in the narrow hallway and slips it over her head, cinching it round her neck with a cable tie, zipping it tight.

While she's suffocating, he moves past her and looks for her laptop. Finds it on the kitchen table. It goes into his bag. Maybe she's uploaded her work to the cloud. But it'll be passworded, and once she's dead nobody will be able to find it anyway.

It takes him ten minutes to find her wallet. He takes the credit cards and the notes, some six hundred kronor in all. It was a mistake not to do this with Brömly. But that was before he'd really thought about what he was doing.

In the bedroom, he opens a wooden jewellery box and takes a few of the more expensive-looking pieces, stuffing them in the bag alongside the laptop. He has no idea if they're valuable. It doesn't matter. They're all going in the lake.

He rifles through her chest of drawers. The top-left drawer is full of surprisingly feminine lingerie. Soft, silky, lacy stuff in pink, cream and black. It doesn't interest him in the slightest, but he strews it around on the bed anyway.

She has a painting by a famous Swedish artist on the wall. He can't remember the name, but he specialises in winter scenes with a birch tree and a Falun-red farmhouse. This one has a grouse in it. He picks up the half-empty jewellery box and hurls it at the picture. A sharp corner pierces the canvas just above the bird's eye.

Has he forgotten anything? He pauses for a moment. Of course! Phone! How could he have missed that? He goes back to the kitchen. The phone's plugged into a charger beside a bowl of apples. Into the bag it goes.

He stands still, closes his eyes and runs through what he's calling his pre-flight checks. The joke amused him when he thought of it, and now, in the adrenaline-soaked excitement of the moment, he barks out a short laugh then claps his gloved hand to his mouth.

He hasn't spilled any blood. The mask will have soaked up any saliva. His hair is contained inside the swimming cap. If he *has* left any trace of his presence in the flat, he doubts the dullards who pass for detectives in Umeå are clever enough to find it.

A final piece of false-trail laying. He returns to the hall, drags the corpse into the bedroom and dumps it on the bed. He pulls the skirt up and drags off the knickers.

He opens her legs. It's a shame he can't leave any semen. But that would run counter to the hygiene measures he's adopted. He clips off the cable tie around her neck and stuffs it, and the plastic bag, into a pocket.

Still, it's not a bad piece of deception. Now it's a robbery-turned-sexual assault that ended in murder.

He checks his watch. Twenty-three minutes, start to finish.

He leaves the flat, closing the door quietly behind him and is strolling down *Dressyrgatan* five minutes later.

38

UMEÅ

Stella spent half the night sitting at the desk in her hotel room, reading and re-reading all her notes on the investigation.

The combined feelings of fatigue and caffeine-induced hyper-alertness were playing havoc with her heart rate. It sped along one minute as if she were having a panic attack, then seemed to disappear altogether the next.

That the sun didn't even start setting until way after ten didn't help matters.

She'd called Johanna in Stockholm and asked her to find out if Kerstin had taken a flight to London in the last month. Then she'd taken Josef Dahl's rifles to the forensics department and asked them to determine if either had been fired recently.

The trouble was, in the absence of the slugs from the Hedlunds' murders, that wouldn't prove anything. Or not beyond the obvious fact, of zero evidential value, that someone had recently fired a hunting rifle in a hunting area of Sweden.

The couple Kerstin had named, the Söderströms, had confirmed on the phone that they had indeed shouted to the Dahls from their boat at around 8.30 a.m. on the day of the Hedlunds' murders.

The evidence was all pointing to Mattsson as the killer.

Unless.

Annika Ivarsson had been quite open that she was writing an article that would expose the men and women who'd sterilised her on her sixteenth birthday.

Stella had seen murders committed on slenderer motives than that. And what better cover for a murderer than to research your intended victims while pretending to write about them?

She checked the time. It was now after one, and she still felt wide awake. Knowing she was closing in on the killer, she knew she should at least try to get some sleep. She had a bath then slid between the cool cotton sheets and closed her eyes.

It felt ridiculous. Lying there absolutely wide awake as if it were the middle of the day not the middle of the night.

Thoughts chased each other round her head, too fast to catch them, powered by planet-sized caffeine molecules.

And then, suddenly, as if the accumulated chemicals keeping her in a state of permanent hyper-alertness had all been metabolised at once, they vanished.

Seemingly seconds later, she opened her eyes. The room was suffused with a pale light from behind the curtains. She felt rested, despite not being able to remember dreaming and therefore whether she had actually slept or not.

She resolved to visit Mattsson and Ivarsson in the morning. If Oskar was busy, she'd drag along one of the other detectives. She frowned, and turned to check the clock-radio by the bedside. The green digits read 4.31 a.m. OK, *later* that morning.

Realising she wasn't going to get any more sleep, she pulled on her running gear and was outside, slipping into a familiar rhythm as she turned towards the river.

She turned left and jogged along a wide tarmac path – *Strandpromenaden* – that tracked just to the south of *Västra Strandgatan*, the wide highway separating north Umeå from its southern half.

As she ran, and her heart and lungs came on song, pumping oxygen-rich blood to her muscles, she nodded and smiled to other early morning runners.

They smiled back, cheerfully shouting '*Morgon*' back.

When a young guy in all-black running gear shouted out '*Hur är läget?*' she was delighted to realise she understood him directly, without translating his question.

How was she?

She was fine. Far from London. Far from Jamie. Far from Roisin. Far from all the shit life had evidently decided to throw at her all at once. Free to focus on the one thing she was good at. Catching murderers.

She smiled back and called, '*Jag mår bra, hur mår du?*' 'I'm good, how are you?'

She ran on, picking up speed, crossing a piece of ground covered with a boardwalk and dodging a couple of dog walkers before turning back for the hotel.

Feeling a little more human after her run, and a breakfast of ham, cheese, hot rolls and tea, rather than coffee, Stella was at the station by 8.04 a.m.

She called Annika's mobile. After ten rings, it switched to voicemail.

'*Hej. Det här är Annika Ivarsson, frilansjournalist. Lämna ett meddelande. Tack.*'

Even with her limited, though growing, Swedish, Stella understood the first part of the voicemail greeting well enough. 'Hi. This is Annika Ivarsson, freelance journalist.' The second half she could translate by context. 'Leave a message. Thanks.'

'Annika, this is DCI Cole. I need to speak to you about the case. Please call me as soon as you can. *Tack.*'

Next she tried Annika's home number. It, too, rang out before playing an identical voicemail greeting. Stella left the same message.

Annika would have answered one of her phones, surely? Freelancers of any kind, but especially journalists, wouldn't want to miss a call, would they? She knew Vicky wouldn't.

Stella frowned. She ought to cut the poor woman a little slack. Maybe she was on the loo. Or putting her makeup on. There could be all sorts of reasons why she hadn't picked up.

As the office filled up with detectives, her restlessness got the better of her and she made her way down to the forensics department.

Compared to Lucian's little empire in Paddington Green, the forensics department here was small-scale. But they'd said they'd fast-track Dahl's rifles for her as the case was so important.

She went over to the female CSI who'd booked in the rifle the previous day. Her name was Alicia, a plain, plump girl in her late twenties. She wore a discreet silver nose-ring and had a tattoo peeping out from under the cuff of her white coat. Something in black and pink that might have been cherry blossom.

Alicia smiled as Stella approached her workstation.

'*Hej*, Stella! We tested the rifles first thing for you. Both have been thoroughly cleaned but I would say not recently. We didn't find any GSR and only the faintest traces of cleaning agents.'

Later that morning, Johanna called her. None of the airlines running flights between Sweden and the UK had any record of a Kerstin Dahl checking in on the dates in question. Of course, that didn't exclude the possibility she'd travelled on false documentation, but really, could Stella see it? No, came the instant answer. She could not.

The ballistics evidence, or lack of it, and the flight records confirmed Kerstin's account and Stella's gut feel. Kerstin was innocent.

She tried Annika again, on both numbers. And got both voicemail greetings again. She didn't leave messages this time.

Something was wrong. She looked around. Most of the detectives were out in the field, knocking on doors. No sign of Oskar. She approached a youngish male detective busy on the phone. He frowned as she approached, and pointed at the handset. The meaning was clear. I'm stuck with this. Find somebody else.

There wasn't time. Bugger protocol.

She headed downstairs to her car. A fizz of nerves in her belly was more than she needed to know she should get herself over to Annika's place urgently.

The apartment block had an entryphone system. Stella buzzed

Annika's flat and waited. Nothing. She buzzed again, for longer this time.

After ten seconds, she pulled out her phone called Annika's mobile again. At the first syllable of the voicemail greeting, she ended the call. She tried the landline. It rang ten times then switched to voicemail.

Something felt off and she wasn't about to hang about. Pulse elevated, and this time not from coffee, she pressed every single button on the front panel in sequence, top to bottom on both rows.

In answer, a handful of voices spoke over each other in a cacophony of Swedish. When they died down, waiting for her to answer, Stella recited a phrase she'd looked up earlier.

'*Det här är polis. Öppna dörren, tack.*'

The latch buzzed immediately. She pushed through and headed straight for the stairs, running up two at a time. On each half-landing a large plate-glass window gave onto the city. Stella had time as she made each turn to look out over the rooftops and wide, straight roads, and the river, sliding sinuously through the middle of it all.

Outside Annika's flat she pushed the door buzzer hard, simultaneously hammering with her fist. She waited for five seconds, hammered again. Another five. Nothing. Shit! This felt bad. Somewhere in her detective's brain, Stella was reassigning Annika from the category of 'suspect' to 'victim'.

'Annika!' she shouted, cupping her hand against the door. 'Annika? It's Stella Cole. Are you there? Can you hear me?'

The door to the next flat along opened and a young, mixed-race guy ambled out into the corridor. A loose grey singlet and flower-printed yoga pants clad his skinny but muscular frame. His wiry ginger hair was teased into an afro and his skin was a pale brown, spattered with copper-coloured freckles. His eyes were pink and she caught the distinctive, herby, sweetish aroma of marijuana.

'I don't think she's in,' he said in a soft voice. 'I haven't heard her at all since last night. Normally she goes out for coffee and she always knocks to ask if I want anything.'

Stella nodded, forcing herself to smile.

'Thanks.'

'Is everything OK?' he asked, moving as if to come towards her.

She held her hand up, palm outwards. 'It's fine. Go back inside, please. This is police business.'

He shrugged. 'Whatever. *Namaste*,' he added, pressing his palms together over his breastbone.

Stella thought for a moment. She could call William and request a method of entry team, or whatever they called the beefy cops with the big red key in Sweden. But that would take too long. And she really, really needed to get inside Annika's apartment.

Muttering, 'exigent circumstances' to herself, and hoping the Swedes looked kindly on foreign cops destroying private property, she reared back and kicked out at the door, just above the lock.

The door held, and all she achieved was to send an electric shock of pain from her heel to her groin. Swearing, she prepared to try again, when the young guy next door reappeared.

He was holding up a key. 'Annika's spare,' he said, laconically, looking at her upper thigh, which she realise she was rubbing.

'Oh. Yes, thanks,' she said, berating herself for not having asked him in the first place. A neighbour who offered to bring you coffee would trust you with their spare front door key.

He stood behind her as she put the key in the lock and turned it. She smelled it as soon as she stepped over the threshold. Faint, but unmistakeable.

A body in the early stages of putrefaction. In time it would deepen and ripen into a stomach-churning odour, like sewage combined with rotting meat. Mistaken by a member of the public, but not an experienced police officer.

She turned to the neighbour. 'I need you to go back to your flat, please. Stay there until I come to talk to you.'

He frowned and scratched at his left shoulder, wrinkling his nose.

'Why, what's happened? Is Annika all right?'

'Just go. Please. I'll handle things from here.'

He nodded, still scratching and left her alone to enter the flat.

Her first job was to locate the body. Because she knew that Annika was dead. And her suspect pool had just shrunk to one.

Inside, she was faced with a narrow, dark hallway, off which led four doors. Three were open, and, as she peered in, she identified the kitchen, bathroom and living room.

The rooms were neither large, nor cluttered, and Stella didn't see a body. Knowing she'd find Annika in the bedroom, she resisted the temptation to rush in, contaminating the primary crime scene in the process.

Instead, she went to the kitchen, and found a roll of plastic food bags in a drawer. She fashioned a pair of crime scene booties, securing them with twist-ties. She put on rubber gloves from the sink and knotted a white tea towel around her mouth and nose. In her improvised CSI gear, she returned to the bedroom.

Annika was lying on her back on a smallish double bed. Her eyes were wide open and her lips were drawn back from her teeth. A dark red line around her neck indicated that the murderer had used a ligature of some kind.

Stella looked down at the dead journalist, and sighed. Without taking her eyes off the corpse, she called William and told him they'd need to muster a full team and start another murder enquiry. 'Linked,' she added.

Now she felt able to consider the scene before her with a clinical cop's eye. Annika's clothes had been pulled around, but it looked staged to Stella. And that word was important.

Serial killers with a sexual fetish would often *pose* their victims. Drawing attention to their breasts and genitals, sometimes in the most disgusting ways imaginable. Or tying them in elaborate patterns of knots, the further to display their humiliation.

But that was from a compulsion linked to their disturbed mind. Annika's murderer had attempted to present her body in a way he imagined was typical of a sex murderer. But he'd got it wrong.

Normally, sex-killers or even the average heterosexual burglar who found himself presented with an opportunity, would yank up a woman's top and pull her bra up, exposing her breasts. Sometimes they'd cut them or bite them or masturbate over them, but Annika's top was snug around her chest with no signs of having been moved.

And although her skirt was rucked up around her hips and her knickers removed, her vagina appeared untouched. No bruising, no bite marks, no blood, no semen on the outside.

Stella shook her head. This wasn't a sexual assault at all. This was someone's idea of what the aftermath of one would look like.

She stood and looked around. An ornate wooden box with a blue-velvet lined lid lay on its side on the bed between Annika's feet. Bright costume jewellery spilled out onto the counterpane. Above the bed's headboard, a painting of a winter scene had been knocked askew. A four-inch-long gash marred the canvas.

She began a methodical walk-through of the flat, and found an emptied-out wallet in the hallway. No sign of a laptop or phone anywhere although there were chargers plugged into the wall by the kitchen table.

All in all, a credible attempt to stage the scene as a robbery plus sexual assault gone wrong. But that's all it was. An attempt.

She heard a shout from the front door.

'Stella? It's William.'

Then footsteps.

She met him in the kitchen and jerked her head towards the bedroom.

'She's in there. She's been murdered.'

He nodded. 'We'll start processing the scene. What are you going to do?'

'I'm not sure. I want to talk to Mattsson again.'

As CSIs, uniformed officers and detectives arrived, Stella threaded her way between them and went back to her car.

This was it. The endgame. Mattsson thought he was being clever, choking off all possibilities of exposure. But he'd been stupid. By eliminating every other suspect, he'd shone a spotlight directly onto himself. She wanted to make sure he'd be at home before driving out to see him, though. Something that would allay his suspicions.

She called Mattsson from her driver's seat.

'*Hallå?*'

'This is DCI Cole, *Herr* Mattsson. I just wanted to let you know that the investigation has moved in a different direction. I had a few last questions for you about Tomas then we'll be able to leave you in peace.'

'I'm sorry, I'm painting, *Detektivinspektor.*'

'I won't keep you from your easel for very long.'

Mattsson laughed. 'I did not make myself clear to you. I'm not painting in the garden. I'm up in the hills. I always do a painting on *Midsommar*. It's a little tradition of mine. I'll be back at eleven tonight. We're having a late dinner then going to the village party. Why don't you come then? Stay for dinner. You'd be most welcome as a guest in our home as well as our country.'

'Thank you. I'll be stopping by just before eleven, then.'

'See you then.'

The rest of the day passed in a flurry of case meetings, evidence reviews and conversations with Malin Holm about the arrest strategy should they decide they wanted to pull in Ove Mattsson for the three murders.

* * *

Roisin slammed her fist down on the desk. She'd just checked flight times from Stockholm to Umeå, only to discover she'd missed the last flight of the day and there wouldn't be another until 8.30 the following morning. She checked her watch: 5.51 p.m.

She went to talk to Nik, and, ten minutes later, was sitting behind the wheel of a three-month-old silver Volvo in pursuit tune with a full tank and plenty of blue lights. According to Google Maps it was a seven-hour drive from Stockholm to Umeå. She reckoned the souped-up engine and the blues and twos would cut that to more like six.

No way was she going to let Stella get away from her. She was in Umeå and that's where Roisin would bring her down.

She turned the key in the ignition, blipped the throttle to produce a satisfying roar from the engine, and pulled out of the space in the carpark onto *Kungsholmsgatan*. She pointed the long bonnet north.

* * *

Oskar stopped by Stella's desk at 7.05 p.m.

'Still here?'

'I'm close, Oskar, I can feel it. I'm going out to talk to Mattsson again at eleven tonight.'

'I'll have to come with you.'

'Fine. If I can get him to incriminate himself, you can arrest him. Game over.'

Oskar grunted. 'I hope you're right. Do you want to pick up a gun from the armoury after all? The paperwork's all been done. We'd just need a signature.'

She shook her head. 'No, thanks. Look at him. He's an old man. I'm half his age and fitter. And I won't give him any reason to suspect he's the one we're looking at.'

Oskar nodded. 'What are you going to do between now and then?'

'Go back to the hotel and order a pizza on room service. Then try to get some sleep.'

'Not doing so well in this northern light?' he asked with a smile.

'I don't know how you do it.'

'Eye masks. And vodka. I'll meet you in reception at ten-thirty.'

At the hotel, Stella ordered her pizza, ate half, washed it down with a miniature of vodka and lay on the bed, fully dressed. She slept fitfully, dreaming of doctors in surgical scrubs and screaming children.

39

UMEÅ

Too much coffee. Too much sunlight. Not enough sleep.

Stella's nerve-endings were sending confusing messages to her overstressed brain. She felt hyper-alert and also half-distanced from reality.

It was 10.28 p.m., yet as bright as day. At least the lateness of the hour had given her a chance to get her head down. But the hotel bed was no more comfortable now than it had been on her first night in Umeå. She'd only managed forty-five minutes of sleep, from which she kept waking in disorientating thirty-second jolts.

Oskar drove through a village where every house was bedecked with flowers and multicoloured ribbons fluttered from a maypole on a central patch of grass. A group of women and girls, aged from five to ninety, walked along one side of the road, wearing white dresses and garlands of wild flowers in their hair. They were laughing and chatting excitedly.

He turned down the forest track towards the Mattssons' place, keeping up a stream of what sounded like Swedish Tourist Board-approved banalities about *Midsommar*. When he started talking about the maypole dancing for a second time, she had to interrupt him.

'What's wrong? You haven't paused for breath for the last five minutes.'

'Sorry. Nervous. Big case. The biggest I've ever worked, actually. Most murders in Sweden are domestic or drug and alcohol-related. I'm under a lot of pressure. Malin told me pretty clearly I have to close this one before anyone else is killed.'

'She's probably got the high-ups breathing down her neck.'

Oskar burst out laughing. 'Breathing down her neck! Like for sex?'

Stella's mouth dropped open. 'No! I mean, watching everything she does really closely. You know—'

Oskar adopted a husky voice he presumably thought was sexy. 'Oh, *Detectivinspektor* Holm, you smell so nice. Can you feel my hot breath on your neck?'

Stella slapped his shoulder. 'No, dummy! It's a perfectly OK phrase in English.'

Still smiling, Oskar shook his head.

Stella checked her watch: 10.45 p.m. The shafts of sunlight flickering through the birch trees gave the forest a dreamlike quality. How could it be this bright, this late?

Clearly the birds were as confused as she was: their songs filled the air. She led the way up to the house and rang the bell. But when the door opened, it wasn't Mattsson behind it.

The man who opened the door was dressed like some sort of pagan priest in a flowing cream smock that reached to mid-thigh over white trousers. His feet were encased in leather sandals. Around his neck he wore a flowered wreath.

He looked to be in his mid-sixties. His hair, dark-brown with just a hint of silver at the temples, was cut in a fashionable style and showed no signs of receding. His eyes were a clear blue, almost turquoise, flecked with hazel.

She introduced herself and Oskar. After checking he spoke English, she switched languages.

'I was looking for Ove Mattsson,' she said.

'Ove's out at the moment, but I'm expecting him back very soon,' he croaked. He touched his neck and smiled apologetically.

'Sorry. Sore throat. We had a long, long choir practice at church yesterday.' He gestured at his smock. 'We're celebrating *Midsommar*. We always dress up and have a nice dinner. Please, come in.'

As they followed him in, she frowned. Was Mattsson gay? Why should that matter? It didn't. Not to her personally. But her cop brain was firing erratically.

She wished she'd been able to get more sleep. Her mind felt simultaneously full of fluff and over-stimulated by all the weapons-grade coffee she'd consumed since arriving in Sweden.

'Do you know when Ove will be back?' she asked.

Sigge rolled his eyes. 'Ove loves his rituals. He'll be back at eleven precisely to present his painting. Sometimes I think he waits down the lane so he can time it properly.'

He took her through the house and into the garden, where a table sat on the terrace laid for dinner.

He looked over his shoulder. 'I have a lot to finish in the kitchen,' he said, in a half-whisper. 'Please make yourselves comfortable.'

Stella leaned back in the chair and surveyed the water. The sun glittered off its mirror-smooth surface.

Unlike earlier, Oskar seemed to be in no mood for conversation, which suited her fine. They sat in silence, each lost in their own thoughts.

The plan in her head was simple. Push Ove on the eugenics question. Rattle him. Ask him again about Brömly's letter. Wait for a misstep. Pounce. Accuse. Push harder. Arrest.

Would it be that simple? Her thoughts were simultaneously filled with certainty and muddy from lack of sleep. Over-stimulated by caffeine and disorientated by the never-ending sunlight.

She stared at the lake. A woman on a paddle board raised an arm and waved at her. She looked familiar. Cropped blonde hair.

She felt a snap inside her head. Had she drifted off? She looked sideways at Oskar. He was checking his phone.

His radio crackled. A panicky voice spoke in rapid Swedish. She caught two words, though. It was easy because they were the same as in English: *Islamist* and *terrorist*. Oskar pulled it off his belt and answered, too quickly for Stella to translate.

His face drained of colour, he turned to her.

'There's been a terror alert in Umeå. They're recalling everyone.'

'What about me?'

He shook his head. 'Stay here. Just ask questions. I'll call you when I know more.'

He ran back up the garden and, seconds later, she heard the car's engine race and tyres spinning in the loose gravel in front of the house.

At that moment, Sigge reappeared carrying a tray bearing two cups of coffee and a plate of *kanelbullar*.

He looked around and frowned. 'Where is your colleague?'

'He had to go. Something came up. But I'll be happy to talk to Ove on my own.'

'Oh well, if you're sure. Try the *kanelbullar*.'

She picked up a bun and nibbled off a piece.

As she chewed the warm doughy treat, she experienced the familiar taste of cinnamon, sugar and dried fruit. Then her front teeth closed on something hard. She bit down and it released a herby, aniseed, almost soapy taste. What the hell was it?

In a flash, her memory fired up.

The waitress at Kafé Valhalla had said the unidentified Swedish customer mentioned that her husband liked the *kannelbullar* baked with caraway. Without the ability to recognise faces, had she taken Mattsson for a woman?

'What is that extra flavour I taste?' she asked, wanting to hear it from Sigge's lips. 'Is it cumin seeds?'

'Caraway. Do you like it?' he asked, then winced and touched his throat again.

Stella nodded and smiled.

'It's nice. Unexpected, but nice.'

Her next question came to her out of nowhere. Or not precisely nowhere. From that instinctive part of her brain that had, over many years, become honed to a sharp edge and supplied insights before she was aware of needing them.

'Did you make them?'

He nodded. 'Ove is many things, but a cook he is not.'

She lifted the little cinnamon bun up. 'Does he like these?'

Sigge smiled. 'Loves them.'

'How about you?'

He waggled his head from side to side. 'I prefer the regular kind, to be honest. The caraway is a northern thing: from Kiruna. Ove was born there. His family moved here when he was still a baby.'

Her mind whirling, she needed somewhere quiet to straighten out her thoughts before Mattsson returned home.

'Can I use your bathroom, please? I've been drinking so much coffee since I've been here...'

Sigge laughed, then winced again. 'Come with me.'

She walked with him for the terrace to the house and into the kitchen. It smelled deliciously of bread baking. He pointed towards the hallway.

'We have a toilet off the boot room,' Sigge said, before reaching for an apron and tying it round his waist.

The boot room was decked out with low, slatted pine benches on two of its sides.

Arrayed in neat rows were pairs of every imaginable kind of footwear, from wellingtons to walking boots and boat shoes in several shades of brown, from tobacco to a pale caramel. Plus long, narrow cross-country skis, fishing waders, tennis shoes and several pairs of gaudy running shoes.

She glanced down at the running shoes. One pair caught her eye. Bright orange, they bore on their tongues a logo: an orange insect.

Looking over her shoulder to check Sigge was out of sight, she squatted and picked up the shoe. The brand was the same as Lucian had shown her: Icebug. She turned it over and felt her heart stutter.

The sole pattern was the same as that impressed on Tomas Brömly's face. Hexagons, interspersed with metal-tipped studs. She replaced it and darted into the guest bathroom and locked the door.

She pulled her jeans and knickers down and sat on the lavatory, eyes closed.

The 'woman' in the cafe back in London had said 'her' husband loved the *kanelbullar* with caraway. But Natasha couldn't recognise faces, instead relying on other cues such as clothing and voices.

So it was entirely possible she'd been talking to a gay man. And although Ove loved the taste of caraway seeds, Sigge did not.

So was it Sigge who'd gone to London and murdered Brömly after all? Not one of his former colleagues, but one of their husbands? It fitted. And motive was staring her right in the face. Perhaps the oldest motive of all. Love.

Brömly was threatening to expose Hedlund, Dahl and Mattsson. The disgrace and, in the social media age, outpouring of hatred and death threats it was sure to cause, would have driven a Volvo SUV through their happy domestic setup.

All it needed was for Sigge to have read Brömly's letter. He didn't even need to have told Ove what he was planning. He could have made an excuse for the trip or just lied and never told Ove he was travelling abroad at all. He was younger and fitter than Ove, too, making the business with the tongue easier to believe as well.

She inhaled deeply and sighed it out again. Scrubbed at her eyes. She consulted her emotions.

Was she frightened? No. Not at all. She'd dealt with far more dangerous characters than Sigge, or Ove for that matter.

He'd shot Brömly in the back and the Hedlunds from long range. Only Annika had been murdered in any way that required a degree of physical strength.

But Annika was in her sixties and while she looked healthy enough, she was smaller than Sigge and undoubtedly less fit. A life behind a desk pecking at a laptop's keys was no preparation for a struggle with a bigger man intent on murder.

No, Stella was confident she could outwit and, if necessary, outfight Sigge Svensson or Ove Mattsson. Hell, she thought with the amount of caffeine coursing through her veins, she could probably take them both on at the same time.

A giggle threatened to burst from her lips and she coughed to hide it in case Sigge was within earshot.

And what about the terror alert? It could have been genuine. But the timing was just a bit too perfect. Just as she and Oskar arrived to interview and potentially arrest Ove, his adoring husband disappears and ten minutes later the call goes in to Umeå's cop shop.

If Sigge was trying to improve the odds, he'd sent the wrong one of them on a wild goose chase.

No, this was only going to go one way. All she needed was to find a single piece of evidence compelling enough to justify arrest and she was home free. She could accept Ove's earlier invitation to stay for dinner, wait for Oskar to return and then give him the nod. Because he would return. She'd no doubt the alert was a hoax.

After relieving herself, she washed her hands, taking her time while she got her thoughts in order.

The CSIs would need to make and compare prints to ascertain whether the wear pattern on the shoe outside the little room in which she was standing matched that from the crime scene. But she was sure in her heart they'd be a perfect match. She dried her hands and unlocked the door.

In the kitchen, Sigge was arranging slices of gravlax on a plate. Stella caught the strong aroma of the dill leaves pressed into the edges of the translucent slices of cured salmon.

She saw antique china dishes in white, pale blue and yellow piled high with potato salad, pickled herrings and various salads.

'You've got enough there for a lot more than three, Sigge,' she said, watching him for any sign he might suspect she was onto him.

He turned, smiling. 'I can't help myself,' he croaked.

To Stella, he seemed utterly unconcerned by her presence. She didn't have him down as a psychopath, able to conceal what limited emotions he possessed behind a veneer of calm. So if he looked unconcerned it was because he *was* unconcerned.

He had a full shot glass of clear liquid by his elbow. Good. The more he drank, the easier he'd be to control.

Sigge beckoned her closer and cut a triangle of the cured

salmon. He offered it to her on a small square of dark-brown bread. She popped it into her mouth. Complex flavours of salmon, dill and picking spices washed over her tongue.

She nodded her appreciation as she chewed and swallowed.

He took a sip from his glass. 'It's a family recipe. Passed down for generations,' he said hoarsely. 'The Svenssons are pure-blooded Swedes back to the time of Håkan the Red.'

Bloody hell! Was he teasing her? Dangling the idea of racial purity in front of her like that. If he was, he was bloody confident. Maybe over-confident.

'Well, they deserve a medal,' she said. 'It's delicious.'

He smiled again. 'As it's Ove you've come to see, I'll let you wander the garden till he arrives.'

Taking the hint, and glad of the space to think, Stella walked down the lawn to look at the lake. A couple of boats were out and a flock of white birds wheeled and dipped over the water, emitting long, drawn-out cries as they skimmed the surface.

40

UMEÅ

Stella checked her watch. It was five past eleven. Mattsson was late, but presumably he'd arrive home at any minute. She desperately wanted something strong enough for her to arrest Sigge on the spot.

In fact, for safety's sake she thought she'd be better off arresting the pair of them.

She wasn't sure of Swedish law, but in the UK she'd have good grounds for arresting him as a suspected accessory to murder. And if he turned out to be innocent, well, he could be released, possibly with a police apology.

She'd researched citizens' arrests and discovered the law in Sweden was much the same as in Britain. As long as she had good reason to suspect he'd committed a crime, it was enough.

So there needed to be an outstanding arrest warrant. She thought Oskar would probably help her out there. He'd said it was his biggest case to date. Well, it wasn't hers, and she knew all about bending the rules to deliver a suspect into custody.

She turned and walked back up the lawn. At the side of the house she saw a wooden outbuilding.

Wondering if she might find a gun cabinet in it, she took a quick look towards the kitchen door. Sigge was bent over the work surface, busy with a knife.

She strode across the grass, stepped right over the gravel path between the house and the outbuilding and went round to the front. The double doors told her it was a garage. There was a side door as well. She tried the handle and it opened on silent hinges.

Sunlight streamed in through the windows, picking out dust particles that floated in and out of the pale yellow beams and revealing the curved contours of what appeared to be an old rally car.

Painted a deep shade of cherry-red with a white roof, it bore a large white roundel on the driver's door enclosing a black number 62. She checked out the front end: a Volvo. Not a scrap of rust anywhere that she could see.

She skirted its curved rear end, looking out for anything that might contain a rifle. A wooden workbench ran along the whole of the back wall. Above it, tools outlined in white hung from a pegboard panel.

In a dark corner where the sunlight didn't reach, she saw a long, narrow, vertical steel cabinet bolted to the wooden frame of the building. Inside, she knew, would be a hunting rifle. Most likely a high-powered hunting model with the sort of high-calibre rounds capable of bursting a person's head like a melon.

She cursed the CSIs for not being able to find either of the slugs Sigge had used to kill the Hedlunds. It was unfair, she knew. They might be in the lake. Or buried in the leaf litter in the birch forest fringing the property.

Would the rifle have Sigge's prints on it? Possibly. In fact, almost certainly. He'd be clever enough, surely, to leave them there. After all, whether the rifle was his or Ove's it would be the most natural thing in the world for him to claim he'd used it recently.

'Of course,' he'd say, when questioned. 'I was out hunting yesterday.'

And if he had GSR on his hands, the same answer would suffice.

She looked under the bench and felt her pulse jerk upwards. She was looking at a red metal tool trolley. She drew it out from under the workbench and lifted the lid.

Staring out at her were two glaring yellow eyes beneath devilish black eyebrows. Teng Tools. Another match with Lucian's findings.

She pulled out the top drawer. Screwdrivers nestled in recesses. The shafts gleamed. Not a speck of oil or dirt on any of them. She tried the next drawer down. Here were the sockets: gleaming chromed cylinders in ascending size order, from tiny pieces the size of 9mm rounds to giants as big as cotton reels.

She slid it back in on greased roller bearings and reached for the third drawer. This one was deeper. It resisted her at first, so she applied more force. With a metallic screech, it shot open. She looked round guiltily, aware she was almost certainly breaking Swedish law by searching uninvited without a warrant. Too late to go back now.

Stella looked down and nodded with satisfaction. Here they were. The variously sized grips without which no car mechanic could practise their trade.

She glanced over her shoulder then back at the drawer. All the shaped slots were filled. She ran her eye over the sizes. The killer had used a twelve-inch pair on Brömly. Obviously he wouldn't have taken his own. But he'd bought ones in London he was familiar with.

She picked up the grips. They fitted her hand comfortably. She opened and closed the jaws, wondering as she did so how Sigge had felt when he used an identical pair to tear out Brömly's tongue.

She heard a car pull up outside. Footsteps on the gravel. Squaring her shoulders, the grips still clutched in her fist, heart thumping, she turned towards the door. She'd have preferred to deal with Sigge alone. Restrain him somehow, before arresting Ove. Now that option had disappeared.

'*Hallå? Vem är där inne?*' Mattsson demanded loudly. Who's in there?

He was standing in the open doorway, a look of puzzlement on his face.

In that moment, her last shred of doubt that Sigge had

murdered Tomas Brömly vanished. Ove's voice didn't fit the description provided by Natasha from Kafé Valhalla in London.

Though it was high for a man, there was a rough undertone that marked it as masculine. A girl who habitually relied on voices to remember people wouldn't be fooled into thinking its owner was female.

'Is that you, Detective Inspector Cole?' he asked in English.

She hadn't planned it this way. But now he'd discovered her snooping around in his garage, her plan had collapsed. She'd arrest him first, then find a way to get to Sigge. She walked around the car to him.

'Ove Mattsson, I am arresting you for being an accessory to the murders of Tomas Brömly, Inger and Erik Hedlund and Annika Ivarsson.'

His eyes flash-bulbed.

'What? This is madness! I didn't murder Tomas or Inger or anyone else.'

Here it was. Her chance to get leverage with Sigge. All it required was the right pressure.

'Brömly was going to expose your role in the sterilisation programme here in Umeå. His face bore the imprint of a running shoe exactly like the one in your boot room. His tongue was pulled out with a pair of grips like these,' she said, holding up the Tengs for him to see.

'But, I don't run. I'm too old for that. I paint. They're Sigge's shoes. So are the tools. He uses them on the Amazon there,' he added, pointing at the red-and-white Volvo.

Stella caught the crunch of gravel. Sigge appeared in the doorway behind Ove. He no longer wore an apron. He was holding a small black pistol. His eyes were dark. And he was no longer smiling.

Ove turned and his mouth dropped open. 'Sigge?'

His eyes never leaving Stella's, Sigge smiled.

'There's gravlax and potato salad in the kitchen, darling,' Sigge said. 'Could you put it out on the table for me, please?'

The croak had disappeared, along with Sigge's friendly

286

demeanour. Stella heard the true voice beneath the faked sore throat.

A lighter tone than most men's.

Smooth.

Womanly.

She had her murderer. But he had a gun aimed at her head.

'What are you doing?' Mattsson asked. 'And where did you get that pistol?'

'Now, please,' Sigge said. 'I need to talk to her alone.'

Stella removed her hand from Ove's shoulder, keeping her eyes fixed on the muzzle of the pistol in Sigge's hand. His face unreadable, he turned away from her, squeezed past Sigge and disappeared around the edge of the doorframe.

Sigge watched him go. Which was a mistake.

Stella rushed Sigge, swinging the heavy grips down at his gun arm. He screamed. The pistol fell from his hand and skittered under the Amazon.

She spun him round by the shoulders and kicked the back of his right knee.

He yelped as his leg folded beneath him. Stella shoved him hard between the shoulder blades, sending him sprawling to the concrete floor.

She bent over him, going for his right hand, intending to hold him down until she could free her phone to call Oskar.

She looked down at her pocket for a second. That glance meant she didn't see Sigge's left arm come up holding a length of steel pipe.

He swung it over his head and smashed it against her temple. As dark curtains swung across her vision, and her head exploded with pain, she saw him run.

* * *

The lake was freezing. Adam was pulling her down by her ankle.

'Join us, Stella,' he said, bubbles rising in a swirling column from his tongueless mouth. An eel wriggled out of the hole in his forehead and swam away.

Lynne grinned up at her. The fish had removed all the flesh from her skull.

'Yes. Come on down. The water's lovely.'

Stella screamed. She kicked Adam's hand away and struck out for the surface.

Gasping for breath, Stella popped out of the freezing water like a fishing float.

A hazy shape above her resolved into Ove's face, creased with concern. He pursed his lips as he sponged more cold water onto her forehead.

'Thank god. I thought he'd killed you,' he said.

'How long have I been unconscious?'

'It can't be long, I think. I came back when you and Sigge didn't join me. I thought there must have been a mistake,' he said. 'A practical joke of some kind, for *Midsommar*. Sigge loves them.'

'How long, though?' Stella asked again, wincing as he dabbed at her left temple.

'I don't know. A few minutes. No more than that. Please tell me. What's going on?'

Stella sat up then cried out as a blinding flash of pain speared through her head from her left temple.

'Can you help me up, I need to call someone.'

Mattsson helped her to her feet and together they stumbled back to the house. He dragged over a chair for her to sit in at the kitchen table.

She called Oskar.

'Stella. What's going on?'

'It's not Mattsson we want. It's his husband. His name's Sigge Svensson. He knocked me out then ran. You're looking for a sixtyish white male. Slim build, short dark hair with a bit of silver. Blue eyes. He might have his arm in a home-made sling. I think I broke his wrist.'

'Are you OK?'

'I'm fine. I've got a goose egg on the side of my head but I'll live.'

'Stay put, yes? I'll get everyone on this. I'll get there as soon as I can. I'm sorry for letting you go alone.'

'It's not your fault. It was supposed to be a quiet chat.'

During this conversation, she'd watched Ove's face. His expression revealed utter bewilderment. She'd seen it before. People suddenly confronted with a completely different truth about their spouse to the one they'd believed in.

His eyes searched hers: she knew what he wanted. Reassurance that it was all some dreadful mistake. A mix-up. Sigge wasn't a murderer. How could he be? He played tennis and went for early morning runs. Baked. Prepared delicious *Midsommar* feasts.

'I have to go. Stay here. Do not leave the property,' she said, gritting her teeth against the fresh wave of pain that washed up against the backs of her eyes. 'If he contacts you, or comes back, don't do anything to antagonise him.'

'But, where are you going? How can this be happening? Sigge's a good man.'

'I don't know. Hopefully, I'll have answers for you soon. Have you got any painkillers?'

He nodded. 'Paracetamol, ibuprofen?'

'Anything stronger?'

'There's some codeine in the bathroom cabinet.'

'Those, please. Double dose.'

'That could be dangerous.'

'I'll take the risk.'

He left, reappearing a few minutes later with four white tablets. He ran a glass of water from the tap and handed it to her along with the pills.

She swallowed all four at once, gulping down the water.

Holding the edge of the table and bracing for the pain, she took a deep breath and then left the house by the front door.

Outside she kept her breathing slow and regular and found that the pain had eased off a little as the codeine kicked in.

She looked at the track leading away from the house. He must have taken it. Where else could a fugitive run to? The woods? He'd be found easily. No, he would have run up the track and headed for the village.

She set off at a gentle jog-trot, ignoring the throbbing that came and went behind her eyes, grateful that it was reducing in severity. She picked up speed, taking heart from the scuffed footprints she saw between the wheel tracks each side of the narrow track.

As she neared the village, she heard music. Violins and an accordion. A drum being beaten heartily in a simple one-two-one-two rhythm.

Children's laughter and high-pitched squeals came next.

And then she saw him. In the distance, just on the outskirts of the village where the first wooden houses, Falun-red with white gables, appeared each side of the road.

41

UMEÅ

Bare-chested, Sigge was limping badly, dragging his right foot. The ankle looked grotesquely swollen. Inflated somehow.

She realised he'd bound it with material torn from his smock. He must have sprained it running on the uneven track. He'd have had to stop to strap it up and that's why she'd been able to catch him. His right arm hung uselessly at his side.

'Sigge Svensson!' she yelled. 'Stop! *Sluta!*'

He looked at her and then turned and hobbled on. She ran faster, oblivious of the pain. Because she'd seen a black object in his left hand. The gun. She hadn't thought to check whether he'd left it beneath the car and now she didn't need to.

Cursing her carelessness, she accelerated into a sprint. And then a sound pierced the forest. A young girl's scream. High-pitched like the others, but this time wound around a vibrating core of pure fear.

The first scream was joined by another, and another. She knew what had happened.

Sigge had come amongst some of the village girls, who were expecting nothing from this night but dancing, drinking and being admired for their flowered head-dresses, and he'd terrified them. Maybe even grabbed one.

Men were shouting, and women's screams joined those of the girls.

Stella reached the edge of the village and sprinted into the centre of the crowd. People were running in all directions, and the flower-girls were running towards her, their faces taut with fear.

A gunshot tore through the noise, immensely loud in comparison to the screams, which redoubled a moment later. She ducked, then straightened, looking for Sigge.

In front of her, a young girl in her early teens, blonde hair braided under her wreathes of cornflowers, ivy and daisies, toppled to the ground, blood streaming from her arm. It looked like a flesh wound. It would hurt badly, but she'd live. Two women ran towards the fallen teenager.

Stella ran on after Sigge, who she could see limping away on the far side of the crowd.

He turned and fired again. Everyone but Stella threw themselves to the ground. It was so unified a movement it looked choreographed.

She waved for them to stay down and shouted the order in Swedish for good measure: '*Polis! Stanna nere!*'

Stella leaped over prostrate figures, parents clutching children, couples lying together, their arms over each other's heads, never taking her eyes off Sigge.

He turned and fired wildly. Now Stella did dive for cover as he emptied the magazine.

Bullets whined overhead. One struck a birch tree just a foot from Stella's left ear. Bright splinters of wood flew out, one smacking against her cheek and opening a cut.

She heard the distant click as the hammer hit an empty breech, and jumped to her feet.

Sigge threw the gun aside, turned and broke into a shambling run. Then his legs gave under him and he fell to his knees. He was done.

Maybe he was a decent runner when fed, hydrated, fit and

healthy, wearing the correct footwear and dressed for it. But he was badly hurt, wearing sandals, carrying more than a few glasses of the local firewater inside him, and panicking.

Stella reached him a few seconds later. She knocked him sideways to the ground. She pulled his arms behind him, drawing a scream as she gripped his damaged wrist. It couldn't be helped.

She dragged her belt out through the loops and cinched it around his elbows. Tight enough to immobilise the joints and prevent his attempting to use his hands. Not that he looked in any state to consider running again.

Kneeling beside him, panting, she uttered her first-ever Swedish arrest script. It was short, and she wasn't sure of her accent, but she was certain he'd get the message.

'*Sigge Svensson. Du är arresterad. För mord.*'

Stella heard the roar of a car being driven at top speed and looked up. Seconds later a grey Volvo, blue lights flashing, burst into the village square and skidded to a stop a metre away from her. Sigge lifted his head then let it drop into the dirt.

Oskar climbed out of the car, pistol drawn, and rushed round the front of the car to where Stella knelt with her right hand holding Sigge down.

Before Stella could say anything, Oskar snapped a pair of cuffs home, drawing a howl of pain as the steel bit into Sigge's broken right wrist.

Oskar recited the formal caution in Swedish.

'I think I broke his wrist,' she said. 'You might want to loosen the cuff.'

Oskar nodded, unlocking the right cuff and then leading Sigge round to the side of his car where he folded him into the back seat and cuffed him to the door handle.

Back with Stella he peered at her and stretched out a finger to gently touch her cut cheek. 'You look like shit,' he said with a shaky grin.

'Thank you so much, Oskar. What happened in town?'

'Hoax call. We swept the entire city centre. They're still searching, but Malin released me.'

'I think it was Sigge. He was trying to buy time.'

'Tell me what happened,' he said, leaning on the bonnet of the car.

She sketched in the details, explaining she'd left Ove back at the house with instructions to stay put. Oskar nodded as she outlined each decision she'd made and her rationale for making the citizen's arrest.

When she finished he said, 'Want to hear something interesting about our Sigge Svensson?'

'Go on.'

'He's a member of a far right political party called *Svenska Renhet*. Know what that means?'

'Swedish something?'

'Swedish Purity.'

'Is that the connection between him and Mattsson?'

'I don't know. We'll get into all of that when we interview him,' he said. 'I need to get him back to book him in, but we shouldn't leave Mattsson alone.'

'It's fine,' Stella said. 'You take him in and I'll help out here then get back to the house. He shot a young girl at the *Midsommar* party, too. Flesh wound. You might want to add that to the charges.'

He nodded. 'I'll see you later. Good work, by the way. Looks like you caught the murderer.'

Stella offered a tight smile in return. She wanted to talk to Mattsson. Find out what, if anything, he knew about his husband's actions.

She found him in the garden, sitting by himself at the table laden with *Midsommar* treats. None of the food appeared to have been touched, although a bottle of clear liquid by his right elbow was a third empty.

As she walked up to him, he turned red-rimmed eyes in her direction and saluted her with a raised shot glass. He downed it in a single swallow and immediately refilled it from the bottle, slopping some onto the tablecloth.

'I love him,' he said as she sat down at his left elbow. 'I thought I knew him. Now,' he waved his arm around in a vague sweep she supposed was meant to encompass the wreckage of his life, 'all this.'

She felt for him, this old man with an evil past. She was only human, after all. As, she was forced to admit, was he.

Not a monster. Nor a psychopath bent on causing as much pain and suffering as he could manage. Just a human being, who had once committed atrocities in pursuit of a purer Sweden.

How ironic that Annika had wanted to ruin his life and his beloved husband, Sigge, had done it after all.

'Did you know what he was doing?' she asked him.

Without meeting her eye, he shook his head. 'No. He runs his own business. He is a corporate head-hunter. He travels a lot. And he's much more active than I am. Tennis, running, you know? He goes out, I don't see him for a while. I just read, or paint.'

'How did he find out about Tomas's plan to expose you all?'

'I don't know. You will have to ask him that. He probably found the letter in my study.'

'What about Inger Hedlund?'

'I don't know that either. She came here to see me. I, I might have said something that night. I'm not sure. I have a little problem with alcohol,' he added, tipping the glass into his mouth.

'And Annika Ivarsson? The journalist who was researching what you four did back then?'

He shrugged, refilled his glass and drained it. 'Kerstin called me. She said Ivarsson had been to see her. Maybe Sigge listened in on the conversation. It was on the landline. Maybe she spoke to Sigge when I was painting. I'm sorry. This is all too much to understand for me.'

Kerstin. She'd dodged a bullet. Literally. Stella had no illusions Sigge would have killed her too. He'd gone too far to stop without cleaning house, as he would have seen it.

Ove's eyes drooped, then closed. A few seconds later, he began snoring. He'd been waiting for her to return, as she told him to, but now she was back the stress had kicked in hard. That and the *akvavit* he'd consumed.

The rest of the conversation could wait until he was sober and sitting in an interview room at the cop shop in Umeå.

She left him sleeping and went inside. He was a university professor. So he'd have an office. Would Sigge have one, too, or did they share? She mounted the wooden staircase to find out.

The first room she came to was book-lined. A wooden desk faced a window looking out over the lake. She tilted her head sideways to read a few of the book titles. All covered genetics, genomics, DNA analysis and other topics she knew Lucian would understand far better than she did.

She spotted a group of the same book, then realised the shelf was filled with similar groups of six or more copies. She angled her head again to read the titles and saw why.

Statistical Methods for Genetic Data Analysis Ove Mattsson
Clinical Genomics: An Introduction Prof. Ove Mattsson
Thoroughbreds: Genetics and the Theory of Perfection Ove Mattsson

Ove's office, she concluded.

The room facing it across the narrow hallway was also filled with books. But when she craned her neck to read the titles, a cold weight settled in her stomach.

Mein Kampf
Racial Theories of Purity
The Degeneration of the Race: Mongrelisation and the Threat from Immigrant Blood

Sigge's office, then. Plastic document holders occupied one shelf, each crammed with magazines. She pulled one out. It was titled:
Svenska Renhet

Thanks to Oskar, she could translate this easily enough. It had to be the party magazine.

The cover featured a smiling blonde woman, her hair in braids wound round the crown of her head above a pretty wreath of cornflowers and evergreen foliage. The headline read:

Midsommar: en tid för svenska patrioter att fira vårt rasarv

She got as far as Midsummer: a time for Swedish patriots to…

The rest eluded her. She typed it into Google Translate. The answer didn't shock her…celebrate our racial heritage.

She sat in the comfortable leather chair and stared through the window at the woods beyond.

Had Sigge sat here, planning to murder Brömly and the rest? Why had he done it? Was it really to protect his husband? Or to squash any further discussion of a racial purity programme he still believed in? Maybe Oskar would find out.

She wandered downstairs again, intending to check on Ove. But when she reached the terrace, he'd gone.

The glass was empty, and the bottle was now only a quarter full. He must have woken and stumbled off. She glanced down to the lake.

If he'd headed that way, he'd be at severe risk of toppling off the dock and drowning himself, the silly old fool. Oh, shit! Maybe he was going to do himself in.

For a second she considered allowing it to happen. Then swore and ran down towards the water's edge. Her days of being judge, jury and executioner were behind her. It was why she'd refused – twice – Oskar's offer of a gun.

She reached the dock and looked down into the clear water. It wasn't deep and she was relieved not to see Ove floating face down.

'Ove!' she shouted. 'Where are you? *Var är du?*'

She strained to hear an answering cry, but heard nothing. The sun was lower in the sky now, bouncing blinding flashes off the water and dazzling her. She checked the time. It was after one in the morning. Weird.

She turned around and cupped her hands around her mouth. She inhaled, ready to yell out his name again. Then she stopped dead.

Though her vision was still filled with wobbling orange afterimages from the sunlight off the lake, the figure striding across the lawn towards her looked like…Roisin?

The figure drew closer.

Jesus! It *was* Roisin. What was she doing out here?

'Rosh! What the hell?'

Roisin had a face like a wet Wednesday afternoon, as Stella's mum used to call her teenaged daughter's particularly dark expressions.

She was dressed like she meant business. An all-black outfit from her boots to a T-shirt that disclosed some impressive biceps Stella was sure hadn't been there before.

Stella's gaze fell to Roisin's waist, around which was belted a pistol in a black holster.

'Stella Cole, I am arresting you on suspicion of the murders of Adam and Lynne Collier,' Roisin said, the corners of her mouth curling upwards, just a fraction. 'We have evidence linking you directly to both crimes. You do not have to say anything but it may harm your defence if you do not mention when questioned something which you later rely on in court. Anything you do say may be given in evidence.'

Stella held her arms wide. 'Rosh, look, I don't know what you think I've done but I—'

'Shut the fuck up!' Roisin snapped. 'I've got CCTV footage of you, with a very cute little pixie cut by the way, kidnapping Lynne Collier. I found your boot stud inside Adam's SUV. I don't know why you killed them, but, right now, guess what? I don't care.'

She reached behind her and pulled out a pair of handcuffs.

'Turn around.'

'Please, Roisin. There's an old man out here somewhere. He's off his face on aquavit and I'm afraid he might drown. Help me find him, then I'll come with you. But there's no need for cuffs.'

In answer, Roisin pulled the pistol from its holster and pointed it at Stella's chest.

'You cheated me out of the DCI's job after you pulled that stunt with Callie, faking your own death. I don't know what you two had going on but I'm going to find out,' Roisin said in a hard, tight voice. 'And then maybe I won't even be DCI Griffin for too long, either.'

Stella tried one final time. 'Please, Rosh. You have to help me. We've just arrested a murderer for god's sake. A key witness has just gone AWOL.'

Roisin shook her head. 'I've got powerful friends now, Stella. And they want you brought in just as much as I do. Now turn around or I'll shoot you in the leg and claim you were resisting arrest.'

She pointed the pistol at Stella's right thigh.

Stella doubted Roisin was much of a shot, but at this range she didn't need to be. Point-and-shoot and Stella would have an agonising flesh wound at best; at worst a broken femur or ruptured femoral artery. Then it really would be game over.

She tried one last time to reason with Roisin. 'How did you know where to find me?'

'It wasn't difficult. You're the talk of Umeå CID. Now, for the third and final time,' Roisin said in a voice hard with menace, 'turn, the fuck, around.'

'*Hallå! Vad gör du?*' a man's voice called out.

Oh, thank Christ! It was Oskar. He was back. She found she could understand him. Hey! What are you doing?

She turned to see him running down the lawn, gun drawn.

'*Polis! Släp ditt vapen!*' Police! Drop your weapon!

Roisin whirled round, pistol up. Three shots rang out, deafeningly loud. A warm spray hit Stella in the face. She tasted salt and copper.

Roisin toppled backwards, falling into Stella and knocking her off her feet. Two of Oskar's bullets had penetrated her chest. One had clipped her left shoulder, tearing a chunk of flesh free. That had been the source of the blood that spattered Stella's cheek.

Roisin's face was white. Stella looked on helplessly as Oskar ran up, holstering his weapon.

'Who is she?' he asked, white-faced.

'She's a colleague. From London.' She bent over Roisin. 'Rosh, stay with me, OK? We'll get you an ambulance.'

Roisin's green eyes were wide, and the pupils had blown out to huge black holes in which Stella could see herself reflected in the *Midsommar* sunlight. Her breathing was shallow and rapid.

Stella stripped off her T-shirt, wadded it into a ball and pushed it against the bullet wounds on Roisin's chest. She heard Oskar calling it in and requesting an *ambulans*.

Stella took Roisin's right hand in hers and squeezed.

'Quiet now. Save your strength,' she said.

Roisin's mouth moved. The whisper that escaped was inaudible. Stella leaned closer, putting her ear against her dying DI's bloodless lips so that she could feel them brush against her skin.

'Why?'

Stella looked over at Oskar. He was still on the phone, free hand gesticulating in the air as if batting away a swarm of wasps.

She looked back at Roisin. Blood was still surging from beneath the improvised dressing. She stuck a finger beneath Roisin's jaw. The pulse was fluttery and fast, but faint. Her eyes were rolling up in her skull.

Stella had seen enough death close-up to know Roisin would never see the inside of the ambulance, let alone the hospital.

She made a decision. She bent towards Roisin.

'Deacon didn't kill Richard and Lola,' she murmured. 'He was a fall guy. Collier was in a conspiracy running death squads. That judge, Ramage? He was its leader. I killed him first. Then the others. Adam last.'

Roisin's eyes widened, and flickered left and right. Her pale lips trembled as they tried to form words.

'Lynne?'

'She was standing between us. He killed her to get a clear shot at me.'

Roisin nodded. Her eyes fluttered and closed.

'Thank you.'

The last two words were carried on a long, hoarse outbreath. Without saying another word, she died.

Still holding Roisin's hand, Stella sat back on her haunches. She thought of Jamie's incredulous expression when she'd confessed to killing Ramage.

She thought of Tomas Brömly telling his former friends – or accomplices – of his intentions to confess his sins in the hopes of absolution.

She thought of Richard. His lifelong passion for justice and human rights. Of Lola, too young to have any concept of crime at all.

And of how Stella herself had learned that good and evil, sin and repentance, justice and the law were often easy to define. But not always.

42

UMEÅ

Stella rode in the ambulance with Roisin's body. She felt nothing. No grief. No relief either. Even if Roisin was no longer able to pursue the case, another officer might pick up the reins.

She'd have to call Callie. Not here though. Not in a Swedish ambulance screaming down the motorway.

What would have happened if Oskar hadn't arrived when he did? Would she really have allowed Rosh to take her back to England in cuffs? Have her charged with murder? What option did she have? But then what?

Callie had hinted that powerful people, though acting from a completely different motive to PPM, would never let her get as far as a trial.

Once she'd signed Rosh's body over to the hospital authorities in Umeå, Stella hitched a ride back to her hotel with a uniformed cop. He dropped her off with a solemn nod.

She checked the time. It was 2.05 a.m and finally dark outside. That made it 1.05 a.m. in London. *Sorry, Callie*, she thought as she called her boss.

'What is it, wee girl?'

Callie sounded wide awake. Good. She needed to be for what she was about to hear. Stella had no time for small talk.

'Roisin's dead. Oskar Norgrim shot her while she was trying to arrest me at gunpoint.'

'She's what?'

'Dead.'

'Oh, fuck me, Stel, you're serious, aren't ye?'

'As a funeral. I've just left her at the mortuary. Thought you'd need a heads-up. Get out in front of it.'

'Aye, well, thanks for that. Was it a legitimate shooting?'

'I think so. I mean, from Oskar's point of view. She had a gun on me and he shouted for her to drop it and she just turned with it still in her hand.'

'What about *your* case?'

'Closed. It was the husband of one of the people Brömly wrote to. I'll explain it when I see you.'

'Well done. Look, I know you won't think you can after what's happened, but try to get some sleep,' Callie said. 'How long are you going to be in Sweden for?'

'I don't know. A few days more?'

'Right. Listen to me carefully. I need to let a few people here know about Roisin. You, say nothing. Come to see me the moment you get back. I don't care what time it is. Understand?'

'Yes, Ma'am.'

This time Callie didn't bat away the use of her title.

Stella cracked a couple of miniatures of vodka from the minibar and poured them into a glass. She took it out onto the narrow balcony and sat watching the stars brighten in the sky.

The first slug of neat vodka made her eyes water and suddenly she was crying, a weltering flow of salty tears she didn't fight.

Was it for Roisin? For the Swedes Sigge Svensson had murdered? Or those tens of thousands of people who'd had their chances of parenthood cut out of them by a government intent on preserving the Swedish bloodline?

Stella didn't know. She just let them come, and she wept until they stopped and the stars were bright above her head and the vodka, and two more, were gone.

Finally, she undressed, climbed into bed and slept until nine the next morning.

Oskar met her at the station. He looked shattered. Purplish circles under his eyes, unkempt hair and a greyish cast to his skin that turned his already unlovely features into a death mask.

'How are you?' she asked.

'I feel like shit. I killed a cop, for fuck's sake! A British cop. How could I have been so stupid?'

Stella reached out and put her hand on his shoulder.

'It wasn't your fault. You shouted a warning. I heard you. And she had her gun up.'

'I've been thinking about it all night. I haven't been to bed.'

'There'll be an investigation,' Stella said.

'Yes. I would really appreciate it if you could stay long enough to talk to them.'

'Of course. I know it feels bad, Oskar, but you did nothing wrong. Not really. Try to find a way to live with it. She could have dropped her weapon like you ordered. She didn't.'

'That sounds quite harsh, if you don't mind me saying.'

'It's not meant to. I didn't get much sleep either. We're both tired, OK? Tell me, did they find Ove?'

He nodded. 'Old fool was sleeping it off in a neighbour's boathouse under a tarpaulin. He's back home now. I've put an officer with him for the moment.'

'Good. He's going to need some careful handling. I'm sorry to ask you this after what we just said, but when do you think I'll be able to repatriate my colleague's body?'

'Probably no more than a week. They will do an autopsy here to determine cause of death. Formally, I mean. Then that should be that.'

'Right. Let's try and just leave that for now. There's still our case to wrap up. When are you interviewing Svensson?'

'Today. You'll join me?'

Stella nodded. 'Try and keep me away.'

* * *

Stella waited for Oskar to finish recording the statutory introduction to the interview. She looked at Svensson, who sat erect on the other side of the table, accompanied by his solicitor, a blonde-haired man with piercing blue eyes.

Svensson stared back at her, his face unreadable. A large bruise marked his right cheek and he had cut his lip at some point. She couldn't remember whether she'd done it while arresting him. His right wrist was strapped. He still had on his white trousers and sandals but his torso was covered by a navy-blue sweatshirt with SPA stencilled on the front and back in large white capitals.

'The terror attack. That was you, wasn't it, Sigge?' she began.

He nodded. 'I had it planned for a while. In case you got too close. I intended to kill you then take Ove across the lake in our boat. I have friends on the other side who would have helped us escape.'

'Why did you kill Tomas Brömly?' she asked.

He surprised her by answering readily.

'For Ove. Brömly would have exposed him to the mob,' he answered in flawless English. 'Our life together would have been destroyed.'

'How did you find out about Inger? And Annika?'

'It wasn't difficult. Ove likes his *akvavit*. You've probably noticed he drinks more than is good for him. Things tend to spill out when he's had one too many,' he said. 'Once I knew about Brömly's letter, I had to start keeping a careful watch on Ove. For his own good.'

'Was the tongue a warning to the others?'

'Yes. But I realised it was too indirect. They could have misinterpreted it. Plus when you didn't make it public, I knew I had to be more,' he paused, then smiled, faintly, 'systematic.'

'Did Ove know?'

He shook his head. 'Of course not! He was worried. I didn't want to add to his anxiety.'

'Do you admit to murdering the others? Inger and Erik Hedlund? And Annika Ivarsson?'

'Yes.'

'And you intended to murder Kerstin Dahl, too?'

'I did.'

'But if you'd killed Kerstin, how would Ove ever sleep peacefully again? He'd think the killer was coming for him last.'

Svensson shrugged. 'I thought once the months went by and he was fine, he'd forget about it. I could just tell him it must all have been a coincidence.'

So he *had* done it for love. Nothing to do with his politics or views on the purity of the Swedish nation. That put a thought in her mind. Is that how they'd met?

'Did you meet because of your shared interest in eugenics?'

Svensson actually laughed. A loud sound in the hard-surfaced cube that made his solicitor jump.

'You'd think, wouldn't you? No. Actually we met at a *Midsommar* party ten years ago. I guess you would say it was love at first sight.'

Stella sat back, shaking her head. She looked at Oskar, who took over the interview, switching to Swedish. After a few more minutes, Stella excused herself and left him to it.

When he emerged, it was to tell her Svensson would be held in custody pending an initial hearing. He'd indicated he would plead guilty to the four murders in return for the judge considering a more lenient sentence.

Later that day, Oskar gave Stella some good news. The CSIs had found a microscopic trace of blood on one of the laces of Sigge's running shoes. The blood contained Tomas Brömly's DNA. The hair discovered in Brömly's flat was matched to Sigge.

Confessions could always be retracted at trial, or challenged as having been produced under duress. Forensic evidence was harder to talk away.

She stayed in Sweden for another week, working with Oskar and the prosecutor's office to tie up the investigation.

The Special Investigations Division of the Swedish Police Authority launched its own investigation into the fatal shooting of DI Griffin by *Detektivinspektor* Norgrim. Security footage from the house revealed Roisin aiming her gun at Oskar as he issued a warning to put down her weapon.

Together with Stella's testimony it was enough to convince them that Oskar had acted within the law and with appropriate respect for the rules governing police use of lethal force.

Stella arrived at SPA headquarters on her last morning to find a Post-It note on her desk asking her to visit an N. Olsson on the fifth floor.

Frowning, she made her way up and, after asking someone for directions, knocked on a plain wooden door with the officer's name on the outside on an aluminium plate above a long job title and department name.

'Come!' a male voice barked from the inside.

Interesting. Using English before he knew who was knocking. She opened the door. The thin man behind the desk did not rise to greet her. No smile either. In fact, he looked downright hostile. His mouth was a grim line, close-set eyes boring into hers.

'Sit,' he said. 'Please.'

Stella took an instant dislike to him. She decided to take the initiative. 'Can I ask what this is about?'

'Of course. It's about Roisin Griffin. Well, not so much about *her* as the reason she came to Sweden.'

Stella caught herself in the act of folding her arms and avoided completing the gesture by scratching her left elbow then returning her hands to her lap.

'What's your interest?'

He leaned forward. 'I hear your Swedish has improved greatly since arriving in Stockholm. Could you translate the words on my office nameplate, I wonder?'

Stella hadn't bothered to try. But now she realised in which department she was sitting. In the office of which *head* of department.

'Human Resources?' she asked. 'I saw a few admin types sitting around.'

The dig struck its target. He frowned and his thin lips twitched with irritation.

'Amusing. British humour, I suppose. Well, *Avdelningen för särskilda utredningar* translates as Special Investigations Division. We have just concluded our investigation of *Detectivinspektor* Norgrim for the fatal shooting of DI Griffin.'

'I heard. Given she pointed a pistol at him and appeared to be about to open fire, you found he had acted legally.'

'Indeed we did. Roisin told me why she was here, DCI Cole. It was to arrest you for murder.'

Stella frowned. 'Is that what she told you? Because when we met, she said she had come to kill me.'

There! That wrong-footed him. And since Roisin had threatened to shoot her at one point in their brief conversation, Stella carried off the lie convincingly.

'I don't believe you.'

Stella leaned forward and fixed Olsson with a stare. 'That's your privilege. Was there anything else? Only I have to fly back to England with her body.'

He met her gaze and she detected the intensity of the true believer behind his eyes.

'I hate corrupt police officers,' he said. 'I have devoted my life to exposing them and delivering justice.'

Stella stood and leaned over his desk, hands flat on its bare surface.

'So have I.'

She left without a backward glance and went to find Oskar.

'What did Olsson want?' he asked.

'He just wished me a safe journey home. Said he was sorry I'd lost a colleague.'

Oskar's face fell. 'Shit! I can't tell you how sorry I am, Stella.'

She laid a gentle hand on his shoulder. 'I already told you, it wasn't your fault. Let it go. I'll look after her from now.'

Oskar drove her to the airport. Before leaving her, he shook hands.

'I want to say it was a pleasure and very educational to work with you, Stella,' he said, in oddly formal English. 'If you come back to Sweden, I would like to see you again. You could meet Hedda and Gustav. We could show you around.'

'Thank you. I'd like that.'

He nodded, smiled, and left her to check in.

* * *

As she walked up the jetway from the plane to Heathrow's arrivals terminal, Stella's mobile woke up and started buzzing. She pulled it out and looked down.

We should talk. Call me?

With a lightness in her step that had been missing for the whole time she'd been in Sweden, she made her way to the taxi rank. She checked her watch. It was 10.00 p.m. She gave the driver Callie's home address and texted her boss to let her know she was on her way.

43

LONDON

Sitting in Callie's comfortably furnished sitting room, a glass of brandy in her hand, it took Stella an hour to relate the incidents leading to both the solving of the case and Roisin's death.

When she reached the part where Roisin had materialised in Ove Mattsson's garden, Callie repeatedly asked her to go back and clarify dozens of details. Exactly who said what to whom? Who was positioned where when Oskar fired the fatal shot? And, most crucially of all, how the internal investigation had turned out.

After Stella finished recounting the events of that weird, sunlit night, Callie blew out her cheeks.

'I think we can keep a lid on this. Roisin will get the full Met funeral with honours,' she said.

'Did you tell the ambassador we caught Brömly's killer?'

'Aye, and he said to pass on his thanks to you. I got the feeling there might be an invitation to the next embassy cocktail party for you and Jamie.'

Stella looked down at her lap, then back at Callie, who picked up on her expression immediately.

'Everything OK in that department, Stel?'

Stella was about to tell Callie that she'd confessed to Jamie when something stayed her tongue. If word got around in whatever murky circles Callie had been forced to move in that Jamie knew about PPM, she'd be putting him in danger.

'Yeah,' she said brightly. 'I was just thinking I didn't really have any little black dresses suitable for a diplomatic shindig.'

Callie smiled. 'I'm sure we can give you a day off to have a wee wander down South Moulton Street.'

Stella smiled back. 'I think the Kilburn High Road might be more my level, but thanks.'

'We both know that's not true, Stel. Listen, I'm glad to have you back.'

Stella looked Callie in the eye. 'With Roisin gone, does that mean Gordon Wade and whoever he reports to are going to back off? Leave me alone?'

Callie pursed her lips. 'I bloody well hope so. With Roisin out of the picture and the case transferred from the FBI to us, I'll make sure whatever she found out gets buried where not even our best cadaver dogs could find it.'

* * *

Once Stella had left, Callie went to find her husband. John was watching a YouTube video in their home office on how to fix a leaking lavatory. Typical.

'I have to pop into the office, darling,' she said with a smile. 'Something's come up. Needs yours truly's signature. Won't be too long. Don't wait up.'

He paused the video, turned in his seat and smiled up at her. 'Don't you have underlings to do that sort of thing for you these days?'

She kissed the top of his head. 'I do. But this one calls for the overling.'

She reached Paddington Green thirty minutes later. She used a local minicab firm, not Bash, and gave her name to the controller as Jean Brodie. She paid in cash.

Beneath Roisin's desk Callie found a cardboard carton full of the FBI's evidence, including two handguns. Its exterior bore an address label with FAO Detective Griffin printed on it below the FBI seal.

Inside the desk, shoved right to the back, she found a folder containing photos of scratches in what looked like a car bonnet. A small chrome stud in a sealed plastic evidence bag. And a flash drive.

Callie plugged the little rectangle into a spare USB slot on the PC. It contained photos of the two handguns, one of Stella's Prada bike boots in closeup, minus a stud, plus a CCTV montage in which Stella, sporting a cheeky little blonde crop, could clearly be seen at the wheel.

She pulled out the drive and pocketed it, and placed the folder on top of the cardboard carton.

Twenty minutes later, after she'd searched the rest of Roisin's desk with her fingertips, Callie went to the kitchen and brewed a cup of coffee. She brought the steaming mug back to Roisin's desk, tipped the PC's tower unit onto its front, and emptied the coffee carefully into the fan grille.

At first nothing happened and Callie began to wonder how she could disable the PC. The liquid must have reached a live wire. A tremendous blue spark flashed inside the casing and it started to smoke. Panicking, Callie looked around for a fire extinguisher.

No flames materialised, and the smoke died away. She breathed a sigh of relief. The computer smelled of burnt plastic and ozone. She hoped she'd done enough to fry the hard drive.

Feeling a twinge of guilt that IT, when eventually the fault was discovered, would blame either a clumsy detective or a cleaner, Callie left with the box and the folder. She arrived home at 2.05 a.m. John was deeply asleep and snoring loudly. For once, she was grateful.

She burnt what could be burnt in the sitting room fireplace and dumped the rest in the dustbin. In her office, she spent five minutes gift-wrapping the boxes containing the handguns and added stick-on bows for good measure.

At 4.00 a.m., she left the house and drove west. The chances of being stopped were remote, but she hoped the birthday wrapping paper would deflect any well-meaning enquiries from Traffic about what she had in her bag.

Fifteen minutes later, she parked on the west side of Chiswick bridge. Bag over her shoulder, she walked back to the centre and dropped the 'presents' and the boot-stud into the deep water.

* * *

While Callie was destroying evidence that could have convicted Stella of murder, Stella was changing into her running gear. She'd woken early again, her overstressed brain unable to quieten since Oskar had shot Roisin.

She was wracked with guilt over a colleague's death. Yet she knew that if it hadn't been for Oskar shouting at Roisin when he did, she'd have been brought back to the UK to face formal charges of murder. Then a trial at best, or a sudden death at the hands of a hired killer at worst.

Sliding her phone and a credit card into the zip pocket in the back of her running vest, she left the flat, locking the front door behind her. After her run, she intended to take the rest of the day off.

She emerged onto Lisson Grove and turned towards Regent's Park, settling quickly into her normal warmup pace. Her favourite Asics Gel-Cumulus running shoes didn't so much hit the pavement as kiss it, and she felt the familiar sense of fleet-footed freedom envelop her and her heart and lungs adjusted to the new demands she placed on them.

The sun was still low, and the sky, a deep, bruised purple at the horizon, underwent a gradual transition to a pale, washed-out blue, shot through with streaks of pink. East-facing windows on the tall tower blocks flashed brilliantly in the sunlight.

She loved running early in the morning. London was never truly quiet. Ask any of the uniformed patrols and they'd confirm it. But around dawn it was at its most peaceful. You could relax. Those intent on evil-doing had mostly finished for the night. Even bad guys slept occasionally.

She nodded to an Indian man loading tables with fruit outside his grocery shop. He smiled and nodded back. He was the only other human being she saw.

Reaching a crossroads, she looked over her shoulder before running across the junction. A white transit van was following her about fifty feet back.

She chided herself. Unless it was going in the other direction, it had to drive the same way as her. It didn't mean it was *following* her.

She reached the pavement on the far side and looked back. The van was gone. Proof she was starting to see conspiracies everywhere. She needed to get her head straight or the next few days were going to be impossible. There'd be reports to write and no doubt interviews with high-ups about Roisin's death.

She turned a corner, intending to take a shortcut to the park, and found herself running towards a thickset man leaning against a lamppost about thirty yards distant.

He was smoking what she took, at first, to be a cigarette, then she smelled it and realised it was a joint. Beside him stood a white transit van, one rear wheel up on the pavement.

She thought back to the van she'd clocked a few minutes earlier. That one had been a Ford. So was this. That one had a broken headlight, giving it a lopsided look. So did this.

His head came up like a dog scenting danger. He looked in her direction: no expression on his face. Which worried her.

A tradesman would nod, or offer a smile. She scanned the road behind her. No traffic on this quiet residential road at this time of day. No other pedestrians either. And no CCTV cameras on lamp posts.

He was dressed in dirty jeans and a pale-blue hoodie. She looked at his feet. Where she'd expected to see dirty trainers, she saw heavy black boots.

At once, she knew who she was facing. Not his name. That would come later. But his job.

This was no casual encounter. And he was no random wrong

'un. They had sent him for her. Probably had her under surveillance even before she left for Stockholm. She always ran the same route. It would have been a simple enough matter for him to work it out.

She looked over her shoulder again and moved onto the road, intending to cross and run around the van. He moved into her path, spreading his meaty arms wide.

'Bit early for a run, isn't it?' he asked.

Even though she could have sped up and accelerated past him and out of his reach, that wasn't what she felt like doing. So she didn't.

She slowed.

Close up, she could see the stubble on his jowly face.

Stopping in front of him, she put her hands on her hips.

'I like running before everyone's awake. It's quiet,' she said.

'I like being up and around at this time, too,' he said in a conversational tone of voice.

She noticed the way his eyes flicked down to her breasts then to her face again. Then to his van. For she was sure it was his.

Stella jerked her chin in the direction of his right hand, where the joint smouldered, sending pungent, sweet-smelling smoke coiling into the air above him.

'You shouldn't be doing that.'

He grinned and took a long drag. He blew out a thin stream of smoke at her.

'What are you going to do, call the police?' he asked derisively.

She smiled and shook her head. 'No. But it's bad for you. The modern strains are too powerful. Very high concentration of THCs.'

He laughed at this. Then he stretched out his right hand.

'Here,' he said. 'Take a puff. It'll loosen you up. You look like you could do with it.'

'I'm good, thanks,' she said.

She made no move to leave. Instead, keeping her stance balanced, a little more weight on her left leg, which she'd advanced half a pace, she waited for his next move.

If he'd been thoughtful, or observant, or less confident in his own physical abilities, he might have wondered why this slightly-built woman wearing nothing but a few ounces of Lycra felt no need to put more distance between them.

He did the precise opposite of what he should have done. He moved closer. The grin morphed into a leer.

'I've got a mattress in the back,' he said in a low voice. 'Why don't you and me get in? We could have some fun.'

He was close enough that Stella could see the blackheads on his nose, and the flakes of dry skin in his eyebrows. His eyes were a mid-brown and they were flecked with green, caught by the sun that was now slanting across the street.

She could smell him, too. A sour, unwashed reek.

He reached behind him and brought out a long-bladed knife. Sun glinted off its edge.

She smiled. 'OK.'

His eyes widened. 'What?'

'I hope you're feeling energetic, because I could give a man like you a really good seeing to.' She pointed to the knife. 'No need for that.'

He smiled. And he actually licked his lips. His gaze slid over her body for a second time, lingering on her breasts and the front of her shorts.

He turned away and yanked open the back doors of the van. Inside, as promised, lay a greasy-looking mattress. It was horribly stained in overlapping blotches of grey and pale brown. She saw darker marks, too.

She pushed him aside and hopped into the noisome space which was lit by a pair of overhead courtesy lights. Moving to the back, she turned and crooked a finger.

'Come on, then? What are you waiting for?'

44

LONDON

She watched him lever his bulk into the back and close the doors behind him with a screech from an unoiled lock. He turned around.

And she kicked him hard in the centre of his face.

The crack as his nose broke was sharp in the metal box. He howled, clutching the flattened bulb of flesh. Blood spurted from between his fingers, soaking the front of his hoodie.

Before he could inhale again, Stella leaped at him and drove another kick into his groin. With no more breath left for a scream he buckled, falling sideways onto the mattress.

Stella punched him twice, once in the throat, once in the solar plexus, driving his wind out.

She grabbed the knife from the mattress where he'd dropped it. Kneeling beside him, she pushed the tip against the soft tissue of his neck where the major blood vessels ran.

Sensing a chance to tilt the scales in her favour beyond the confines of the van, she got her phone out and started a video recording.

'Who are you?' she growled.

'What?' he mumbled through his fingers. 'You broke my fucking nose, you cunt.'

Stella paused the recording. 'Call me a cunt again and I'll castrate you like the pig you are.'

She tapped the red circle again and restarted the video.

'What's your name?'

'Dave.'

'Dave, what?'

'Hoyle.'

'For the tape, Dave Hoyle, who sent you to kill me?'

'I don't know what you're talking about.'

She pushed the knife a little harder. The tip broke the skin on his throat and a thin stream of blood trickled sideways onto the mattress.

'Last chance,' she said.

She removed the knife from his throat, reached back with it and pressed the tip hard into his groin, not caring about the precise point of contact. He wheezed out a thin, terrified cry.

'All right, all right. Stop! I'll tell you.' She increased the pressure on the knife. 'It's a cop. In Scotland.'

Stella's heart rate doubled.

'Name.'

'Spring. Alec Spring. He's this really fucking senior guy. Brass.'

Holding the phone as steady as she could manage, Stella pressed on.

'Did he tell you why?'

'No. He said best not ask too many questions. Said to fuck you up properly then kill you. Make it look like one of those creeps who get off on it. Rape you first if I wanted to.'

'Where did he find you?'

'I'm an ex-cop. I got kicked out for brutality. I got a call from a former CI. Said this brass wanted to see me. There was money in it.'

'How much?'

'Five grand.'

Was that all they thought her life was worth? Stella almost laughed. She made a split-second decision. She ended the recording and pocketed her phone. She climbed off him, keeping the knife within striking distance of his face.

'I could kill you right here. I've done it before. But I'm going to let you go. You're going to disappear,' she said. 'You don't report back and you don't get in my way again. If you do—'

He sprang at her – 'Fuck you! Cunt!' – straight into her outstretched fist.

She caught him in the throat again. He fell backwards onto the mattress, clutching his neck and heaving out strange cracked noises.

Rearing up, he clawed at her face. She jerked her head back out of range of his fingers. He kicked out and caught her on the point of her right knee, which exploded in pain.

As she toppled sideways, he grabbed her throat with both hands and started squeezing. His teeth were bared in a feral snarl. Stars flickered around the edge of Stella's vision.

Then she struck. At first his hands stayed locked around her neck. But the shock and pain registered in his eyes. She saw it. Knew that though the van would shortly contain a dead body, it wouldn't be hers.

His grip slackened. His mouth dropped open and he looked down at his belly. Dark-red blood flooded out, drenching the lower part of his hoodie and the front of his jeans.

He looked back at her, a puzzled expression on his face: brows knitted, eyes questioning, mouth half-open.

'It's because you're dying,' she said, pulling the blade out of his stomach.

Then she grabbed a fistful of lank, greasy hair and jerked his head down, folding him double. She drew the blade swiftly under his chin, left to right.

He'd looked after the knife. The edge was as keen as the point was sharp. His thick neck offered little resistance as the blade parted skin, fat, muscle, sinew, artery, vein and cartilage.

A great deal of blood issued from the rent in his throat. The air escaping his lungs hissed and bubbled.

Stella stood back to avoid the blood. The arterial spray was contained by the fold of his neck. Most soaked into the mattress.

When the bleeding stopped, she moved closer and wrapped his right hand tightly around the handle of the knife. Once again, she thanked dear, sweet, heroin-addicted Yiannis Terzi for removing her prints.

She opened the rear door and peered out. The road was still empty. She climbed out and shut it behind her.

She took his baseball cap and pulled it on and down to cover her face, then she got out and went round to the driver's seat. When she started the engine, she was pleased to see the van had a three-quarters full petrol tank.

Checking the mirror, she indicated right and pulled away, feathering the throttle to make as little noise as possible. She didn't want to disturb anyone's last hour of sleep.

As she drove down to the south coast, keeping the van to a steady seventy, Stella let her mind wander. She didn't feel at all strange to be transporting a corpse in a stolen transit van. It wasn't as if she'd never done something like it before. And the killing had been completely justified.

In law, yes. She doubted there was a jury in the land who'd convict her for murder. Reasonable force in the face of a terrifying adversary who'd snatched her off the street with the intent to rape and murder her? She thought so.

But it was also justified because, with backers like Spring, Hoyle would never see the inside of a courtroom.

That was her own, personal code. She believed in the law. Still. Despite everything. But she could also detect when the law lacked the teeth to deliver justice. Did that make her a vigilante? On the whole, she thought not. But if it did, so be it. Even the most liberal-minded citizen could hardly claim the man they'd sent to kill her was innocent.

As she left the outskirts of Brighton, heading east towards Lewes, she rolled her head on her shoulders. Her muscles ached and the pain in her knee had settled into a steady throb.

She reached Beachy Head and drove as close to the edge of the cliff as she dared. So close she could hear the waves crashing sixty or more yards below. She killed the engine and yanked on the handbrake.

A dog walker, or an early morning jogger, would be the first to see the abandoned van. But how long would it take for the smell or a trickle of blood to alert somebody to the truth? She didn't know. She didn't care. They'd call the local cops and they'd force the rear doors and find him. A suicide in the back of a van.

Obvious conclusion: he'd gone to Beachy Head intending to drive over the edge. Bottled it and did himself in with his own knife instead. Maybe eyebrows would be raised at the severity of his self-inflicted wounds, but it wasn't unprecedented. People intent on suicide were capable of unimaginable acts against their own bodies. Every cop knew that.

CSIs would find no fingerprints on the knife but his. None on the door handle but his, and those of the careless local plod. Any CCTV would pick up a lone driver wearing his cap.

The cap!

Stella inspected it carefully, removing two of her own hairs but leaving plenty belonging to the dead man. She left it on the passenger seat. She checked her appearance in the mirror. No obvious blood spatter but she'd clean up at the railway station.

She checked the wing mirrors. Nobody around. So she climbed out and, as if the intervening two and a half hours had been a particularly nasty dream, continued her morning run.

She reached Eastbourne town centre in eighteen minutes, a good time, but by no means her best for a three-mile run.

She had time to wash her face and hands before catching the next train to London Victoria. Her outfit, unconventional for a commuter train, drew a few curious stares from suited business types. But they quickly returned to their phones, laptops and iPads. Nobody read on trains anymore, she thought incongruously.

A tube ride and another short jog later and she was inside her flat in Lisson Grove and locking the door behind her.

She stripped off her running clothes, sports bra and knickers and put them straight into the washing machine on its hottest cycle.

The shoes might never be the same again. She shrugged. Who was? They'd be sacrificed the evening before the dustmen came.

Under a scalding shower she scrubbed every inch of her skin until she felt clean again. She used two palmfuls of shampoo, creating so much lather around her feet that she laughed.

She laughed harder. And louder. She could feel herself tipping over into hysteria. She clapped her palm over her mouth. No! It mustn't happen again. She couldn't lose her shit like before.

She closed her eyes and while the water drummed down on her skull listened out for the voice. *That* voice. The mocking, sardonic voice of Other Stella.

Her head was quiet. What she'd just done she'd done herself. Unaided.

And then another thought intruded. *I need an insurance policy.* She got dressed and called Vicky.

* * *

Vicky made them both a coffee then joined Stella at her kitchen table.

'Last time I saw you, you said you had an idea how you could protect me,' Stella said. 'I think we need to move on that quickly.'

'Why? What's happened?'

'You remember how I told you PPM sent that psychopath to try to kill me?'

Vicky nodded. 'Moxey?'

'That's right. Well, it just happened again.'

Vickey's eyebrows shot up towards her hairline. She put her mug down. 'What?'

Stella recounted the story. Before Vicky could respond to her latest confession, Stella started the video she'd recorded in the scuzzy transit van.

The quality was better than she'd hoped for at the time. His face was clear, and so was every word of what he said. Vicky made Stella play it through a second time.

When she looked up at Stella, her face was pale. Not everyone would cope with their best friend turning up and showing them a snuff movie. But then, not everyone had Stella Cole for a bestie.

Her face was pale, but, in her eyes, Stella saw the kind of resolve she herself felt. Vicky had been exposed to the true evil of which people in power were capable when PPM had sent a gunman to murder her beloved godparents. Ever since, she'd shown a steelier side to her character.

'I wrote up a dossier on everything you told me about PPM,' Vicky said. 'I added some other stuff I researched on my own.'

'Which we will copy and distribute to a few trusted sources.'

Stella nodded. Vicky's plan chimed with her own. The plan that she'd been sorting out in her mind over the previous couple of weeks. The plan that her recent encounter with Dave had brought into sharp focus.

She explained how she thought it could be made to work in a way that would protect both of them.

* * *

At 1.00 p.m. the following day, Stella and Vicky were seated at Callie's meeting table, positioned so that the opening door would hide them from view. Callie came in, talking over her shoulder.

'Thanks for coming down, Gordon, I really appreciate you making the time.'

'You really didn't give me much choice, Callie. Now I'm here, maybe we can drop the cloak and dagger business, eh?'

Wade's voice sounded friendly, but puzzled.

Callie looked at Stella and nodded. It began here. And, hopefully, ended.

As Callie shut the door, Wade looked round for somewhere to put his briefcase. His head jerked back as he registered Vicky's presence, and then Stella's.

He stiffened, and, for a split-second, she thought he might actually turn and run. His mouth opened. The colour drained from his face. Seeing a woman you'd thought murdered alive and well tended to do that to a man. For him, it might have been the first time. For Stella, it was not.

'Hello, Gordon,' she said.

He looked from her to Callie then back again. Caught in a trap, the rat had no option but to sit. Breathing heavily, he joined them at the table. Callie followed him.

'You know Stella,' Callie said. 'Obviously. I'd like to introduce you to Vicky Riley. Vicky's a journalist. So is her husband.'

'I specialise in investigative journalism,' Vicky said. 'I was working with Richard Drinkwater before he was murdered by Pro Patria Mori.'

'As you can see, Gordon,' Callie said, 'we're all on the same page of the script, so we can skip the polite denials sections of the conversation. Stella, I believe you have something you'd like to show us?'

Stella opened her laptop and swivelled it round to face Callie and Wade. 'You might need to get the blinds, Gordon,' she said. 'Not sure you're going to want any curious passersby seeing this. Even without the sound.'

He got to his feet, sighing, and pulled the blind cords to shutter them from the outside world.

Once he'd regained his seat, Stella hit the Play button.

Barely thirty seconds long, the video had a profound effect on Wade. The colour, which had flooded back into his cheeks, left again. His stubble stood out on his pale skin, which was sheened with a film of greasy-looking sweat.

Stella shut the laptop's lid with a sharp clack.

'The bit I didn't record was me killing him. I drove his van down to Beachy Head and left it there. The locals'll be chalking it up as a suicide but you might want to keep an eye on things.'

'What do you want?' he asked in a quiet voice.

'Let's talk about what *you* want first,' Stella countered. 'I'm thinking, you'd prefer this little video nasty remains away from the public gaze.'

'And not posted to social media and the main satellite and terrestrial channels, bloggers and online news outlets,' Vicky added.

He nodded, a tight jerk of his head that spoke volumes of the muscle tension in his neck and shoulders.

'There's an accompanying document that lays out all our roles in dismantling PPM,' Callie said. 'You, me, those higher up the food chain including Alec Spring.'

'And it's all going to stay tucked away where even those annoying little Russian hackers couldn't get to it,' Stella said. 'Unless, and this is where we get to what I want, Gordon, anything happens to me, Vicky, Callie or anyone we care about. Then, and I'm guessing you've probably figured this next bit out for yourself, it all goes online. All any of us needs to do is make a call to one of three people and it's done.'

'The wee girl's been awfully clever,' Callie said, and Stella thought she detected the glimmer of a grin as Callie glanced in her direction. 'Because even if we were somehow all to die simultaneously in a tragic accident of some kind, the person we'd otherwise call would publish it anyway.'

Wade pulled his tie knot down and undid his top button. Stella thought he looked as if he might be sick at any moment.

'You're bluffing,' he said.

Stella regarded him coolly. 'Call it, then. See if your friend Spring knows any more disgraced cops looking to earn an extra five grand.'

After a pause of ten seconds, he wiped his top lip. 'That's all you want?' he asked.

'Not quite,' Stella said. 'I also want to go on working. I like catching murderers. It's what I do. It's what I'm best at. So you tell whoever needs telling to leave me alone.'

'How do I know you'll keep your word?' he asked.

Stella resisted a sudden, powerful urge to rush him and break something important.

She inhaled slowly, willing her pulse to settle.

'You'll just have to trust me.'

ACKNOWLEDGMENTS

I want to thank you for buying this book. I hope you enjoyed it. As an author is only part of the team of people who make a book the best it can be, this is my chance to thank the people on my team.

For being my first readers, Sarah Hunt and Jo Maslen.

For sharing their knowledge and experience of The Job, former and current police officers Andy Booth, Ross Coombs, Jen Gibbons, Neil Lancaster, Sean Memory, Trevor Morgan, Olly Royston, Chris Saunby, Ty Tapper, Sarah Warner and Sam Yeo.

For helping me stay reasonably close to medical reality as I devise gruesome ways of killing people, Martin Cook, Melissa Davies, Arvind Nagra and Katie Peace.

For their brilliant copy-editing and proofreading Nicola Lovick and Liz Ward.

And for being a daily inspiration and source of love and laughter, and making it all worthwhile, my family: Jo, Rory and Jacob.

The responsibility for any and all mistakes in this book remains mine. I assure you, they were unintentional.

Andy Maslen
Salisbury, 2021

ABOUT THE AUTHOR

Photo © 2020 Kin Ho

Andy Maslen was born in Nottingham, England. After leaving university with a degree in psychology, he worked in business for thirty years as a copywriter. In his spare time, he plays blues guitar. He lives in Wiltshire.

READ ON FOR AN EXTRACT FROM *SHALLOW GROUND*, THE FIRST BOOK IN THE DETECTIVE FORD THRILLERS...

EXTRACT FROM SHALLOW GROUND

Summer | Pembrokeshire Coast, Wales

Ford leans out from the limestone rock face halfway up Pen-y-holt sea stack, shaking his forearms to keep the blood flowing. He and Lou have climbed the established routes before. Today, they're attempting a new line he spotted. She was reluctant at first, but she's also competitive and he really wanted to do the climb.

'I'm not sure. It looks too difficult,' she'd said when he suggested it.

'Don't tell me you've lost your bottle?' he said with a grin.

'No, but . . .'

'Well, then. Let's go. Unless you'd rather climb one of the easy ones again?'

She frowned. 'No. Let's do it.'

They scrambled down a gully, hopping across boulders from the cliff to a shallow ledge just above sea level at the bottom of the route. She stands there now, patiently holding his ropes while he climbs. But the going's much harder than he expected. He's wasted a lot of time attempting to navigate a tricky bulge. Below him, Lou plays out rope through a belay device.

He squints against the bright sunshine as a light wind buffets him. Herring gulls wheel around the stack, calling in alarm at this brightly coloured interloper assaulting their territory.

He looks down at Lou and smiles. Her eyes are a piercing blue. He remembers the first time he saw her. He was captivated by those eyes, drawn in, powerless, like an old wooden sailing ship spiralling down into a whirlpool. He paid her a clumsy compliment, which she accepted with more grace than he'd managed.

Lou smiles back up at him now. Even after seven years of marriage, his heart thrills that she should bestow such a radiant expression on him.

Rested, he starts climbing again, trying a different approach to the overhang. He reaches up and to his right for a block. It seems solid enough, but his weight pulls it straight off.

He falls outwards, away from the flat plane of lichen-scabbed limestone, and jerks to a stop at the end of his rope. The force turns him into a human pendulum. He swings inwards, slamming face-first against the rock and gashing his chin. Then out again to dangle above Lou on the ledge.

Ford tries to stay calm as he slowly rotates. His straining fingertips brush the rock face then arc into empty air.

Then he sees two things that frighten him more than the fall.

The rock he dislodged, as large as a microwave, has smashed down on to Lou. She's sitting awkwardly, white-faced, and he can see blood on her leggings. Those sapphire-blue eyes are wide with pain.

And waves are now lapping at the ledge. The tide is on its way in, not out. Somehow, he misread the tide table, or he took too long getting up the first part of the climb. He damns himself for his slowness.

'I can lower you down,' she screams up at him. 'But my leg, I think it's broken.'

She gets him down safely and he kisses her fiercely before crouching by her right leg to assess the damage. There's a sharp lump distending the bloody Lycra, and he knows what it is. Bone.

'It's bad, Lou. I think it's a compound fracture. But if you can stand on your good leg, we can get back the way we came.'

'I can't!' she cries, pain contorting her face. 'Call the coastguard.'

He pulls out his phone, but there's no mobile service down here. 'Shit! There's no signal.'

'You'll have to go for help.'

'I can't leave you, darling.'

A wave crashes over the ledge and douses them both.

Her eyes widen. 'You have to! The tide's coming in.'

He knows she's right. And it's all his fault. He pulled the block off the crag.

'Lou, I—'

She grabs his hand and squeezes so hard it hurts. 'You *have* to.'

Another wave hits. His mouth fills with seawater. He swallows half of it and retches. He looks back the way they came. The boulders they hopped along are awash. There's no way Lou can make it.

He's crying now. He can't do it.

Then she presses the only button she has left. 'If you stay here, we'll *both* die. Then who'll look after Sam?'

Sam is eight and a half. Born two years before they married. He's being entertained by Louisa's parents while they're at Pen-y-holt. Ford knows she's right. He can't leave Sam an orphan. They were meant to be together for all time. But now, time has run out.

'Go!' she screams. 'Before it's too late.'

So he leaves her, checking the gear first so he's sure she can't be swept away'. He falls into an eerie calm as he swims across to the cliff and solos out.

At the clifftop, rock gives way to scrubby grass. He pulls out his phone. Four bars. He calls the coastguard, giving them a concise description of the accident, the location and Lou's injury. Then he slumps. The calmness that saved his life has vanished. He is hyperventilating, heaving in great breaths that won't bring enough oxygen to his brain, and sighing them out again.

A wave of nausea rushes through him and sweat flashes out

across his skin. The wind chills it, making him shudder with the sudden cold. He lurches to his right and spews out a thin stream of bile on to the grass.

Then his stomach convulses and his breakfast rushes up and out, spattering the sleeve of his jacket. He retches out another splash of stinking yellow liquid and then dry-heaves until, cramping, his guts settle. His view is blurred through a film of tears.

He falls back and lies there for ten more minutes, looking up into the cloudless sky. Odd how realistic this dream is. He could almost believe he just left his wife to drown.

He sobs, a cracked sound that the wind tears away from his lips and disperses into the air. And the dream blackens and reality is here, and it's ugly and painful and true.

He hears a helicopter. Sees its red-and-white form hovering over Pen-y-holt.

Time ceases to have any meaning as he watches the rescue. How long has passed, he doesn't know.

Now a man in a bright orange flying suit is standing in front of him explaining that his wife, Sam's mother, has drowned.

Later, there are questions from the local police. They treat him with compassion, especially as he's Job, like them.

The coroner rules death by misadventure.

But Ford knows the truth.

He killed her. *He* pushed her into trying the climb. *He* dislodged the block that smashed her leg. And *he* left her to drown while he saved his own skin.

DAY ONE, 5.00 P.M

SIX YEARS LATER | SUMMER | SALISBURY

Angie Halpern trudged up the five gritty stone steps to the front door. The shift on the cancer ward had been a long one. Ten hours. It had ended with a patient vomiting on the back of her head. She'd washed it out at work, crying at the thought that it would make her lifeless brown hair flatter still.

Free from the hospital's clutches, she'd collected Kai from Donna, the childminder, and then gone straight to the food bank – again. Bone-tired, her mood hadn't been improved when an elderly woman on the bus told her she looked like she needed to eat more: 'A pretty girl like you shouldn't be that thin.'

And now, here she was, knackered, hungry and with a three-year-old whining and grizzling and dragging on her free hand. Again.

'Kai!' she snapped. 'Let go, or Mummy can't get her keys out.'

The little boy stopped crying just long enough to cast a shocked look up into his mother's eyes before resuming, at double the volume.

Fearing what she might do if she didn't get inside, Angie half-turned so he couldn't cling back on to her hand, and dug out her keys. She fumbled one of the bags of groceries, but in a dexterous act of juggling righted it before it spilled the tins, packets and jars all over the steps.

She slotted the brass Yale key home and twisted it in the lock. Elbowing the door open, she nudged Kai with her right knee, encouraging him to precede her into the hallway. Their flat occupied the top floor of the converted Victorian townhouse. Ahead, the stairs, with their patched and stained carpet, beckoned.

'Come on, Kai, in we go,' she said, striving to inject into her voice the tone her own mother called 'jollying along'.

'No!' the little boy said, stamping his booted foot and sticking his pudgy hands on his hips. 'I hate Donna. I hate the foobang. And I. Hate. YOU!'

Feeling tears pricking at the back of her eyes, Angie put the bags down and picked her son up under his arms. She squeezed him, burying her nose in the sweet-smelling angle between his neck and shoulder. How was it possible to love somebody so much and also to wish for them just to shut the hell up? Just for one little minute.

She knew she wasn't the only one with problems. Talking to the other nurses, or chatting late at night online, confirmed it. Everyone reckoned the happily married ones with enough money to last from one month to the next were the exception, not the rule.

'Mummy, you're hurting me!'

'Oh, Jesus! Sorry, darling. Look, come on. Let's just get the shopping upstairs and you can watch a *Thomas* video.'

'I hate *Thomas.*'

'*Thunderbirds*, then.'

'I hate them even more.'

Angie closed her eyes, sighing out a breath like the online mindfulness gurus suggested. 'Then you'll just have to stare out of the bloody window, like I used to. Now, come on!'

He sucked in a huge breath. Angie flinched, but the scream never came. Instead, Kai's scrunched-up eyes opened wide and swivelled sideways. She followed his gaze and found herself facing a good-looking man wearing a smart jacket and trousers. He had a kind smile.

'I'm sorry,' the man said in a quiet voice. 'I couldn't help seeing your little boy's . . . he's tired, I suppose. You left the door open and as I was coming to this address anyway . . .' He tailed off, looking embarrassed, eyes downcast.

'You were coming *here?*' she asked.

He looked up at her again. 'Yes,' he said, smiling. 'I was looking for Angela Halpern.'

'That's me.' She paused, frowning, as she tried to place him. 'Do I know you?'

'Mummee!' Kai hissed from her waist, where he was clutching her.

'Quiet, darling, please.'

The man smiled. 'Would you like a hand with your bags? I see you have your hands full with the little fellow there.' Then he squatted down, so that his face was at the same level as Kai's. 'Hello. My name's Harvey. What's yours?'

'Kai. Are you a policeman?'

Harvey laughed, a warm, soft-edged sound. 'No. I'm not a policeman.'

'Mummy's a nurse. At the hospital. Do you work there?'

'Me? Funnily enough, I do.'

'Are you a nurse?'

'No. But I do help people. Which I think is a bit of a coincidence. Do you know that word?'

The little boy shook his head.

'It's just a word grown-ups use when two things happen that are the same. Kai,' he said, dropping his voice to a conspiratorial whisper, 'do you want to know a secret?'

Kai nodded, smiling and wiping his nose on his sleeve.

'There's a big hospital in London called Bart's. And I think it rhymes with' – he paused and looked left and right – 'farts.'

Kai squawked with laughter.

Harvey stood, knees popping. 'I hope that was OK. The naughty word. It usually seems to make them laugh.'

Angie smiled. She felt relief that this helpful stranger hadn't seen fit to judge her. To tut, roll his eyes or give any of the dozens of subtle signals the free-and-easy brigade found to diminish her. 'It's fine, really. You said you'd come to see me?'

'Oh, yes, of course, sorry. I'm from the food bank. The Purcell Foundation?' he said. 'They've asked me to visit a few of our customers, to find out what they think about the quality of the service. I was hoping you'd have ten minutes for a chat. If it's not a good time, I can come back.'

Angie sighed. Then she shook her head. 'No, it's fine . . . Harvey, did you say your name was?'

He nodded.

'Give me a hand with the bags and I'll put the kettle on. I picked up some teabags this afternoon, so we can christen the packet.'

'Let me take those,' he said, bending down and snaking his fingers through the loops in the carrier-bag handles. 'Where to, madam?' he added in a jokey tone.

'We're on the third floor, I'm afraid.'

Harvey smiled. 'Not to worry, I'm in good shape.'

Reaching the top of the stairs, Angie elbowed the light switch and then unlocked the door, while Harvey kept up a string of tall tales for Kai.

'And then the chief doctor said' – he adopted a deep voice – '"No, no, that's never going to work. You need to use a hosepipe!"'

Kai's laughter echoed off the bare, painted walls of the stairwell.

'Here we are,' Angie said, pushing the door open. 'The kitchen's at the end of the hall.'

She stood aside, watching Harvey negotiate the cluttered hallway and deposit the shopping bags on her pine kitchen table. She followed him, noticing the scuff marks on the walls, the sticky fat spatters behind the hob, and feeling a lump in her throat.

'Kai, why don't you go and watch telly?' she asked her son, steering him out of the kitchen and towards the sitting room.

'A film?' he asked.

She glanced up at the clock. Five to six. 'It's almost teatime.'

'Pleeease?'

She smiled. 'OK. But you come when I call you for tea. Pasta and red sauce, your favourite.'

'Yummy.'

She turned back to Harvey, who was unloading the groceries on to the table. A sob swelled in her throat. She choked it back.

He frowned. 'Is everything all right, Angela?'

The noise from the TV was loud, even from the other room. She turned away so this stranger wouldn't see her crying. It didn't matter that he was a colleague, of sorts. He could see what she'd been reduced to, and that was enough.

'Yes, yes, sorry. It's just, you know, the food bank. I never thought my life would turn out like this. Then I lost my husband and things just got on top of me.'

'Mmm,' he said. 'That was careless of you.'

'What?' She turned round, uncertain of what she'd heard.

He was lifting a tin of baked beans out of the bag. 'I said, it was careless of you. To lose your husband.'

She frowned. Trying to make sense of his remark. The cruel tone. The staring, suddenly dead eyes.

'Look, I don't know what you—'

The tin swung round in a half-circle and crashed against her left temple.

'Oh,' she moaned, grabbing the side of her head and staggering backwards.

Her palm was wet. Her blood was hot. She was half-blind with the pain. Her back met the cooker and she slumped to the ground. He was there in front of her, crouching down, just like he'd done with Kai. Only he wasn't telling jokes any more. And he wasn't smiling.

'Please keep quiet,' he murmured, 'or I'll have to kill Kai as well. Are you expecting anyone?'

'N-nobody,' she whispered, shaking. She could feel the blood running inside the collar of her shirt. And the pain, oh, the pain. It felt as though her brain was pushing her eyes out of their sockets.

He nodded. 'Good.'

Then he encircled her neck with his hands, looked into her eyes and squeezed.

I'm so sorry, Kai. I hope Auntie Cherry looks after you properly when I'm gone. I hope . . .

* * *

Casting a quick glance towards the kitchen door and the hallway beyond, and reassured by the blaring noise from the TV, Harvey crouched by Angie's inert body and increased the pressure.

Her eyes bulged, and her tongue, darkening already from that natural rosy pink to the colour of raw liver, protruded from between her teeth.

From his jacket he withdrew an empty blood bag. He connected the outlet tube and inserted a razor-tipped trocar into the other end. He placed them to one side and dragged her jeans over her hips, tugging them down past her knees. With the joints free to move, he pushed his hands between her thighs and shoved them apart.

He inserted the needle into her thigh so that it met and travelled a few centimetres up into the right femoral artery. Then he laid the blood bag on the floor and watched as the scarlet blood shot into the clear plastic tube and surged along it.

With a precious litre of blood distending the bag, he capped it off and removed the tube and the trocar. With Angie's heart pumping her remaining blood on to the kitchen floor tiles, he stood and placed the bag inside his jacket. He could feel it through his shirt, warm against his skin. He took her purse out of her bag, found the card he wanted and removed it.

He wandered down the hall and poked his head round the door frame of the sitting room. The boy was sitting cross-legged, two feet from the TV, engrossed in the adventures of a blue cartoon dog.

'Tea's ready, Kai,' he said, in a sing-song tone.

Protesting, but clambering to his feet, the little boy extended a pudgy hand holding the remote and froze the action, then dropped the control to the carpet.

Harvey held out his hand and the boy took it, absently, still staring at the screen.

DAY TWO, 8.15 A.M.

Arriving at Bourne Hill Police Station, Detective Inspector Ford sighed, fingering the scar on his chin. *What better way to start the sixth anniversary of your wife's death than with a shouting match over breakfast with your fifteen-year-old son?*

The row had ended in an explosive exchange that was fast, raw and brutal:

'I hate you! I wish you'd died instead of Mum.'

'Yeah? Guess what? So do I!'

All the time they'd been arguing, he'd seen Lou's face, battered by submerged rocks in the sea off the Pembrokeshire coast.

Pushing the memory of the argument aside, he ran a hand over the top of his head, trying to flatten down the spikes of dark, grey-flecked hair.

He pushed through the double glass doors. Straight into the middle of a ruckus.

A scrawny man in faded black denim and a raggy T-shirt was swearing at a young woman in a dark suit. Eyes wide, she had backed against an orange wall. He could see a Wiltshire police ID on a lanyard round her neck, but he didn't recognise her.

The two female civilian staff behind the desk were on their feet, one with a phone clamped to her ear.

The architects who'd designed the interior of the new station at Bourne Hill had persuaded senior management that the traditional thick glass screen wasn't 'welcoming'. Now any arsehole could decide to lean across the three feet of white-surfaced MDF and abuse, spit on or otherwise ruin the day of the hardworking receptionists. He saw the other woman reach under the desk for the panic button.

'Why are you ignoring me, eh? I just asked where the toilets are, you bitch!' the man yelled at the woman backed against the wall.

Ford registered the can of strong lager in the man's left hand and strode over. The woman was pale, and her mouth had tightened to a lipless line.

'I asked you a question. What's wrong with you?' the drunk shouted.

Ford shot out his right hand and grabbed him by the back of his T-shirt. He yanked him backwards, sticking out a booted foot and rolling him over his knee to send him flailing to the floor.

Ford followed him down and drove a knee in between his shoulder blades. The man gasped out a loud 'Oof!' as his lungs emptied. Ford gripped his wrist and jerked his arm up in a tight angle, then turned round and called over his shoulder, 'Could someone get some cuffs, please? This . . . gentleman . . . will be cooling off in a cell.'

A pink-cheeked uniform raced over and snapped a pair of rigid Quik-Cuffs on to the man's wrists.

'Thanks, Mark,' Ford said, getting to his feet. 'Get him over to Custody.'

'Charge, sir?'

'Drunk and disorderly? Common assault? Being a jerk in a built-up area? Just get him booked in.'

The PC hustled the drunk to his feet, reciting the formal arrest and caution script while walking him off in an armlock to see the custody sergeant.

Ford turned to the woman who'd been the focus of his newest collar's unwelcome attentions. 'I'm sorry about that. Are you OK?'

She answered as if she were analysing an incident she'd witnessed on CCTV. 'I think so. He didn't hit me, and swearing doesn't cause physical harm. Although I am feeling quite anxious as a result.'

'I'm not surprised.' Ford gestured at her ID. 'Are you here to meet someone? I haven't seen you round here before.'

She nodded. 'I'm starting work here today. And my new boss is . . . hold on . . .' She fished a sheet of paper from a brown canvas messenger bag slung over her left shoulder. 'Alec Reid.'

Now Ford understood. She was the new senior crime scene investigator. Her predecessor had transferred up to Thames Valley Police to move with her husband's new job. Alec managed the small forensics team at Salisbury and had been crowing about his new hire for weeks now.

'My new deputy has a PhD, Ford,' he'd said over a pint in the Wyndham Arms one evening. 'We're going up in the world.'

Ford stuck his hand out. 'DI Ford.'

'Pleased to meet you,' she said, taking his hand and pumping it up and down three times before releasing it. 'My name is Dr Hannah Fellowes. I was about to get my ID sorted when that man started shouting at me.'

'I doubt it was anything about you in particular. Just wrong place, wrong time.'

She nodded, frowning up at him. 'Although, technically, this *is* the right place. As I'm going to be working here.' She checked her watch, a multifunction Casio with more dials and buttons than the dash of Ford's ageing Land Rover Discovery. 'It's also 8.15, so it's the right time as well.'

Ford smiled. 'Let's get your ID sorted, then I'll take you up to Alec. He arrives early most days.'

He led her over to the long, low reception desk.

'This is—'

'Dr Hannah Fellowes,' she said to the receptionist. 'I'm pleased to meet you.'

She thrust her right hand out across the counter. The receptionist took it and received the same three stiff shakes as Ford.

The receptionist smiled up at her new colleague, but Ford could see the concern in her eyes. 'I'm Paula. Nice to meet you, too, Hannah. Are you all right? I'm so sorry you had to deal with that on your first day.'

'It was a shock. But it won't last. I don't let things like that get to me.'

Paula smiled. 'Good for you!'

While Paula converted a blank rectangle of plastic into a functioning station ID, Hannah turned to Ford.

'Should I ask her to call me Dr Fellowes, or is it usual here to use first names?' she whispered.

'We mainly use Christian names, but if you'd like to be known as Dr Fellowes, now would be the time.'

Hannah nodded and turned back to Paula, who handed her the swipe card in a clear case.

'There you go, Hannah. Welcome aboard.'

'Thank you.' A beat. 'Paula.'

'Do you know where you're going?'

'I'll take her,' Ford said.

At the lift, he showed her how to swipe her card before pressing the floor button.

'If you don't do that, you just stand in the lift not going anywhere. It's mainly the PTBs who do it.'

'PTBs?' she repeated, as the lift door closed in front of them.

'Powers That Be. Management?'

'Oh. Yes. That's funny. PTBs. Powers That Be.'

She didn't laugh, though, and Ford had the odd sensation that he was talking to a foreigner, despite her southern English accent. She stared straight ahead as the lift ascended. Ford took a moment to assess her appearance. She was shorter than him by a good half-foot, no more than five-five or six. Slim, but not skinny. Blonde hair woven into plaits, a style Ford had always associated with children.

He'd noticed her eyes downstairs; it was hard not to, they'd been so wide when the drunk had had her backed against the wall. But even relaxed, they were large, and coloured the blue of old china.

The lift pinged and a computerised female voice announced, 'Third floor.'

'You're down here,' Ford said, turning right and leading Hannah along the edge of an open-plan office. He gestured left. 'General CID. I'm Major Crimes on the fourth floor.'

She took a couple of rapid, skipping steps to catch up with him. 'Is Forensics open plan as well? I was told it was a quiet office.'

'I think it's safe to say it's quiet. Come on. Let's get you a tea first. Or coffee. Which do you like best?'

'That's a hard question. I haven't really tried enough types to know.' She shook her head, like a dog trying to dislodge a flea from its ear. 'No. What I meant to say was, I'd like to have a tea, please. Thank you.'

There it was again. The foreigner-in-England vibe he'd picked up downstairs.

While he boiled a kettle and fussed around with a teabag and the jar of instant coffee, he glanced at Hannah. She was staring at him, but smiled when he caught her eye. The expression popped dimples into her cheeks.

'Something puzzling you?' he asked.

'You didn't tell me your name,' she said.

'I think I did. It's Ford.'

'No. I meant your first name. You said, "We mainly use Christian names," when the receptionist, Paula, was doing my building ID. And you called me Hannah. But you didn't tell me yours.'

Ford pressed the teabag against the side of the mug before scooping it out and dropping it into a swing-topped bin. He handed the mug to Hannah. 'Careful, it's hot.'

'Thank you. But your name?'

'Ford's fine. Really. Or DI Ford, if we're being formal.'

'OK.' She smiled. Deeper dimples this time, like little curved cuts. 'You're Ford. I'm Hannah. If we're being formal, maybe you *should* call me Dr Fellowes.'

347

Ford couldn't tell if she was joking. He took a swig of his coffee. 'Let's go and find Alec. He's talked of little else since you accepted his job offer.'

'It's probably because I'm extremely well qualified. After earning my doctorate, which I started at Oxford and finished at Harvard, I worked in America for a while. I consulted to city, state and federal law enforcement agencies. I also lectured at Quantico for the FBI.'

Ford blinked, struggling to process this hyper-concentrated CV. It sounded like that of someone ten or twenty years older than the slender young woman sipping tea from a Spire FM promotional mug.

'That's pretty impressive. Sorry, you're how old?'

'Don't be sorry. We only met twenty minutes ago. I'm thirty-three.'

Ford reflected that at her age he had just been completing his sergeant's exams. His promotion to inspector had come through a month ago and he was still feeling, if not out of his depth, then at least under the microscope. Now, he was in conversation with some sort of crime-fighting wunderkind.

'So, how come you're working as a CSI in Salisbury? No offence, but isn't it a bit of a step down from teaching at the FBI?'

She looked away. He watched as she fidgeted with a ring on her right middle finger, twisting it round and round.

'I don't want to share that with you,' she said, finally.

In that moment he saw it. Behind her eyes. An assault? A bad one. Not sexual, but violent. Who did the FBI go after? The really bad ones. The ones who didn't confine their evildoing to a single state. It was her secret. Ford knew all about keeping secrets. He felt for her.

'OK, sorry. Look, we're just glad to have you. Come on. Let's find Alec.'

He took Hannah round the rest of CID and out through a set of grey-painted double doors with a well-kicked steel plate at the foot. The corridor to Forensics was papered with health and safety posters and noticeboards advertising sports clubs, social events and training courses.

Inside, the chatter and buzz of coppers at full pelt was replaced by a sepulchral quiet. Five people were hard at work, staring at computer monitors or into microscopes. Much of the 'hard science' end of forensics had been outsourced to private labs in 2012. But Wiltshire Police had, in Ford's mind, made the sensible decision to preserve as much of an in-house scientific capacity as it could afford.

He pointed to a glassed-in office in the far corner of the room.

'That's Alec's den. He doesn't appear to be in yet.'

'*Au contraire*, Henry!'

The owner of the deep, amused-sounding voice tapped Ford on the shoulder. He turned to greet the forensic team manager, a short, round man wearing wire-framed glasses.

'Morning, Alec.'

Alec clocked the new CSI, but then leaned closer to Ford. 'You OK, Henry?' he murmured, his brows knitted together. 'What with the date, and everything.'

'I'm fine. Let's leave it.'

Alec shrugged. Then his gaze moved to Hannah. 'Dr Fellowes, you're here at last! Welcome, welcome.'

'Thank you, Alec. It's been quite an interesting start to the day.'

Ford said, 'Some idiot was making a nuisance of himself in reception as Hannah was arriving. He's cooling off in one of Ian's capsule hotel rooms in the basement.'

The joviality vanished, replaced by an expression of real concern. 'Oh, my dear young woman. I am so sorry. And on your first day with us, too,' Alec said. 'Why don't you come with me? I'll introduce you to the team and we'll get you set up with a nice quiet desk in the corner. Thanks, Henry. I'll take it from here.'

Ford nodded, eager to get back to his own office and see what the day held. He prayed someone might have been up to no good overnight. Anything to save him from the mountains of forms and reports that he had to either read, write or edit.

'DI Ford? Before you go,' Hannah said.

'Yes?'

'You said I should call you Ford. But Alec just called you Henry.'

'It's a nickname. I got it on my first day here.'

'A nickname. What does it mean?'

'You know. Henry. As in Henry Ford?'

She looked at him, eyebrows raised.

He tried again. 'The car? Model T?'

She smiled at last. A wide grin that showed her teeth, though it didn't reach her eyes. The effect was disconcerting. 'Ha! Yes. That's funny.'

'Right. I have to go. I'm sure we'll bump into each other again.'

'I'm sure, too. I hope there won't be a drunk trying to hit me.'

She smiled, and after a split second he realised it was supposed to be a joke. As he left, he could hear her telling Alec, 'Call me Hannah.'

DAY TWO, 8.59 A.M.

The 999 call had come in just ten minutes earlier: a Cat A G28 – suspected homicide. Having told the whole of Response and Patrol B shift to 'blat' over to the address, Sergeant Natalie Hewitt arrived first at 75 Wyvern Road.

She jumped from her car and spoke into her Airwave radio. 'Sierra Bravo Three-Five, Control.'

'Go ahead, Sierra Bravo Three-Five.'

'Is the ambulance towards?'

'Be about three minutes.'

She ran up the stairs and approached the young couple standing guard at the door to Flat 3.

'Mr and Mrs Gregory, you should go back to your own flat now,' she said, panting. 'I'll have more of my colleagues joining me shortly. Please don't leave the house. We'll be wanting to take your statements.'

'But I've got aerobics at nine thirty,' the woman protested.

Natalie sighed. The public were fantastic at calling in crimes, and occasionally made half-decent witnesses. But it never failed to amaze her how they could also be such *innocents* when it came to the aftermath. This one didn't even seem concerned that her upstairs neighbour and young son had been murdered. Maybe she was in shock. Maybe the husband had kept her out of the flat. Wise bloke.

'I'm afraid you may have to cancel it, just this once,' she said. *You look like you to could afford to. Maybe go and get a fry-up, too, when we're done with you. Put some flesh on your bones.*

The woman retreated to the staircase. Her husband delayed leaving, just for a few seconds.

'We're just shocked,' he said. 'The blood came through our ceiling. That's why I went upstairs to investigate.'

Natalie nodded, eager now to enter the death room and deal with the latest chapter in the Big Book of Bad Things People Do to Each Other.

She swatted at the flies that buzzed towards her. They all came from the room at the end of the dark, narrow hallway. Keeping her eyes on the threadbare red-and-cream runner, alert to anything Forensics might be able to use, she made her way to the kitchen. She supported herself against the opposite wall with her left hand so she could walk, one foot in line with the other, along the right-hand edge of the hall.

The buzzing intensified. And then she caught it: the aroma of death. Sweet-sour top notes overlaying a deeper, darker, rotting-meat stink as body tissues broke down and emitted their gases.

And blood. Or 'claret', in the parlance of the job. She reckoned she'd smelled more of it than a wine expert. This was present in quantity. The husband – what was his name? Rob, that was it. He'd said on the phone it was bad. 'A slaughterhouse' – his exact words.

'Let's find out, then, shall we?' she murmured as she reached the door and entered the kitchen.

As the scene imprinted itself on her retinas, she didn't swear, or invoke the deity, or his son. She used to, in the early days of her career. There'd been enough blasphemy and bad language to have had her churchgoing mum rolling her eyes and pleading with her to 'Watch your language, please, Nat. There's no need.'

She'd become hardened to it over the previous fifteen years. She hoped she still felt a normal human's reaction when she encountered murder scenes, or the remains of those who'd reached the end of their tether and done themselves in. But she left the amateur dramatics to the new kids. She was a sergeant, a rank she'd worked bloody hard for, and she felt a certain restraint went with the territory. So, no swearing.

She did, however, shake her head and swallow hard as she took in the scene in front of her. She'd been a keen photographer in her twenties and found it helpful to see crime scenes as if through a lens: her way of putting some distance between her and whatever horrors the job required her to confront.

In wide-shot, an obscene parody of a Madonna and child. A woman – early thirties, to judge by her face, which was waxy-pale – and a little boy cradled in her lap.

They'd been posed at the edge of a wall-to-wall blood pool, dried and darkened to a deep plum red.

She'd clearly bled out. He wasn't as pale as his mum, but the pink in his smooth little cheeks was gone, replaced by a greenish tinge.

The puddle of blood had spread right across the kitchen floor and under the table, on which half-emptied bags of shopping sagged. The dead woman was slumped with her back against the cooker, legs canted open yet held together at the ankle by her pulled-down jeans.

And the little boy.

Looking for all the world as though he had climbed on to his mother's lap for a cuddle, eyes closed, hands together at his throat as if in prayer. Fair hair. Long and wavy, down to his shoulders, in a girlish style Natalie had noticed some of her friends choose for their sons.

Even in midwinter, flies would find a corpse within the hour. In the middle of a scorching summer like the one southern England was enjoying now, they'd arrived in minutes, laid their eggs and begun feasting in quantity. Maggots crawled and wriggled all over the pair.

As she got closer, Natalie revised her opinion about the cause of death; now, she could see bruises around the throat that screamed strangulation.

There were protocols to be followed. And the first of these was the preservation of life. She was sure the little boy was dead. The skin discolouration and maggots told her that. But there was no way she was going to go down as the sergeant who left a still-living toddler to die in the centre of a murder scene.

Reaching him meant stepping into that lake of congealed blood. Never mind the sneers from CID about the 'woodentops' walking through crime scenes in their size twelves; this was about checking if a little boy had a chance of life.

She pulled out her phone and took half a dozen shots of the bodies. Then she took two long strides towards them, wincing as her boot soles crackled and slid in the coagulated blood.

She crouched and extended her right index and middle fingers, pressing under the little boy's jaw into the soft flesh where the carotid artery ran. She closed her eyes and prayed for a pulse, trying to ignore the smell, and the noise of the writhing maggots and their soft, squishy little bodies as they roiled together in the mess.

After staying there long enough for the muscles in her legs to start complaining, and for her to be certain the little lad was dead, she straightened and reversed out of the blood. She took care to place her feet back in the first set of footprints.

She turned away, looking for some kitchen roll to wipe the blood off her soles, and stared in horror at the wall facing the cooker.

'Oh, shit.'

KEEP READING

Printed in Great Britain
by Amazon

82304077R00210